Winning his Heart

CARA COLTER
ALISON ROBERTS
MELISSA McCLONE

First Published in Great Britain 2017
By Mills & Boon, an imprint of HarperCollins*Publishers*
1 London Bridge Street, London, SE1 9GF

The Millionaire's Homecoming, *The Maverick Millionaire* and *The Billionaire's Nanny* were first published in Great Britain by Harlequin (UK) Limited.

ISBN: 978-0-263-92961-4

05-0417

Our policy is to use papers that are natural, renewable and recyclable products and made from wood grown in sustainable forests.The logging and manufacturing processes conform to the legal environmental regulations of the country of origin.

Printed and bound in Spain
by CPI, Barcelona

THE MILLIONAIRE'S HOMECOMING

BY

CARA COLTER

Cara Colter lives in British Columbia with her partner, Rob, and eleven horses. She has three grown children and a grandson. She is a recent recipient of an *RT Book Reviews* Career Achievement Award in the Love and Laughter category. Cara loves to hear from readers, and you can contact her or learn more about her on her Facebook page.

This story is for my sister, Anna,
for my brother-in-law, Dale,
and especially for Courtenay.
You are my greatest teachers.

CHAPTER ONE

Blossom Valley. In a fast-paced world, David Blaze thought, a trifle sardonically, his hometown was a place unchanging.

Built on the edges of a large bay that meandered inland from Lake Ontario, it had always been a resort town, a summer escape from the oppressive July humidity and heat for the well-heeled, mostly from Canada's largest city, Toronto.

The drive, two hours—with the top down on David's mint 1957 two-seater pearl-gray ragtop convertible—followed a route that traveled pleasantly through rolling, lush hills dotted with contented cattle, faded red barns, weathered fruit stands and sleepy service stations that still sold ice-cold soda pop in thick, glass bottles.

Upon arrival, Blossom Valley's main street welcomed. The buildings were Victorian, the oldest one, now an antiques store, had a tasteful bronze plaque that said it had been built in 1832.

Each business front sparkled, lovingly restored and preserved, the paned windows polished, the hanging planters and window boxes spilling rainbow hues of petunias in cheerful abundance.

Unfortunately, the main street had been constructed—no doubt by one of David's ancestors—to accommodate horses and buggies and the occasional Model T. It was too narrow at the best of times; now it was clogged with summer traffic.

David, though he had been here only on visits since leaving after high school, found himself uncharmed by the quaintness of the main street, pretty as it was. He still had a local's impatience with the congestion.

Plus, once there had been two carefree boys who raced their bicycles in and out of the summer traffic, laughing at the tourists honking their horns at them....

David shook it off. This was the problem with being stuck in traffic in his hometown. In Toronto, being stuck in traffic was nothing. He had a car and driver at his disposal twenty-four hours a day, and it was a time to catch up on phone calls and sort through emails.

He was accustomed to running Blaze Enterprises, his Toronto-based investment firm, and he had only one speed—flat out. His position did not lend itself, thank God, to ruminating about a past that could not be changed, that was rife with losses.

Then, up ahead of him, as if mocking his attempts to leave the memories of those kids on bicycles behind, he saw a girl on a bike, threading her way through traffic with a local's panache.

The bicycle was an outlandish shade of purple, and the old-fashioned kind, with a downward sloping center bar, high handlebars and a basket. Pedaling away from him, the girl was in a calf-length, white, cotton skirt. The midday sun shone through the thinness of the summer fabric outlining the coltish length of her legs.

She was wearing a tank top, and it was as if she'd chosen it to match the bike. The girl's narrow, bare shoulders had already turned golden from the sun.

She had on a huge straw hat, the crown encircled with a thick, white ribbon that trailed down her back.

He caught a glimpse of a small, beige, wire-haired dog, or maybe a puppy, peeping around her with a faintly worried expression. The dog was sharing the bicycle basket with some green, leafy lettuce and a bouquet of sunflowers.

For a moment, David's impatience waned, and he felt the innocence of the picture—all the things that had been so good about growing up here. The girl herself seemed familiar, something about the slope of her shoulders and the way she held her head.

He could feel himself holding his breath. Then the girl shoulder checked, and he caught a glimpse of her face.

Kayla?

Someone honked at a jaywalker, and David began to breathe again and yanked his attention back to the traffic.

It wasn't Kayla. It was just that his hometown stirred a certain unavoidable melancholy in him. The loss of innocence. The loss of his best friend.

Kayla. The loss of his first love.

Grimly, David snapped on his sound system and inched forward. The street, if he followed it a full six blocks, would end at Blossom Valley's claim to fame, its lakefront, Gala Beach, named not because galas were held there, but after a popular brand of apples that grew in the local orchards.

Gala Beach was a half kilometer stretch of perfect white sand in a protected cove of relatively calm, shallow water. The upper portions, shaded by fifty-year-old cottonwoods, held playground equipment and picnic tables, concessions and rental booths.

It had been a decade since David had been a lifeguard on that beach, and yet his stomach still looped crazily downward when he caught a glimpse of the sun-speckled waters of the bay sparkling at the end of Main Street.

David Blaze hated coming home.

He turned left onto Sugar Maple Lane, and the difference between it and Main Street was jarring. He was transported from the swirling noise and color and energy of Main Street to the deep, shaded silence of Sugar Maple: wide boulevards housed the huge, century-old trees that had given the street its name.

Set well off the road in large, perfectly manicured yards were turn-of-the-century, stately homes—Victorians. Solid columns supported roofs over deeply shadowed verandas. On one he caught a glimpse of white wicker furniture padded with overstuffed, color-splashed cushions that made him think of sugary ice tea in the heat of the afternoon.

And there was the girl on her bike again, up ahead of him, pedaling leisurely, fitting in perfectly with a street that invited life to slow down, to be savored—

He frowned. There *was* something familiar about her. And then, as he watched, the serenity of the scene suddenly dissolved.

The girl gave a small shriek and leaped from the bike. It crashed down, spilling sunflowers out onto the road. The puppy, all five pounds of it, tumbled out of the basket and darted away, tiny tail between tiny legs.

The girl was doing a mad jig, slapping at herself. It momentarily amused, but then David realized there was an edge of desperation in the wild dance. Her hat flew off, and her hair, loosely held with a band, cascaded out from under it, shiny, as straight as the ribbon around the brim of her hat, the soft light filtering through the trees turning its light brown tones to spun gold.

David felt his stomach loop crazily for the second time in a couple of minutes.

Please, no.

He had slowed his car to a crawl; now he slammed on the brake and shoved the gear stick into Neutral in the middle of the street. He jumped out, not even bothering to shut the door. He raced to the girl, who was slapping at her thighs through the summer-weight cotton of the skirt.

His shadow fell over her and she went very still, straightened and looked up at him.

It wasn't a girl. While he had denied it could be her, his deepest instincts had recognized her.

Despite the snub of the nose and the faint freckles that dusted it, making her look gamine and eternally young, it was not a girl, but a young woman.

A woman with eyes the color of jade that reminded him of a secret grove not far from here, a place the tourists didn't know about, where a waterfall cascaded into a still pond that reflected the green hues of the surrounding ferns that dipped into its waters.

Of course, it wasn't just any woman.

It was Kayla McIntosh.

No, he reminded himself, Kayla *Jaffrey,* the first woman he had ever loved. *And lost.* Of course, she had been more a girl than a woman back then.

He felt the same stir of awareness that he had always felt when he saw her. He tried to convince himself it was just primal: man reacting to attractive woman.

But he knew it was more. It was summer sunshine bringing out freckles on her nose, and her racing him on her bike. *Look, David, no hands.* It was the way the reflection from a bonfire turned her hair to flame, and the smell of woodsmoke, and stars that she could name making brilliant pinpricks of light in the inky black blanket of the sky.

David Blaze hated coming home.

"David?"

For a moment, the panic of being stung was erased from Kayla's mind and replaced with a different kind of panic, her stomach doing that same roller-coaster race downward that it had done the very first time she had ever seen him.

Except for the sensation in her stomach, it felt as if the world had gone completely still around her as she gazed at David Blaze.

She tried to tell herself it was the shock of the sting—knowing that she was highly allergic and could be dead soon—that made the moment seem tantalizingly suspended in time. Her awareness of him was sharp and clear, like a million pinpricks along her arms.

Kayla didn't feel as if she were twenty-seven, a woman who knew life, who had buried her husband and her dreams. No, she felt as if she were fifteen years old all over again, the new girl in town, and the possibility for magic shimmered in the air around her that first time she looked at David.

No, she told herself, firmly. She had left that kind of nonsense well behind her. That pinprick feeling was the beginning of the allergic reaction to the sting!

Still, despite the firm order to herself, Kayla felt as if she drank him in with a kind of dazed wonder. It seemed that everyone she ran into from the old days had changed in some way, and generally for the worse. She'd seen Mike Humes in the hardware store—her new haunt now that she had been thrust into the world of home ownership—and the former Blossom Valley High senior year class president had looked so comically like a monk with a tonsure that she had had to bite her lip to keep from laughing.

Cedric Parson ran Second Time Around—an antiques store that she also haunted, ever on the lookout to furnish her too-large house—and the ex-high school football star looked as if he had an inflated tire tube inserted under his too-tight shirt.

Cedric was divorced now, and had asked her out. But even though she had been a widow two years, she was so aware she was not ready, and that she might never be. There was something in her that was different.

Even the fact that she judged her two high school pals in such a harsh and unforgiving light told Kayla something about herself. Not ready, but also harder than she used to be, more cynical.

Or maybe "unforgiving" said it all.

But trust David Blaze to have gotten better instead of worse. Of course, she knew what he did—the whole town took pride and pleasure in following the success of a favored son.

Even though she'd been back in Blossom Valley less than two weeks, one of the first things Kayla had seen was his picture on the cover of *Lakeside Life.* The magazine was everywhere: in proud stacks at the supermarket, piled by the cash registers of restaurants, in leaning towers of glossy paper at the rental kiosks.

The magazine had recently done a huge spread about his company, and the cover photo had been of David standing in front of the multimillion-dollar Yorkton condo he had developed, in a suit—even her inexperienced eye new it was custom—that added to his look of supreme confidence, power and success.

Though she had contemplated the inevitability of running into him, given where she lived, the photo hadn't really prepared her for the reality of David Blaze in his prime.

How was it that someone who made investments, presumably from behind a desk, still had the unmistakably broad build of a swimmer: wide shoulders, deep chest, narrow waist, sleekly muscled limbs?

David was dressed casually in a solid navy-colored sport shirt and knife-creased khaki shorts, and despite the fact a thousand men in Blossom Valley were dressed almost identically today, David oozed the command and self-assurance—the understated elegance—of wealth and arrival.

His coloring was healthy and outdoorsy. That combined with that mouthwatering physique made Kayla think his appearance seemed more in keeping with the lifeguard he had once been than with the incredibly successful entrepreneur he now was.

His hair, short enough to appear perfectly groomed despite the fact he had just leaped from a convertible with the top down, was the color of dark chocolate, melted. His eyes were one shade lighter than his hair, a deep, soft brown that reminded her of suede.

It had been two years since she had seen him. At her husband, Kevin's, funeral. And that day she had not really noticed what he looked like, only felt his arms fold around her, felt his warmth and his strength, and thought, for the first time, and only time: *everything will be all right.*

But that reaction had been followed swiftly by anger. Where had he been all those years when Kevin could have used a friend?

And she could have, too.

Why had David withheld what Kevin so desperately needed? David's chilly remoteness after a terrible accident, days after they had all graduated from high school, had surely contributed to a downward spiral in Kevin that nothing could stop.

Not even her love.

The trajectory of all their lives had changed forever, and David Blaze had proven to her he was no kind of friend at all.

David had let them down. He'd become aloof and cool—a furious judgment in his eyes—when Kevin had most needed understanding. Forgiveness. Sympathy.

Not, Kayla reminded herself bitterly, *that any of those things had saved my husband, either, because everyone else—me, his parents—had given those things in abundance.*

And had everything been all right since the funeral? Because of Kevin's insurance she was financially secure, but was everything else all right?

Not really. Kayla had a sense of not knowing who she really was anymore. Wasn't that part of why she had come back here, to Blossom Valley? To find her lost self? To remember Kevin as the fun-loving guy she had grown up with? And not…

She was weakened by the sting. And by David's sudden presence. She was not going to think disloyal thoughts about her husband! And especially not with David Blaze in the vicinity!

"Where's your kit?" David asked with an authoritative snap in his voice that pulled her out of the painful reverie of their shared history.

"I don't need your help."

"Yes, you do."

She wanted to argue that, but the sense of languid clarity left her and was replaced rapidly by panic. Was her throat closing? Was her breathing becoming rapid? Was she swelling? And turning red? And where was her new dog, Bastigal?

She dragged her eyes from the reassuring strength in David's—that was an illusion, after all—and scanned the nearby shrubs.

"I don't need your help," she bit out again, stubbornly, pushing down her desire to panic and deliberately looking away from the irritation in his lifted eyebrow.

"Bastigal," she called, "come here! My dog. He fell out of the basket. I have to find my dog."

She felt a finger on her chin, strong, insistent, trying to make her look at him. When she resisted, masculine hands bracketed her cheeks, forcing her unwilling gaze to his.

"Kayla." His voice was strong and sure, and very stern as he enunciated every word slowly. "I need to know where your bee-sting kit is. I need to know *now.*"

CHAPTER TWO

DAVID BLAZE WAS OBVIOUSLY a man who had become way too accustomed to being listened to.

And Kayla was disgusted with herself for how easily she capitulated to his powerful presence, but the truth was she felt suddenly dizzy, her blood pressure spiraling downward in reaction to the sting. At least she hoped it was the sting!

She divested herself from the vise grip of David's hands on her cheeks, not wanting him to think it was the touch of his strong hands that had made her so light-headed.

He was not there for Kevin, she reminded herself, trying to shore up her strength…and her animosity.

She lowered herself to the curb. "Purse. In the bike basket." It felt like a cowardly surrender.

She watched David, and reluctant admiration pierced her desire for animosity. Even though he was far removed from his lifesaving days, David still moved with the calm and efficiency of a trained first responder.

His take-charge attitude might have been annoying under different circumstances, but right now it inspired unenthusiastic confidence. Feeling like every kind of a traitor, Kayla allowed David's confidence to wash her with calm as she attempted to slow her ragged breathing.

How was it he could feel so familiar to her—the dark glossiness of his hair, the perfect line of his jaw, the suede of his eyes—and feel like a complete stranger at the same time?

David strode over to where she had thrown down her bike, picked through the strewn sunflowers and green-leaf lettuce until he found the purse where it had fallen on the ground. He crouched, unceremoniously dumping all the contents of her bag out on the road. If he heard her protested "Hey!" he ignored it.

In seconds he had the "pen," an emergency dose of epinephrine. He lowered himself beside her on the curb.

"Are you doing this, or am I?" he asked.

He took one look at her face and had his answer. His fingers tickled along the length of her leg as he eased her skirt up, exposing her thigh. She closed her eyes against the shiver of pure awareness that was not caused by reaction to the sting or the feel of the warm summer sunshine on her skin.

She wanted to protest he could have put the pre-loaded needle, concealed within the pen, through the fabric of the skirt, but she didn't say a word.

She excused her lack of protest by telling herself that her throat was no doubt swelling shut. It felt as if her eyes were!

She felt the heat of his hand, warmer than the sun, as he laid it midway up the outside of her naked thigh and pressed her skin taut between his thumb and pointer finger.

"I think I'm going to faint," she whispered, any pretense of courage that she had managed now completely abandoning her.

"You're not going to faint."

It wasn't an observation so much as an order.

She attempted to glower at his arrogance. She knew if she was going to faint! He didn't! But instead of resentment, Kayla was aware, again, of feeling a traitorous clarity she attributed to near death: his shoulder touching hers, the light in the glossy chocolate of his hair as he bent over her, his scent masculine, sharply clean and tantalizing.

Still, some primal fear made her put her hand over the site on her leg where he had pulled the skin taut with his bracketed fingers as the perfect place to inject the epinephrine.

He took her hand and put it firmly out of his way. When she went to put it right back, he held it at bay, his strength making her own seem puny and impotent.

"I'm not ready!" she protested.

"Look at me," he commanded.

She did. She looked into the strength and calm of those deep brown eyes and all of it felt like an intoxicating chemical cocktail so strong it made a life-threatening beesting feel like nothing.

The years dropped away. He was woven into the fabric of her life, the way he cocked his head when he listened, the intensity of his gaze, the ease of his laughter, the solidness of his friendship, the utter reliability of him.

She could feel her breathing slow.

But then with her hand still in the grip of his, her eyes drifted to the full, sensuous curve of his lower lip and she could feel her heart and breath quicken again.

Once, a long time ago, she had tasted those lips, giving in, finally, to that *want* he had always made her feel. Though by then they had both been seventeen, she had been like a child drinking wine and it had been just as heady an experience.

She remembered his taste had felt exotic and compelling; she remembered how he had explored the hollows of her mouth as if he, too, had thought of nothing else for the two years they had known each other.

What a price for that kiss, though! After that exchange, he had gone cool toward her. Frosty. It had changed everything in the worst of ways. They had never been able to get back to the easy camaraderie that predated that meeting of lips.

David had started dating Emily Carson, she, Kevin.

And yet, even knowing the price of it, sitting here on the curb, Kayla had the crazy thought: if she was going to die and had just one wish, would it be to taste David's lips again? She found herself, even though it filled her with self-loathing, leaning toward him as if pulled on an invisible thread.

David leaned toward her.

His eyes held hers as he came closer. She could feel her own eyes shutting, and not just because they were swelling, either. Her lips were parting.

He jammed the pen, hard, against the outer edge of her upper thigh.

The needle popped out of its protective casing and injected the epinephrine under her skin.

"Ouch!" The physical pain snapped her back to reality, and her eyes flew open as Kayla yanked herself back from him, mortified, trying to read in his face if he had seen her moment of weakness, her intention.

It didn't look like he had. David's face was cool, remote.

The indifference of his expression reminded her of the emotional pain she had felt that night after they had shared that kiss. She had thought, on fire with excitement and need, that it was the beginning of something.

Instead, she had become invisible to him.

Just as Kevin had become invisible to him. That was

what Kayla needed to remember about David Blaze: he seemed like one thing—a man you could count on with your life, in fact—and yet when there was any kind of *emotional* need involved, he could not be relied on at all.

The moment of feeling intoxicated by David was gone like a soap bubble that had floated upward, iridescent and ethereal, and then *pop*—over.

"That hurt," she said. It was the memories of all the ways he had disappointed her as much as the injection, not that he needed to know.

"Sorry," he said with utter insincerity. He hadn't cared about her pain or Kevin's back then, and he didn't care now. He got up, moved to his car with efficiency of motion. It seemed as if he were unhurried and yet he was back at her side almost before she could blink.

He settled back on the curb, and Kayla ordered herself not to take any more comfort from the strength in the shoulder that touched hers. She saw David had retrieved a small first-aid kit from the glove box of his car, and he unzipped it and rummaged through, coming up with a pair of tweezers.

"I'm just going to see if I can find the stinger."

"You are not!" she said, yanking her skirt down over her naked thigh and pressing the fabric tight to her legs.

"Don't be ridiculous. The stinger could still be pumping poison into you."

She hesitated and he, sensing her hesitation, pressed. "I already saw the sting site. And your panties. They're pink."

To match the blush she could feel moving up her cheeks. Kayla sputtered ineffectually as he easily overpowered her attempts to hold her skirt down.

"There it is. Quit jumping around like that."

"Give me those tweezers!" She made a grab for them.

"Stay calm, Kayla," he ordered, amused. "It's like being bitten by a snake. The more excited you get, the worse it is."

"I don't want you messing around under my skirt and talking about excitement," she said grimly.

But for the first time, his stern mask fell. He gave a small snort of laughter, and that damned grin made him more astoundingly attractive than ever! "Just be grateful you didn't get stung somewhere else."

"Grateful," she muttered. "I'll be sure and add it to my list."

"Got it!" he said with satisfaction, inspecting the tweezers and then holding them up for her to see. Sure enough, a hair of a stinger was trapped in them.

The amusement that had briefly made him so attractive had completely evaporated.

"Get in the car."

That's what she had to remember. The very qualities that made David a superb rescuer—detachment, a certain hard-nosed ability to do what needed to be done—also made him impossible to get close to.

What had she been thinking, leaning toward him, thinking of his kiss?

She was in shock, that was all. Riding her bike with her dog and sunflowers on a perfect summer day when out of nowhere, a bee. And him.

She, of all people, should know that. When you least expected it, life wreaked havoc. It was a mistake to surrender control, and the circumstances were no longer life-threatening, so she simply wasn't giving in.

"My dog," she reminded him. "And my bike. My purse. My stuff is all over the road. The phone is new. I need to—"

"You need to get in the car," David said, enunciating every word with a certain grim patience.

"No," she said, enunciating every word as carefully as he did, "I need to find my dog. And get my bike off the street. And retrieve my phone. It is a very expensive phone."

He frowned, a man who moved in a world where his power was absolute. He was unaccustomed to anyone saying no to him, and she felt a certain childish satisfaction at the surprised, annoyed look on his face.

Slowly, as if he was speaking to a child, and not a very bright one at that, David said, "I'm taking you to the emergency clinic. I'm doing it now."

"Thank you. You've given me the shot. I undoubtedly owe you my life, but—"

"I'll take care of the dog and the bike and the purse and the phone after I've made sure you are all right."

"I *am* all right!"

That was, in fact, a lie. Kayla felt quite woozy.

And she got the impression he was not the least bit fooled as he looked at her carefully.

"Get in the car," he said again.

He was quite maddening in his authoritative approach to her. Her gaze went to her personal belongings scattered all over the road. "The EpiPen bought me time," she said, tilting her chin stubbornly at him.

His sigh seemed long-suffering, though their encounter had lasted only minutes. "Kayla, you need to listen to me. I'll take care of your stuff after I've taken care of you."

She scanned his face, the stern, no-nonsense cast of his features, and felt a somewhat aggravating sense of relief swell in her. Why would it feel quite good to surrender control to him? To let someone else be in charge? To let someone else take care of her?

David was just *that* guy, and he always had been. The one who did everything right. The one who knew what to do. The one who could be counted on to look after things. The one you would choose to have with you in an emergency: when the hurricane arrived, or the boat capsized or the house caught fire.

Except he hadn't done the right thing by Kevin, the time it had really counted.

"My dog is on the loose somewhere. He could be picked up by a stranger or run over by a car. My bike could be stolen. The new phone could be crushed by a passing vehicle!"

Irrationally, she trusted David, in some areas, at least. If he said he'd take care of it, he simply would. His strength of purpose had always been nothing less than amazing.

And intolerant of those less strong.

Like Kevin, who had never taken care of anything.

The thought, breathtaking in its disloyalty, came out of nowhere, blasted her and made her feel guilty. And, oddly, angry at David all over again.

Okay, so Kevin had not been overly responsible. He'd had many great qualities!

Hadn't he? The whisper of disloyalty, again, made her feel angry with David as if his presence was nursing these forbidden thoughts to the forefront.

"I need to find my dog," she said, folding her arms over her chest. She was not going to have these thoughts, or surrender control to David Blaze—who was overly responsible—without so much as a whimper.

Had she learned nothing from life? No, she had learned to rely on herself!

"I'm okay now," she said, and it felt like an act of supreme bravery, in light of his darkening features. "David,

I appreciate you playing knight in shining armor to my damsel in distress."

The look on his face darkened so she rushed on, shooting a look at his car, "I appreciate your riding in on your shining gray steed, but really, I'll take it from here. I don't need any more help from you."

CHAPTER THREE

DAVID CONTEMPLATED KAYLA, and it was hard not to shirk from the impatience that yanked at the muscle in his jaw and darkened his eyes to a shade of brown so dark it bordered on being black.

He looked totally formidable, and not a single remnant of the carefree boy of Kayla's adolescence appeared to remain in him.

When had he become this? A man so totally certain of his own power, a man not to be messed with?

"I'm not playing a game here," he said quietly. "I am not playing knight to your princess. Not even close. Life is not a fairy tale."

"I'm the last person who needs to be reminded of that," she said, and he flinched, ever so faintly, but still she had to hide a shiver at his intensity, and her face felt suddenly hot.

She was not blushing at the thought of sharing a fairy tale with him! It occurred to Kayla that, despite the shot, her face might be swelling. In fact, with each passing second she probably was looking more like poor Quasimodo, with his misshapen face, than a princess.

"You are highly allergic to beestings," he said, his patience worn thin, like a scientist trying to explain a highly complicated formula to a fool. "Anaphylaxis is a life-threatening emergency."

She touched her forehead. She could feel the puffiness in it.

"We have stopped the emergency for now," he went on. "A secondary reaction is not uncommon. You need to be under medical observation."

"But my dog," she said, weakly. She knew he had already won, even before he snapped *"Enough,"* with a quiet authority that made her stomach dip.

"Kayla, either get to the car under your own power, or I'll throw you over my shoulder and put you there with mine."

She scanned his face, and could feel the heat in her own intensify. There was no doubt at all in her mind that he meant it.

Or that her forehead felt like it was swelling like a balloon filling with helium.

"Humph." She stuck her chin out, but it was a token protest. As annoying as it was, he was absolutely right.

By the time his hand went to her elbow and he used his easy strength to leverage her up, Kayla had no resistance in her at all.

Annoyed with herself, she shook off his hand, marched to his car, opened the passenger-side door and slid in. The deep leather seat had been warmed by the sun, and the rich scent of the luxurious car enveloped her.

It was possibly the nicest car Kayla had ever been in. Her car, now, was a presentable, fairly new economy model that Kevin's insurance had allowed.

She didn't even want to think about the cars before that—a string of dilapidated jalopies that always seemed to need repairs she and Kevin could never afford.

That made her even more determined not to give David

the satisfaction of thinking his beautiful car made any kind of impression on her.

Apparently not any more interested in small talk than she was, David got in the driver's side. He checked over his shoulder, pulled out into the empty street, did a tight U-turn and headed back toward downtown, though he had a local's savvy for navigating a path around the congested main street toward the beach.

Kayla settled her head against the back of her seat and felt a subtle, contented lethargy. The aftermath of the sting, or the drug hitting her system, or surrendering control or some lethal combination of all of those things.

She had always had a secret desire to ride in a convertible, and even though the circumstances were not quite as she had envisioned, she did not know if the opportunity would ever arise again.

She tugged at the elastic that most of her hair had fallen out of anyway, and freed her hair to the wind. If the circumstances had been different, she had a feeling this experience would be intoxicatingly pleasurable.

David glanced at her, and his eyes seemed to hold on her hair before he looked at her face and a reluctant smile tugged at the beautiful corner of his mouth.

Kayla flipped down the sun visor on her side, and it explained the smile. Despite the adrenaline shot, her brow bone had disappeared into puffiness that was forming a shelf over her eyes. She could have hidden under her hat if it wasn't lying back there on the road waiting to get run over with the rest of her things!

Including her dog. Surely, he could have taken a moment to find the dog.

But no, she came first.

A long time since she had come first. Not that it was personal. It was an emergency responder prioritizing.

She cast David a glance. Thankfully, he had turned his attention back to the road. He was an excellent driver, alert and relaxed at the same time, fast but controlled. His face had a stubborn set to it. He had, in that infernally aggravating way of his, put his priorities in order, and a dog was not among them!

"Can I borrow your cell phone?" Her voice came out faintly slurred over a thick tongue, and much as the admission hurt, Kayla knew he had made the right decision.

He fished the phone out of his pocket and tossed it to her casually.

Who to call about the dog? She barely knew anyone here anymore. The neighbors across the street had their name on their mailbox. And children home for the summer.

She navigated his phone to a local directory, looked up her neighbor's number and asked whether her kids could look for the dog. She offered a reward, and then as an afterthought, payment if they would go collect her bike and belongings.

"I said I'd look after it," he said when she clicked off.

She gave him a frosty look that she hoped, despite the swollen brow, let him know she would look after her own life, thank you very much.

Despite her discomfort, Kayla could not help but notice the details of the gorgeous vehicle. Sleek and posh, the subtle statement of a man who had parlayed his substantial talent for being able to discern the right thing into a sizable fortune and an amazing success story.

Not like Kevin.

Again, the thought came from nowhere, as if somehow David's close proximity was coaxing to the surface feelings she did not want to acknowledge about her late husband.

Guilt washed over her. And then she just felt angry. She had tried so, so hard to put Kevin back together again, and not a word from David.

The ride with him was mercifully short given that his scent—masculine and clean—was mingling with the scent of sun on leather, and tickling at her nostrils. In minutes, his driving fast, controlled and superb, they arrived at the small village emergency clinic.

For practical purposes it was located adjacent to the public beach where the huge influx of summer visitors didn't always recognize the dangers hidden beneath the benign scene of a perfect summer.

But David knew them. He knew those dangers intimately. Kayla was aware of David's shoulders tightening as he pulled into the parking lot.

He got out of the car and she followed, watching as he went still and gazed out over the nearby beach.

Fried onion and cooking French fries smells wafted out of the concession and the sand was dotted with the yellow-striped sun umbrellas rented from a stand. Out on the water, people who didn't have a clue what they were doing paddled rented kayaks and canoes.

Teenagers had laid claim to the floats that swayed on sparkling waters, and bikini-clad girls shrieked as boys splashed them or tried to toss them in the water.

Toddlers played with sand buckets, mothers handed out sandy potato chips and farther back, among the cottonwoods, grandmothers sat in the deep shade engrossed in books or crossword puzzles.

The lifeguards, alone, were not in fun mode. They sat in high chairs, watching, watching, watching.

She hadn't been there that day it had happened. The day that had changed all of them forever. David was looking at one of the lifeguards, frowning.

What did David see? She saw a young man who was slouched in his chair, looking faintly bored behind sunglasses, as he endlessly scanned the waters between the sand and the buoys that ended the designated swimming area.

For a moment the expression on David's face was unguarded, and she could see sorrow swim in the depths of those amazing eyes. Her animosity toward him flagged. Was it possible that like Kevin, he could not put it behind him?

"David?" She touched his arm.

He broke his gaze and looked at her, momentarily puzzled, as if he didn't know who she was or where he was.

"It was a long time ago," she said softly.

He flinched, and then shook off her arm. "I don't need your pity," he said quietly, his voice cold and hard-edged.

"It wasn't pity," she said, stung.

"What was it, then?" His voice sounded harsh.

She hesitated. "A wish, I guess."

"A wish?"

"That it could somehow be undone. That we could have been the same people we were before it happened."

For a moment he looked like he was going to say something, and that he bit it back with great effort.

"Wishes are for children," he said grimly.

"And that's the day childhood ended for you," she noted softly.

"No, it isn't. I wasn't a child anymore." He didn't say *neither was Kevin,* but she heard it as clearly as if he had spoken it. "It was the day childhood ended for her. Not us. That little girl who drowned."

"It wasn't your fault."

"No," he said firmly, "It wasn't."

Which left the cold, hard truth about whose fault it had been. It had been an accident. A terrible tragedy.

But somehow he had always blamed Kevin, never forgiven him. David's hard attitude had been part of what destroyed him.

That's what Kayla needed to remember when she was leaning toward him, thinking illicit thoughts about his lips and admiring how posh his car was.

"It was an accident," she said, "There was a full investigation. Ultimately, it was an accident. Her parents should have been watching more closely."

His eyes narrowed on her. "How long did he tell you that before you started believing it?"

"Excuse me?"

His tone was furious. "Her parents weren't trained lifeguards. How would they know that drowning isn't the way it is in the movies? Would they know sometimes there is not a single sound? Not a scream? Not a splash? Not a hand waving frantically in the air?

"He knew that. He knew that, but you know what? He wasn't watching."

Kayla could feel the color draining from her face. "You've always blamed him," she whispered. "Everything changed between the two of you after that. How could you do that? You were his best friend. He needed you."

"He needed to do his job!"

"He was young. He was distracted. Anybody could be distracted for a second."

"The end of our friendship doesn't just fall on my shoulders," David said quietly. "Kevin wouldn't talk to me after the investigation. He was mad because I told the truth."

"What truth?"

He drew in his breath sharply, seemed to consider.

"Tell me," she said, even though she had the childish desire to put her hands over her ears to block what he was going to say next.

"He was flirting with a girl. Instead of doing his job."

She knew David rarely swore, but he inserted an expletive between *his* and *job* that could have made a soldier blush.

"He was over there by the concession not even looking at the water."

"He was already going out with me!" she said, her voice a squeak of outrage and desperation. "That's a lie."

"Is it?" he asked quietly. "I was coming on shift. I wasn't even on duty. I looked out at the water and I knew something was wrong. I could feel it. There was an eeriness in the air. And then I saw that little girl. She had blond hair and she was facedown and her hair floating around her head in the water. I yelled at him as I went by and we both went out."

"You're lying," she whispered again.

He looked at her sadly. "It was too late. By the time we got to her."

"Why would you tell me something so hurtful?" she demanded, but her voice sounded weak in her own ears. "Why would you lie to me like that?"

His eyes were steady on her own.

"Have I ever lied to you, Kayla?" he asked quietly.

"Yes!" she said. "Yes, you have."

And then she turned and practically ran from him before he could see the tears streaming down her face.

CHAPTER FOUR

DAVID'S HAND LANDED on her shoulder, and he spun her around.

"When?" he demanded. "When did I ever lie to you?"

"We kissed that one night on the beach," Kayla said, carefully stripping her voice of any emotion.

His hand fell away from her shoulder, and he stuffed it in the pocket of his shorts and looked away from her.

"And then," she said, her voice a hiss, "you would barely look at me after that. That, David Blaze, is the worst kind of lie of all!"

He drew in his breath, sharply, and looked like he had something to say. Instead, his expression closed.

That same cool, shutting-her-out expression that she remembered all too well from after their ill-fated kiss!

"I don't want to talk about it," he said. "I don't want to talk about any of this."

His tone was dismissive, his eyes that had been so expressive just a moment ago, were guarded. His features were closed and cold, his mouth a firm line that warned her away from the place he did not want to go. Which was their shared history.

And that was not a problem. Because Kayla didn't want to go there, either.

"You brought it up," she reminded him tightly.

He scraped a hand though his hair and sighed, a sound heavy with weariness. "I did. I shouldn't have. I'm sorry."

"Thank you for your help," Kayla said with stiff formality. "I can take it from here. I've taken enough of your time. You should go."

David was aware Kayla was taking her cues from him. Slamming the door shut on their shared past.

David was aware he had managed to hurt her feelings, and make her very angry and he was genuinely sorry for both.

Her husband was dead. What momentary and completely uncharacteristic lack of control had made him tell her, after all these years, about what had happened that day?

He supposed it was because she had taken Kevin's word and way, absolved him of responsibility by blaming those poor parents, as innocent in the whole thing as their child had been.

The drowning *had* been ruled an accident. But the tension between him and Kevin had never been repaired.

It was only the fact that he had just saved Kayla's life that was making her struggle for even a modicum of courtesy. In other circumstances, David was aware that he probably would have found that struggle, so transparent in her face and eyes, somewhat amusing.

You should go. That was a good idea if David had ever heard one.

He still could not believe the anger he felt when she said that about it being the parents' responsibility, his anger at how completely she had bought into Kevin absolving himself.

Still, it *was* all a long time ago. Her voice saying

that, soft with compassion, was something worth escaping from.

It *was* a long time ago.

Sometimes months could go by without him thinking of it.

But that was not while looking at the beach, with Kayla at his side. He didn't like it that she had seen, instantly, that it still bothered him.

And he liked it even less that her hand had rested on his wrist, her touch gentle and offering understanding.

Kayla. Some things never changed. She was always looking for something or someone to save, Kevin being a case in point.

Kevin had died in a car accident on a slippery night, going too fast, as always. Had he not cared that he had responsibilities? The accident had happened very late at night. Why hadn't he been home with his beautiful, young wife?

David shook it off. It was none of his business, but he wished she had not brought up that kiss. He remembered every single thing about it: the sand of the day clinging to them both, the bonfire, the sky star-studded and inky, the night air warm and sultry, the velvety softness of her cheek nestled into his hand as she gazed at him with those huge, liquid-green eyes. His lips had been pulled to her lips like steel to a magnet. And when he had tasted them, they had tasted sweetly of the nectar that gave life.

Until that precise moment, that electrifying meeting of lips, they had just been friends in a circle of friends. But they had been at that age when awareness is sharpening...where the potential for everything to change is always shimmering in the air.

It was true. What he had done after was the worst kind of lie.

Because the next day, Kevin, who had not been at the bonfire the night before, had told David *he* had fallen for Kayla. That he'd known forever that she was the girl for him, that he had asked her to the prom and she had said yes.

Obviously, Kevin had asked her to the prom before David had kissed her.

He'd felt the dilemma of it; his best friend was staking a claim, *had* a prior claim. Since his own father had died, David had practically lived at the house next door. He and Kevin were more than friends. They were brothers. Plus, what had Kayla been doing kissing David when she'd agreed to go with Kevin to the prom?

David had done the only possible thing. He'd backed off. In truth, he had probably thought he might have another chance to explore the electricity that had leaped so spontaneously between him and Kayla.

He had thought the thing between her and Kevin would play itself out. Kevin never stuck with anything for long.

But then the little girl had drowned. On Kevin's watch. And the days of that summer had become a swiftly churning kaleidoscope that they all had been sucked into. A kaleidoscope of loss and of pain and guilt and remorse and sadness. And of anger.

And somehow, when the kaleidoscope had stopped spinning and had spit them all out, Kayla and Kevin were engaged.

It occurred to David that he had been angry at Kevin long before that child had drowned.

"You need to go."

Kayla said it again, more firmly.

David wanted to get away from her, and from the anger in her eyes, and the recrimination, and the pain that shaded the green to something deeper than green.

She dismissed him, turning her back on him, marching through the doors of the clinic.

The easiest thing would have been to let her go.

But when had David ever done what was easy?

He had promised to see to her dog and her things, and the fact that his word was solid gold was part of what had allowed him to go so far in the world. Blaze Enterprises had been built on a concept of integrity that was rare in the business world.

He followed her through the doors of the clinic.

The ancient nurse, Mary McIntyre, insisted that Kayla take one of the beds in the empty clinic, and so, even though Kayla had dismissed him, he followed them as Mary fussed around her, asking questions, taking her pulse and her blood pressure and listening to her heart.

"We'll just keep an eye on you, dear. There's a doctor three minutes away if we need him."

"Okay," Kayla said, settled on the cot, her arms folded across her chest. She glared at David. "Why are you still here?"

"Just making sure."

She raised a comically puffy eyebrow at him. "You don't need my pity. I don't need your help. I'm chaperoned. I can't possibly get into any more trouble. The neighborhood kids are out looking for my dog and are retrieving my purse, so you can go."

It was like coming through a smoky building fraught with danger, and finally catching sight of the red exit sign.

"Do you want me to pick you up in a couple of hours?"

David contemplated the words that had just come out of his mouth, astounded. He wasn't even planning on being here in a couple of hours. A quick check on his mother, a consult with her care aides and gone.

The urgency to get back to *his* world felt intense.

Especially now that he'd had this run-in with Kayla.

But in a moment of madness he had promised to look after her dog, and bike and purse. He had tangled their lives together for a little while longer. But escape was just postponed, not canceled.

And apparently, she was just as eager not to tangle their lives as he was.

"I've got the neighborhood kids on the case of my dog. I mean it would be nice if you checked, but no, don't feel obligated. And no, definitely don't come back. I'll just walk home. It's not far."

She had been riding her bike on Sugar Maple. Did she live close to there?

"Where are you staying?"

She gave him a puzzled look. "I thought your mom would have told you."

"Told me what?" he said cautiously.

His mother, these days, told him lots of things. That someone was sneaking into the house stealing her eye-glasses. And wine decanters. That she'd had the nicest conversation with his father, who had been dead for seventeen years.

That was part of the reason he was here.

One of the live-in care aides had called him late last night and said, in the careful undertone of one who might be listened to, *You should come. It may not be safe for her to be at home anymore.*

He had known it was coming, and yet been shocked by it all the same. Wasn't he back in his hometown hoping it was an overreaction? That if he just hired more staff he would not have to take his mother from the only home she had known for the past forty years?

It seemed to David, of all the losses that this town had handed him, this was the biggest one of all.

He was losing his mother. But he was not confiding that in Kayla, with her all-too-ready sympathy!

"You thought my mother would tell me where you lived?"

"David, I'm her next-door neighbor."

His mouth fell open and he forced it shut. That was a rather large oversight on his mother's part.

"The house was too much for Kevin's folks," Kayla said.

He'd known that. The house had been empty the last few times he had visited; he had noticed the Jaffreys were no longer there the next time he'd returned to Blossom Valley after Kevin's funeral. It probably wasn't the house that was too much, but the memories it contained.

David had his fair share of those, too. He'd felt a sense of loss, to go with his growing string of losses that he felt when he came home, at seeing the house empty. He had practically grown up in that house next door to his, he and Kevin passing in and out of each other's kitchens since they were toddlers.

Both of them had been only children, and maybe that was why they had become brothers to each other as much as friends.

There was no part of David's childhood that did not have Kevin in it. He was part of the fabric of every Christmas and birthday. They had learned to ride two-wheelers and strapped on their first skates together. They had shared the first day of school. They had chosen David's puppy together, and the dog that had been on their heels all the days of their youth had really belonged to both of them.

They had built the tree fort in Kevin's backyard, and swam across the bay together every single summer.

When David's dad had died, Mr. Jaffrey had acted like a father to both of them.

No, maybe not a father. More like a friend. Had that been part of the problem with Kevin? A problem David had successfully ignored for years?

No rules. No firm hand. No guidelines. An only child, totally indulged, who had, despite his fun-loving charm, become increasingly self-centered.

The Jaffreys' empty house had looked more forlorn with each visit: paint needing freshening up, shingles curling, porch sagging, yard overgrown.

That house had once been so full of love and laughter and hopes and dreams. The state it was in now made it seem like the final few words in the closing chapter of a book with a sad ending.

David wondered if maybe the reason he had stayed so angry at Kevin was because if he ever let go of that, the sadness would swallow him whole.

"The Jaffreys got a condo on the water," Kayla continued. "The house would have gone to Kevin, eventually. They wanted me to have it."

He let that sink in. Kayla was his mother's next-door neighbor. She was living in the house he and Kevin had chased through in those glorious, carefree days of their youth.

He didn't want to ask her anything. He didn't want to know.

And yet he annoyed himself by asking anyway, "Doesn't that house need quite a lot of work?"

He hoped she would hear his lack of enthusiasm. And he thought he caught a momentary glimpse of the fact she was overwhelmed by the house in something faintly worried in her eyes. But she covered it quickly.

"Yes!" she said, her enthusiasm striking him as faintly forced. "It needs everything."

Naturally, she would never walk away from that particular gift horse. She was *needed.*

He couldn't stop himself. "Do you ever give up on hopeless causes?"

CHAPTER FIVE

KAYLA LOOKED BRIEFLY WOUNDED and then she just looked mad. David liked her angry look quite a bit better than the wounded one. The wounded expression made her look vulnerable and made him feel protective of her, even though he had caused it in the first place!

"Are you talking about the house?" she asked dangerously.

He answered safely, "Yes," though he was aware, as was she, that he could have been talking about Kevin.

"Do you ever get tired of being a wet blanket?"

"I prefer to think of it as being the voice of reason."

"I don't care to hear it."

David didn't care what Kayla cared to hear. She obviously was in for some hard truths today, whether she liked it or not. Maybe somebody did have to protect her. From herself! And apparently, no one had stepped up to the plate to do that so far.

"That house," he said, his tone cool and reasonable, "is doing a long, slow slide into complete ruin."

"It isn't," she said, as though he hadn't been reasonable at all. "And it isn't a hopeless cause!"

There. He'd said his piece. Despite the fact that he dealt in investments, including real estate, all the time, his expertise had been rejected.

He could leave with a clear conscience. He had tried to warn her away from a house that was a little more—a lot more—of a project than any thinking person would take on, let alone a single woman.

"I've already ordered all new windows," she said stubbornly. "And the floors are scheduled for refinishing."

A money pit, he thought to himself. He ordered himself to shut up, so was astounded when, out loud, he said drily, "Kayla to the rescue."

She frowned at him.

Stop! David yelled at himself. But he didn't stop. "I bet the dog is a rescue, too, isn't it?"

He had his answer when she flushed. He realized Kevin wasn't the only one he was angry with.

"There was quite a large insurance settlement," she said, her voice stiff with pride. "Can you think of a better use for it than restoring Kevin's childhood home?"

"Actually, yes."

She was in his field of expertise now. This is what he did, and he did it extremely well. He counseled people on how to invest their money. Blaze Enterprises was considered one of the most successful investment firms in Canada.

"A falling-down house in Blossom Valley would probably rate dead last on my list of potential places to put money."

"Are you always so crushingly practical?"

"Yes."

"Humph. Well, I'm going to buy a business here, too," she said stubbornly, her swollen brows drawing together as she read his lack of elaboration for what it was: a complete lack of enthusiasm.

"Really?" he said, not even trying to hide the cynical note from his voice.

"Really," she shot back. Predictably, his cynicism was only making her dig in even deeper. "I'm looking at an ice cream parlor."

"An ice cream parlor? Hmm, that just edged the house out of the position of dead last on my list of potential investments," he said drily.

"More-moo is for sale," she said, as though she hadn't heard him. "On Main Street."

As if the location would change his mind.

He told himself he didn't care how she spent her money. Didn't care if she blew the whole wad.

But somehow he did. Given free rein, Kayla would rescue the world until there was not a single crumb left for herself.

There was no doubt in his mind that More-moo was one more rescue for her, one more thing destined for failure and therefore irresistible. It was time for him to walk away. And yet he thought if he did not try to dissuade her he might not be able to sleep at night.

Sleep was important.

"Nobody sells a business at the top of its game," he cautioned her.

"The owners are retiring."

"Uh-huh."

She looked even more stubborn, her attempts to furrow her brow thwarted somewhat by how swollen it was.

It was none of his business. Let her throw her money around until she had none left.

But of course, that was the problem with having tasted her lips all those years ago. And it was the problem with having chased with her through endless summers on the lake. It was the problem with having studied with her for exams, and walked to school with her on crisp fall days, and sat beside her at the movies, their buttered fingers accidentally touching over popcorn.

It was the problem with having surrendered the first girl he had ever cared about to his best friend, only to watch catastrophe unfold.

There was a feeling that he had dropped the ball, maybe when it mattered most. He couldn't set back the clock. But maybe he could manage not to drop the ball this time.

Whether he wanted to or not, David had a certain emotional attachment to her—whether he wanted to or not, he cared what happened to her.

At least he could set Kayla straight on the ice cream parlor.

"There is no way," he said with elaborate patience, "to make money at a business where you only have good numbers for eight weeks of the year. You've seen this town in the winter. And spring, and fall, for that matter. You could shoot off a cannon on Main Street and not hit anyone."

"The demographics are changing," she said, as if she hoped he would be impressed by her use of the word *demographics.* "People are living here all year round. It's become quite a retirement choice."

"It's still a business that will only ever have eight good weeks every year. And even those eight weeks are weather dependent. Nobody eats ice cream in the rain."

"We did," she said softly.

"Huh?"

"We did. We ate ice cream in the rain."

David frowned. And then he remembered a sudden thunderstorm on a hot afternoon. Maybe they had been sixteen? Certainly it had been the summer before the kaleidoscope, before he had kissed her, before Kevin had laid claim, before the drowning.

A group of them had been riding their bikes down Main Street and had been caught out by the suddenness of the storm.

It had felt thrilling riding through the slashing rain and flashing lightning, until they had taken cover under the awning of the ice cream store as the skies turned black and the thunder rolled around them.

How could he possibly remember that Kayla's T-shirt had been soaked through and had become transparent, showing the details of a surprisingly sexy bra, and that Cedric Parson had been sneaking peeks?

So David had taken his own shirt off and pulled it over Kayla's head, making her still wetter, but not transparently so. He could even remember the feeling: standing under that awning on Main Street, bare chested, David had felt manly and protective instead of faintly ridiculous and cold.

How could he possibly remember that he'd had black ice cream, licorice flavored? And that her tongue had darted out of her mouth and mischievously licked a drip from his cone? And that he had deliberately placed his lips where her tongue had been?

How could he possibly remember that he had felt like the electricity in the air had sizzled deep inside him, and that ice cream had never since tasted as good as it had that electric afternoon?

David shook off the memory and the seductive power it had to make him think maybe people would eat ice cream in the rain.

"Generally speaking, people are not going to go for ice cream if the weather is bad," he said practically. "One season of bad weather, you'd be finished. A few days of bad weather would probably put an ice cream parlor close to the edge."

"Well, I like the idea of owning an ice cream parlor," Kayla said firmly. "I like it a lot."

He took in her eyes peering at him stubbornly from under her comically swollen forehead, and knew this wasn't the time.

"Your ambition in life is to be up to your elbows, digging through vats of frozen-solid ice cream until your hands cramp?"

"That sounds like I'm selling a lot of ice cream," she purred with satisfaction.

"Humph."

"My ambition," she told him, something faintly dangerous in her tone, "is to make people happy. What makes anyone happier than ice cream on a hot day?"

Or during a thunderstorm, his own mind filled in, unbidden.

He said, "Humph," again, more emphatically than the last time.

"It's a simple pleasure," she said stubbornly. "The world needs more of those. Way more."

He had a feeling if he wanted to convince Kayla, he had better back his argument with hard, cold facts: graphs and projections and five years' worth of More-moo's financial statements. What would it hurt to have one of his assistants do a bit of research?

"I would like to bring in specialty ice creams. Did you know, in the Middle East, rose petal ice cream is a big hit?"

He felt she had already given her ice cream parlor dreams way more thought than they deserved.

David was pretty sure he felt the beginnings of a headache throbbing along the line of his forehead and into his temples.

"I bet people would drive here from Toronto for rose petal ice cream," she said dreamily.

David stared at her. She couldn't possibly believe that! Why did he feel as if he needed to personally dissuade her from unrealistic dreams?

Because he had failed to do so when it had really mattered.

Don't marry him, Kayla.

Tears streaming down her face. "I have to."

He could only guess what that fateful decision had put her through. He was going to guess that being married to Kevin had been no bed of roses. Or rose petals, either.

And yet here she was, still dreaming. Was there a certain kind of courage in that?

He hated coming home.

"I'll go see how the kids are doing with finding the dog," David said gruffly.

He could clearly see she wanted to refuse this offer—a warning she wasn't exactly going to embrace his unsolicited advice about the ice cream parlor with open arms—but her concern for the little beast won out.

"You have a cell?" he asked her.

"In pieces on the road, probably," she said wryly.

"I'll call here to the clinic, then, when I find out about the dog. Is he a certain breed?"

"Why?"

"If the kids haven't found him, or I don't find him hiding under a shrub near where you got stung, I'll find a picture on the internet and have my assistant, Jane, make a poster. She can email it to me, and I'll have it printed here."

Under her comical brows, Kayla was transparent. She was both annoyed by his ability to take charge and his organizational skills, and relieved by them, too. No doubt it would be the same reaction when he presented her with the total lack of viability for operating an ice cream parlor in Blossom Valley.

"He's a toy Brussels Griffon," she said, hopeful that he would find the dog, yet reluctant to enlist his aid and hating that she was relying on him. But Kayla was as emotional as he was analytical, her every situation driven by her heart instead of her head.

He put it into his phone. A picture of the world's ugliest dog materialized, big eyes, wiry hair popping out in all the wrong places. The hair springing from the dog's ears and above his eyes reminded him of an old man, badly in need of an eyebrow and ear trim.

"Is it just me, or does this dog bear a resemblance to Einstein?" he muttered, showing her the picture.

"Hence the name," she said, and he smiled reluctantly. Damned if the dog didn't bear a striking resemblance to the high school teacher, Mr. Bastigal, who had emulated his science hero right down to the crazy gray hair and walrus mustache.

When she nodded that the dog on the screen resembled hers, he slipped the phone into his pocket and vowed to himself he would find it. He ran a multimillion-dollar empire. Trouble-shooting was his specialty. One small dog was no match for him. It *looked* like Einstein. That didn't mean it was smart.

And while he was tracking down the doggie, an assistant could do the homework on More-moo, not that it mattered. He was willing to bet Kayla would find another failing business to ride to the rescue of once she was given the reality check on More-moo.

"I'll leave Mary a business card with my cell number on it. You can call me if you change your mind about the ride home."

"I won't."

He scanned her face, nodded and left the room, leaving the card with Mary, as promised. Mary seemed to want to catch up—she'd been the nurse here way back when he was lifeguarding, and she'd seemed old then—but he begged off, claiming responsibility for the dog.

David Blaze had had enough of old home week. Except, as he walked back out into the sultry heat of the July day, he glanced at his watch. He hadn't been here a week. Nowhere near. It had been thirty-two whole minutes since he had last checked his watch in the snarled traffic of Main Street.

CHAPTER SIX

KAYLA WAS AT HOME, and in bed. She could not sleep. She ordered herself not to look at the bedside alarm, but she did, anyway.

It was 3:10 a.m.

She was exhausted, and wide awake at the same time, possibly from the drugs in her system.

But possibly sleep eluded her because she had become used to her little dog cuddled against her in the night, his sweet snores, his wiry whiskers tickling her chin, his eyes popping open to make sure she was still there, staring deeply at her, his liquid gaze holding nothing but devotion and loyalty.

Unlike her husband.

Wasn't that why she was really awake? Contemplating what David had told her about the day of the drowning?

She had called David a liar.

But in her heart, she had felt the sickening reverberation of truth.

That, Kayla decided, was what was hateful about being awake at this time of night. She was held hostage by the thoughts that she could fend off during the day. During the day there was so much this old house needed, it was overwhelming.

But being overwhelmed was not necessarily a bad

thing. It could occupy her every thought and every waking hour. Between that, the new dog and looking for the perfect investment opportunity, she was blessedly busy.

But on a night like tonight, thoughts crowded into her tired mind. Even before David had said that about Kevin flirting with a girl instead of doing his job, Kayla had lain awake at night and contemplated her marriage.

She tried to direct her thoughts to good things and good memories, like the night he had proposed, so sweet and serious and sincere.

I want to do the honorable thing. For once.

She frowned. She hadn't thought of that part of it for a long time, and not in the light she was thinking of it now. Had he loved her, or had he done the honorable thing?

Crazy thoughts. Middle of the night thoughts. Of course he had loved her.

In his way. So what if his way bought flowers when they needed groceries? That was romantic! And he had been a dreamer. That was a good memory. Of them sitting at the kitchen table, in the early days of their marriage sipping the last of their coffee, his face all intense and earnest as he described what he wanted for them: a business of their own, a big house, a great car.

Disloyal to think his dreams had been grandiose and made it impossible for him to settle for an ordinary life. Within days of finding a job, it would seem his litany of complaints would begin. He wasn't appreciated. He wasn't being paid enough. His boss was a jerk. His coworkers were inferior, his great ideas weren't being listened to or implemented.

She never stopped hoping and praying that he would find himself, that he would grow up to be a man with all the best characteristics of that boy she had grown up with—so fun-loving and energetic and full of mischief.

Kevin had rewarded her unflagging belief in him by increasingly taking her for granted. He had become careless of her feelings—though the old charm would return, temporarily, when she threatened to leave or when it managed to bail them out of one of his predicaments yet again.

The old charm. The one thing he was good at. What had David meant about Kevin flirting with a girl? Had he been talking to her? Or more? Touching her? Kissing her?

Had Kevin had affairs during their marriage?

There. She was there, at the place she had refused to go since her husband's death. It felt like she had just plunged into a hard place at the core of her, that did not go away because she pretended it was not there, that had not been a part of her makeup before she had married Kevin.

Was it this very suspicion that had caused it? This suspicion, and *so* much disappointment that it felt so disloyal to look at?

She had wondered about Kevin's fidelity even before David's shocking revelation outside of the clinic that afternoon. It seemed to her the more Kevin failed at everything else, the more she had become lonely within their marriage, the more he had exercised his substantial charm outside of it.

Where had he been, when speeding toward home too late at night, the car sliding on ice and slamming into a tree?

No seat belt. So like Kevin.

He had been chronically irresponsible, and others had picked up the tab for that.

It felt like David's fault, David's sudden unexpected presence in her life, and his revelations of this afternoon that had brought these thoughts, lurking beneath the surface, surging to the top.

Kayla blinked back tears. It had just all gone so terribly, terribly wrong. The tears felt weak, and at the same time, better than that hard, cold rock she carried around where her heart used to be.

And now David was back, and words she had not allowed herself to think of in those five long years of marriage to Kevin were at the forefront of her mind.

Don't marry him, Kayla.

She considered the awful possibility that David, who had withheld his forgiveness, had not been the cause of Kevin's downward spiral, but that he had seen something about his oldest friend that she had missed.

And who was withholding forgiveness now? It was pathetic. But now that her feelings had surfaced, she was aware one of them was anger. It was useless to feel that way. Kevin was dead. It could never be fixed.

"Stop it," Kayla ordered herself, but instead she thought of how David's hand had felt on her thigh, how she had leaned toward him, wanting, if she had only seconds left, one last taste of him.

Those thoughts made her feel restless, and hungry with a hunger that a midnight snack would never be able to fill.

Irritated with the ruminations of an exhausted mind, she yanked off the sheet that covered her, sat up and swung her legs out of the bed.

She padded over to her open window, where old-fashioned chintz curtains danced slowly on a cooling summer breeze. The window coverings throughout the house were thirty years behind the current styles, and one more thing on the long "to-do" list.

Which Kayla also didn't want to be thinking about in the dead of night, a time when things could become overwhelming.

She diverted herself, squinting hopefully at her backyard. The moon was out and bright, but the massive, mature sugar maple at the center of the yard, and overgrown shrub beds, where peonies and forsythia competed with weeds, cast most of the yard in deep shadow where a small dog could hide.

Her little dog was out there somewhere. She had no doubt he was afraid. Poor little Bastigal was afraid of everything: loud noises and quick movements, and men and cats and the wind in leaves.

It was probably what was making him so hard to find. All afternoon he had probably been quivering under a shrub, hidden as the hordes of Blossom Valley children ran by, calling his name.

And it was hordes.

Walking home from the clinic there had been a poster on every telephone pole, with a picture of a Brussels Griffon on it that looked amazingly like Bastigal.

Under it had been the promise of a five-hundred dollar reward for his return.

And *David's* cell phone number. Well, she could hardly resent that. Her own cell phone had been left with her bicycle, her purse, her hat and her crushed sunflowers on her front porch. Blossom Valley being Blossom Valley, her purse was undisturbed, all her credit cards and cash still in it. But her cell phone had been shattered beyond repair, and since she had opted not to have a landline, it was the only phone she had.

So she could not resent the use of his number, but she did resent the reward. Obviously, she could not allow him to pay it, and obviously she did not have an extra five hundred dollars lying around. It hadn't been a good idea, anyway. She had no doubt the enthusiasm of the children, reward egging them on like a carrot on a stick before a donkey, was frightening her dog into deeper hiding.

She looked out the window, willing herself to see

through the inky darkness. Was it possible Bastigal would have found his way to his own yard? Would he recognize this as his own yard? They'd only been back in Blossom Valley, in their new home, for a little over two weeks. She hadn't even finished unpacking boxes yet.

But through the open window, Kayla thought she heard the faintest sound coming from between the houses, and her heart leaped.

Grabbing a light sweater off the hook behind her closet door, glad to have an urgent purpose that would help her to escape her own thoughts, Kayla moved through her darkened, and still faintly unfamiliar, house and out the back door into her yard.

Hers.

Despite the loss of the dog and her undisciplined thoughts of earlier, the feeling of having a place of her own to call home calmed something in her.

She became aware it was a beautiful night, and her yard looked faintly magical in the moonlight, not showing neglect as it did in the harsh light of day. It was easy to overlook the fact the grass needed mowing and just appreciate that it was thick and dewy under her feet. There was a scent in the air that was cool and pure and invigorating.

She heard, again, some slight noise around the corner of her house, and her heart jumped. Bastigal. He had come home after all!

She rounded the corner of her house, and stopped short.

"Mrs. Blaze?"

David's mother turned her head and looked at her, smiling curiously. And yet the smile did not hide a certain vacant look in her eyes. She was in a nightgown that had not been buttoned down the front. She also wore a straw gardening hat, and bright pink winter boots. She was holding pruning shears, and a pile of thorny branches were accumulating at her feet.

Kayla noticed several scratches on her arms were bleeding.

It occurred to her she hadn't really seen Mrs. Blaze since taking up residence next door. She had meant to go over and say hello when her boxes were unpacked.

In a glance she could see why David's mother had not told him who had moved in next door. She was fairly certain she was not recognized by the woman who had known Kayla's husband all of his life, and Kayla for a great deal of hers.

"It's me," Kayla said, gently. "Kayla Jaffrey."

Mrs. Blaze frowned and turned back to the roses. She snapped the blades of the pruners at a branch and missed.

"It used to be McIntosh. I'm friends with your son, David." *Why did I say that, instead of that I was Kevin's wife?*

Not that it mattered. Mrs. Blaze cast her a look that was totally bewildered. A deep sadness opened up in Kayla as she realized she was not the only one in Blossom Valley dealing with major and devastating life changes.

She stepped carefully around the thorny branches, plucked the dangerously waving pruners from Mrs. Blaze's hands and set them on the ground. She shrugged out of her sweater and tucked it lightly around Mrs. Blaze's shoulders, buttoning it quickly over the gaping nightie.

"Let's get you home, shall we?" Kayla offered her elbow.

"But the roses…"

"I'll look after them," Kayla promised.

"I don't know. I like to do it myself. The gardener can't be trusted. If roses aren't properly pruned…" Her voice faded, troubled, as if she was struggling to recall what would happen if the roses weren't properly pruned.

"I'll look after them," Kayla promised again.

"Oh. I suppose. Are you a gardener?"

What was the harm in one little white lie? "Yes."

"Don't forget the pruners, then," Mrs. Blaze snapped, and Kayla saw a desperate need to be in control in the sharpness of the command.

She stooped and picked up the pruners, then took advantage of the budding trust in Mrs. Blaze's eyes to offer her elbow again. This time Mrs. Blaze threaded her fragile arm through Kayla's and allowed Kayla to guide her through the small wedge of land that separated the two properties. They went through the open gate into the Blaze yard.

Kayla had assumed, looking over her fence at it, that Mrs. Blaze gardened. The lawn was manicured, the beds filled with flowers and dark loam, weed free. Now she realized there must be the gardener Mrs. Blaze had referred to.

Kayla led David's mother up the stairs and onto the back veranda. Again, she had been admiring it from her own yard. Everything here was beautifully maintained: the expansive deck newly stained, beautiful, inviting furniture scattered over its surface, potted plants spilling an abundance of color and fragrance.

She had been holding out the hope her own property was going to look like this one day. Now she wondered just how much time—or staff—it took to make a place look this perfect. Once she had her own business, would she be able to manage it? She tried not to let the thought make her feel deflated.

Kayla knocked at the door, lightly, and when nothing happened, louder. She was just about to put her head in the door and call out when from within the house she heard the sound of feet coming down the stairs.

She knew from the sound of the tread it was likely David—and who else would it be after all—but still, she did not feel prepared when the door was flung open.

David Blaze stood there, half-asleep and half-naked, unconsciously and mouthwateringly sexy, looking about as magnificent as a man could look.

CHAPTER SEVEN

DAVID'S CHOCOLATE HAIR was sleep tousled, and his dark eyes held faint, dazed amusement as he gazed at the two nightie-clad women in front of him.

Kayla gazed back. He stood there in only a pair of blue-plaid pajama pants that hung dangerously low over the faint jut of his hips.

He didn't have on anything else. His body was magnificent. He was deeper and broader than he had been all those years ago when he had been a lifeguard. The boyish sleekness of his muscle had deepened into the powerful build of a man in his prime. There was not an ounce of superfluous flesh on him.

In the darkness of the night he looked as if he had been carved from alabaster: beautiful shoulders, carved, smooth chest, washboard abs on his stomach.

Kayla gulped.

David came full awake, and the faint amusement was doused in his eyes as he took them both in, lingering on Kayla's own nightie-clad self a second more than necessary. It occurred to her the nightie, light as it was and perfect for hot summer nights, was just a little sheer for this kind of encounter. Her shoulders felt suddenly too bare, and she could feel cool air on the thighs that had already been way too exposed to him.

David seemed to draw his eyes away from her reluctantly. Kayla could feel her pulse hammering in the hollow of her throat.

"Mom," he said gently, swinging open the screen door, "come in the house."

His mother looked at him searchingly and then her expression tightened. "I don't know who you are," she snapped, "but don't think I don't know my wallet is missing."

"We'll find your wallet." His voice was measured, and the tone remained gentle. But Kayla saw the enormous pain that darkened his eyes as his mother moved toward him.

"And the roses need pruning," Mrs. Blaze snapped at her son.

He winced, and at that moment, a woman came up behind them, dressed in a white uniform.

"Mr. Blaze, I'm so sorry. I—"

He gave her a look that said he didn't want to hear it, and passed his mother into her care. "It looks like she has some scratches on her arms, if you could tend to those."

"Yes, sir."

There was something faintly shocking about hearing David—the boy who had romped through the days of summer with her, and played tricks on their teachers, and sat in with her at bonfires licking marshmallow off his fingers—addressed in such a deferential tone of voice.

The door shut behind his mother and the care aide, and he stepped out onto the porch. His face was composed, but Kayla saw him draw in a deep, steadying breath, and then another.

It filled his chest and drew her eyes to the masculine perfection of that surface.

"Thank you," he said quietly. "Where was she?"

Her eyes skittered away from his chest, and to his face. The lateness of the hour and the pain in his face made all the hurts between them seem less important somehow. She found that she wanted to reach up and ease the stern, worried lines that had creased around his mouth.

"In my yard, pruning the roses." Kayla handed him the pruning shears, and he took them and stared down at them for a moment, then looked out at the garden shed, the door hanging open.

"I guess that needs to be locked," he said.

"I didn't know," Kayla said softly. "I haven't been over yet since I got back. The house and yard looked so beautifully maintained, I just assumed your mom was going as strong as ever."

"One of my property managers makes sure the maintenance gets done, and the yard is looked after." He looked around sadly. "It does look like normal people live here, doesn't it?"

"I'm so sorry, David," she said softly, and then again, "I didn't know."

He smiled a little tightly. "No pity," he warned her.

"It wasn't pity," she said, a little hotly.

"What, then?"

"It was compassion."

"Ah." He didn't look convinced, or any more willing to accept whatever she was offering no matter what name she put on it. "What are you doing out here, anyway? What time is it?"

"After three." No sense confessing all the terrible thoughts that had kept her from sleeping. "I was worried about my dog. I couldn't sleep. I heard a noise out here and thought it might be Bastigal."

"And it was Mom. It's a mercy that you found her before she wandered off or hurt herself with the pruners."

He shook his head. "She can't remember what she had for breakfast—"

Or her own son, Kayla thought sadly.

"—but she worked her way past two security locks, a dead bolt and a childproof handle on the door."

Kayla was afraid to tell him, again, how sorry she was.

"There's a live-in aide, but obviously she was distracted by something. I think she sneaks the odd cigarette out here on the deck. Maybe she left the door open behind her."

Kayla shivered a little at his tone, very happy she was not in the aide's shoes.

"How long has your mom been like that?" Kayla asked softly.

It looked like a conversation he didn't want to have, but then he sighed, as if it was a surrender to confide in her.

"She's been deteriorating for a couple of years," he said softly. "It starts so small you can overlook it, or wish it away. I'd notice things when I visited: toothpaste in the refrigerator, mismatching socks, saying the same thing she just said. When I wasn't here, she'd phone me. She lost the car. Where was Dad? That was when she could still remember my phone number."

David stopped abruptly, took a deep breath, as if he was shaking off the need to confide. His voice cooled. "I've had live-in help for her for nearly two months. The last few weeks, the decline has seemed more rapid. I don't think she's going to be able to stay here any longer."

So what could she say, if not "sorry"? But Kayla had dealt with her own grief, and sometimes she knew how words, intended to help, could just increase the feeling of being lonely and alone.

Instead of words she reached out and placed her palm over his heart. She wasn't even sure why. Perhaps to let him know she could feel it breaking?

His skin felt beautiful under her fingertips, like silk that had been warmed in the sun. And his heartbeat was steady and strong. She didn't know if the gesture comforted him, but it did her. She could feel his strength, and knew he had enough of it to cope with whatever came next.

For a moment he stood gazing down at her hand, transfixed. And then he covered it with his own.

Something more powerful than words passed between them, and she felt a shiver of something for David she had not felt ever before.

Certainly not with her own husband.

Shaken, and trying desperately not to show it, she withdrew her hand from under the warm, resilient promise of his.

For a moment, an electric silence ran between them. Then David ran his freed hand through the crisp darkness of his hair. "No dog, I assume?"

Kayla was inordinately relieved at the change of subject, at the words sliding like cooling raindrops into the place that sizzled like an electrical storm between them. "No. I hoped he might have found his way back to the yard."

"I'm sorry I didn't find him."

"It's not for lack of trying. Thank you for the posters—they brought out an army of children. I'll reimburse you, of course."

He shrugged. "Whatever."

"And naturally, I'll pay the reward when we find him."

"It's okay, Kayla. I offered it, I'll pay it."

"No."

"It's probably a moot point, anyway."

"You think we aren't going to find him?" she asked,

trying to keep the panic from her voice. David obviously had bigger things to think about than her dog.

"Oh, I think you'll find him. I just don't think the kids will. He's a timid little guy, isn't he?"

"Yes. How did you know?"

"Well, I saw him scurry away after he fell out of the basket when you got stung."

"Did he look hurt?"

"Not at the rate he was running, no. I had spotted you before that. Riding down Main Street. Even then the dog had a distinctly worried look on his face."

Despite herself, she chuckled. "That's him—my little worrier. I'll probably never get him to ride in the basket again!"

"A pair well matched. You're both worriers!"

To be standing with such a gorgeous man and pegged as a worrier! What did she want to be seen as? Carefree? Lively? Happy?

But David always saw straight to the heart of things, and the last few years of her life had been rife with worry. Kayla self-consciously touched her brow, wondering if there was a permanent mark of it there.

Thankfully, David was scanning the bushes. "I don't think he's going to come out for the reward-hungry children running through the streets shrieking his name. Sorry. A misstep on my part."

"He'll show up," she said, but she could hear the wistfulness—and worry—in her own voice.

"I hope so." She knew she should say good-night and leave his porch, cross the little strip of grass that separated their properties and close the gate firmly between them.

But she didn't.

When had she become this lonely? She felt like she ached for his company. Anyone's company, probably. She didn't want to return to that empty house, the wayward direction of her restless thoughts.

He was looking at her, smiling slightly.

"What?"

"There is a quality about you that begs to be painted."

"What?" She wanted to press her brow again!

"I noticed it when I saw you on the bike. I could almost see a painting of you—Girl on a Bicycle.

"And now, out here in your white nightdress on the porch. Girl on a Summer Night." He shrugged, embarrassed.

But she felt as if she drank in the words like a flower deprived too long of water.

In that *Lakeside Life* feature on David and Blaze Enterprises, it had said, almost as an aside, that David had one of the largest private collections of art in the country. Again, the man who stood in front of her did not seem like the same boy who had raced her on bicycles down these tree-lined streets.

This David, this man of the world and collector of art, thought she was worthy of a painting? He saw something else in her besides a furrow-browed worrier?

Kayla could feel tears smarting her eyes, so she said swiftly, carelessly, turning her head from his gaze and pressing her fingers into her forehead to erase any remaining worry lines,"I guess the swelling has gone down, then." She pretended she was concerned about the swelling from the beesting rather than the worry lines!

She felt his fingers on her chin, turning her unwilling gaze back to him.

He searched her face, and she felt as if she was wide open to him: the loneliness, the crushing disappointment, the constant worry, all of it. She felt as if he could see her.

And she realized, stunned, she had always felt like that. As if David could see her.

The longing that leaped within her terrified her. The longing and the recrimination. She suddenly felt as if every choice she had ever made had been wrong.

And she probably still could not be trusted with choices!

Kayla reminded herself she had made a vow that she was not going to offer herself on the altar of love anymore.

She had vowed to be content with the house Kevin's parents had given her—restoring it to some semblance of order, never mind its former glory, should be enough to fill her days! Add to that her dog, when she found him, and eventually her business when she discovered the right one.

Those things would fill her, complete her, give her purpose, without leaving her open to the pain and heartache of loving.

She hated it that the night was working some odd magic on her, that she would even think the word *love* in the presence of David.

She broke free of his fingers and his searching gaze, darted down the steps and across the back lawn.

"Kayla," he called. "Stop."

But she didn't. Stop why? So that he could dissect her heartbreak? Lay open her disappointments with his eyes? No, she kept on going. Nothing could stop her.

Except his next words.

"Kayla, stop. I think I see the dog."

CHAPTER EIGHT

AT FIRST KAYLA THOUGHT it was a trick. Kevin had not been above using what she wanted most to get his own way.

Once we get established, in our new town, then we can talk about a baby.

She whirled, already angry that something about David being here was bringing all this *stuff* up. She was prepared to be very angry if David had used her dog to make her do what he wanted.

He was not looking at her, but had gone to the railing of his deck and was watching something intently. She followed David' gaze, and though it was dark, she saw Bastigal's little rump, tail tucked hard between his legs, disappearing through the Blazes' hedges and heading out onto the street.

Kayla's heart leaped with hope.

David stepped back inside the door, shoved his feet in a pair of sneakers and went down the back porch steps two at a time. He blasted through the boxwood, careless of the branches scraping him.

Kayla looked down at her own bare feet, and contemplated the skimpy fabric of her nightgown. By the time she went and got shoes on, or grabbed a sweater to cover herself—her sweater had gone inside with Mrs. Blaze—

the dog would be gone. She doubted Bastigal would come to David even if he did manage to catch up to him.

It was the middle of the night. It was not as if anyone was going to see her.

Except him. David. And he thought I should be painted.

Without nearly enough thought, with a spontaneity that felt wonderfully freeing, Kayla took off through the hedge after David.

She saw he was crossing the deserted street at a dead run. If Kayla had had any doubt that he had maintained the athleticism of a decade before, it was vanquished. He ran like the wind, effortless, his strides long and ground covering. In the blink of an eye, David had crossed the silvered front lawn of a house across the street. Without breaking stride he charged around the side of a house and disappeared into the backyard.

She followed him. She thought her feet would give her grief, but in actual fact she had spent all the summers of her life barefoot, and she loved the feeling of the grass on them, velvety, dewy, perfect lawns springing beneath her feet.

She arrived in the backyard just in time to watch David hurdle effortlessly over a low picket fence into the next yard. She scrambled over it, catching her nightie. She yanked it free and kept running. She didn't see Bastigal, but David must have seen the dog, because he was chasing after something like a hound on the scent.

She caught up with David after finding her way through a set of particularly prickly hedges. They were in the middle of someone's back lawn. She cast a glance at the darkened windows.

"Do you see him?" she whispered.

He held a finger to his lips, and they both listened, and heard a rustle in the thick shrubs that bordered the lawn.

"Bastigal!" Kayla called in a stage whisper, both not wanting to frighten the dog or wake the neighbors.

Twigs cracked and leaves rustled, but she didn't catch so much as a glimpse of her dog, and the sound was moving determinedly away from them.

David moved cautiously toward it. She tiptoed after him. And then David was off like a sprinter out of the blocks, and Kayla kept on his heels.

Three blocks later, she had done the fast tour of every backyard in the neighborhood, and they now found themselves on Peachtree Lane, in the front yard of a house that was on Blossom Valley's register of most notable heritage homes.

"I think we lost him," David said, and put his hands on his knees, bent forward at the waist and tried to catch his breath.

"Dammit." She followed his lead and rested her hands on her knees, bent over and gasping for air. She was so close to him she could see the shine of perspiration on his brow, the tangy, sweet scent of a clean man's sweat tickled her nostrils.

"Don't move a muscle," David whispered. He nodded toward the deep shadow of a shrub drooping under the weight of heavy purple blossoms.

One of the blossoms stirred in the windless night. The leaves parted.

Kayla stopped gasping and held her breath.

A little beige-colored bunny came out, blinked its pinky eyes at them and wiggled its nose.

"Is that what we've been chasing?" she asked.

"I think so."

"Dammit," she said for the second time.

But despite her disappointment, Kayla was aware that

her blood felt as if it were humming through her veins, and that she felt wonderfully, delightfully alive.

She began to laugh. She tried to muffle her laughter so as not to disturb the sleeping neighborhood.

David straightened, watched her, arms folded over his chest. He shook his head, and then smiled. Then he chuckled.

She collapsed on the grass, on her back, knees up. She tugged her nightie, now torn at the hem where it had snagged, down over her bare knees, and then spread her arms wide, giggling and still panting, trying to catch her breath.

After a moment, David flopped down on his back beside her, his arm thrown up over his forehead.

Their breathing became less ragged, and the night seemed deeply silent. Some delicious fragrance tickled her nostrils. The stars were magnificent in an inky black sky.

"This is one of the things I missed after we moved to Windsor," Kayla whispered. "You don't see the stars like this in the city."

"No," he agreed softly, "you don't."

The silence was deep and companionable between them. "Why did you move to Windsor?" he asked. "You always liked it here."

I hoped for a fresh start. I hoped a baby could repair some of the things we had lost.

Out loud, she said, "Kevin got a job there."

She didn't say that Kevin's job had not lasted, but by then they could not afford to move back, let alone have a baby. She did not say the kind of jobs she had done to keep them afloat. She had waitressed and cleaned and babysat children and even done yard work.

She did not say how she had longed for the sweetness

of the life she had left behind in her hometown. Didn't David long for it like that? She asked him.

"Do you miss it here? Ever?"

His silence was long. "No, Kayla. I don't have time to miss it."

"If you did have time, would you?"

Again the silence was long. And then, almost reluctantly, he said, "Yeah, I guess I would. Blossom Valley was the place of perfect summers, wasn't it?"

The longing was poignant between them.

"I can't remember the last time I looked at the stars like this," she murmured. But she thought it was probably in those carefree days, those days before everything had changed.

"Me, either."

It was one of those absolutely spontaneous perfect moments. His bare shoulder was nearly touching hers. Peripherally, she was aware of the rise and fall of his naked chest, and that it was his scent, mingled with the pure scent of the dew on the grass and the night air and those flowers drooping under their own weight, that had made the night so deliciously fragrant.

"Is that Orion above us?" he asked.

"Yes," she said, "the hunter."

"I remembered how you impressed me once by naming all the stars in that constellation."

She laughed softly. "Zeta, Epsilon, Delta. That's his belt."

"Go on."

So she did, naming the stars of the constellation, one by one, and then they lay in silence, contemplating the night sky above them.

"I always thought you'd become a teacher," he said

slowly. "You had such an amazing mind, took such delight in learning things."

She said nothing, another road not taken rising up before her.

"I at least thought you'd have kids. You always loved kids. You were always a counselor at that awful day camp. What was it called?"

"Sparkling Waters. And it wasn't awful. It was for kids who couldn't afford camp."

"Naturally," he said drily. "One of the most affluent communities in Canada, and you find the needy kids. I didn't even know there were any until you started working there."

"That whole neighborhood south of the tracks is full of orchard workers and people who clean rooms at the motels and hotels." She didn't tell him that now that she had been one of those people she had even more of an affinity for them. "It was Blossom Valley's dirty little secret then, and it still is today."

"And how are you going to fix that?" he asked.

Instead of feeling annoyed, she felt oddly safe with him. She replied, "I bet I could think of some kind of coupon system so the kids can come for ice cream."

"Ah, Kayla," he said, but not with recrimination.

"That's me. Changing the world, one ice cream cone at a time."

"No wonder those kids adored you," he remembered wryly. "What I remember is if we saw the kids you worked with during the day at night, they wanted to hang out with you. I hated that. Us ultracool teenagers with all these little tagalongs."

"Maybe you were ultracool. I wasn't."

"I probably wasn't, either," he said, that wryness still

in his voice. "But I sure thought I was. Maybe all guys that age think they are."

Certainly Kevin had thought he was, too, Kayla remembered. But he never really had been. Funny, yes. Charming, absolutely. Good-looking, but not spectacularly so. Athletic, but never a star. Energetic and mischievous and fun-loving.

Kevin had always been faintly and subtly competitive with his better-looking and stronger best friend.

When David signed up for lifeguard training, so did Kevin, but he didn't just want to be equal to David, he wanted to be better. So if David swam across the lake, Kevin swam there and back. When David bought his first car—that rusting little foreign import—Kevin, make that Kevin's father, bought a brand-new one.

The faint edge to Kevin's relationship with David seemed like something everyone but David had been aware of.

Hadn't Kayla spent much of her marriage trying to convince Kevin he was good enough? Trying to convince him that she was not in the least bowled over by David's many successes that were making all the newspapers? Trying to forgive Kevin's jealousy and bitterness toward his friend, excuse it as *caused* by David's indifference to the man who had once been his friend?

But Kayla remembered David *really* had been ultra-cool. Even back then he'd had something—a presence, an intensity, a way of taking charge—that had set him apart.

And made him irresistible to almost every girl in town. *And on one magic night, I'd been the girl. That he had shared his remarkable charisma with.*

I tasted his lips, and then he hardly looked at me again.

"I adored them back," she said, wanting to remember

the affection of those moments and not the sense of loss his sudden indifference had caused in her.

"They were pesky little rascals," David said. "You never told them to go away and leave you—us—alone. I can remember you passing out hot dogs—that I had provided—to them at a campfire."

Maybe that was why he had stopped speaking to me.

"Did I?"

"Yeah. And marshmallows. Our soda pop. Nothing was safe."

"I love kids," she said softly. "I probably couldn't bear to think of them hungry."

"Our little do-gooder." He paused and looked at her. "You did love kids, though. That's why I thought you'd lose no time having a pile of them of your own. Especially since you seemed in such a hurry to get married."

Kayla bit her lip. For the first time since they had lain down beneath the stars, she was certain she heard judgment there.

Marry in haste, repent at leisure.

"So why didn't you have kids?" he persisted.

Kayla begged herself not to even think it. But the soft night air, and this unexpected moment, lying in the coolness of the grass beside David, made the thought explode inside of her.

She had wanted a child, desperately. Now she could see it was a blessing she had not had one.

"The time was just never right," she said, her tone cool, not inviting any more questions.

"Aw, Kayla," he said, and as unforthcoming as she thought her statement had been, she felt as if David heard every unhappy moment of her marriage in it.

She felt an abrupt, defensive need to take the focus off

herself. “So why aren’t you married, David? Why don’t you have a wife and kids and a big, happy family?”

“At first it was because I never met anyone I wanted to do those things with,” he said quietly.

“Come on. You’ve become news with some of the women you dated! Kelly O’Ranahan? Beautiful, successful, talented.”

“Insecure, superficial, wouldn’t know Orion if he shot her with an arrow.”

The moment suddenly seemed shot through with more than an arrow. Heat sizzled between them as his gaze locked on hers.

“What do you mean, ‘at first’?” she whispered.

He didn’t answer—he just reached out and slid a hand through her hair, and looked at her with such longing it stole her breath from her lungs.

The air felt ripe with possibilities. Kayla again felt seen, somehow, in a way no one had seen her for years.

Somehow, feeling that way made her feel more intensely guilty than her disloyal thoughts about her husband.

And then, thankfully, the uncomfortable intensity of the moment was shattered when the darkness exploded around them, and they were both frozen in an orb of white light.

“End to a perfect day,” she said, happy for the distraction from the intensity. “Beesting, hospital emergency room, lost dog—” *disloyal thoughts about my deceased husband* “—now alien kidnapping.”

He didn’t smile at her attempt to use humor to deflect the intensity between them.

“Don’t forget the stargazing part,” he said softly.

She looked at him. Not many people would look better under the harsh glare of the light that illuminated them, but he did. It brought the strength of his features into sharp relief.

It occurred to her that the stargazing was the part she was least likely to forget.

David broke the gaze first, sat up and shielded his eyes against the bright light that held them.

"Police! Get up off that grass."

CHAPTER NINE

THEIR PREDICAMENT STRUCK KAYLA as hilarious, but she suspected her sudden desire to laugh was like biting back laughter at a funeral. Her nerves were strung tight over the moments they had just shared. Her emotions felt electric, overwhelming and way too close to the surface.

Could David possibly think she was more attractive than Kelly O'Ranahan, the famous actress?

Of course not! She was reading way too much into his hand finding her hair and touching it. He probably felt nothing but sorry for her.

"Put your hands in the air where I can see them."

Poor David. She cast a look at his face. If David had been ultracool back then, he was even more so now. A proven track record of ultracoolness.

It occurred to her she was about to get one of Canada's most respected businessmen arrested. It was no laughing matter, really, but she couldn't help herself.

She laughed.

David shot her a look that warned her he wasn't finding it in any way as amusing as she was. His expression was grim as he reached for her hand and found it. Then he got his feet underneath him and jumped up lithely, yanking her up beside him.

She noticed he stepped out just a little in front of her,

shielding her torn nightie-clad body from the harshness of the police searchlight with his own.

It reminded her of something a long time ago—a thunderstorm, and seeking shelter under the awning of the ice cream store. She remembered him pulling off his shirt and putting it over her own, which had become transparent with wetness.

Was it in some way weak—a further betrayal of her marriage—to enjoy his protective instincts so much? He let go of her hand only after he had put her behind him, and then shaded his eyes, trying to see past the light.

"Sir, I need you to put your hands up in the air. You, too, ma'am."

The light they were caught in was absolutely blinding. Kayla squinted past the broadness of David's shoulder and into the brightness. She could make out the dark outline of Blossom Valley's only patrol car.

She did as asked, but the laughter had started deep inside her and she had to choke it back. She slid a look at David. His expression was grim as he put his hands up, rested them with laced fingers on the top of his head.

The spotlight went off, and a policeman came across the lawn toward them. He looked grumpy as he stopped a few feet away and regarded them with deep suspicion. He took a notepad from his pocket, licked his pencil, waiting.

When neither of them volunteered anything, he said, "We've had a report of a prowler in this area."

Kayla bit her lip to try and stop the giggle, but she made the mistake of casting a glance at David's face. Naturally, he was appalled by their predicament, his face cast in stone. A snort of laughter escaped her.

"Have you folks been drinking?"

"No," David bit out, giving her a withering glance when another snort of laughter escaped her.

"I'm sorry," she managed to sputter.

"Is this your house?"

"No," David snapped.

"Have you got any ID?"

"Does it look like we have any ID?" David said, exasperated and losing patience fast. She cast him a glance, and saw instantly that he was not intimidated, that he was a man who was very accustomed to being in authority, not knuckling under to it.

"Well, what are you doing half-dressed in front of a house that isn't yours? How do you know each other?"

David sucked in a harsh breath at the insinuation that they might have been doing something improper. He took a step forward, but Kayla stepped out of his protection and inserted herself, hands still on top of her head, between him and the policeman. She sensed David's irritation with her.

"We're neighbors. We're looking for my dog," Kayla said hastily, before David really did manage to get himself arrested. "We thought we saw him and gave chase. I'm afraid we did trespass through several backyards. It turned out to be that bunny over there."

"What bunny?"

Kayla turned and lowered one arm to point, but the bunny, naturally, had disappeared. "There really was one. We haven't been drinking." She could feel a blush moving up her cheeks as she realized a nightie that was perfectly respectable in her house was not so much on the darkened streets of Blossom Valley.

"Or doing anything else," she said, lowering her other arm and folding both of them over the sheerness of her nightie.

The policeman regarded them both, then his suspicion died and he sighed.

"You can put your hands down. My little girl has been looking for that dog since the posters went up. She went to sleep dreaming about the reward. She wants a new bicycle." He squinted at David. "Do I know you?"

David lowered his arms and lifted an eyebrow in a way that said *I doubt it.* How could he manage to have such presence, even in such an awkward situation?

"Are you that investor guy?" the cop asked. Deference, similar to that Kayla had heard in the care aide's voice, crept into the policeman's tone. "The one I saw the article about in *Lakeside Life?*"

"That would be me."

"You don't look much like a prowler, actually."

"Do most prowlers not go out and about in their pajamas?" David asked a bit drily.

"Well, not Slugs and Snails pajamas," the officer said, recognizing the name brand of a Canadian clothing icon that produced very sought after—and very, very expensive—men's casual clothing.

Kayla squinted at David's pajama bottoms. They did, indeed, have the very subtle label of the men's designer firm, and she had to admire the officer's professional powers of observation.

She also had to bite back another giggle as she realized her own attire, her summer-weight, white nightie, might be worthy of a painting, but it was way too revealing. She maneuvered back into the shadow cast by David.

David shot her a warning look over his shoulder when she had to bite back another giggle.

"What do you think of AIM?" the policeman asked, putting the dark writing pad he'd held in his hand back into his shirt pocket. He snapped a flashlight onto his belt.

"Personally, I think it's a dog," David said.

"Unfortunately, not the dog we are looking for," Kayla inserted helpfully.

David gave her a look over his shoulder, and then continued as if she hadn't spoken, "If you have it, now's the time to dump it. If you don't have it, don't buy it. Try—" he smiled a bit "—Slugs and Snails. It trades as SAS-B. TO."

"Really?"

David lifted a shoulder. "If you're into taking advice from a half-naked man in his pajamas in the middle of the night."

The policeman finally relaxed completely. Now it was all buddy to buddy. He laughed. "Well, the pajamas are Slugs and Snails. How far are you from home?"

"Sugar Maple," David said.

"I can give you a lift back over there."

"No!" David's answer was instant. "Thanks anyway."

"Speak for yourself," Kayla said firmly. "It's a perfect finish for this day—a ride in the backseat of a police car. Plus, it's on my bucket list."

David glared at her. "Why would that be on your bucket list?"

"Because it's what everyone least expects of me."

"You got that right," David growled.

But a deeper part of the truth was that Kayla knew David wouldn't get in the police car because he would be aware, as she was, that everyone had phones and cameras these days. He was the CEO of a company that relied on his reputation being squeaky clean. He was publically recognizable because of his success and his involvement with well-known and high-profile people. Kelly O'Ranahan was only one of a long list.

David Blaze was a public figure. Kayla didn't really blame him for not getting in, but she was aware as she smiled at him, as the policeman opened the door for her and she slid into the backseat, that she needed for this encounter with David to be over.

She felt she had, somehow, revealed too much of herself on the basis of a starry night and an old friendship.

Now she felt the vulnerability of her confessions, felt faintly ashamed of herself and as if she had betrayed Kevin.

But worse than any of that? The yearning she had felt when David had reached out and touched her hair.

Kayla felt she had to escape him.

Being determined that he would not see any of that, she gave David a cheeky wave as she drove away in the police car.

And then she let the relief well up in her, a feeling as if she was escaping something dangerous and unpredictable and uncontrollable.

She liked being in control. Especially after Kevin.

"Hey, good luck with your dog," the cop said, a few minutes later. He very sweetly got out and opened the car door for her before he drove away.

Despite the fact her day had unfolded as a series of mishaps, and her dog was missing, and she had discovered, within herself, an unspoken bitterness toward Kevin, Kayla was uncomfortably aware of something as she climbed the dilapidated stairs to her house.

She felt alive. She felt intensely and vibrantly alive, possibly for the first time since she had left Blossom Valley.

She could not even remember the last time she had laughed so hard as when the police light had been turned on her and David.

Her life, she realized, had been way too serious for way too long. When had she lost her ability to be spontaneous?

But she already knew. Her marriage had become an ongoing effort to control everything— fun had become a distant memory.

Yearning grabbed her again. To feel alive. To laugh.

Despite the hour, Kayla didn't feel like sleeping. She didn't feel ready, somehow, to leave the night—with its odd combination of magic and self-discovery and discomfort—behind. She went into the kitchen, turned on the light, opened the fridge.

Somehow, drinking lemonade on her front porch and watching the sun come up sounded wonderful in a way it would not have even a day ago.

And who knew? Maybe she would even see Bastigal wandering home from his own adventure.

But it was the thought that maybe she was really waiting to see David again that made her rethink it. She closed the fridge door—and the door on all her secret longings. She turned off the lights and ordered herself to bed.

But not before having one last peek out the window. She told herself she was having one last look for Bastigal, and yet her stomach did a funny downward swoop when she watched David come down the street.

Kayla sank back in the shadows of her house as she watched David take the front steps of the house next door. He pulled up the screen and tried the handle.

Kayla realized the care aide had decided to do her job *now.* The front door was locked up tight.

Telling herself it was none of her business, she went to a side window and watched him go to the back door of his house. It was the same. Locked.

He tried a window. Locked. Kayla noticed all the windows were closed, which was a real shame on such a beautiful night—but she realized all sorts of precautions would be in place to try and ensure his mother's well-being.

As she continued to watch, David went back to the door and knocked lightly. Kayla could tell he did not want to wake his mother if she was sleeping. Presumably the care aide was not, but she did not come to the door, either. Watching television, maybe?

He stepped back off the steps, and Kayla could tell he was contemplating his options.

She could offer him her couch, of course. He had rescued her today—no, given the lateness of the hour, that was yesterday already—after she'd been stung.

She'd only be returning the favor.

But she remembered his deeply sarcastic tone when he had said earlier today: *Kayla to the rescue.*

And then, a certain wryness in his tone, he had remembered her working at that camp, those children trailing her through town.

Really, more of the same.

Kayla to the rescue. It made her aware that she *needed* to resist whatever was going on in her.

She was going to go to bed, and she was going to mind her own business and not feel the least bit guilty about it, either.

Not even when she peeked back out her window and saw him dragging a thick cushion off the patio furniture down the deck steps and onto the lush grass of his mother's backyard.

She watched him lay it out a few feet from the bottom of the steps, and then lie down on top of it, on his back, his face toward the sky as if he could not get enough of the stars tonight. Some tension left him, and she was not sure she had ever seen a person look more relaxed.

And she envied him for the place he had among the stars. Had she offered her couch and had he taken it, she would have deprived him of this moment.

It occurred to her that maybe that's what rescuing did: gave the rescuer a feeling of power while keeping the rescued person from their own destiny, from finding their own way to where they were supposed to be.

And in light of her relationship with Kevin, that was a deeply distressing thought.

Kayla decided, right then and there, that she was going to avoid David for the rest of the time he spent here with his mother.

She did not need the kind of introspection he seemed to be triggering in her. And she certainly did not need the complication of a man who could cause her to ache with yearning just by touching her hair!

CHAPTER TEN

DAVID CONTEMPLATED THE STARS above his head. He could sleep in his car, except he had put the roof up at dark and locked it. His keys were inside the house. Ditto for his wallet, or he could go get a hotel room somewhere, though of course hotels would be booked solid at this time of year in Blossom Valley.

If his mother managed to get out the back door again, he had her escape route, and the route to the garden shed, blocked.

What do you mean "at first"? Kayla had asked him about his choice not to marry, not to have children.

At first it had been because he had never found the right person. Now it went so much deeper. Some forms of his mother's illness had a genetic component. What if he had it?

And his father had died young of heart disease, plunging the family he had protected so diligently into a despair deeper than the ocean.

David's doctor had assured him his own heart was the heart of an athlete. And the other? There was a test they could do to determine the presence of the "E" gene.

But so far, David had said no. Did you want to know something like that? Why would you? Just for yourself, no. If there was someone else involved in his life…?

Was it the strangely delightful evening with Kayla making him have these wayward thoughts?

He decided firmly, and not for the first time, that he was not going there, that these kind of thoughts were counterproductive. They had snuck by his defenses only because he was exhausted. He closed his eyes, drew in one long breath and ordered himself to sleep. And it worked.

David woke up feeling amazingly refreshed. The sun was already warm on his face, and he glanced at his watch, astounded by how late he had slept and how well. He realized he was glad to have slept outside.

The inside was not really a house anymore: doors locked, cleaning supplies hidden, windows never opened, stove unplugged. One of the live-in care aides had moved into his boyhood bedroom, and he was relegated to a tiny den with a pullout sofa when he came.

David got up swiftly, not wanting to dwell on all the depressing issues inside his mother's house. He returned the cushions to the deck that was never used anymore, except by that care aide he suspected of slipping outside to sneak cigarettes.

What had he said last night to Kayla? That his mother's house looked like normal people lived here. He was aware, the feeling of being refreshed leaving him, that he had probably kept that particular illusion alive too long.

It wasn't safe for his mother to be here anymore.

He would look at options for her today. He was aware of feeling that there was no time to lose.

He would look after it and leave here. For good, this time.

David knocked on the door, and this time it was opened by a new aide, who must have arrived to help the live-in with morning chores. She looked at him with an expression as bewildered as his mother's.

"It's a long story," he said and moved by the aide.

His mother was in the kitchen, toying with her breakfast, an unappetizing-looking lump of porridge that had been cooked in the microwave. At one time David had hired a cook, but his mother had become so querulous and suspicious of everyone that staff did not stay no matter what he offered to pay them. Then there had been the issue of her sneaking down in the night and turning on the stove burners.

But this morning his mother was dressed, and everything matched and was done up correctly and her hair was combed so he knew she'd had help. The thorn scratches on her arms had been freshly treated with ointment but were a reminder of what he needed to do.

He left the house as soon as he had showered and put on a fresh shirt and shorts from a suitcase he did not bother to unpack. He went downtown and had breakfast. His mother, obviously, had no internet, and for many years he hadn't stayed long enough to miss it. Now, after a frustrating phone call, he found out it would take weeks to get it hooked up.

He drove down to the beach, still quiet in the morning, and began to make phone calls.

The first was to his assistant, Jane, a middle-aged girl Friday worth her weight in gold.

With her he caught up on some business transactions and gave instructions for putting out a few minor fires. Then, aware of feeling a deep sadness, he told Jane what he needed her to research. A care home, probably private, that specialized in people with dementia.

"See if you can send me some virtual tours," he said, stripping the emotion from his own voice when she sounded concerned. Then, as an afterthought, maybe to try and banish what he was setting in motion, he said,

"And see what you can find out about an ice cream parlor for sale here in Blossom Valley. It's called More-moo."

He was aware, as he put away his phone, that his heart was beating too fast, and not from asking his assistant to find out about the ice cream parlor.

From betraying his mother's trust.

Not that she trusted me, he reminded himself, attempting wryness. But it fell flat inside his own heart and left the most enormous feeling of pain he'd ever felt.

Unless you counted the time he'd witnessed Kayla say *I do* to the wrong man.

"I hate coming home," he muttered to himself. He stepped out of the car and gazed out at the familiar water.

And suddenly he didn't hate coming home quite so much. The water. It had always been his solace.

After a moment he locked the phone in the car and went down to the beach. He took off his shirt and left it in the sand. The shorts would dry quickly enough. He dove into the cool, clear water of the bay and struck out across it.

An hour and a half later he crawled from the water, exhausted and so cold he was numb. And yet, still, he could not bring himself to go home.

No point without a Wi-Fi connection, anyway, he told himself. He drove downtown, bought some dry shorts and looked for a restaurant that offered internet.

It happened to be More-moo, and David decided he could check out some of the more obvious parts of their operation himself.

He managed to conduct business from there for most of the day. Jane sent him several links to places with euphemistic names like Shady Oak and Sunset Court, which he could not bring himself to open. She sent him the financials for More-moo, which he felt guilty looking at, with that sweet grandmotherly type telling him, *No, no, you're no bother at all, honey.* And keeping his coffee cup filled to the brim.

Whatever reason they were selling, it wasn't their service, their cleanliness or their coffee. All three were excellent.

He brought dinner home for his mother, rather than face the smells of some kind of liver and broccoli puree coming out of the microwave.

She had no idea who he was.

That night, it seemed so easy just to go and drag the cushions back off the deck furniture and lie again, under the stars, protecting the back exit from his mother's escape.

He was aware of a light going on in Kayla's house, and then of it going off again. He both wanted to go see her and wanted to avoid her.

He hadn't had a single call about the dog, but he was pretty sure it wasn't his failure keeping him away.

It felt like the compassion in her eyes could break him wide open.

And if that happened? How would he put himself back together again? How?

Tomorrow he was going to force himself to look at some of the websites for care homes. Tomorrow he was going to force himself to call some of the numbers Jane had supplied him with.

Tonight he was going to sleep under the stars, and somehow wish that he were overreacting. That when he went in the house tomorrow he would see his mother was better, and that it was not necessary to make a decision at all.

But in the morning, after he'd showered and shaved and dressed, he went into a kitchen that smelled sour, and his mother had *that* look on her face.

She looked up from her bowl of porridge—surely at Shady Oak they would manage something more appetizing—and glared at him.

David braced himself. She held up a sweater she'd been holding on her lap, stroking it as though it were a cat.

"Where did this come from, young man?"

"I'm sure it's yours, Mom."

"It's not!" she said triumphantly. "It belongs to Kayla McIntosh."

He tried not to look too surprised that she remembered Kayla's name. It had been a long time since she had remembered his. Even if it was Kayla's maiden name, it made him wonder if he was being too hasty. Maybe no decisions had to be made today.

"You go give it back to her. Right now! I won't have your ill-gotten gains in this house, young man."

He took the sweater. Of course he didn't have to go give it to Kayla—it probably wasn't even hers. But he caught a faint scent overriding the terrible scents that had become the reality of his mother's home.

The sweater smelled of freshness and lemons, and he realized Kayla must have given it to his mother the other night when she had found her in the roses.

Was it the scent of Kayla that made him not pay enough attention? Or was it just that a man couldn't be on red alert around his own mother all the time?

The porridge bowl whistled by his ear and crashed against the wall behind him. All the dishes were plastic now, but the porridge dripped down the wall.

"Mrs. Blaze!" the attendant said, aghast. The look she shot David was loaded with unwanted sympathy.

He cleared his throat against the lump that had risen in it, that felt as if it was going to choke him.

He said to the caregiver, his voice level, "When I was a

little boy, my mother took the garden hose and flooded the backyard in the winter so I could skate. She made lemonade for my stand, and helped me with the sign, and didn't say a word that I sold five bucks worth of lemonade for two dollars. She never missed a single swim meet when I was on the swim team, and they must have numbered in the hundreds.

"She stayed up all night and held me the night my father died, worried about my grief when her own must have been unbearable. She lent me the money to buy my first car, even though she had been putting away a little bit of money every week trying to get a new stove.

"My mother was the most amazing person you could ever meet. She was funny and kind and smart. At the same time, she was dignified and courageous.

"I need you to know that," he said quietly. "I need you to think about what she once was. I need that to be as important to you as what she is now."

"Yes, sir," the aide said.

"I remember the skating rink," his mother whispered. "My mittens got wet and my hands were so cold I couldn't feel them. The bottom of my pants froze, like trying to walk in stovepipes. But I wouldn't stop. Wanted to surprise him. The ice froze funny, all lumpy. But he was out there, every night, skating. My boy. My boy."

David had to squeeze the bridge of his nose, hard.

"I'll return the sweater right now," he said, as if nothing had happened. He went out the door, gulping in air like a man who had escaped a smoke-filled building. He heard the locks click in place behind him.

He drew in a long breath, contemplating his options, again. He tucked the sweater under his arm and went out his gate. He paused in that familiar stretch of lawn between the two houses.

As much as he logically knew the illness was making terrifying inroads on her mind, it hurt that his mother saw him as a thief and untrustworthy, that she could remember Kayla's name, but not his. It hurt that she had become a person who would throw her breakfast at anyone, let alone at her son.

But she remembered the skating rink, and so did he, and the pain he felt almost made him sorry he had brought it up.

He thought, *This is why, now, I will not get married and have children. I cannot do this to another person. I cannot pass this on to another person.*

Was he thinking these kind of thoughts because Kayla, at some level, was making him long for things he was aware he could not have?

Drawing in a deep breath, David went through Kayla's back gate. He would hang the sweater on her back door, then walk to the lake and swim. He was developing a routine of sorts, and he loved the cold water in the morning, when the beach was still deserted.

He went up the stairs to Kayla's back deck and eyed the patio furniture—four old Adirondack chairs, grouped together. Once, he seemed to remember, they had been light blue, but now the wood was gray and weathered. The chairs looked like they would offer slivers rather than comfort. The deck was in about the same condition as the chairs. It had not been stained in so long that the exposed wood had rotted and was probably past repair.

He went to hang the sweater on the back door handle. He noticed only the screen door was closed, the storm door open behind it, leaving a clear view into the cheeriness of the kitchen.

Was that safe? Even in Blossom Valley?

He had just decided it was none of his business when

Kayla came to the door. She didn't have a scrap of makeup on and had her honey-colored hair scraped back in a ponytail. She was wearing a bib apron tied over a too-large T-shirt and faded denim shorts.

The contrast to his world of super sophistication—women who wore designer duds even when they were dressed casually, and who were never seen in public without makeup on and hair done—was both jarring and refreshing.

Kayla looked *real.* She also looked as if she had been up for hours, and the smell of toast—so normal it hurt his heart—wafted out the door.

For a moment she looked disconcerted to see him—not nearly as pleased to be caught in such a natural state as he had been to catch her in it—but then her expression brightened.

"Have you heard something about Bastigal?" she asked eagerly.

"No, I'm sorry. I just brought you back your sweater."

"Oh." She looked crushed. "Thanks."

She opened the door, and it screeched outrageously on rusting hinges. He noticed she didn't even have the hook latched on it.

"Do you have a phone yet?" he asked.

"Not yet."

"You should get one," he said, "and you should lock your door. At least do up the latch on the screen."

She looked annoyed at his concern, rather than grateful. "This is Blossom Valley," she said. "You and I 'prowling' was probably the biggest news on the criminal front in years."

"Bad stuff happens everywhere," he said sternly.

"If it's safe enough for you to sleep out under the stars, it's safe enough for me to leave my screen door unlatched."

He glared at her.

"The latch is broken," she said with a resigned sigh. "The wood around it is rotted."

"Oh."

She bristled under what she interpreted as sympathy or judgment or both. "And how are you sleeping in the great outdoors? Fending off mosquitoes?"

Did she mutter a barely audible "I hope"?

Was he trying to control the locks on Kayla's doors because his own world seemed so unsafe and unpredictable—beyond saving—at least where his mother was concerned?

Several retorts played on his tongue, *never better, reminds me of my boy scout days*—but it shocked him when the truth spilled out.

"I hate it in that house," David said, his voice quiet. "I hate how the way it is now feels like it could steal the way it once was completely from my mind. Steal Christmas mornings, and the night I graduated from high school and the way my mom looked when my dad pinned that rose corsage on her for their fifteenth anniversary, right before he died. The way that house is now could steal the moment the puppy came home, and the memories of the dog he grew to be."

He blinked hard, amazed the words had come out past the lump that had been in his throat since his mother had thrown her porridge at him, but then remembered the backyard skating rink.

David was both annoyed with himself and relieved to have spoken it.

Kayla's bristling over her unlocked door, and her glee at his sleeping arrangements, melted. "Oh, David, I'm so sorry."

He ordered himself to walk away, to follow his original plan to go to the lake and let the ice-cold water and the physical exertion take it all.

Instead, when the door squeaked open and Kayla stepped back, inviting him into her house, he found himself moving by her as if he had no choice at all.

He entered her kitchen like a man who had crossed the desert and known thirst and hardship, and who had found an oasis that promised cool protection from the harshness of the sun, and that promised a long, cold drink of water.

He looked around her kitchen. He had spent a lot of his growing-up years in this room and this room was as unchanged as his own house was changed.

A large French-paned window faced the backyard. It was already a bright room, but Mrs. Jaffrey had painted the walls sunshine-yellow, and though the yellow had faded, the effect was still one of cheer.

The cabinets were old and had seen better days, and nobody had that kind of countertop anymore. The table had been painted dozens of times and every one of the color choices showed through the blemishes in the paint. It was leaning unsteadily, one of the legs shorter than the others. The appliances were old porcelain models, black showing through the chipped white enamel.

The kitchen was unchanged, but still he felt something catch in his throat. Because although the room was the same, wasn't this just more of the same of what was going on next door?

He could practically see Kevin sitting at that table, gulping down milk and gobbling down still-warm cookies, leaving dribbles of chocolate on his lips.

He could see Kevin's devil-may-care smile, almost hear his shout of laughter.

David realized he had lied to Kayla when she had asked him why he had never chosen marriage and a family.

And when she had asked him if he ever missed *this,* for this kitchen was really the heart and soul of what growing up in Blossom Valley had been.

Right now, particularly vulnerable because of what had just happened with his mother, he missed how everything used to be so much that he felt like he could lay his head on that table and cry like a wounded animal.

Kevin was dead, but even before his death, had been the death of their friendship, which had been just as painful. Now, the Jaffreys had moved. It seemed shocking that Kayla was Mrs. Jaffrey now.

Really, with the death of his father, David felt as if he had begun to learn a lesson that had not really stopped since: love was leaving yourself open to a series of breathtaking losses.

And still, this kitchen softened something in him that did not want to be softened.

The kitchen was a mess of the nicest kind: recipe books open, mixing bowls out, blobs of yellowy batter—lemon chiffon cake, at this time of the day?—spattering the counter. David was painfully aware that there was a feeling of homecoming here that he no longer had at home.

He realized some of it was scent: Kayla's scent, lemony and sweet, that clung to her, and the sweater he was holding. There was the fresh smell of the toast she'd had for breakfast, but underneath that he remembered more good things. He swore he could smell all the cookies that had ever been baked in that archaic oven, and Thanksgiving dinner, and golden-crusted pies that lined the countertops after the original Mrs. Jaffrey had availed herself of Blossom Valley's apple harvest.

He compared that to the hospital smells of his mother's house—disinfectants and unappetizing food heated in the microwave and smells he did not even want to think about—and he felt like he never wanted to leave this kitchen again.

"Mom asked me to return your sweater," he said past the lump in his throat. "She remembered your name."

Kayla scanned his face and took the sweater wordlessly from his hands, hanging it on the back of one of the chairs.

There. He'd done what he came to do. He needed to be in the water, to swim until his muscles hurt and until his mind could not think a single thought. Instead, he found himself reluctant to leave this kitchen that said home to him in a way his mother's home would never do again.

Instead, he found himself wishing Kayla would press her hand over his heart again.

"Are you okay?" she asked him.

No. "Yes."

But she seemed to hear the *no* as if he had spoken it.

She regarded him thoughtfully. It was as if she could see every sorrow that he carried within him.

"I'm trying out recipes in an effort to keep busy and keep my mind off Bastigal. Would you like to try some homemade ice cream?"

He thought of the congealed porridge at his house. He thought he had to say no to this. He was in a weakened state. This could not go anywhere good.

But suddenly none of that mattered. He had carried his burdens in solitude for so long and it felt, ridiculously, as if they could be eased by this kitchen, by her, by the appeal of homemade ice cream.

He could not have said no to her invitation if he wanted to.

CHAPTER ELEVEN

To admit Kayla's kitchen, and her invitation, and Kayla herself, were proving impossible to say no to felt as if it would be some kind of defeat, so instead of saying yes, David just lifted a shoulder as if he could care less whether he ate her ice cream or not.

Kayla did not seem to be fooled, and her eyes were gentle as they lingered on his face. Then she acted just as if she had heard the *yes* that he had not spoken.

"It's not quite ready. Give me a second."

"I hope it's not rose petal," he said, needing her to know he had not surrendered to her charms or the charms of her kitchen completely.

"Oh, way better than that."

"But what could be?" he said drily.

"I bought this at a yard sale," she said, turning away from him and back to her crowded countertop. She lifted off her counter a bowl big enough to bathe a baby in.

At first he thought she meant she had purchased the bowl at a yard sale but then she trundled over to a stainless-steel apparatus that squatted on her floor with a certain inexplicable air of malevolence. He wasn't sure how he hadn't noticed it before since it took up a whole corner of the kitchen.

"What is it?" he asked warily, and gratefully, as something in him shifted away from that awful picture of porridge dripping down the wall in his house next door.

"It's called a batch freezer!" Kayla said triumphantly. "What are the chances I would find one just as I'm contemplating buying an ice cream store?"

"Cosmically ordained," he said.

She either missed his sarcasm or refused to acknowledge it. "Exactly."

"It reminds me of HAL from *2001: A Space Odyssey.*"

"That's ridiculous. If I remember correctly, HAL was not nice."

"You slept through ninety percent of that movie. And you were the one who insisted we rent it."

"I was in my all-things-space stage." She sniffed. "It disappointed."

But what David remembered was not disappointment, but that there had been a bunch of them in somebody's basement rec room gamely watching the vintage sixties movie Kayla had rented.

Somehow she'd ended up crammed next to him on a crowded couch. And partway through—after gobbling down buttered popcorn and licking the extra butter off her fingers—he realized she had gone to sleep and her head was lolling against his shoulder, and the cutest little pool of drool was making a warm puddle on his shirt.

And that he hadn't embarrassed her by mentioning it when she woke up.

"How much did you pay for this contraption?" he asked gruffly, moving over to inspect it.

"Fifteen hundred dollars," she said happily. "That's a steal. New ones, of commercial grade, start at ten grand. This size of machine is eighteen thousand dollars."

He realized, uncomfortably—and yet still grateful to have his focus shifting—that Kayla was way more invested in the idea of owning the ice cream parlor than she had originally let on.

"Presumably," he said carefully, "More-moo already has one."

"They don't," she crowed triumphantly. "They buy their ice cream from Rolling Hills Dairy, the same as you can buy for yourself at the grocery store. There is nothing special about that. Why go out for ice cream when you can have the same thing at home for a fraction of the price?"

"Exactly. Why?"

"That's how I plan to be different. Homemade ice cream, in exotic flavors that people have never had before."

She frowned at his silence, glanced back at him. "And, of course, I'll offer the old standbys for *boring* people. Chocolate. Vanilla. Strawberry. But still homemade."

"So what flavor is this that you're experimenting with?" he asked, curious despite himself.

"Dandelion!"

"And that's better than rose petal?" he asked doubtfully.

She nodded enthusiastically.

"Have you done any kind of market research at all?"

"Don't take the fun out of it," she warned him.

"Look, fun is playing volleyball on the beach, or riding a motorcycle flat out, or skinny-dipping under a full moon."

Something darkened in her eyes when he said that, and he wished he hadn't because a strange, heated tension leaped in the air between them.

"Fun is fun, and business is business," he said sternly.

And he was here on business. To return a sweater. But ever since he had walked in the door and felt almost swamped with a sensation of homecoming, his mission had felt blurry.

"That's not what you said in the article for *Lakeside Life,*" she told him stubbornly. "You said *if a man does what he loves he will never work a day in his life.*"

What did it mean that she had read that so closely? Nothing, he told himself.

"I'd play with the name," she said, ignoring his stern note altogether. "That's part of the reason I like it better than rose petal, well, that and the fact it would be cheaper to produce. I'd call this flavor Dandy Lion."

His look must have been blank, because she spelled it out for him. "D-A-N-D-Y L-I-O-N."

"Oh."

"Cute, huh?"

"Not to be a wet blanket but in my experience, *cute* is rarely a moneymaker. Look, Kayla, if ever there was a time to worry, this would be it. I don't think people are going to line up to eat dandelion ice cream, no matter how you spell it."

"Oh, what do you know?" she said, and her chin had a stubborn tilt to it. "They drink dandelion wine."

"They do? I can't imagine why."

"Well, maybe not the people you hang out with."

"I haven't seen any of the good wineries with dandelion wine," he said, keeping his tone calm, trying to reason with her. "And you can bet they do their homework. In fact, Blaze Enterprises is invested in Painted Pony Wineries and—"

But she turned her back to him, and turned on the machine and it drowned out his advice. He was pretty sure it was deliberate. She freed one arm to open a lid on the top of the stainless-steel machine, then tried to heft the huge bowl up high enough to pour the contents in a spout at the top.

At her grunt of exertion, he stepped up behind her and took the bowl. He gazed down into the bright yellow contents.

"Hell, Kayla, it looks like pee," he said over the loudness of the machine.

Her face scrunched up in the cutest expression of disapproval. "It doesn't! It looks bright and lemony."

"Which, if you think about it, is what—"

She held up her hand, not wanting to hear it. He shrugged. "Whatever. In here?"

She nodded and he dumped the contents of the bowl in the machine through an opening she would have had to stand on a chair to reach.

Unlocked doors. Precarious balancing on chairs. And no phone to call anyone if she found herself in an emergency. Plus, spending fifteen hundred dollars on an idea that seemed hare-brained, and that should still be in the research stages, not the investing-in stages.

Why did he feel so protective of her? Why did he feel like she needed him? She had made it this far without his help, after all.

Though good choices were obviously not her forte.

It occurred to David that he felt helpless to do anything for his mother. And he hated that out-of-control feeling.

Not that Kayla would appreciate his trying to control her. But if he could help her a little bit—find her dog, pour her recipe for her so she didn't risk life and limb climbing on one of her rickety chairs with this huge bowl, save her from throwing away any more money on ice-cream-themed machinery—those could only be good things.

Right?

The machine gobbled up the contents of the bowl with

a huge sucking sound. David had to stand on his tiptoes to look inside. The mustard-yellow cream was being vigorously swished and swirled, and the machine was growling like a vintage motorcycle that he owned.

"How long?" he called over the deafening rumble.

"It's going to come out here!" She showed him a wide stainless-steel spigot and handle. "It will be six to twelve minutes, depending on how hard I want the ice cream. We'll try a sample after six."

He peered back in the hole where he had dumped the cream. "Is this thing supposed to close?"

"I'm not sure all the parts were there. I need to look up the manual online. It didn't come with the manual. I saved over sixteen thousand dollars—I can live with that."

The stickler in him felt like now might be a really good time to point out to her that she hadn't actually *saved* sixteen thousand dollars. She had *spent* fifteen hundred dollars.

He had a feeling she wouldn't appreciate the half-empty perspective.

That was one of the glaring differences between them. That and the fact he would have looked up the manual *before* pouring several gallons of pricey cream into the vat.

"You can turn up the beater speed here," she said proudly, and touched a button.

The growl turned into a banshee wail and then the yellow mixture was vomited out of the top of the machine through the same opening he had put it in. It came out in an explosive gush.

He yanked back his head from the opening just in time to avoid having his eyes taken out. A fountain of yellow slush sprayed out with the velocity of Old Faithful erupting. It hit the ceiling and rained down on them and every other surface in the kitchen.

He scrambled for the off switch on the ice cream maker and hit it hard.

The room was cast into silence.

Kayla stood there wide-eyed, covered from head to toe in yellow splotches. One dripped down from the roof and landed on David's cheek.

She began to giggle. He was enchanted by her laughter, and it made him realize there was something somber in her and that she had not been like that before. Not just somber. And not quite hard.

Serious and studious, but not so…well, worried, weighed down by life. As if she had built a wall around herself to protect herself from life.

Suddenly, her laughter felt like a wave that was lifting him and carrying him away from his own troubles. He found himself laughing with her. It felt so good to stand there in the middle of her kitchen and see the hilarity in the situation, to let go of all the dark worry that had plagued him since he arrived home.

Then the laughter died between them.

And then she stepped up to him, and ran her finger across his cheek. She held the yellow smudge up for his inspection, and then, still smiling, she touched it to his lips.

The substance on her finger was already surprisingly chilled, and not quite liquid anymore, but like a frothy, cold mousse.

He hesitated, and then touched his tongue to the yellow glob. In an act of startling intimacy, he licked the substance off the tip of her offered finger.

Was it possible he had wanted to taste her finger ever since she had licked the butter off it all those years ago?

No. That was not even remotely possible.

Still, he was aware that the mess all around him had evaporated. It didn't matter that he was covered in pee-colored mousse, or that it dripped from the ceiling, and spotted the walls and the countertops. It didn't matter that it was splashed all across Kayla's apron and clinging in clumps to her hair.

The flavor on his tongue made him feel as if he was about to die of sheer delight.

Or was the delight because his tongue had touched her finger?

"Well?" she demanded.

"I can't believe I'm about to say this," he confessed, "but Kayla, I think you may be onto something. Don't call it Dandelion. Or Dandy Lion. Call it Ambrosia."

Her smile put the very sun to shame.

So he didn't bother to tell her that her finger was probably a very important ingredient in the ambrosia he had just experienced.

CHAPTER TWELVE

HIS LIPS WERE still way too close to her finger! Kayla wondered whatever had possessed her to touch his cheek, to hold her finger out to him, to invite his tongue to touch her. Something shivered along her spine—an electric awareness of him that was like nothing she had ever felt before.

She could feel her smile dissolving, her pleasure at his approval giving way to something else altogether.

She wasn't an innocent young girl anymore, but the power of her hunger astounded her. She *wanted* him.

It felt like a kind of crime to want someone who had hurt her husband so badly. But had he really? Or had Kevin hurt himself over and over again, and then blamed the whole world in general and David in particular?

She shivered at the thought, and then thankfully, any kind of decision—to lean toward him, to touch his lips with her lips instead of her finger—was taken from her.

He, too, sensed the sudden sizzle of chemistry between them, but he had the good sense to back abruptly away from it.

He turned from her quickly, grabbed a dishcloth from the sink and began to clean up the mess.

That was David. All the time she had known him he

had always stepped up to the plate, done what needed to be done.

Especially after the danger of having her finger nibbled, Kayla knew she needed to send him on his way, even if he hadn't received any of the promised ice cream—unless you counted that one taste.

"According to what I read in *Lakeside Life,*" Kayla said, "you have better things to do than help me with my messes."

"Don't believe everything you read."

He got a chair and climbed up on it and began to tackle the mess on her ceiling. She saw his shirt lifted and she saw the hard line of his naked tummy.

That hunger unfolded in her, even more powerful than before.

"You should go home." It was self-protection and it was desperately needed!

"I'll just give you a hand with this first."

Kayla wanted to refuse and found that she couldn't. It had been so long since she had had help with anything. Someone to share a burden with was as least as seductive as the sight of his naked skin. For so long she had carried every burden, large and small, all by herself.

An hour later her kitchen had been restored to order. Every surface shone. David had even ferreted out yellow cream in the toaster and wiped it from the inside of the light fixture.

But if the kitchen shone, they were a mess!

"I hope that isn't a Slugs and Snails shirt," Kayla said, but now that she was looking, she could see the distinctive small snail over the left breast.

"Of course it is," he said, glancing down at the yellow blotches that she was fairly certain had already set on his very expensive shirt and shorts. "My company was their start-up investor. I always use the products of the companies we invest in."

A reminder that the man standing here, in her kitchen, covered in yellow stains, was the CEO of a very prestigious company!

He misread her distressed expression. "I'm sure the stains will come out."

"You don't know the first thing about dandelions, do you?" she said, sadly. "When you do your laundry, that stain is not an easy fix."

"I don't do my own laundry," he said, a little sheepishly.

It was a further reminder of who she was sharing her kitchen with. "Well, you could tell whoever does it to try lemon juice."

"Is that why you smell like lemons?" he asked. "Because this is not your first experiment with dandelions?"

He had noticed her scent. Somehow it was headier than dandelion wine.

So when he said what he said next, she should have resisted with all her might. But she didn't have a single bit of might left in her.

"I was on my way down to the lake to swim. Why don't we just go jump in? Like the old days?"

A small smile was playing across the sensuous line of the mouth she had been foolish enough to touch.

She knew exactly what he was talking about. The last day of school, every year, all the kids in Blossom Valley went and jumped in the lake, fully clothed.

And suddenly he did not seem like the CEO of one of Canada's most successful companies. David seemed like what she needed most in the world and had tried, pathetically perhaps, to find in a dog.

He seemed like a friend, and nothing in the world could

have kept her from going and revisiting the most carefree time of her life by jumping in the lake with him!

"Hang on," she said, "I'll grab my lemon juice."

They didn't go to the public beach, but snuck down a much closer, but little-known lake access, between two very posh houses.

He stood patiently while she doused the stains on both their clothes with lemon juice. She set down the empty bottle and then rubbed the lemon into the stains. His skin beneath the fabric struck her as velvet over steel.

She heard his sharp intake of breath and looked up. He was watching her, his lips twitching with amusement but his eyes dark with something else.

Kayla gulped, let go of his shirt and backed away from him, spinning.

"Race you," she cried over her shoulder, kicking off her flip-flops and already running. With a shout he came up behind her, and they hit the cold water hard. He cut the water in a perfect dive, and she followed. The day was already so hot that the cold water felt exquisite and cooling.

The water had been her second home since she had moved here. Beaches and this lake were the backdrop to everything good about growing up in a resort town.

It seemed the water washed away the bad parts of their shared past, and gave them back the happy-go-lucky days of their youth. They gave themselves over to play, splashing and racing, dunking each other, engaging in an impromptu game of tag, which he won handily, of course. He tormented her by letting her think she could catch him, and then in one or two powerful strokes he was out of her reach.

Kayla had known, when she had seen David run the other night, that he had lost none of his athleticism. But the water had always been his element.

His absolute strength and grace in it were awe-inspiring.

That and the fact his wet shirt had molded to the perfect lines of his chest. His hair was flattened and shiny with water, and the beads ran down the perfect plane of his face.

But the light in his eyes was warmer than the sun. That awareness of him that she had been feeling all morning—that had been pushed to the breaking point when she had scrubbed at his lemony shirt—was kept from igniting only by the coldness of the water.

Finally, gasping from exertion and laughter, they rolled over and floated side by side, completely effortless on their backs, looking up at a cloudless sky, the silence compatible between them. Even the awareness that had sizzled seemed to have morphed into something else, like the rain after the electrical storm, calm and cooling.

Finally, she broke the silence.

"I know you didn't lie about him," she said quietly. "David, I'm sorry I called you a liar."

It felt so good that he said nothing at all, rolled his head slightly to look at her then rolled it back and contemplated the blueness of the sky.

The cold of the water finally forced them out. On the shore, she inspected his dripping clothes. The dandelion stains were unfazed by her lemon treatment.

"That will have to be your paint shirt," she said, just as if he was a normal person who actually painted his own home when it needed it.

"Good idea," he said, going along with her. Then, "For two relatively intelligent people, one of us could have remembered towels."

"Watch who you're calling relatively intelligent," Kayla said, and shook her wet hair at him.

"This is a private beach," a voice called.

They looked up to see a woman glaring at them from her deck.

In their youth, they would have challenged her. They would have told her there was no such thing as a private beach. That the entire lake and everything surrounding it to the high water mark—which would take them up to about where her lawn furniture was artfully displayed—belonged to the public. In their youth, they might have eaten their sandwiches on her manicured lawn.

But David just gave the sour-faced woman a good-natured wave, took Kayla's hand, scooped up the empty lemon juice bottle and walked her back out between the houses.

They began the walk home, dripping puddles as they went. Somehow, David didn't let go of her hand. They laughed when her flip-flops made slurping sounds with every step.

She tried to remember the last time she had felt so invigorated, so alive, so free. Oh, yeah. It had been just the other night, lying beside him in the cool grass, looking at the stars.

A siren gave a single wail behind them and then shut off.

They both whirled.

"Oh, no," Kayla said. "It's the same guy."

"She called the police because we were on her beach?" David said incredulously.

Kayla could feel the laughter bubbling within her. "You and I have become a regular two-person crime wave," she said. "Who would have thought that?"

The policeman got out of his car and looked at them. And then he reached back inside.

Kayla squealed.

"Bastigal!"

She raced forward and the dog wriggled out of the policeman's arms and into her own. Her face was being covered with kisses and she realized she was crying and laughing at the same time.

But even in her joy it occurred to her that her dog had been returned to her only when she had learned the lesson: Bastigal was no kind of replacement for human company, for a real friend.

"Did your daughter find him?" David asked. Kayla glanced at him. He was watching her with a smile tickling the edges of that damnably sexy mouth.

"Yeah."

"I guess she's going to be getting that new bike," David said.

"She'll have to find another way to get her new bike."

"What? Why?"

"I told her she can't take the reward. You do good things for people because it's right, not because there's something in it for you. To me, teaching her that is more important than a new bike. Though at the moment, she hates me for it."

"I'm going to buy an ice cream parlor," Kayla said, the tears sliding even faster down her face.

"Maybe you're going to buy an ice cream parlor," David growled in an undertone.

Kayla ignored him. "Tell your daughter she gets free ice cream for life."

The policeman lifted a shoulder, clearly trying to decide if that was still accepting a reward. Finally, he said, with a faint smile, "Sure. Whatever. Hey, by the way, you were called in for trespassing."

"Really?" She shouldn't be delighted, but what had happened to her life? It had surprises in it!

"As soon as I heard *two fully clothed people swimming,*

I somehow knew it was you," he said wryly. "I told the complainant she only owns to the high water line."

And then all of them were laughing and the dog was licking her face and Kayla wondered if she had ever had a more perfect morning.

The policeman left and they continued on their way, Bastigal content in her arms.

David reached over and scratched his ears. "He's so ugly he's cute," he said.

"I prefer to think that he's so cute, he's ugly," she retorted. "I think that nice policeman should let his daughter have the reward."

"Do you?"

"Don't you?"

"I don't know. That kind of stand reminded me of what my dad was like," David said quietly.

"I never met your dad," Kayla said.

"No. I think he died a year or two before your family moved here. Completely unexpected. He seemed in every way like a big, strong guy. He had a heart attack. It was instant. He was sitting there having his supper, joking around, and he got a surprised look on his face and keeled over."

"Oh, David."

"No sympathy, remember?" he said. "But keep that in mind. Bad genetics."

He said it lightly, but there was something in his eyes that was not light at all. As if she had been considering him as partner material, that should dissuade her.

How could she address that without making it seem as if she *were* looking at him as partner material?

She didn't have to address it because he went on, his voice quiet, "In the last little while, I've actually felt grateful that he didn't live to see my mom like this."

She wanted to say *Oh, David,* again, but didn't. She was so aware that he was giving something of himself to her, sharing a deeply private side that she suspected few people, if any, had ever seen.

"My dad," he went on, "would have been just like that policeman. He knew right from wrong and he taught me that, and he didn't care if I was happy about it or not. My happiness was secondary to my being a good person."

"Mine, too," she said, "now that I think about it."

"It's nice to see you looking so happy, Kayla," David said quietly, as if they had spoken Kevin's name out loud, as if he knew how desperate she had often felt in her marriage.

She felt as if the tears were going to start again, so she bit the side of her cheek and buried her face in her dog's fur and said nothing.

"It's your turn," he said quietly, as if it were an order. And then, as if she might have dismissed it the first time, he said it again, even more firmly. "Kayla, it's your turn for happiness."

CHAPTER THIRTEEN

HER TURN FOR HAPPINESS?

"I feel guilty when I'm happy," Kayla blurted out.

David nodded. "I remember feeling that way after my dad died. How dare the world hold laughter again?"

She nodded. That was how she felt exactly, but it was layered with even deeper confusion because her feelings about her husband's death were not all black and white.

"But then I remembered something my dad said to me," David said thoughtfully. "My dad said you could never be guilty and happy at the same time. Or afraid and happy at the same time. That's why he was such a stickler for doing the right thing. That's what he saw as the stepping stones to building true happiness. And that's what he would have wanted me to do. To choose happiness. And that's what I want you to do, too."

She stared at David. He could have said a million things, and yet the thing he had said was so right.

Despite herself, she shared something else.

"David?"

"Hmm?"

"I'm scared of happiness. Remember you said wishes are for children? I'm afraid that the things you wish for just set you up for disappointment. And heartbreak."

They had arrived in front of her house, and he glanced

at his and then, as if it were the most natural thing in the world, went and sat in his wet clothes on her front step. He patted the place beside him.

"It was awful, wasn't it?" he asked.

And she was going to say "what?" as if she didn't know what he was talking about, but she did know, and she could not bear to bring dishonesty between them.

She had known this time was coming when they would have to address the history between them.

And she had expected that exploration would be like there was an unexploded mine buried somewhere in the unexplored ground between them.

"Yes," she whispered. "Being married to Kevin was awful in so many ways. I mean, there were good things, too, don't get me wrong."

"Tell me," he said.

And she knew he didn't mean the good things. She ordered herself not to, but she could not disobey the command in his voice.

And so she found herself telling him. Slowly at first, like water that was seeping out a hole in a dam, the steady, small flow making the hole larger until the water was shooting through it with force, faster and faster.

She told him about the late nights waiting for Kevin, not knowing where he was, about the terrible houses they had lived in and the bills not paid. She talked about working as a waitress and a cleaning lady, about babysitting children and raking leaves, trying to hold it all together long after she should have let it fall apart.

And the more she worked at holding it together the more Kevin seemed to sabotage everything she had done, lose interest in her, treat her shabbily, at first in the privacy of their own home, and then in front of other people.

"Sometimes," she said, finally, "I feel relieved that he died."

It should have been her biggest secret. But it wasn't. There was one left, still.

She waited for him to react with horror to this revelation that she had never admitted out loud to anyone.

Instead, they sat silently on the front steps with the sun pouring down hot on their heads, drying their clothes so that the lemon stains and wrinkles would probably never come out. Her dog snoozing in her arms, Kayla was aware she did not feel judged at all.

There. They were out. Her shameful and most closely guarded secrets. It *was* like a mine exploding, but instead of feeling destructive, it felt like a relief.

Before it exploded she waited. And wondered. And every step was guarded. And every breath was held.

Suddenly it felt as if she could breathe.

And suddenly it felt as if she were free to walk across the field that was her memory without being caught in an explosion.

Instead of rejecting her, David put his arm around her shoulder and pulled her into the solidness of his body.

And Kayla, in that moment of shared strength and sunshine, realized it had not been so much Kevin she had withheld forgiveness from.

In fact, she had forgiven Kevin again and again and again.

Except when he had died, taking with him any chance that they would find their way, that the love she still had for him would somehow see them through, would fix things—then she had felt angry and beyond forgiveness.

Betrayed by his carelessness in a way she could no longer fix. But now she could see most of her anger was at her own powerlessness.

She realized that more so than with Kevin, it was herself she had never forgiven. She had never forgiven herself for her own bad choices, for making everything worse instead of better.

But there, with David's arm around her shoulder, she felt strong and warm, and for the first time in very, very long, optimistic.

And not in a superficial way. Not about starting an ice cream business or saving a house from ruin. She felt changed in a way that went to her soul.

"Why did you marry him?" David asked, his voice hoarse with caring, knowing instinctively somehow there was one last thing she needed to tell.

She shuddered. The last secret. The thing no one had ever known. Not her parents. Or Kevin's. Not her best girlfriend.

"I was pregnant."

"Shoot," he said softly.

"You would have been proud of him," she said. "He wanted us to get married. He wanted to do the honorable thing."

But wasn't this also what she had to forgive herself for? That she had accepted his attempt at honor instead of love? That she had allowed it all to go ahead, when there had been a million signs that maybe it would have been better to let it go, even if there was a baby, maybe especially if there was a baby?

"I miscarried the baby a month after we were married. But I still thought I could save Kevin," she whispered. "After that summer, when he changed so much, I thought I could save him."

This was met with silence.

"Love conquers all," she said with a trace of self-derision. "We'd only been together that way once. After that little girl drowned, he was in so much pain. I was comforting him. One thing led to another."

There. Of all of it. That was the thing she had never forgiven herself for.

David's hand found hers, and he squeezed, but then he didn't let go.

"You knew," she whispered. "You knew it was going to be a disaster. You knew Kevin was a runaway train that nothing could stop. You told me not to marry him."

"After that little girl died, it was as if I started seeing Kevin for who he really was," he said, his voice ragged with regret. "He was in pain after it happened. But it wasn't about *her.* It was about how it was affecting *him.* He begged me not to tell the investigators that he hadn't been paying attention that day.

"But I had to do what I had to do. And I could never see him the same after that. I didn't see 'carefree' anymore. I saw 'careless.' I didn't see 'fun-loving.' I saw 'irresponsible.' I didn't see 'charming.' I saw 'self-centered.'

"And still." His voice cracked. "If he would have once expressed remorse for that day, I would have loved him all over again."

His voice firmed and became resolute. "But he didn't. It was always all about him. It gave birth to this cynicism in me that has never been altered. That people will always act in their own self-interest. Myself included. I'm sorry, Kayla. I'm sorry to talk about your husband that way."

But despite the things they both had said, they sat there bathed in more than sunlight.

They sat there bathed in truth and the special bond of a burden shared. They had shared the burden of loving someone who was grievously flawed and all the choices that entailed.

For Kayla, hopeful and romantic, this had meant

moving closer. For David, pragmatic and guarded, moving away.

She had judged David's choice, and even hated him for it, but now she wondered if it hadn't been the right one after all. He had saved himself.

And she had lost herself. She had become something she had never been before: cynical and hard and a survivor.

But had she really?

Because sitting here with the warmth of the sun and the warmth of his shoulder being equally comforting, she realized she had never really stopped being that softhearted person who rescued impossible men, and old houses and orphaned dogs.

She had just tried to hide all that was soft about her, because it felt as if it left her open to hurt.

But now she felt soft all over again. She felt soft to her soul and the hard armor around her heart had fallen away, leaving it exposed.

And acknowledging she was those things—someone who believed, still, in the power of love—did not feel like a weakness.

It felt like a homecoming.

Kayla felt as close to David as she had ever felt to another human being. Close and connected.

She tilted her head and looked at him. Really looked. He turned and looked back at her. She saw the most amazing thing in his eyes.

Wonder.

As if he knew he had seen her at her rawest and most real, and *still* liked what he saw.

In David's eyes she saw a truth that stole her breath away. If she were standing with her back against the wall, with the enemy coming at her with knives in their teeth, he would stand beside her.

If they were on a ship that was going down in a stormy sea, he would make sure she was safe before he got off.

If the building were burning and filled with smoke, he would be the one finding her hand and leading her out into the cool, clean air.

He was the one who could lead her to life.

Her newly softened heart was so filled with gratitude that she leaned toward him. She did not know how else to express the magnitude of what she was feeling, what she was awakening to, what she knew of herself that she had not known ten minutes ago.

Kayla found the courage to do what she had wanted to do since the moment she had first laid eyes on him again, after the bee had stung her.

If she'd been dying, she wanted to taste him, to feel the soft firmness of his lips tangling with her own.

Why would she not feel the same way about living?

He read her intent. And instead of backing away, he moved his hand to the small of her back and brought her in to himself. He tilted his head down so that it was easy for her to reach his lips.

And then they touched.

She touched the soft openness of her lips to the hard line of his. Only his lips were not hard.

Not at all.

The texture was velvety and plump, like a peach, warmed by the sun and ready to be picked.

At first the kiss was gentle, a welcome. But it quickly deepened to reflect the hunger between them, a long-ago fire that still had embers glowing.

Kayla's sense of being alive intensified thrillingly. Her blood felt as if it were on fire. It was *more* than she remembered from that night long ago, because they were both *more.*

More mature, more aware, more experienced. And it felt as if they both brought everything that they were to that kiss, left nothing behind, gave it all. Heart and soul and blood and bone. Hurts and triumphs and all of life.

Her dog woke in her arms, getting squished between them.

Bastigal growled, and then barked and then snapped at David's hand, missing by a hair.

They drew apart. Kayla laughed nervously. "I'm sorry. He's never done that before."

But did David look faintly relieved as he reeled back from her and ran a hand through his sun-dried dark hair?

He was a man who liked a plan. How would he react to the spontaneous passion that had just erupted between them?

It was an earthquake, and he could feel something shifting between them, or the shift in her heart. He let go of Kayla's hand and stood up abruptly. "I should go home and change."

At first she thought he was rejecting her after all. But she couldn't have been more wrong.

"But then I'll come back," he said softly, watching her steadily, letting her know he had seen her and he was not afraid and not scared off by what he had seen, or by what had just leaped up between them, igniting both their worlds.

"You will?"

David nodded. "I need to fix that chair in your kitchen. When I was standing on it, reaching the ceiling, it wobbled pretty badly. I don't want you to get hurt the next time you stand on it to pour something down HAL's throat."

But with her newly opened heart, she saw it wasn't

about the chair, really. Maybe it wasn't about her or that kiss, as much as she hoped, either. She saw the look he cast toward his own house.

Something in her said to let him go—but it was the old part, that part of her that somehow had stopped believing that good things could happen and that it was okay to be happy.

The newer part felt stronger. Kisses aside, Kayla could see David *wanted* to have an excuse not to spend time in his mother's house.

He did not have a home to go to, at least not the one next door. She realized he was looking for reasons not go back to the house he had grown up in, not the way it was now.

And whether he knew it or not, or could acknowledge it or not, something about what had just passed between them had let him know she would stand by him.

That she had his back.

Just as she had become so aware that he would stand by her, no matter what.

Kayla had seen the pain and desperation in him this morning. She had nearly wept when he had spoken about how the way his mother was now was threatening to wipe out everything that had happened before.

And she saw the truth. This morning she had been a different person than the one she was now. When had she become that person? The one who would turn away from someone in need to protect herself?

That was what the hardness inside her had done. That was what the bitterness of her marriage had done. That was what being so unforgiving had done.

But those were things that had happened to her. Only she could decide if they could change who she really was.

Really, did anything change the essence of who a person was?

Once, a long time ago, she and David and some other kids had hiked in to Cambridge Falls, not far from town.

But when they had gotten there, someone had left garbage along the edges of the jade-green pool at the bottom of the falls.

She had been incensed, but David had simply picked up the trash and stowed it in his backpack.

"It's temporary," he'd said, seeing her face. "It can't change this." He gestured at the beauty of the fall cascading into the greenness of the glade.

"Even if I didn't pick it up," he'd insisted softly, "five years from now, or twenty, or a hundred, the garbage would be gone, and this would remain."

This would remain. The essence. Water hammering down over moss-covered rocks created a cooling mist and prisms of light, falling into a pool that was the deepest shade of green she had ever seen. Like emeralds.

Like her eyes, David had said.

The essence: what was at the heart of each thing in the universe.

And Kayla felt the garbage had kept her from seeing hers. Now, just as then, David had seen past the garbage, to who she really was.

And had allowed her to glimpse it again, too.

Kayla could feel something fresh and hopeful unfolding in herself. And it made her want to be a better person, even if that meant taking risks.

Surely she could trust herself to be the friend David needed just as he had been the friend she needed this morning?

Or could they ever be just friends after what had just transpired between them?

She drew in a steadying breath at the thought. She remembered his mother in her pink winter boots and her gaping nightgown, and him sleeping on the lawn.

She guessed he was sleeping out there, not just because he didn't like it inside the house, but in case his mother got out again.

He was a warrior protecting his camp, and somehow Kayla had fallen inside that ring of protection.

The tenderness she felt for this strong, strong man who was having his every strength tried nearly overwhelmed her.

Kayla drew in a deep breath. If she could help him get through that, she was going to, even if it meant putting herself in danger.

And being around him did make the very air feel as if it were charged with danger. She was just way too aware of him right now: the rain-fresh scent of the lake clinging to him, his wet shirt and shorts molding the fine cut of his muscles.

And then there was the way his lips had felt on her finger. And then on the tenderness of her lips.

In fact, the place where his lips had tasted her and touched her and claimed her felt, still, tingling, faintly singed as if she had been branded by the electricity of a storm.

"I'd appreciate it if you could fix that chair," she said. "You're right. I would have stood on it to put the cream in HAL."

He nodded, knowing.

"And while you fix the chair, I'll see if I can rescue any of the cream from that machine. We might have homemade dandelion ice cream yet today."

She was pleased that her voice sounded calm and steady, a complete lie given the hard beating of her heart as she recognized a new start, a second chance, a return to herself.

A homecoming.

He shot her a look. “Stay away from HAL,” he warned.

“I’m going to rescue my ice cream from the jaws of HAL,” she muttered, and heard his snort of reluctant laughter.

“Okay, but don’t do it until I get there.”

She should have protested at his controlling behavior. Instead, knowing it might be a weakness, she savored someone caring for her.

And she savored caring for someone right back.

“Aye-aye, David,” she said, and gave him a mock salute. His grin was sudden, warm, spontaneous, completely without guards; it was the cherry on top of the sundae of what they’d just shared.

“I prefer the French pronunciation,” he said, “Duh-veed.”

It was an old, old joke between them, a leftover from their high school days, a reminder of the people they both had been, and perhaps, could be again.

CHAPTER FOURTEEN

"AYE-AYE, DUH-VEED," she said, and her laughter felt rich and warm and real as she watched him cross the lawn between their two houses. Then she turned and went around her walkway to her back door, Bastigal tucked close to her heart. She was aware of the dog's heart beating. But even more aware of the beating of her own.

Life.

She was aware she was alive, and glad of it.

A little while later, feeling joyous with her dog back in his little basket watching her, Kayla tried to decide what to wear and what to do with her hair.

Momentarily, guilt niggled at her. What was she doing?

But she brushed the guilt aside and decided right then and there that she had had enough guilt to last her a lifetime. David had said guilt and happiness could not coexist. He had said fear and happiness could not coexist.

When was the last time she had just taken the moments life gave her as a gift? In the past days, lying out under the stars, getting sprayed with yellow globs, swimming fully clothed in the chilly and refreshing waters of the lake she had felt something she had not felt for so long.

Happy.

And then when she had given in to the temptation to taste his lips?

Alive.

And if it was some kind of sin to *want* that feeling, to chase it, even though it was connected to him, well, then she was going to be a sinner.

She had tried for sainthood for the first twenty-some-odd years of life. She was going to try playing for the other side.

And so, she looked at her wardrobe with a critical eye, and she passed over the knee-length golfing shorts and the button-down blouse.

She put on, instead, shorty-shorts and a tailored plaid top that she left one button more than normal undone on.

She scooped up her hair into a loose bun, letting the tendrils fall out and curl around her face. She dusted her eyes with makeup that made them look like they were the color of emeralds, and she dabbed lip gloss onto her lips and admired how puffy and shiny they looked.

She looked at herself in the mirror. She felt attractive and womanly for the first time in how long?

"What the heck are you doing?" she whispered.

Given the hunger David Blaze made her feel, and the happiness, what the heck *was* she doing?

It was obvious. She was playing with fire. And she was startled by how much she liked it, especially when she let him into her house a half hour later and saw the deep male appreciation darken the brown of his eyes to near black.

And then he turned his attention, swiftly, to her rickety chair, and to the heap of tools he had unearthed at his mother's house and brought with him.

For a moment she felt an old wound resurfacing: his turning his attention so deliberately away from her made her feel the same way she had felt after he had kissed her all those years ago, and then turned away.

Suddenly, she wondered about that. Had he turned

away then because he felt too little? Or because he had felt too much?

She reminded herself that she had invited him here for him, not for her.

And for now she was going to free herself from all that; she was just going to enjoy the moment. She would navigate the other stuff when it surfaced.

And hope that it didn't blow everything around it to smithereens!

"There," he said, a half hour later, righting the chair, resting his hand on the back of it and looking supremely satisfied with himself when it did not wobble. "Done."

"That's great, David. Hey, do you think you could mow my lawn? I've let it get too deep. I can't even push the mower through it."

He shot her a look like he was going to protest. She deliberately busied herself rescuing the remains of the Dandy Lion ice cream, then snuck a look at him.

As she suspected, David looked nothing but relieved that she had given him another excuse not to go home.

Two days later, on her back deck, Kayla snuck another look at the man in her yard. Terrible as it was to admit—like a weakness, really—it was nice to have a man around. Of course, it didn't hurt that it was a man like David.

They had fallen into a routine of sorts. He came over in the morning, and she made coffee and toast.

He sat out on her deck with his laptop and used her internet, and then, as if it were a fair trade, did some chores around the house. Her screen door didn't squeak anymore—he'd replaced and reinforced the latch; the kitchen faucet didn't drip.

Yesterday, when the hardware store had delivered planks to fix her back deck, she had protested.

"David, no. I feel as if I'm taking advantage of you and all your manly skills."

He had lifted an eyebrow at her to let her know that he had manly skills she had not begun to test yet. The awareness between them was electric. But despite long, lingering gazes, and hands and shoulders and hips "accidentally" touching, they had not kissed again.

But then his gaze had slid to his own house.

She saw how her initial assessment of the situation had been bang on: he needed to be busy right now.

And his initial assessment of her situation had also been correct: her house was a project that was too big for her to undertake.

"I am so grateful for your help," she admitted.

He smiled and Kayla appreciated the slow unfolding of the new relationship between them. Even if she would have given in to the temptation, Bastigal had an intuitive sense of when the hum of electricity was growing too intense between them, and would become quite aggressive toward David.

His message was clear: *I am the man of this house.* But in a way it was a blessing that he was chaperoning them.

She had made the mistake of intimacy too quickly once before and the results had been disastrous.

If there was something here to be explored, she wanted to do it slowly, an unfolding of herself and of him.

Now she watched him out on her lawn. David was doing her lawn in sections, mostly because her lawn mower—which he had dubbed HAL Two—had, like the name suggested, a mind of its own.

It would roar to life, work for five or ten minutes and then sputter to a halt. From the first day, she had liked watching David fiddle with her cranky lawn mower.

Every time it broke down he would do the manly things

required with such ease: checking the oil, turning it over and cleaning out underneath it. As she looked on he would run his finger along the blade and frown, but then apparently decide it was okay and flip it back up again.

Moments later the air would be filled with the sound of the mower once more. She had always liked that sound and the smell of fresh-mown grass.

Kayla had told herself to keep busy. She could look up the manual for her batch freezer on the internet after all! But there was no reason she could not do that from her perch on the deck.

So she ended up, day after day, taking the computer out on the deck, liking the feeling of being close to him, of covertly watching him work.

Seeing David—willingly working, liking to help out—was such a poignant counterpoint to the life that she had had and the choices she had made.

After watching David struggle through her jungle of a lawn until he was wiping the sweat from his brow, Kayla took pity on him and went in and made lemonade. She had it done by the time the lawn mower shut off, and she called him up from the yard.

He eyed her offering with pretended suspicion.

"This looks suspiciously like pee, too. Is it the Dandelion ice cream reincarnated?"

"No, but what a great idea! Fresh squeezed lemonade at More-moo."

"You need to let me do some homework before you go any further on the More-moo thing."

She went still. Oh, it felt so good to have someone offering to do things for her! But it was a weakness to like it so much, a challenge to her vow to be totally independent.

"Duh-veed," she said, her tone teasing, "I can do my own homework."

He lifted an eyebrow and put down his lemonade in one manly gulp. He handed her the empty glass. "I have people who do nothing else all day long. You should let them have a look at it."

To refuse would be churlish, pure stupid pride. "I'd have to pay," she decided.

"At least that would be a better investment than the batch freezer."

"The ice cream eruption was just a minor glitch," she said. "I can fix it. I've been on the internet looking at that model. The snap-down lid is missing, that's all."

"It's kind of putting the cart before the horse, getting that contraption before you know about the ice cream parlor."

"It was a good deal!"

He rolled his eyes but took the glass from her. He casually wiped the sweat off his brow. She refilled the glass and he took a long, appreciative swig.

There was something about the scene that was so domestic and so normal that she wanted to just stay here, in this sunny moment, forever.

His phone buzzed and he took it out of his pocket, frowned, read a message and put it back. "Could I tap into your internet for a few minutes? A video is coming through that I'd like to look at on my laptop instead of my phone."

"Of course."

He went and retrieved his laptop from where it was now stored on her kitchen counter. He sat outside on one of her deck chairs. He looked uncharacteristically lost.

Kayla refilled his lemonade one more time. "I hope you don't get a splinter," she said when he thanked her and settled more deeply into the chair.

He looked like he hadn't even heard her.

"Because, Duh-veed, it would be very embarrassing for you if I had to pull a sliver out of your derriere."

"That would be awful," he agreed, but absently.

Suddenly, she was worried about him. He seemed oddly out of it since he had taken that phone call. Now he was scowling at his computer screen.

"Hey," she said softly.

When he looked up he could not hide the stricken look on his face.

"David? What's wrong?"

"Nothing."

"That's a bald-faced lie," she said.

"You've got to quit calling me a liar," he said, but even that was a lie, because while the words were light, his tone sounded as if his heart was breaking.

She had never known a stronger man than him. Not ever. And so it was devastating to watch him turn his computer to her so she could see what he was looking at.

The strongest man she knew put his head in his hands, and she thought he was going to weep.

CHAPTER FIFTEEN

KAYLA TURNED HER ATTENTION to the screen to give David a moment to compose himself. It took her a minute to figure out what she was looking at. And then she knew. It was some kind of retirement home. Unbelievably posh, and yet…

"Oh, David," she whispered.

"I have to put her name on a list. If they have an opening," he said, his voice a croak, "I have to decide right away. I need to go meet with the director and look at the facility in person this afternoon. I'll come back in the morning."

"I'm going with you," she said.

She could not leave him alone with the torment she saw in his face.

He looked at her as if he was going to protest. But then he didn't.

"Thank you," he said quietly.

"I'll go pack an overnight bag. And make arrangements for Bastigal to go to the kennel."

And it wasn't until she was in her room packing that bag that Kayla considered the implications of it. She sank down on the bed.

Life seemed, suddenly, to have been wrested from

her grasp, to have all these totally unexpected twists and turns in it.

But there was something about making this decision to go with David that felt as if she had been lost in a forest and suddenly saw the way out.

She *needed* to be there for him. His need and his pain were so intense, and she needed to be there, to absorb some of that, to ease his burden.

Kayla realized there was the potential for pain here, tangling herself deeper in his world. And yet, she had to do it.

The word *love* whispered through her mind, but she chased it away. Now was not the time to study this complication.

Wasn't it enough to know that something amazing was happening, and that it was happening to both of them?

She didn't have to—or want to—put a label on it. She just wanted to sink into the sensation that they weren't, either of them, as alone as they had been just a short time ago.

And she wanted to sink into the feeling of gratitude, that all the events of her life, even her difficult marriage—or maybe especially that—had prepared her for this, made her exactly the person she needed to be to rise to this challenge and more: embrace it.

David was so grateful that Kayla was there with him. It took his mind off what he was about to do. As they drove to Toronto she was the most pleasant of diversions—the way the wind caught in her hair with the top down, how childish she was in her wonder about the car, her lemony scent—what kind of ice cream stain was she trying to get rid of now?—tickling his nostrils.

He wanted to take her for lunch at a place he favored

downtown, which was coincidentally close to the "retirement" home, but she took one look at his face and knew he was not up to even the rudiments of ordering a meal.

Instead she had him stop by a food truck, got out and ordered for both of them, and they sat in his car and ate.

"I'll try not to spill, Duh-veed," she said, but quickly saw he was not even up to teasing. She put out her hand and he took it, and it seemed after that he would never let go.

He left the car—she insisted he put the roof up, otherwise he was so distracted he might have left it down—and they walked to Graystone Manor. David knew from the video that it was a converted sandstone house that had belonged to a lumber baron at the turn of the century. It had a specialized wing for dementia and Alzheimer's patients.

The director, Mark Smithson, met them at the door. He was kind and soft-spoken, but nonetheless it reminded David of consulting with a funeral director over his father's ceremony many years ago.

It was a beautiful facility. The rooms were like good hotel suites, the colors were warm and muted, the quality of the furniture and art was exquisite.

As Mr. Smithson talked about their programs for patients with all forms of dementia—people first, illness second, life maps and memory boxes, gardening and crafts—David knew he had come to the right place. He wondered if he should have made this decision long ago.

Still, it was with great sadness that he made the deposit and filled out the forms for his mother.

"We could have a vacancy very quickly," Mr. Smithson warned him, kindly. "You will only have forty-eight hours to make up your mind."

A vacancy. David realized his mother could come

here when someone else died. He could not trust himself to speak.

Again he was aware of his hand in Kayla's, and that that alone was giving him the strength to do the unthinkable and unspeakable.

When they left, she remained silent. She did not try to reassure him, or comment on the visit.

Fifteen minutes later, Kayla led him past the uniformed doorman into the lobby of his building. David felt as if he were the Alzheimer's patient, dazed and disoriented.

His condo was Yorkton—arguably Toronto's most affluent neighborhood—at its finest. His company had bought an aging hotel and completely gutted and refurbished it into condos. The lobby, with its Swarovski crystal chandelier, artfully distressed leather furniture and authentic Turkish rugs, could easily compete with the best five-star hotels in the world.

Each condo took up an entire floor of the building; their size was part of the reason they had commanded the highest prices ever paid in Yorkton for real estate.

The elevator, using the latest technology, was programmed to accept his fingerprint. He touched the panel and it began to glide upward to his penthouse.

"But what about company?" Kayla asked, her voice hushed as if she was in a church.

"I can give them a code."

"Oh." She seemed subdued. As the elevator doors whispered open, Kayla looked like a deer frozen in headlights. Her eyes went very wide and David saw his living space through her perspective.

"This is like a movie set," Kayla said.

"Feel free to look around," he invited.

Kayla glanced at him and then moved into his space, her mouth a little round O of astonishment and awe.

The space the elevator opened onto was large and open. The original plank flooring had been restored to distressed glory, stained dark, and it ran throughout.

Low-backed and sleek, two ten-foot white leather sofas, centered on a hand-knotted carpet from Tajikistan, faced each other over a custom-made coffee table, the glass top engineered around a base of a gnarled chunk of California Redwood.

Floor-to-ceiling windows—the window coverings could darken the room by remote control if needed—showed the skyline of Toronto, lights beginning to wink on as dusk fell.

Outside the windows was a generous deck with invisible glass rails. There was a good-sized pool—for a private pool in a condo, anyway—the infinity edge making it seem like the water cascaded off into the city lights. The pool lights on sensors were just beginning to come on, turning the water into a huge turquoise jewel.

The kitchen, open to the living room but separated from it by an island with a massive gray-veined granite countertop, was as sleek and modern as his living room furniture.

"Copper?" she said of the double ovens mounted into the cabinetry. "I've never even heard of that."

"Everybody has stainless," he said.

"Not me," she shot back. "Where's your fridge?"

He moved by her and showed her how the fridge and dishwasher were blended into the cabinetry, artfully hidden behind panels.

"I don't think a fridge like this should be hidden, necessarily," she decided after a moment.

She stared at the built-in espresso maker— also copper—then turned to inspect the copper-topped, eight-burner gas range. She tentatively pushed a button and the range fan silently appeared out of the granite.

"Wow," she murmured. "HAL Three."

He smiled despite himself, glad for the distraction, taking pleasure in her awe of his space. And yet as she looked around in amazement it occurred to him that in the short time he had been in Blossom Valley, her house, with all its unpacked boxes and its old yellow kitchen, felt more like home than this.

This was a space made for entertaining, personally, occasionally. Mostly professionally. The space was designed to impress and it did just that.

She looked at the wine cooler—copper—a dual-zone with French doors.

"How many bottles does that hold?"

"Forty-eight."

"Do you want a drink?" she asked.

He shook his head, "I think that is the last thing I need right now."

She looked so relieved that that was not how he dealt with stress, and he got another hint of what it must have been like with Kevin.

He reminded himself that it was her turn to be happy.

She moved out of the kitchen. When he had designed the condo he had loved it; that by necessity, the windows were only on one wall.

That meant all the rest of the walls, soaring to fifteen feet in height, could be used to display art. Systems of invisible wires, not unlike clotheslines except tauter, displayed dozens of canvasses that he could switch out at any time for others that he kept in a museum-quality storage facility.

"I don't know anything about art," she finally said, "But I stand in amazement. You don't have to understand it. You can *feel* it."

It pleased him that she got it so completely. For a moment a future shimmered before him, the two of them on that couch, sipping wine and…

He made himself stop.

"If you're into a quiet evening in, I'll order us a great dinner," he offered. It occurred to him that Kayla was the only woman he had ever said that to, where he didn't have an agenda.

She crossed over to him and put her hand on his arm. "Right now," she told him sternly, "you do not need to look after me. You need to look after you. What do you need to do for you?"

"I need to swim," he said, nodding toward the pool. "I need to swim and swim and swim. I hope you'll come with me. There's a hot tub, too."

"I didn't bring a suit."

"I keep a supply of them for visitors in the guest suite."

"Ah." She said this a little sadly, as if she was figuring out she did not belong in his world.

And yet the truth for him? His apartment had never felt as much like home as it did with her looking through his kitchen.

"Will you swim with me?"

For a moment she looked as though she was going to bolt for the door. But then she drew in a deep breath and nodded solemnly.

"I'll show you the guest suite," he said. "Suits are in the top drawer, left hand side, in the closet."

Kayla heard the door of the guest suite whisper shut behind her. She looked around at the opulence, almost shocked by it.

There were in here, as elsewhere, floor-to-ceiling

windows. The same beautiful, dark, aged hardwood ran throughout.

An antique four-poster bed, centered on a deep area carpet and beautifully made up with modern-patterned bedding that contrasted the age of the bed, looked incredibly inviting.

It was a walk-in closet with built-in shelves and drawers and hangers. She went to the top drawer on the left and found a huge selection of bathing suits, all brand-new and all sizes, from children's to men's.

Somehow it was a relief that he didn't just entertain women here!

Tempted as she was to snoop through the other drawers, Kayla chose several suits that might fit her and went into the bathroom.

Again, she was nearly shocked by the opulence. There was a fireplace! In the guest bathroom! A beautiful painting hung above it. There were dove-gray marble floor tiles, honed, instead of polished. Despite the fireplace, the focal point of the room was definitely an egg-shaped, stand-alone soaker tub. Two lush and obviously brand-new white robes hung from hooks. Towels, plush and plump, also pure white, were rolled into a basket by the tub.

Kayla tried on three of the suits, feeling just a bit like Goldilocks. The first one was too skimpy, the next one was too frumpy and the third one was just right.

Darkness had fallen almost completely when, wrapped in one of the housecoats, she slid open the door of her suite that went directly onto the patio.

The view was breathtaking and the pool was gorgeous, lights inside it turning the water to winking turquoise.

Aware David was already in the water watching her, she slipped off the housecoat and slid into the water.

She made her way over to him and sat on an underwater bench beside him.

"Thank you for coming today," he said hoarsely, "I don't think I could have made it through without you." And then wryly, "Kayla to the rescue."

"She'll be safe there," Kayla told him. "And as happy as can be expected. I liked the memory box idea. What will you put in it, I wonder?"

David was silent for a long time. When he spoke his voice was so low that Kayla had to strain to hear it.

"I'll put the pinecone Christmas ornament I made in the second grade in it," he said. "And the corsage my dad gave her for their fifteenth anniversary that she dried and always kept by the bed. I'll put the dog's worn old collar that she kept long after he died and that still sits on the mantel. I'll put in my graduation diploma. I'll put her favorite recipe book in there, and a picture of her sister and the old sepia photo of the farm she grew up on in Saskatchewan. I'll put in the ugly dish that she made in ceramics that we all laughed about, and the earrings I gave her for her birthday when I was ten, and that she wore even though they looked like Ukrainian Easter eggs.

"A whole life," he said, his voice breaking. "How can I put her whole life in a box? How do I put in Canada Day fireworks, and the look on her face as she looked upward? How do I put in the memory of her fingers on my back as she smoothed cream on a sunburn? How do I put in waking up to the smell of bacon and eggs? How do I put her laughter when the snowman toppled over? How do I —" But he didn't finish.

He was crying.

She had never seen a man cry. It seemed to her it was the strongest thing she had ever seen a man do.

It seemed to her she had never seen a man so capable of deep love and the sorrow that it brought.

She slowly moved her hand and caught one of his tears and lifted the saltiness to her lips with gentle reverence and tasted it.

He caught her hand and he kissed it and then he moved away from Kayla, sliced cleanly through the water and began to swim.

And after a moment she dove into the water and she swam beside him, silently, matching him stroke for stroke, swimming through the silent beauty of a dark city night, swimming through the memories that swirled around them, swimming through the pain.

She would not have chosen to be anywhere else at that moment but beside him, swimming through life in all its grief and all its glory.

CHAPTER SIXTEEN

When it seemed like they had swum for hours, David hoisted himself out of the pool and then helped her out.

His body was extraordinary, beaded with water, the city lights and the reflections from the pool casting it in bronze. His swimming trunks clung to the perfect muscle of his legs.

"Can I interest you in that dinner now? I'm hungry."

"Liar," she said, softly. "You're just saying that because you think I should eat something."

He smiled tiredly.

"Why don't you go to bed?" she said. "I'll look after myself tonight."

"Are you sure?"

She nodded. After he had gone, she sat on his big couch and watched the lights outside.

After a while, she went into that opulent guest suite, put on her pajamas and got into the giant bed. She could not sleep and got up, took the housecoat from where she had dropped it on the floor, wrapped it around herself and wandered restlessly around the gorgeous apartment. She was drawn to the art.

Even in the darkness, it held light. She moved slowly from one amazing piece to the next. It was almost too much beauty to take in.

Then Kayla froze when she heard a sound. She moved out of the living room and went down a wide hallway in the direction she thought the sound had come.

It was a different wing than the guest room was in, and she realized it was his wing, where his private bedroom suite was.

She found herself standing outside his bedroom door.

It was slightly ajar and she could hear the steadiness of his breathing behind it. She was going to move away when the sound came again, a stifled sound of pain, like a wounded animal.

She gave David's bedroom door a faint shove with her fingertips and it whispered open. Like the rest of the apartment, the bedroom could have been from a movie set, or a hotel suite that rented for thousands upon thousands of dollars a night.

He had not bothered to close the drapes, and the floor-to-ceiling windows looked out over the dazzling lights of the city. The pool lights were reflecting in the room, making it seem like an underwater dream.

It was a deeply masculine room, done in many shades of gray, but saved from being too cold or too modern by an exquisite large abstract painting—an explosion of warm colors—that hung above a bed that was enormous.

The bed, despite its kingly proportions, struck Kayla as being faintly sad, like two people who didn't like each other very much could sleep here and never know of the other's presence.

The sound came again, a muted sound of torment, and she slipped deeper into the room and tiptoed over to the bed.

He was fast asleep, his lashes long and thick and casting faint shadows against his cheeks. A faint bristle was rising along the line of his jaw. The covers were thrown back and David was bare-chested.

The masculine lines of his chest put the beauty of the canvas above his head to shame!

His legs, clad in Slugs and Snails pajama bottoms in a different shade than the other ones she had seen, were tangled in the sheets. It was obvious, from the messiness of the bed coverings that his sleep was restless and troubled.

In his sleep, David's brow furrowed, and he made that sound again, tormented.

Tentatively, she put her hand on his forehead and was satisfied when, under her touch, he was soothed and the line of distress left his brow.

It felt like a stolen moment, a guilty pleasure, to study him like this without his knowledge, to drink in the now oh so familiar planes of his ruggedly handsome face. It was with the utmost of reluctance that Kayla turned away.

"I don't want you to go."

At first she thought he was talking in his sleep, talking about the decision he had made for his mother, that he did not want her to have to leave her home of forty years and go to Graystone Manor.

But when she turned back, prepared to soothe again, David was awake, if groggy. He drank her in, then propped himself up on one elbow and drank her in some more.

It was probably only the lateness of the hour, the magical light reflected from the pool outside his bedroom, but it seemed to her that the look in his eyes might be identical to the one she had just looked at him with.

He scooted over in the bed and tapped the empty place beside him with the palm of his hand. Her mouth went dry. She felt as if she were standing on the edge of a cliff, deciding whether to jump or to back away.

To jump held the danger—and the thrill—of the unknown. To back away did not really feel like an option at all.

Feeling powerless she slipped in beside him, and felt not the danger of a leap into the unknown at all. She lay on her back, studying the ornate plaster work on his ceiling, feeling the exquisite touch of linen warmed through by his skin.

She felt that softness within her swell like a bud in early spring about to burst.

He covered her with the sheet. "What have you got on underneath that housecoat?" he asked gruffly.

"My pajamas."

"Are they sexy?"

"No."

He growled something that she was pretty sure was *thank God.*

She nestled into him, cherishing this moment, feeling as if she were in a dream that she didn't want to wake up from.

"David," she said after a long time, trusting the sense of intimacy between them, "I need to know something."

"Anything."

"Why did you stop talking to me that night after you kissed me?" she whispered, needing, finally, to address the last of the unfinished business between them.

He closed his eyes again. She heard a ragged regret in the quietness of his deep voice.

"Kevin told me he'd asked you to the prom. To me, it was an honor thing between friends. You don't take your best friend's girl. He had spoken for you. I took the step back."

She was silent as she contemplated this. Kevin had not asked her to the prom until after David had kissed her.

She had only said yes because it was evident that David regretted the kiss, and had no intention of taking his relationship with her anywhere. Maybe she had even hoped it would make him jealous.

Certainly, picking out the prom dress, she had been thinking of David as much as Kevin. That she would be gorgeous, and he would be sorry that he had let her get away.

But David had not reacted to her at all that night. He'd seemed engrossed in Emily Carson, who had been wearing a pure black strapless gown that made her seem sophisticated and worldly and that had made Kayla feel like a small-town girl and a hick that a guy like David would never look at.

This knowledge—that Kevin had betrayed her, betrayed both his friends, manipulated and lied to have his own way—did not have any taste of bitterness to it.

She had already forgiven him.

And she had already forgiven herself.

She saw no point in telling David. Wouldn't the knowledge just cause him more pain when he was dealing with enough?

Plus, it was as if knowing that final truth about Kevin set her totally free.

To love another. Or perhaps to return to the love her heart had first recognized.

"David?"

"Hmm?"

"You loved him, didn't you?"

There was a long silence, and then he said, "Yeah. He was not just my friend. He was my brother."

A floodgate that had been closed opened between them.

The water of forgiveness flowed out of it and washed over both of them.

"Tell me something wonderful that you remember about your brother," she said softly. "Remind me of the Kevin he once was."

And so he did. And then she did. And then he did. And by the time the morning light had softened the room, they were exhausted.

"I always thought," David said, "if I stopped being angry with him that all that would remain would be a pool of sadness so deep I would drown in it."

"And?" she whispered.

"It doesn't feel like that at all. It feels as if the love remains, strong and true, even after all we went through. I wish I could tell him."

"I think you just did," she said softly. "I think you just did. He gave us more than he took, didn't he? Even his flaws helped shape both of us into the people we are today.

"Do you think," Kayla went on, "that is what love does? Performs this kind of alchemy, where it turns lead into gold?"

No answer. She turned and gazed at him. David was sleeping, not restlessly now, his arm curled around her, his nose buried in her hair.

"I love you," she whispered.

Maybe he was not sleeping after all because she felt a sudden tension ripple through him and she braced herself for his rejection.

But it did not come. Instead, he sighed and relaxed, and the arm that was curled around her touched her hair, and then pulled her in yet closer to his heart.

Any thought about going back to her own room evaporated. She could not resist lying beside him, just for a moment, just to drink in his scent and the feel of his skin, to feel the heartbeat of the man she had come to love so completely.

His essence.

But somehow, her eyes closed and she fell asleep beside him.

David awoke feeling groggy, as if he had a hangover, when he knew he had not had a drop to drink. That was the power of grief.

He stretched and then froze, opened one eye and then the other cautiously.

Kayla was in his bed, her small frame wrapped in the plushness of the housecoat, her face squished against his skin, her beautiful honey-colored hair scattered across his naked chest. If he was not mistaken, there was the tiniest little pool of drool on his chest.

The feeling of grogginess left him, as did the feeling of being hungover.

It seemed to David, in a life that had everything—glamour and adventure and success beyond his wildest dreams—that he had never had a moment sweeter than this one.

It occurred to him he loved her.

And that maybe he always had, from that first kiss.

And so he savored her head on his chest, and the lemony scent of her. Had she said those words last night?

Had she whispered *I love you* to him?

The moment of sweetness was replaced with sadness. There was a responsibility with loving someone. As she had said last night, loving Kevin had shaped them both. Even his flaws had shaped them. And this was one of the things David had learned.

To love someone was to protect them from harm.

It made David feel like a colossal failure, given the decision he was about to make concerning his mother.

To love someone was to protect them from pain, not to cause it.

He thought of what that meant in terms of what he had been discovering over the long, lazy days of summer, about what he felt for Kayla.

There was no chance—absolutely none—that they would grow to love each other less. No, he knew that.

He knew each tumbling snowman, and each summer night lit with fireworks intensified the love. He knew that old dogs died and new puppies came home, and that these events intensified the love.

And so did making ice cream.

And so did cleaning up messes that dripped from the ceilings and covered their clothes in yellow splotches.

And lying on the lawn looking up at Orion and listening to her name the stars.

And swimming fully clothed in a cold lake on a hot summer day.

And what did that mean, that the love kept deepening and intensifying? It meant it would hurt Kayla more when that day came.

When the doctor's reassurances about his heart proved incorrect and, just as it had done for his father, that vital organ exploded inside his chest and left him lying on the floor, keeled over, dying in front of her, all the chest compressions in the world not enough.

Or when they were walking through someplace like Graystone, only this time it was her decision to make. About him. About what to do with him.

All the money in the world and all the success could not stop the march of time. All the money in the world could not rip the "E" gene from your body and replace it with something else.

All the money in the world could not prevent the inevitability of causing those you loved pain.

Kayla woke up slowly and he cherished her waking. He cherished her slow blink, and then nodding back off, a stir of her leg, and then her arm, her hand pushing her hair from her face.

And then that hand settling on his chest. And going still. Her eyes popping open wide, taking it all in.

And then her smile.

He would hold that smile in his heart forever. And then she leaned over and kissed him. And for one horribly weak moment, he let himself believe he could have this. That he could really have it all.

And then he yanked himself back from her, sat up, swung his legs off the bed and kept his back to her.

In a voice stripped of emotion, he said, "What are you doing in my bed?"

He could not turn and look, but he could feel the sudden stillness in the air.

"Isn't that exactly what got you in trouble before?" he said into her stricken silence. "Weren't you trying to make someone feel better who was in pain?"

Again, the silence that was worse than words.

He made himself look at her. He made his voice as hard and cold and mean as he could. He said, "I don't need you to rescue me, Kayla. I don't need you at all."

All those times she had seen him so clearly, all those times she had called him a liar. He held his breath hoping, maybe even praying, that she would see the lie he was telling her now.

But she didn't.

Her face went blank with pain. After the intimacies of their conversation last night—of finally reaching that place where the love and forgiveness flowed, instead of the anger—he felt his own treachery deeply.

And then she got up out of his bed, stiffly, and with her head held high, without glancing back, she walked out of his room, shutting the door quietly behind her.

It was only after she was gone that he let himself feel the pain of what he had just done. And he couldn't just let her go. How the hell was she going to get home? Walk? Take a bus?

He went and threw open his bedroom door, folded his arms over his naked chest, watched her heading for his door, her little overnight bag so quickly and haphazardly packed that something pink—the panties he had caught sight of that first day—were caught in the zipper.

When she heard him open his bedroom door, she tucked her head down so that her hair fell in a smooth curtain over her face, and hurried faster toward the elevator.

"I'll have a car sent around for you," he said, his voice still stripped of emotion, cool.

Her head shot up and she looked at him.

"Let me tell you something, David. Kevin never asked me to the prom until *after* we kissed that night."

He schooled his features not to show the distress that made him feel, not to let the thousand *what-ifs* that leaped instantly to his mind show on his face.

With humongous effort, with a kind of negligent carelessness, David lifted one shoulder, as if he didn't care.

Through the tears, she said a word he suspected she had never ever said before.

And she added a very emphatic *you* to the end of it.

And then she was gone.

CHAPTER SEVENTEEN

KAYLA HAD NOT BEEN out of her pajamas in a long time. Weeks? Her eyes were nearly as swollen from crying as they had been from the beesting. She was afraid to look at the calendar. How many days of summer had she let slip away while she nursed this heartbreak?

"Pathetic," she told herself. "You are pathetic."

Bastigal, her stalwart companion, licked her tears and looked worried.

Kayla took another spoonful of the ice cream out of the big tub on the coffee table in front of her.

It was bright yellow. It *did* look like pee. But it tasted surprisingly good, even after consuming nearly a gallon of it, solo.

Bastigal liked it, too, and uncaring about what it said about how pathetic her life had become, she let him share the spoon with her.

She had known the truth all along. The heartbreak had been completely preventable. David was completely out of her league after all. Look at that car. And the way he dressed. And that apartment. There was a fireplace in his bathroom, for Pete's sake.

David Blaze was straight out of a magazine spread, Kayla reminded herself glumly. He dated actresses, and ran a multimillion-dollar corporation. They *still* had stacks of that magazine all over town. She could not avoid his handsome mug, even when she ventured out ever so reluctantly to get dog food.

It made her mad that she had *hoped.* It made her even madder that David had presented himself as a regular guy who could mow the lawn and fix the door.

Who, even though he owned a zillion-dollar condo, had slept on his back grass to protect his mother.

Ten days after she had left his Yorkton condo, an ambulance had pulled up next door. She had raced to put on her shoes and get over there to see what was wrong with Mrs. Blaze, but as she had opened her front door, David had pulled up.

In a different car. Sleek and black and very, very expensive-looking. A uniformed driver had gotten out and held the back passenger-side door open for him then waited at a kind of respectful distance while David went into the house.

And she had sunk back in the shadows, realizing the ambulance had not come with its sirens on, so it was not an emergency. His mother was being transported to Graystone.

And she realized the difference in their two worlds.

Kayla realized he was this man: in the expensive suit, with the chauffeur holding open the door for him.

And yet, when he had come back out, his mother strapped to the ambulance gurney, the stricken look on his face had nearly made her go to him.

But his words that morning, brutal, had come back to her.

Isn't this exactly what got you in trouble before? Weren't you trying to make someone feel better who was in pain? I don't need you to rescue me, Kayla. I don't need you at all.

And so she had resisted the impulse to watch him from behind the sheer curtain in her living room, to see if he would even glance this way. Instead, she had turned away from the terrible tragedy of the scene unfolding next door, and gone to her couch.

And she had rarely been off it since.

The dog was a safe bet. The best bet. She had been on the right track when she had sworn devotion to her dog and her house and her business.

Would she buy More-moo? What if David was right? It was just risky business, one more hopeless rescue.

Her doorbell rang, and Kayla started, and the dog leaped off her lap and raced in crazy circles in front of the door.

She couldn't go to the door. She was in her pajamas. She had barely combed her hair since she had come back from Toronto. She had not brushed her teeth today. And possibly not yesterday, either. She had yellow splotches down the front of her pajamas.

Then it occurred to her.

It was him. It was David. His mother was settled in Graystone. He was coming out of that terrible crisis with a new understanding of what mattered. He had come to declare the error of his ways. He had come to get down on bended knee, beg her forgiveness, perhaps ask her hand in marriage.

Her heart thudding crazily as she contemplated a world once again ripe with possibility, Kayla slid off the couch and crept to her living room window, lifted the shade a hair.

It was another bright summer day and the brightness hurt her eyes. A courier van was pulling away.

So it was a written declaration of error, a written proclamation of undying love.

She went and flung open the door and looked at the parcel that lay there in its plastic envelope. The return address, Blaze Enterprises, seemed to be blinking in neon.

She picked it up and hugged it to herself, waltzed through to the kitchen—which was a disaster of ice cream and HAL experimentation—and went to her cutlery drawer. She found a butter knife and slit open the envelope.

She pulled out a thick binder and frowned. That would be quite a lengthy apology. And declaration of love.

She flipped it over and read: More-moo, A Financial and Business Analysis.

The self-pity evaporated instantly and was replaced with furious anger. Without opening the cover of the binder, Kayla went over to her garbage can, stepped on the lever that opened the lid and tossed the whole thing in.

It landed amongst the empty cream containers.

She stared at it for a moment, and then said a word she was saying for only the second time in her life. She added a most emphatic *you* after it.

And then she went into her bedroom and took off the stained pajamas, and decided, after looking at the stains, that they would be best beside the Business Analysis binder in the garbage.

She showered, put on her favorite white skirt, a dusting of makeup and her big, white sun hat that only a little while ago had made her feel independent and carefree and faintly Bohemian. She kissed Bastigal goodbye, knowing it would be a struggle to get him back in the basket, and then went and wheeled her bike out of the shed.

She rode downtown.

She felt a love for Blossom Valley swell in her heart as she rode down Main Street. The July sun had gentled into the cooler days of August. The leaves on the trees hinted at changes, and the summer crowds were thinning as people headed back to the city to do their before-school shopping.

She parked her bicycle in the rack outside More-moo, and looked hard at the place. The awning looked tired and the petunias had gotten leggy.

Still, she looked beyond that. It was only cosmetic, after all. Kayla took a deep breath and setting her shoulders, she went and opened the door.

It was a screen door on squeaky hinges, and a bell croaked a raspy greeting as she entered. Inside it was dark and cool after being in the bright sun.

It smelled good, and the little old lady beaming welcome at her from behind the counter reminded her of the grandmother she had always adored.

It wasn't as crowded as it would have been in the height of summer. She was sure that would be in the report.

But something the report wouldn't have captured was a young family of three sitting at one of the round tables, on the wrought iron, curly-backed chairs with the round seats padded in red-checked vinyl. The baby, in a baby seat, was covered in chocolate ice cream, the whites of his eyes showing like those of a miner coming up from the coal, the mom and dad laughing at him as he yelled for more.

In the booth in the corner, a boy and a girl sat across from each other, their fingertips intertwined in the center of the table. They were so delightfully young—maybe fifteen—and a single shake, in thick glass showing above metal shaker, was between them, with two straws but they were just using one, taking turns.

She recognized Mr. Bastigal, the science teacher, long since retired, nursing a coffee and looking forlornly out the window. He still looked like the spitting image of

Albert Einstein. Someone had told her his wife had died last year, and he looked lost. His gaze flickered to her but without recognition. Had she known she was going to bump into him from time to time, she probably would not have named the dog after him.

All of it: the smells and the sounds and the people, the unfolding of life's beautiful, simple vignettes filled her with a feeling.

No business report in the world could give you this: the feeling that something was just right.

Kayla walked up to the counter. The woman smiled at her as if she were a long-lost relative who had found her way, finally, home.

"I'd like to talk to someone about buying your business," she said firmly.

CHAPTER EIGHTEEN

UP UNTIL NOW in his life, David Blaze had been blessedly unaware that it was possible for a human being to feel as bad as he felt.

He barely slept. And he barely ate.

Guilt gnawed at him. And it wasn't guilt for the decision he had made about his mother. That had been a decision absolutely necessary to her health and well-being. It hadn't really been a decision at all, the choices narrowing until there were none left.

Now that his mother was settling at Graystone, he really wondered why he had waited so long. They were set up beautifully for her care. She was safe there. And relatively happy. Plus, she was closer. He could stop in and spend a few minutes with her every day.

Sometimes they went through the memory box, and it brought him great comfort to see her fingers gently stroking the petals of that dried rose corsage, as if the details of what it meant might be lost to her, but the essence was not.

He had put in an old nozzle from a garden hose to remind her of the skating rink, and then an old photo of him and Kevin standing in that rink, looking at the camera. That photo, of them leaning with fake ferociousness on their sticks, seemed to be her favorite thing in the box.

She touched David's younger face in the photo with

such tenderness. "This is my son," she said. Some days she remembered his name, and other days she didn't, and she almost never made the connection it was that same son who sat beside her now. And yet by her face, David was reassured that she remembered the most important part about the skating rink, too.

The devotion that had built it.

And the boys who had skated there had known that love built it, even if they had not ever said that. The boys had loved each other, even if they had never said that, either.

And when she touched his face in that long-ago photo, he felt she remembered what was crucial, at the heart of it all, the essence.

The love.

What he felt guilty about was that he had chased Kayla away and made her feel as if it was in any way about her.

He had made her feel her ability to love and to hope were a defect of some sort, and his regret was sharp and intense, a companion that rode with him and tormented him daily.

It was just wrong. He was a man who had built his whole life and his entire career on integrity, and the lie he had said to Kayla ate at him.

He had made it sound as if he didn't care about her. It had been for her own good, but it still didn't sit well with him. He had a sensation of having to set it right.

His assistant, Jane, came in.

"How's your mom today?" she asked, her face crinkled with concern.

He knew she was seeing the changes in him: weight loss, dark circles around his eyes. He had snapped at her more in the last few weeks than he had in all the years they had worked together.

She was putting it down to stress over the decisions he had made about his mother, and he was content to leave it at that. He didn't think he could handle one more woman thinking he needed rescuing.

"What's up?" he asked her, not answering about his mother, who was, in fact, having an off day.

"This just arrived by courier. I know you were waiting for it."

David looked at the sealed envelope she handed him. The return address was from Billings and Morton, an independent laboratory. It could take weeks and even months to get this kind of information. Though he rarely used his power or wealth to circumvent the system, he had this time.

"Thanks," he said, setting the envelope aside.

Jane turned to leave, and then turned back. "Oh, one more thing. Do you remember that ice cream parlor you asked me to do the analysis on?"

He nodded, hoping the sudden tension did not show in his face.

"The one that, in the final analysis, was about the worst investment anyone could ever make?"

He didn't nod this time, only held his breath.

"Somebody bought it," Jane said with a faint derisive giggle. "Can you believe that?"

Actually, he could.

"Just a sec," she said, "I've got the name of the person out on my desk."

"Never mind," David said. "I already know."

And he waited until she had closed the door behind herself before he contemplated the completeness of his failures when it came to Kayla McIntosh Jaffrey.

He thought, to his own detriment, he was always so

colossally sure of himself. He always was sure he was doing the right thing.

Look at all those years ago, when he had backed off Kayla for Kevin, thinking it was the honorable thing between friends.

And it had been based on a total lie.

Kevin hadn't asked Kayla to the prom by then. Someone else who had been at the campfire that night must have told him about what had happened between David and Kayla. And Kevin, ever competitive, ever with something to prove, had scooped him on the girl.

To Kevin, it had probably all been a game.

Until Kayla was pregnant.

Still, he knew that he was experiencing a miracle of sorts, that when he thought of Kevin these days, it was never with anger. It was with the quiet tolerance of knowing he had loved someone flawed, and that he had grown from it.

Once he had thought his love for Kevin had only given him the gift of cynicism. Now he saw that it had given him many gifts, but that was the one he could leave behind.

He hoped all that love that was part of his history would show him the right thing to do now. When he opened this envelope, wouldn't he know he had done the right thing by love? David reached for the envelope, turned it over in his hands and yet could not bring himself to open it.

It was time to set everything right that had gone wrong. It was time to end the lies. There was no place in life for deceit.

The next thought came unbidden, *Maybe it was time to let someone else into my world. Maybe there was less chance of making a mistake with a decision when it was not made alone, and when all parties were armed with the facts.*

That thought gave him pause. He *always* made the final decision alone.

Why did it feel like such a relief to even be contemplating a different way?

"Bastigal, stay away from the paint. Oh, for Pete's sake." Kayla got down off the ladder, caught Bastigal and wiped the creamy white paint from where his tail had dipped in the open bucket. She secured the lid on the bucket and headed back up her ladder, paint brush in hand.

From her perch there, she paused and looked around.

Really, if she was going to be painting, she could have started at home. But no, she was excited about More-moo. She had kept it open until the long weekend in September, learning all she could from the outgoing owners, and giving out samples of flavors she was experimenting with. She was excited about the response.

Then she had shut it down completely to freshen up the inside and bring in new equipment before reopening with a brand-new menu and services. She would be reopening in October.

She could almost hear a cynical voice saying, *Who comes to Blossom Valley in October?* That thing happened in her heart that happened every single time David crossed her mind, which was still pathetically often.

The new copies of *Lakeside Life* had replaced the old, but that didn't help as much as she had hoped it would.

Because it seemed the very streets held memories, of their younger selves, yes, but of the time they had just shared, too.

She could not look out her back window without picturing him stretched out on the back lawn at his mother's house. She could not open the screen that did not squeak anymore without thinking of him. Or secure the latch without remembering his dark head bent over it, the tip of his tongue caught between his teeth in concentration. She couldn't get the lawn mower going at all, and that made her think of him, too.

There were streets she avoided altogether, like Peachtree Lane, where they had lain on their backs after chasing the bunny they thought was Bastigal, and she had named the stars on Orion's belt for him.

Even on the hottest day, Kayla would not swim in the lake, because the memory of swimming with him, fully clothed, and the sense of awakening that had come with that, were painful.

When she was not busy painting or chipping fifty-year-old linoleum off the floor of her new business, she tried to stay busy so she wouldn't think so much, fall into the trap of feeling sorry for herself.

Kayla was experimenting with all kinds of flavors of ice cream—rose petal, jalapeño jelly, nasturtium, even dark ale—but for some reason the Dandy Lion flavor seemed to be on hold.

The door jingled, and she realized she had forgotten to lock it, and even a small thing like that made her think of David, and that he would be irritated with her for giving safety such a low priority.

"Sorry," she called from her perch on the ladder, "we're closed."

Bastigal began to growl, that low, throaty sound she had only heard him make on a few occasions before—mostly when she and David were getting too close to each other!

She turned on the ladder, felt the shock of who was there as if she had conjured him by thinking of him so much!

Her fingers felt strangely numb and she nearly dropped

her container of paint. In her attempt to keep her hold on it, she lost her balance.

He was beside her in a second, lifted her easily from around the waist and settled her solidly on the floor.

The dog, of course, went crazy as soon as David touched her, and ran a frantic circle around them, barking.

"I got paint on your nice suit. Sorry." She stepped away from him, trying not to stare, trying not to drink in his features like she was parched and he was a long, cold drink of water.

"David," she said, and heard some softness in her voice—the softness she had revealed to him and he had then used to hurt her. Keeping that in mind, she recovered, set down her paint and folded her arms over her chest.

She tried not to feel dismayed that he looked so unwell. Had he been sick? He looked like he had lost fifteen pounds, and there had not been any extra flesh on him to begin with! There were dark circles under his eyes, and his cheeks were whisker shadowed. His hair was a little long in the back, touching his white shirt, curling a little around his ears.

Kayla realized she wouldn't be much to look at at the moment, either. She really regretted the disposable painter's coverall that made her look a little bit like a snowman.

"What are you doing here?" she demanded, so afraid to hope for anything anymore, steeling herself against the crazy flip-flopping of her heart.

"Full price, Kayla? Are you crazy? You could have waited for spring to buy. That's closer to your very small money-making season."

She should have known that's why he would have come! A poor business decision was as irresistible to him as she had once hoped she would be!

She stripped the disappointment from her voice. "How

do you know I paid full price? Have you been spying on me?"

He looked a little sheepish.

She had no intention of letting him know that her heart quickened at the very thought he was keeping tabs on her, that he cared even a little bit. She wanted desperately to ask him how his mom was doing, and how he was coping, but his last words reared up in her head.

And he was right. Feeling for people was always what got her in trouble—trying to fix their pain was her worst flaw.

"You should have offered less if you were taking it at the end of the season. You think people are going to be eating ice cream for Thanksgiving? If, by some miracle, you manage to reopen by then?"

"I'll be open by then," she said stubbornly. "I'm doing two specialty ice creams for Thanksgiving, a pumpkin and a cranberry."

"Appealing," he said sarcastically.

"I don't care what appeals to you," she lied.

He flinched, and she wanted to take it back, but she didn't. She stood there waiting to see why he had come.

He drew in a deep breath, shoved his hands in his pockets and studied his shoes, which looked very expensive. Bastigal ventured in and sniffed them, backed off growling. He managed to leave a white paint mark on the toe of one.

"Understandable," David said, "that you would not care what appeals to me. I'm afraid I hurt you."

"Nonsense," she said quickly, but her voice had a little squeak in it.

He went on as if she had not denied it. "The last time I saw you, I was a jerk, Kayla."

"Yes, you were."

"You aren't going to make this easy for me, are you?"

"No, I'm not."

"I wanted to hurt you," he said slowly. "I wanted to drive you away."

"I'd say that worked. I had a very nasty bus ride back to Blossom Valley."

"I offered you a driver."

"Big of you. I made the most of my bus ride. I thought of ice cream flavors the whole way," she lied, and then, as if she could convince him it was not a lie, "Hot Banana Pepper, Cinnamon and Pear, French Champagne, Chinese Noodle."

She had not really thought of any of those flavors until just this second. All of a sudden it penetrated the almost panicky sensation that she could not let him know how she really felt, what he had actually said.

I wanted to hurt you.

That was not David.

I wanted to drive you away.

"I couldn't leave it the way it was," he said. "Kayla, I could not leave you with the impression that it was about you. That it was because I didn't care about you. Or need you."

Her heart felt like it stopped in her chest. What was he saying? That he *did* care about her? That he *did* need her?

She took in his ravaged features, and suddenly saw, as if a light had been turned on in a dark room.

She saw so clearly it felt as if she would explode.

David Blaze *loved* her.

CHAPTER NINETEEN

"KAYLA," DAVID SAID, his voice barely a whisper. "My family has a long history of health problems. I wouldn't wish them on anyone."

From her memory bank she pulled a sentence. *No sympathy, remember?* he said. *But keep that in mind. Bad genetics.*

He had said it lightly, but there had been something in his eyes that was not light at all.

It had been that day when they were walking home, dripping from the lake, and the young policeman had reminded him of his father.

And he had told her how his father had died.

"You think you're going to have a heart attack. Like you dad," she said softly. She was aware her voice was trembling as the truth of why he had come here filled her up. To the top. And then to overflowing.

"That might be a mercy compared to the other thing."

"The other thing?"

"It can be genetic," he said softly. "What my mother has. They've isolated a gene. It's called the E gene."

He pulled an envelope from his pocket and handed it to her. She took it, not understanding. She glanced at if briefly and read the return address: Billings and Morton. It meant nothing to her.

"It's from a laboratory. They do independent genetic analysis."

"Oh, boy," she said. "And you're lecturing me on wasting money foolishly? What did this cost?"

"That's not the point!"

"I bet this cost nearly as much as my new flooring," Kayla said.

"You are missing the point. This is very serious business, Kayla," he said tersely. "I was tested. Open it. And then we'll know."

"Know what?"

"Whether," he said softly, "I am worth taking a chance on."

She stared at him, and then she began to laugh. Into his astonished features, she said, "Oh, you stupid, stupid man."

He looked stunned. Well, obviously as the head of one of Canada's most successful companies he had never heard that before.

Then he looked annoyed, and folded his arms over his chest.

Who was really the stupid one, Kayla asked herself? She should have figured this out. She'd known from the moment she saw him sleeping on his mother's back lawn, guarding the door, that this was what he did. He protected those he loved.

And when he could not protect? When it was not in his power?

Then he retreated, to nurse his sense of failure, impotence in the face of what mattered most to him.

She saw in a brand-new light why he had never renewed their friendship after she had married Kevin. Had it ever been about Kevin at all? Or had it been about his own love for her? And how he would hide that, especially when he saw she was unhappy or needed his protection.

The love had been there between them for so long, constrained, and now it was breaking free.

She felt her love for David quicken within her. It felt as if a light had gone on, that was filling her and then expanding beyond her, filling the room and then beyond that, the street.

It felt as if the love within her could, unleashed, reach out and fill up the whole world.

Kayla looked down at the envelope in her hands, and then, without opening it, she ripped it to shreds.

"Hey!"

"No," she said firmly, throwing the pieces of paper up in the air and watching them scatter. "We're going to pretend we opened it. And we're going to pretend it said yes."

"Yes?" he said, flummoxed.

"Yes." She nodded emphatically, and crossed the space that separated them. She reached up and ran her palm over the rough surface of his whisker-bristled cheek.

"We're going to pretend it said yes. And that you went to the doctor and he told you that you had heart disease, too. We're going to pretend you could die any second."

He stared at her, baffled. And annoyed.

And yet she could see the hope in his eyes, too, so she went on, her confidence and her certainty increasing with each word she spoke.

"And while we're at it," Kayla said, "we're going to pretend I went to someone who could tell the future. Who is famous for it and never gets it wrong. A gypsy woman with a head scarf and too much makeup and earrings as big a pie plates looked into her crystal ball—"

"You are not comparing a legitimate medical laboratory like Billings and Morton to a fortune teller!"

"Yes, I am," she continued, unperturbed by the interruption. "The gypsy woman said I was going to get hit by a car and die instantly."

"Stop it," he said.

"No, you stop it."

He looked stunned. Really, being the head of a large company had made David Blaze far too accustomed to being listened to, even when he was wrong.

"Don't you see?" Kayla asked him, suddenly serious. "Don't you get it, David? We are going to live like it said *yes*. We are going to live each and every day as if one of us could be gone. Instantly. Or just disappear without warning from the face of the earth. Or change beyond recognition.

"And that is going to allow us to celebrate this moment. We are going to drink each other in, as if this day, this very second, might be our last together. As if everything could change in a moment.

"And we're going to start like this."

She stood on her tiptoes and she took his lips with her own. For a moment, he held himself stiffly, resisting.

And then with a moan of complete surrender, he kissed her back. He wrapped his hands in her hair and pulled her so close to him that not even air could squeeze in between them, and certainly not her overexcited dog!

Bastigal ran frantic circles around them, yapping hysterically.

"Bastigal," David said, taking his lips from hers for just a second. "Hush up and get used to it."

The dog fell silent. Then he sat down abruptly and stared at them, worried. And then his tail began to thump cautiously, then joyously, on the floor.

If there is anything a dog recognizes, it is the absolute essence of what is going on.

* * *

David let go of his last need to control, to protect Kayla from the folly of loving him. He drank in what she was giving him.

She loved him. She loved him completely and deeply and he realized, astounded, that he needed the *way* she loved him.

Kayla's way of looking at the world was opposite to his own.

He was pragmatic. She was whimsical. He was sensible. She was impulsive. He was ruled by his mind. She was ruled by her heart.

Her way was not wrong. And neither was his. But each of them only formed half a picture. They needed each other to come into perfect balance.

And he was aware that maybe he needed her a whole lot more than she needed him. He had walked alone for too long, battered by the ravages of love: his father, Kevin and now, his mother.

She, too, was battered. But she was the one with the courage to say yes to all of it. To the storm, and to the rainbow. To the tears and to the laughter.

It occurred to him that Kayla would show him the very heart of what love meant. And as he took her offered lips, it felt as if he was sealing a deal.

That would give him the life he had always dreamed of, and been afraid to ask for. A life that was so much more than a great condo and a fleet of cars and a successful business.

A life that was full in a different way, and a better way.

A life that was full in the only way that really counted.

And so David began his courtship of the girl he had always loved. And he courted her as if she might be gone from him at any second, or he from her, and as if it was a sacred obligation to cram as much joy and as much life into those seconds as they could.

He soon realized it didn't matter what they were doing, whether they were jumping into the amazing colors of the sugar maple leaves that they had raked in her yard in Blossom Valley, or attending a black-tie art auction in New York.

It didn't matter if they were throwing snowballs at each other after the first snow, or getting ready for the charity Christmas Ball Blaze Enterprises held every year. It didn't matter if they were having a quiet glass of wine in his apartment, watching the New Year's Eve fireworks explode over the city or sitting with his mother, taking pleasure from her enjoyment in the CD Kayla had picked out for her.

It didn't matter if they were having a croissant at a bakery, after he'd convinced her they should go to Paris for springtime, or whether they were supervising the installation of the new ice cream cooler at Dandy Lion's Roaring Good Ice Cream getting ready for the grand reopening.

It didn't matter if he was watching the awe on her face as she saw the Louvre for the very first time, or if they were paddling a canoe across the lake, trying to keep Bastigal from jumping in after the ducks that swam beside them.

It didn't matter if she was asleep with her head on his shoulder in the airport lounge after their flight had been delayed because of fog, or if he was covered in grease from trying to get that old lawn mower going for one more season. She wouldn't let him buy a new one. She claimed that old lawn mower was going in her memory box someday.

"Everybody else gets a memory box," he teased. "Trust you to get a memory crate."

But the truth was they were going to need a crate to store all these memories in!

As spring began to turn to summer once more, David watched his calendar, and a year to the day that he had seen Kayla riding her bike down the main street of Blossom Valley, a year to the day that she had been stung by the bee, he proposed.

He had the ring put in a special box that he had custom made. The box was yellow and black and shaped like a bumble bee.

For the ring he had chosen a perfect, brilliant white diamond mined in the Canadian arctic. He had consulted on the design of the setting, wanting it to reflect Kayla's personality, simple but complex, light but deep.

On the day that marked the anniversary of their meeting again, while Kayla was busy overseeing things at her astonishingly busy ice cream parlor—people were actually driving from Toronto to sample some of those crazy flavors like jalapeño Havarti, for Pete's sake?—he brought a team into her backyard.

And they transformed it.

White fairy lights were threaded by the thousands through the trees and shrubs. A structure was erected at the center of her yard, a gauzy tent, and inside it was a table set on a carpet that covered the lawn. The table was covered in sparkling white linen, set exquisitely for two.

Every available surface inside that tent was either full of candles or flowers.

A chef was working magic in her kitchen and at her barbecue. A waiter stood by, elegant in tails and white gloves. A string quartet was set up in one corner of the yard to supply music.

David had even managed to get Bastigal into a tux that matched his own, right down to the subtle pink of the bow tie, and pleased with himself for this detail, he had fastened the ring box onto the back of Bastigal's suit, and then locked him in the house.

And that's where things went wrong.

Or right, depending what kind of memories you wanted to put in your memory box.

Because everything had gone perfectly. The dinner was exquisite. The music was beautiful. The summer evening night was soft with warmth and fragrance.

Kayla was gorgeous, sitting across from him, in her white Dandy Lion uniform, laughing and crying, and then laughing again.

Once, he had seen himself as pragmatic, and her as the believer in miracles.

But wasn't he living a miracle? He and Kayla had had a chance to love each other once, and circumstances had taken that chance from them.

Now they had been given what he saw as the rarest and most beautiful of gifts.

"Here's to second chances," David said, lifting his champagne flute to Kayla's.

A second chance that was made better by the fact that both their lives had given them things that had made them stronger and ultimately better, more ready for what an adult love required.

On cue, just as they finished dinner and before dessert, when he could not wait another second with his secret, with a quickly lifted finger from David, the waiter casually went across her back deck and let Bastigal out of the house.

David knew the little dog, having missed her all day, would make a beeline for Kayla and deliver the ring.

Except at the very moment when the dog was hurtling

himself across the yard in a paroxysm of excited welcome for Kayla, the chef was flambéing dessert at their table.

At the sudden poof of blue flame, Bastigal stopped. Then he tucked his tail between his legs and with a single startled yip, ran away and, though it seemed impossible, squeezed himself underneath the gate and was gone.

It seemed like a full minute of stunned silence fell between them.

And then David leaped up and took chase, with Kayla hard on his heels, and the chef scowling at their departing backs and his ruined finale.

It seemed it was hours later that they finally caught up with the little dog after doing a backyard and alleyway tour of most of Blossom Valley.

They captured the dog and Kayla admired his little outfit and David retrieved the ring, and she laughed at the little bumble bee box and she laughed right until the moment that David got down on bended knee in front of her.

Then the tears came. She had Bastigal clasped to her chest and tears running down her face, whether from laughing or crying, he wasn't too sure.

And he wasn't too sure it really mattered which it was, either. Because the essence of that moment was startling in its clarity, more multifaceted and brilliant than the ring he was about to give her.

"Will you marry me?"

The look on her face was a look that could make any man find the courage in himself to believe in the future.

She had not said yes, yet, when a spotlight caught them in the harshness of its glare.

"Sheesh," David heard a voice behind him say, "I should have known."

Kayla's laughter was better than a yes. It was the laughter of a woman who wasn't the least bit guilty about her happiness. It was the laughter of a woman who did not have one ounce of fear in her.

Her joy filled her eyes with a light that drenched him, and that drenched the world around him, turning it from black and white to pure gold.

This, then, was what his future held.

EPILOGUE

ONCE, DAVID BLAZE THOUGHT, he had been the most arrogant of men. Had he really believed that he knew the things that intensified love? Had he really been convinced he knew of the things that should be included in a memory box?

Now he was humbled by how little he had known.

The moment Kayla and he had stood on a beach in the Caribbean, she in a sundress and a spaghetti-strapped T-shirt and a hat that reminded him of the day she had bicycled back into his life, he had felt the love between them intensify to what he believed was a breaking point.

But then, when she had whispered *I do,* his love had intensified to such a point that he did not know how a heart so full could not explode. He had been sure it could never get fuller. Or better. Or more intense.

When the doctor had sat him and Kayla down, and smiled slightly and said *congratulations,* that was the moment he realized something in him was expanding to hold a whole new level of intensity.

But it surely had reached its limit now? His heart was fuller than full. It could not expand any more.

But then it did. Any other intensity David had ever experienced had been eclipsed by the ultrasound pictures.

And then that had been eclipsed *again* by that terrifyingly beautiful night when David would have done anything to take the pain from his wife.

And then *that* moment moved into the shadows when he held the baby in his arms, that wrinkly, loud, ugly, hair-sticking-up-every-which-way bundle of life that was his daughter.

And now, Kayla punched the code on the door, simple one-two-three, but more complicated than anyone on the wing could figure out, and they went down the hall to his mother's room.

His mother was sitting in a chair, and when they came in, she looked at them blankly. He was thankful that today, at least, she had her clothes on.

But then she saw the baby, and something soft bloomed in her face.

Not recognition of them, perhaps, and perhaps that was not what was as important as what she recognized, anyway.

She looked eagerly at the bundle he was holding, and held out her arms.

He glanced at Kayla. Was it okay to give their daughter to his mom? Who admittedly was not all there? Could this poor addled soul be trusted with something so fragile as a baby, less than a week old?

But Kayla nodded without the slightest hesitation.

David passed the baby to his mother, ready to rescue her in an instant if something went wrong, but it did not.

He felt himself relax as something went beautifully, wonderfully right.

It occurred to him that this was a moment he would put in his memory box, the way his mother's instinct was still there, and her one hand went naturally to cradle the baby's neck while the other supported her tiny body.

This would surely always be in his memory box, his

mother's face when she held her granddaughter. It was as if everything else they had been through was gone, and there was only this moment of shining truth left.

What the memory box held—the only thing of any importance at all—was the love.

An experience so intense that by some miracle it took the limits off a human heart, letting it expand beyond measure to hold it.

"Her name is Polly," he said softly.

"But that's my name," his mother said, bewildered.

"Yes," he said quietly. "Yes, it is."

The two Pollys regarded each other solemnly. And then the baby wrinkled up her face, opened her eyes and blew spit bubbles from her lips. She made a cooing sound and she blinked and she wriggled a little bit, tiny fists finding their way out a pale pink blanket and flailing at the air.

And the light that came on in his mother's face held every Christmas morning, and every fireworks display they had ever seen together, and it held the puppy he had brought home. It held safe the memory of his father, and all that they had been as a family. It held his friendship, his brotherhood, with the boy next door.

The light in his mother's face held joy and tears, and sorrow and laughter.

And Kayla's hand crept into David's and he looked down at her and saw the contented smile on her face.

Of all the gifts she had given him, and those were many, he was aware of how tenderly she had revealed his dishonesties to him.

And this was the biggest one: once, he had convinced himself that he could not go to her because he was protecting her from his bad genetics.

Now he saw not that he had wanted to protect her, but that he had wanted to protect himself. Because to love greatly meant a man had to open himself to the possibility of great loss.

Unbearable loss, even.

And yet, that same love he feared, when he turned his face to its sunshine, did not burn him, but day by day lifted him up and filled him with a simple faith.

It was a faith that for all the bad, the good still won out, still outweighed the bad ten to one. Or maybe a hundred to one. Or maybe even a million to one.

And in the end, it seemed to David, when everything else was gone, even the memories, you could trust one thing.

The love remained.

In the end, you could trust that the intensity of love, the essence of it, remained and traveled—relentlessly, unstoppably, breathtakingly—toward the future it had helped to shape.

* * * * *

grand, for such a man to lay open himself to the possibility of greater [illegible].

Unfathomably so, even.

And you, that someone loved her, that when he turned his face to its sunshine, did not burn him. But day by day lifted him up and filled him with a simple faith.

It was a faith that taught him that there could still be wonder without a guarantee, that it was worth the risk, a hundred to one. Or maybe even a million to one.

And in the end it came down to David, when everything else was gone, even the memories, you could trust one thing.

The love remains.

In the end you could trust that the intensity of love, the essence of it, remained and traveled unbreakably, unstoppably, unshakably, toward the future it had helped to shape.

* * * * *

THE MAVERICK MILLIONAIRE

BY
ALISON ROBERTS

Alison Roberts lives in Christchurch, New Zealand, and has written over sixty Mills & Boon Medical Romances. This is her debut for the Romance line.

As a qualified paramedic she has personal experience of the drama and emotion to be found in the world of medical professionals, and loves to weave stories with this rich background—especially when they can have a happy ending.

When Alison is not writing you'll find her indulging her passion for dancing or spending time with her friends (including Molly the dog) and her daughter Becky, who has grown up to become a brilliant artist. She also loves to travel, hates housework, and considers it a triumph when the flowers outnumber the weeds in her garden.

Alison Roberts lives in Christchurch, New Zealand, and has written over sixty Mills & Boon Medical Romances. This is [illegible] for the Romance [illegible].

As a qualified paramedic, she has personal experience of the drama and emotion to be found in the world of medical professionals, and loves to weave stories with this special background—especially when they can have a happy ending.

When Alison is not writing you'll find her [illegible] for [illegible] of [illegible] with her friends, including [illegible] the dog and her daughter [illegible]. She also loves to [illegible] and [illegible] where her favourite [illegible] the world [illegible] in her garden.

[illegible]

CHAPTER ONE

No. NOT THIS TIME.

Jacob Logan was not going to let his older brother assume responsibility for sorting out the mess they were in. Not again. Not when he was still living with the scars from the last time.

Ben was only the elder by twenty minutes and their parents were long gone. Why was it so incredibly hard to break free of the beliefs that had got embedded in childhood?

But this time it was *his* turn to take charge. Yet again, it had been his bright idea that had got them into this mess and it was a doozy. So bad that it might be the only chance he ever got to look out for Ben for once.

This was more terrifying than the aftermath of their father's wrath for any childhood scrape they'd got themselves into. Worse than being in the thick of it in Afghanistan after they'd both escaped by running off to join the army. This was a life or death battle and the odds were getting higher that they weren't going to win.

There'd been warnings of possible gale-force winds yesterday and they'd known they could be in for a rough day, but nothing like this. Cyclone Lila had changed course unexpectedly overnight and dawn had broken to mountainous seas, vicious winds and driving rain that almost obliterated visibility. The strong currents made the waves unpredictable, and the fleet of yachts in this Ultraswift-Round-the-World Challenge had been caught, isolated and exposed in the open seas east of New Zealand's north island.

They'd caught some of the stats on the radio before the yacht had finally been crushed under a mountain of water and they'd had to battle to get into their bubble of a life raft. Winds of sixty-five knots and gusts up to two hundred miles per hour. Waves that towered up to fifty feet, dwarfing even the biggest boats. Competitors were retiring from the race in droves and turning to flee, but not fast enough. Boats had overturned. Masts had snapped like matchsticks. Mayday calls had gone out for men overboard. Bodies had already been recovered. There were search aircrafts out all over the place, but the only thing the Logan brothers had heard over the sound of an angry sea had been the deep drone of an air force Orion and that had been a long way away.

The Southern Ocean was a big place when you were in trouble.

They'd been drifting for hours now. Being tossed like a cork in the huge seas.

By some miracle, they'd finally been spotted. A helicopter was overhead and a crewman was being lowered on a winch. Jake could see the spare harness dangling.

One harness.

No way could more than one person get winched up at a time.

And he wasn't going to go first. This weather was getting worse by the minute. What if the chopper *couldn't* get back?

'You're going first,' he yelled over the noise of the sea and the chopper.

'Like hell I am. You're going first.'

'No way. You're hurt. I can wait.'

The guy on the end of the winch had disappeared behind the crest of a wave. Caught by the water, he was dragged through and suddenly swinging dangerously closer. Someone was putting their life on the line here to rescue them.

'Look—it was my stupid idea to do this. I get to decide who goes first.'

He didn't have to say it out loud. It was his fault. Things that turned to custard had always been his fault.

Desperation had him yelling loud enough to be really heard as the rescuer got close enough to shove a harness into his hands. He pushed it towards Ben. Tried to wrestle him into it.

'Just do it, Ben. Put the harness on. You're going first.'

But Ben pushed it back. Tried to force Jake's arm into a loop.

'Someone's got to look out for you,' he yelled.

'I'll be okay. I can wait.'

'This isn't make-believe, Jake. It's not some blockbuster *movie.*'

'You think I don't know that?'

'I know you don't. You wouldn't know reality if it bit you. You're just like Mom.'

And now it was their rescuer yelling. Helping Ben to shove the harness onto Jake.

'There's no time for this.' Good grief…was this person risking life and limb to rescue them *female?*

Jake was still resisting. Still focused on his brother. 'What the hell is that supposed to mean?'

'She couldn't face reality. Why do you think she killed herself?'

That did it. The shock took the fight out of Jake. The harness was snapped into place.

'The chopper's full,' the rescuer yelled at Ben. 'We'll

come back for you as soon as we can.' She was clipping heavy-duty carabiners together and she put her face close to Jake's. 'Put your arms around me and hang on. Just hang on.'

He had no choice. A dip into icy water and then they were being dragged into the air. Spinning. He could see the bright orange life raft getting smaller and smaller, but he could still see his twin brother's face looking up at him. The shock of his words was morphing into something even worse. Maybe he'd never find out the truth even if he wanted to go there.

Dear God… *Ben…*

This shouldn't be happening. Would he ever see his brother again?

CHAPTER TWO

THE WAVE WAS the last straw.

As though the adrenaline rush of the last few hours was simply being washed away as Eleanor Sutton faced the immediate prospect of drowning.

How much adrenaline could one person produce, anyway? She'd been burning it as fuel for hours as the rescue helicopter crew she was a part of had played a pivotal role in dealing with the stricken yachts caught up in this approaching storm. They'd pulled two people from a life raft and found another victim who'd had nothing more than his life jacket as protection as he rode the enormous swells of this angry sea.

Then they'd plucked a badly injured seaman from the deck of a yacht that was limping out of trouble with the broken mast that had been responsible for the crewman's head injuries. The chopper was full. Overfull, in fact, which was why Ellie had been left dangling on the winch line until they could either juggle space or get to a spot on land.

With her vantage point of being so much closer to the water as the chopper had bucketed through the menacing shark-gray sky, she'd been the one to spot the bright orange bubble of a life raft as it had crested one of the giant swells and then disappeared again. In the eerie light of a day that was far darker than it should be for the time, it had been all too easy to spot the two pale faces peering up at the potential rescue the helicopter advertised.

The helmet Ellie wore had built in headphones and a microphone that sat almost against her lips. Even in the howl of driving wind and rain and helicopter rotors, it was easy to communicate with both her pilot, Dave, and fellow paramedic, Mike.

'Life raft at nine o'clock. At least two people on board.'

'We can't take any more.' It was Dave who responded. 'We'd be over limit in weight and this wind is picking up.'

There was a warning tone in those casual last words. Dave was a brilliant pilot, but he was already finding it a challenge to fly in these conditions. Some extra weight with the approaching cyclone getting ever closer might be enough to tip the balance and put everybody in even more danger.

But they couldn't leave them behind. The full force of Cyclone Lila wouldn't be felt for a good few hours yet, but they shouldn't still be in the air as it was. All aircraft would be grounded by the time they reached land again. It was highly unlikely that this life raft would be spotted by any other boats and, even if it was, it would be impossible to effect a rescue.

If they didn't do something, they were signing the death warrants of another two people. There had already been too much carnage in this disastrous leg of the Ultraswift-Round-the-World yacht race. At least one death had been confirmed, a lot of serious injuries and there were still people unaccounted for.

'We can get one,' Ellie said desperately. 'He can ride with me on the end of the line. We're so close to land. We can drop him and try going back for the other one.'

There was a moment's silence from above. It was Mike who spoke this time.

'You really want to try that, Ellie?'

Did she? Despite the skin-tight rescue suit she was wearing under her flight suit, Ellie knew she was close to becoming hypothermic. Would her fingers work well enough to manipulate the harness and carabiner clips to attach another person to the winch safely? She was beyond exhaustion now, too, and that old back injury was aching abominably. What if the victim was terrified by this form of transport and struggled? Made them swing dangerously on the end of the line and make a safe landing virtually impossible?

But they all knew there was no choice.

'Let's give it a try, at least,' Ellie said. 'We can do that, can't we?'

And so they did, but Dave was having trouble keeping the chopper level in the buffeting winds, and the mountainous swells of the sea below were impossible to judge. Just as they got close enough to hover near the life raft, the foaming top of a wave reached over Ellie's head and she was suddenly underwater, being dragged through the icy sea like a fish on a line.

And that did it.

She wasn't under the water for very long at all, but it was one of those moments where time seemed to stand still. Where a million thoughts could coalesce into surprising clarity.

Eleanor Sutton was totally over this. She was thirty-two years old and she had a dodgy back. Three years ago this hadn't been the plan of how her life would be. She would be happily married. At home with a gorgeous baby. Working part time, teaching one of the subjects she was so good at. Aeromedical transport or emergency management maybe.

The fact that she could actually remember this so clearly was a death knell. This kind of adrenaline rush had been what had got her through the last three years when that life plan had been blown out of the water so devastatingly. Losing personal priorities due to living for the ultimate challenge of risking her life for others had been the way to move forward.

And it wasn't working any more.

If she could see all this so clearly as she was dragged through the wave and then swinging in clear air again over the life raft, Ellie knew it would never work again. She shouldn't be capable of thinking about anything other than how she was going to harness another body to her own in the teeth of the approaching cyclone and then get them both safely onto land somewhere.

This was it.

The last time she would be doing this.

She might as well make it count.

Unbelievably, the men in the life raft weren't ready to cooperate. Ellie had the harness in her hands. She shoved it towards one of them, holding it up to show where the arm loops were. The harness was taken by one of the men, but he immediately tried to pass it to the other.

'Just do it, Ben. Put the harness on. You're going first.'

But he pushed it back and there was a brief struggle as he tried to force the other man's arm into one of the loops. Too caught up arguing over who got to go first, they were getting nowhere.

'I'll be okay,' one of them was yelling. 'I can wait.'

'This isn't make-believe,' the other yelled back.

Static in her ears made Ellie wince.

'You still on the air?' Dave's voice crackled. 'That radio still working after getting wet?'

'Seems to be.' Ellie put her hand out to stop the life raft

bumping her away. It was dipping into another swell. And the men were still arguing. Good grief—had one just accused the other of being just like his *mother?*

She thought the terrifying dunk into that wave had been the final straw, but this was just too much. Ellie was going a lot further than the extra mile here, making her potentially last job as a rescue helicopter paramedic really count. She shouldn't be doing this and this lack of cooperation was putting them in a lot more danger. Suddenly Ellie was angry.

Angry with herself for endangering everybody involved in the helicopter hovering overhead.

Angry with these men who wanted to save each other instead of themselves.

Angry knowing that she had to face the future without the escape from reality that this job had provided so well for so long.

She was close enough to help shove the harness onto one of the men. To shout at them with all the energy her anger bestowed.

'There's no time for this.'

But they were ignoring her. 'What the hell is that supposed to mean?' one yelled.

There was another painful crackle of static in Ellie's headphones. 'What's going on?' Dave asked in her ear.

'Stand by,' Ellie snapped. She was still angry. Ready to knock some sense into these men, but whatever had been said while Dave had been making contact had changed something. The man she'd been helping to force the harness onto had gone completely still. Thankfully, Ellie's hands were working well enough to snap the clips into place and check that he was safely anchored to the winch line.

'The chopper's full,' she shouted at the other man.

'We'll come back for you as soon as we can.' She clipped the last carabiners together and put her face close to her patient's. 'Put your arms around me and hang on,' she instructed him grimly. 'Just hang on.' She knew they would have been listening to every word from above. Hopefully, they'd think the lack of reassurance she was providing was due to the tension of the situation, not the anger that was still bubbling in her veins like liquid lava.

'Take us up, Dave. Let's get out of here.'

'Ben...'

The despairing howl was whipped from Jacob Logan's lips by the force of the wind as he felt himself pulled both upwards and forwards in a violent swinging movement. It was also drowned by the stinging deluge of a combination of rain and sea spray, made all the more powerful by the increasing speed of the helicopter rotors above.

It was too painful to try and keep his eyes open. Jake squeezed them shut and kept them like that. He tightened his grip around the body attached to his by what he hoped was the super-strong webbing of the harnesses and solid metal clips. There was nothing he could do. However alien it felt, he had no choice but to put his faith in his rescuers and the fact that they knew what they were doing.

Shutting off any glimpse of the outside world confined his impressions more to what was happening internally, but it was impossible to identify a single emotion there.

Fear was certainly there in spades. Terror, more like, especially as they were spinning in sickening circles as the direction of movement changed from going up to going forward, interrupted by drops and jerks that were probably due to the turbulence the aircraft was having to deal with.

There was anger there as well. Not just because he'd

lost the fight over who got rescued first. Jake was angry at everything right now. At whoever had come up with the stupid idea of encouraging people to take their expensive luxury yachts out into dangerous seas and make the prize prestigious enough to make them risk their lives.

At the universe for dropping a cyclone onto precisely this part of the planet at exactly this time.

At fate for ripping him apart from his twin brother. The other half of himself.

But maybe that anger was directed *at* Ben, too. Why had he said such a dreadful thing about their mother? Something so unbelievable—so *huge*—it threatened to rip the brothers apart, not just physically but at a much deeper level. If what he'd said was true and he'd never told *him,* it had the potential to shatter the bond that had been between the men since they'd arrived in this world only twenty minutes apart.

Was life as he knew it about to end, whether or not he survived this dreadful day?

And there was something else in his head. Or his heart. No…this was soul-deep.

Something that echoed from childhood and had to be silenced.

Dealing with it was automatic now. Honed to a talent that had made him an international star as an adult. The ability to imagine the way a different person would handle the situation so that it would all be okay in the end.

To *become* that person for as long as he needed to.

This was a scene from a movie, then. Reality could be distorted. He was a paratrooper. This wasn't a dreadful accident. He was supposed to be here. It wasn't him being rescued, it was a girl. A very beautiful girl.

It was helpful that he knew that this stranger he had his arms wrapped around so firmly was female. Not that she felt exactly small and feminine, but he could work around that.

He'd never had this much trouble throwing the mental switches to step sideways out of reality. A big part of his brain was determined to remind him that this horrible situation was too real to avoid. That even if it was a movie, there'd be a stuntman to do this part because his insurance wouldn't cover taking this kind of a risk. But Jake fought back. If he could believe—and make countless others believe, the way he had done so far in his stellar career—didn't that make it at least a kind of reality?

He was out to save the world. The chopper would land them somewhere and he'd unclip his burden. He'd want to stay with the girl, of course, because he was desperately in love with her, but he'd have to go back into the storm. To risk his life to rescue…not his twin brother, that would be too corny. This was the black moment of the movie and he was the ultimate hero so maybe he was going back to rescue his enemy.

And, suddenly, the escape route that had worked since he'd been old enough to remember threw up a barrier so solid Jake could actually feel himself crashing against it.

Maybe Ben *was* the enemy now.

Even if it hadn't been a success, the effort of trying to catch something in the maelstrom of thoughts and emotions and turn it into something he could cope with had distracted him for however long this nightmare ride had been taking. Time was doing strange things, but it couldn't have been more than a few minutes.

Close to his head, he could hear his rescuer trying to talk to the helicopter pilot. The wind was howling like a wild animal around them and she was having to shout, even though she had a microphone against her lips. As close as he was, Jake couldn't catch every word.

Something about a light. A moon.

Was she kidding?

In even more of a fantasyland than he'd been trying to get into?

'The lighthouse,' Ellie told Dave, her words urgent. 'At five o'clock. It's Half Moon Island.'

'Roger that.' Dave's voice in her ears sounded strained. 'We're heading southeast.'

'No. The beach…'

'What beach?'

'Straight across from Half Moon Island. The end of the spit. Put us down there.'

'What? It's the middle of nowhere.'

'I know it. There's a house…'

It was hard enough to communicate through the external noise and the internal static without trying to explain. This area was Ellie's childhood stamping ground. Her grandfather had been the last lighthouse-keeper on Half Moon Island and the family's beach house was on an isolated part of the coast that looked directly out at the crescent of land they'd all loved.

The history didn't matter. It was the closest part of the mainland they could put her down and she knew they could find shelter. It was close enough, even, for them to drop their first victim and try to go back for the other one.

He still had her in a grip that made it an effort to breathe. An embrace that would have been unacceptably intimate from a stranger in any other situation. His face was close enough to her own to defy any concept of personal space but, curiously, Ellie didn't have any clear idea of what he looked like.

The hair plastered to his head looked like it would be very dark even if it was dry and it was too long for her taste for a man. The jaw was hidden beneath a growth of beard that had to be weeks old and his eyes were screwed shut so tightly they created wrinkles that probably made him look a lot older than he was.

He was big, that much she could tell. Big enough to make Ellie feel small and that was weird. At five feet ten, she had always towered over other women and many men. She'd envied the fragility and femininity of tiny women—until she'd needed to be stronger than ever. That had been when she'd finally appreciated the warrior blood that ran in her veins from generations past.

No man was ever going to make Eleanor Sutton feel small or insignificant again.

She put her mouth close enough to the man's ear to feel the icy touch of his skin.

'We're going to land on the beach. Keep your legs tucked up and let me control the impact.'

Dave did his best to bring them down slowly and Ellie did her best to try and judge the distance between them and the solid ground, but it had never been so difficult. The crashing rolls of surf kept distorting her line of sight and the wind was sending swirls of sand in both horizontal and vertical directions.

'Minus twenty…no…twenty-five…*fifteen*…' This descent was crazy. They were both going to end up with badly broken legs or worse. 'Ten… Slow it down, Dave.'

He must have done his absolute best, but the landing was hard and a stab of pain told Ellie that her ankle had turned despite the protection of her heavy boots. There was no time to do more than register a potentially serious fracture, however. She fell backwards with her patient on top of her and for a split second she was again aware of just how big and solid this man was.

And that she couldn't breathe.

But then they were flipped over and dragged a short distance in the sand. Ellie could feel it scraping the skin on her face like sandpaper. Filling her mouth as her microphone snapped off. The headphones inside her helmet were still working, but she didn't need Dave's urgent orders to know how vital it was that she unhook them both from the winch line before they were dragged any further towards the trees that edged the beach.

Before they both got killed or—worse—the line got tangled and brought the helicopter down.

Somehow she managed it. She threw the hook clear so that it didn't hit her patient as it was retracted and the helicopter gained height. Once she'd unclipped herself from this man, she could get into a clear position and they could lower the line to her again.

But it was taking too much time to unclip him. Her hands were so cold and she was shaking violently from a combination of the cold, pain and the sheer determination to get back and save the other man as quickly as possible.

He was trying to help.

'No,' Ellie shouted, spitting sand. 'Let me do it. You're making it harder.'

His hands fisted beside his face. 'You're going back, aren't you? To get Ben?'

'Yes. Just let me...' Finally, she unclipped the last carabiner and they were separated. Ellie almost fell the instant she tried to put weight on her injured ankle but somehow managed to lurch far enough away from her patient to wave both arms above her head to signal Dave. There was no point in shouting with the microphone long gone, but she did it anyway.

'Bring the line down. I'm ready.' She wouldn't need to worry about her ankle once she was airborne again. It shouldn't make it impossible to get the other man from the life raft.

'Sorry, El. Can't do it.' Dave's voice was clear in her ears. 'Wind's picking up and we've got a status one patient on board under ventilation.'

The helicopter was getting smaller rapidly. Gaining some height and heading down the coast.

'No...' Ellie yelled, waving her arms frantically. *'No-o-o...'*

The man was beside her. 'What's going on?' he shouted. 'Where's he going?' He grabbed Ellie's shoulders and it felt like he was making an effort not to shake her until her teeth rattled. 'You've got to go back. For Ben.'

His face was twisted in desperation and Ellie knew her own expression was probably close to a mirror image of it.

'They won't let us. It's too dangerous.'

The man had let her go in order to wave *his* arms now. 'Come *back,*' he yelled. 'I *trusted* you, dammit...'

But the bright red helicopter was vanishing into the darkening skies. Ellie could still hear Dave.

'We've got your GPS coordinates. Someone will come as soon as this weather lifts. Get to some shelter. Your other radio should still work. We'll be in touch.' She could hear in his voice that he was hating leaving her like this. It broke all the unspoken rules that cemented a crew like this together. 'Stay safe, Ellie.'

The helicopter disappeared from view.

For what seemed a long, long time, Ellie and the rescued man simply stood on this isolated, totally deserted stretch of coastline and stared at the menacing cloud cover, dark enough to make the ocean beside them appear black. The foam of the crashing breakers was eerily white.

The man took several steps towards the wild surf. And

then he stopped and let out a howl of despair that made Ellie's spine tingle. He knew he'd lost his friend. The lump in her throat was big enough to be painful.

'I would have gone back,' she yelled above the roar of the wind and surf. 'If they'd let me.'

He came closer in two swift strides. 'I would have *stayed,*' he shouted back at her.

He was angry at *her?* For saving his life?

His words were a little muffled. Maybe she'd heard wrong. Dave was too far away for radio contact now and the communication had been one-sided anyway, thanks to the broken microphone. Ellie undid the chin strap of her helmet and pulled it off. The man was still shouting at her.

'Who gave *you* the right to decide who got rescued first?'

Ellie spat out some more sand. '*You're* lucky to be alive,' she informed him furiously. 'And if we don't find any shelter soon we'll probably both die of hypothermia and then all this would have been for nothing.' He wasn't the only one who could be unreasonably angry. 'Who gave *you* the right to put *my* life in danger?'

She didn't wait to see what effect her words might have had. Ellie turned and tried to pick out a landmark. She had to turn back and try to catch a glimpse of Half Moon Island to get any idea of which direction they needed to go. The lighthouse was well to her left so they had to go north. The beach house was in a direct line with the point of the island where the lighthouse was.

Confident now, Ellie set off up the beach. She didn't look to see whether he was following her. He could have his autonomy back as far as she was concerned. If he wanted to stay out here and die because she hadn't been able to rescue his friend then maybe that was *his* choice. She was going to survive if she could, thank you very much.

Except that she didn't get more than two steps away. Her ankle collapsed beneath her and she went down with a shout of anguish.

'What's the matter?' The man was crouched over her in an instant. 'What's happened?'

'It's my ankle. I… It might be broken.'

If he was swearing, the words were quiet enough for the wind to censor them. Ellie felt herself being picked up as if she weighed no more than one of those tiny women she'd once mistakenly envied. Now she was cradled in the arms of this big man as if she was a helpless child.

'Which way?' The words were as grim as the face of the man who uttered them.

'North.' Ellie pointed. 'About a mile.'

A gust of wind, vicious enough to make this solid man stagger, reminded her that this was only the beginning of this cyclone. Things were going to get a whole lot worse before they got any better.

The stabs of pain coming up her leg from her ankle were bad enough to make her feel sick. On top of her exhaustion and the knowledge that they were in real trouble here, it was enough to make her head spin. She couldn't faint. If she did, how would he know how to find the beach house, which was probably their only hope of surviving?

'There's a river,' she added. 'We turn inland there.'

She could feel his arms tighten around her. It had to be incredibly hard, carrying somebody as tall as she was in the face of this wind and on soft sand, and they had a long way to go.

Could he do it?

Ellie had no choice but to put her faith in him, however hard that was to do. With a groan that came more from defeat than pain, she screwed her eyes shut and buried her face against his chest as he staggered along the beach.

It had been a very long time since she had felt a man's arms around her like this.

At least she wouldn't die alone.

CHAPTER THREE

SHE WAS NO lightweight, this woman in his arms.

Jake had to lean forward into the fierce wind and his feet were dragging in the soft sand that was no match for these conditions. It swirled around enough to obscure his feet completely and it would have reached his nose and eyes if the rain hadn't been heavy enough to drive it down again.

Another blast of wind made Jake stagger and almost fall. He gritted his teeth and battled on. They had to find shelter. She'd been right. He might wish it was Ben instead of him, but he *was* lucky to still be alive and he owed it to her to try and make sure the heroic actions of his rescuers weren't wasted to the extent that one of them lost her life.

A river, she'd said. Good grief. He didn't even know the name of the woman he was carrying. A person who had risked her life for his and he'd been ungrateful enough to practically tell her he wished she hadn't. That he would have stayed with Ben if he'd been given a choice.

His left leg was dragging more than the right and a familiar ache was tightening like a vice in his thigh.

Another vice was tightening around his heart as his thoughts were dragged back to Ben, who would still be being tossed around in the ocean in that pathetically small life raft.

The combination of his sore leg and thoughts of his brother inevitably dragged his mind back to Afghanistan. They'd only been nineteen when they'd joined the army. Sixteen years ago now but the memories were as fresh as ever. Had it been his idea first that it was the ideal way to escape their father?

Charles Logan's voice had the ability to echo in his head with all the force of the gunfire from a war zone.

You moronic imbeciles, you're your mother's children, you've inherited nothing from me. Stupid, stupid, stupid...

No. They'd both wanted to run. Both had needed the brutal reality of the army to find out what life was like outside an overprivileged upbringing. To find out who *they* really were.

But *he* had been more excited about it, hadn't he? In the movies, the soldiers were heroes and it always came out all right for them in the end.

They weren't supposed to get shipped home with a shattered leg as the aftermath of being collateral damage from a bus full of school kids that had been targeted by a roadside bomb.

His brother's last words still echoed in his head.

Why do you think she killed herself?

It *had* been Ben who'd found her, all those years ago, when the boys had been only fourteen.

Did he know something he'd never told *him?* Had he found evidence that it hadn't been an accidental overdose of prescription meds washed down with alcohol?

A *note,* even?

No. It couldn't be true. She wouldn't have deserted her children with such finality. She'd *loved* them, even if she hadn't been around often enough to show them how much.

A cry was ripped from Jake's lips. An anguished denial of accepting such a premeditated abandonment.

Denial, too, of what was happening right now? That his brother was out there somewhere in that merciless ocean? Too cold to hang on any longer?

Drowned already, even?

No. Surely he'd know. He'd feel it if his other half was being ripped away for eternity.

The cry of pain was enough to pull Ellie from the mental haze she'd been clinging to as she kept her face buried from the outside world, thinking of nothing more than the comfort of being held in strong arms and, hopefully, being carried to safety.

What had she been thinking? Eleanor Sutton wasn't some swooning heroine from medieval times. She didn't depend on anyone else. She could look after herself.

'Put me down,' Ellie ordered.

But he kept lurching forward into the biting wind and rain.

'No. We're not at the river.'

'I need to see where we are, then.' She twisted in his arms to look towards the sea.

Taking her helmet off had probably been a bad idea. The wind was pulling long strands from the braid that hung down over Jake's arm. They were plastered against her face the moment they came free and she had to drag them away repeatedly to try and see properly.

'I can't see it. The waves are too high.'

'See what?'

'The light from the lighthouse. The bach is in a direct line with the light, just before the river mouth.'

'The *what?*'

'The bach. A holiday house.' Ellie had finally picked up the drawl in the man's voice. 'Are you American?'

'Yep.'

'A cabin, then. Like you'd have by a lake or in the woods. Only this one's near the beach and it's the only one for a hundred miles.'

'How do you know it's even there?'

'Because I own it.' Maybe it wasn't dark enough for the automatic light to be triggered, but she'd seen it earlier, hadn't she? When she'd told Dave where to drop them?

Maybe she'd only seen the lighthouse itself and it had been childhood memories that had supplied the flash of light. The flash she'd watched for in the night since that first time she'd stayed on the island with her grandfather. A comforting presence that had assured a small girl she was safe even if she was on a tiny island in the middle of a very big sea.

'We'll have to keep going till we get to the river. I can find the way from there.'

How long did he keep struggling against the wind before they finally reached the river mouth? Long enough for Ellie to know she'd never felt this cold in her life. At least they had the wind behind them as they turned inland, but there was a new danger when they reached the forest of native bush that came to meet the coastline in this deserted area. The massive pohutukawa trees were hundreds of years old and there were any number of dead branches coming loose in the vicious wind to crash down around them. Live bits were breaking off, too, leafy enough to make it impossible to see the old track that led to the bach.

Ellie had to rely on instinct. Her fear was growing. Had she made a terrible mistake, telling Dave they could find shelter here? The little house that Grandpa and her father had built had seemed so solid, wedged into the bush that had provided the wood to make it. A part of the forest that would always be here even if she had never come back. A touchstone for her life that was a part of her soul.

But how many storms had there been in the years that had passed? Had the tiny dwelling disintegrated—like all the hugely important things in her life seemed to have a habit of doing?

No.

They almost missed it. They were off to one side of the patch of land she owned. She might have let herself get carried right past if she hadn't spotted the tiny hut that sat discreetly tucked against the twisted trunk of one of the huge pohutukawas.

'We're here,' she shouted.

The man looked at the hut. If he went inside the bleached wood of its walls, he would have to bend his head and he wouldn't be able to stretch out his arms. 'Are you *kidding* me? *That's* your cabin?'

Ellie actually laughed aloud.

'No. That's the dunny.'

'The *what?*'

'The long drop. Toilet.' Oh, yeah…he was American. 'It's the *bathroom*.'

She didn't wait to see a look of disgust about how primitive the facilities were. The track from the outhouse to the real house was overgrown, but Ellie knew exactly where she was now. And if the outhouse had survived, maybe everything else was exactly as it should be. Within a few steps they could both see the back porch of the beach house, with its neatly stacked pile of firewood. The relief of seeing it look just like it always had brought a huge lump to Ellie's throat.

She felt herself being tipped as he leaned down to grasp the battered iron knob of the door. He turned and pushed. The door rattled but didn't open.

'It's *locked*.'

She couldn't blame him for sounding shocked. It wasn't

as if another living soul was likely to come here when the only access was by boat so why would anybody bother locking it?

Another childhood memory surfaced. The door that had been purchased in a city junkyard had been roped to the deck of the yacht, along with an old couch and a pot-belly stove.

'The door's even got a lock and a key.' Her father had laughed. *'That'll keep the possums out.'*

A family joke that had become a tradition. Unlocking the bach meant they were in residence in their tiny patch of paradise. Locking it meant a return to reality.

'I know where the key is. Put me down.'

This time he complied and it was Ellie's turn to be shocked as she felt the loss of those secure arms around her, along with the chill of losing his body warmth that she hadn't been aware of until now. She staggered a little, but her ankle wasn't as bad as it had been. Hellishly painful but it didn't collapse completely when she tested it with a bit of weight. Maybe it was a bad sprain rather than a fracture.

'Can you walk?'

'I only need to get to the meat safe. The key's in there.'

The wire netting walls of the meat safe were mangled, probably by possums, and the box frame was hanging by only one corner, but the big, wrought-iron key was still on its rusty nail. Getting it inside the lock was a mission for her frozen hands, though, and turning it seemed impossible.

'It must be rusty.' Ellie groaned with the effort of trying to turn the key.

'Let me try.' His hands covered hers and pushed her fingers away so that he could find the end of the key. She was still wearing her rescue gloves and his hands had to be a lot colder than hers were, but the pressure of the contact felt like it was skin to skin. Warm.

Maybe it was the reassurance that she wasn't alone that was so comforting?

He was shivering badly, Ellie noticed, but when he jiggled the key and then turned it, she could hear the clunk of the old lock opening.

And then they were inside and the sound of the storm was suddenly muffled.

Safety.

They might be frozen to the bone and in the middle of nowhere, but they had shelter.

Jake was safe, thanks to this woman. Thanks to her astonishing courage. She'd not only risked her life to get him out of that life raft, she'd battled the elements, despite being injured, to lead him here. To a place where they had four walls and a roof and they could survive until the storm was over.

She seemed as stunned as he was. They both stood there, staring at each other, saying nothing. It couldn't be nighttime yet, but it was dark enough in here to make it difficult to see very clearly. She was tall, Jake noted, but still a good few inches shorter than his six feet two. Eyes dark enough to look black in this light and her lips were deathly pale but still couldn't hide the lines of a generous mouth. A rope of wet hair hung over one shoulder almost as far as her waist.

'What's your name?' He'd been so used to shouting to be heard outside that his voice came out loudly enough to make her jump.

'Eleanor Sutton. Ellie.'

'I'm Jacob Logan. Jake.'

'Hi, Jake.' She was trying to smile but loosening

her facial muscles only made her shiver uncontrollably. 'P-pleased to m-meet you.'

'Likewise, Ellie.' Jake nodded instead of smiling.

His name clearly didn't mean anything to her and it was a weird feeling not to be instantly recognised. He didn't look much like himself, of course. Even his own mother probably wouldn't have recognised him in this dim light with the heavy growth of beard and the long hair he'd had to adopt for his latest movie role. But instant demotion from a megastar to a…a *nobody* was very strange.

Jake wasn't sure he liked it.

And yet it was oddly comforting. It took him back to a time when he had only been known for being 'one of those wild Logan boys.' Closer to Ben, somehow.

Should he tell her? Was it being dishonest not to? Would Ben consider this a form of play-acting as well?

Keeping silent didn't feel like acting a part. Just being the person he used to be. And there would be no reason for this Ellie to present herself as anything other than who she really was and, in Jake's experience, that wasn't something he could ever trust. This might be the only time in his life that he got to see how a stranger reacted to him as a person without the trappings of extreme wealth or fame. He was curious enough to find this almost a distraction from his desperate worry about Ben.

'We need to get warm.' She wasn't even looking at him now. 'There should be enough dry wood to get the fire and the stove going. Hopefully the possums won't have been inside. There'll be plenty of blankets on the beds. And there's kerosene lamps if the fuel hasn't evaporated or something. It's been a fair few years since I was here.'

Beds? For the first time, Jake took a good look around himself.

The dwelling was made of rustic, rough-hewn boards

that had aged to a silvery-gray that made it look like driftwood. An antique glass-and-metal lamp hung from a butcher's hook in the ceiling and there was a collection of big shells lined with iridescent shades of blue and purple attached to the wall in a curly pattern. Beside that was a poster of a lighthouse, its beam lighting up a stormy sky while massive waves thundered onto rocks below. There was a kitchen of sorts in one corner of the square space, with a bench and a sink beside the potbelly stove close to a small wooden table and spindle-back chairs.

The other half of the space was taken up with an ancient-looking couch and an armchair, positioned in front of an open fireplace. Two doorless openings in the walls on either side of the fireplace led to dark spaces beyond. The bedrooms?

'Don't just stand there.' The authority in her voice made Jake feel like he was back at school. Or under the charge of one of the many nannies the Logan boys had terrorised. Incredibly, he had to hide a wry smile. No woman had ever spoken to him like this in his adult life. And then he remembered being shouted at on the beach. Being told that no one would be going back to rescue his brother.

What did it matter whether Ellie knew who he was? Or what she thought of him?

Nothing would ever matter if he'd lost Ben.

Ellie was opening a cupboard in the kitchen. She pulled out a big tin. 'Do something useful. You'll get even colder if you don't move. You can get some wood in from the porch.' She prised open the lid of the tin. '*Yes*...we have matches.'

A fire. Warmth. This basic survival need drove any other thoughts from Jake's head as he obeyed the order. He took an armful of small sticks in first to act as kindling and then went back for the more solid lumps of wood. His brain felt as frozen as his fingers. Worry about Ben was still there along with the anger of no attempt being made to rescue him, but he couldn't even harness the energy of that anger to help him move faster. And then something scuttled away as he lifted a piece of wood. Did New Zealand have poisonous spiders, like Australia did? Or snakes?

Man, he was going to have some story to tell Ben when he saw him again.

If he saw him again.

There was a puddle of water on the floor where Ellie was crouching to light the fire and he could see how badly her hands were shaking, but she'd managed to arrange small sticks on a nest of paper and while the first two matches spluttered and died, the third grew into a small flame.

She looked up as he walked towards her with the wood. He saw the way her eyes widened with shock.

'You're limping.' Her tone was accusing. 'You're hurt. And I let you carry me all that way. Why didn't you *tell* me?'

'I'm not hurt.' He dumped the wood on the floor beside her. His old injury was hardly a state secret, but it wasn't something he mentioned if he could avoid it.

'I'm a paramedic, Jake. I've got eyes. I can *see*—'

'Drop it,' he growled. 'I told you. I haven't been injured. Not in the last ten years anyway.'

'Oh…' She caught her bottom lip between her teeth. Maybe she was attempting a smile. 'Old war wound, huh?'

He glared at her. 'First time anyone's found it funny.'

Her face changed. Was she embarrassed? Not that she was about to apologise. There was an awkward silence as she turned her attention back to the fire and then she must have decided that it was best ignored.

* * *

'Some rats or mice had shredded the paper for me,' Ellie said. 'Good thing, too, because my fingers are still too cold to work properly.' Her tone was deliberately lighter. Impersonal, even. 'Don't think we'll use the beds, but the blankets might be okay.'

The wood sizzled a little, but the flame was still growing. The glow caught Ellie's face as she leaned in to blow gently on the fire. Water dripped from her long braid to add to the puddle at her feet. Smoke puffed out and made her cough.

'There could well be a bird's nest or two in the chimney, but they should burn away soon. We'll get the potbelly going, too, if we can, and that should get things toasty in no time.'

Jake had to forgive the dismissal of his old injury as some kind of joke. She didn't know the truth and, if he wasn't prepared to enlighten her, it would be unfair to hold a grudge. And he had to admire her. She was capable, this Eleanor Sutton, but that was hardly surprising given what she did for a job. Jake was given the task of feeding larger sticks into the fire as it grew while Ellie limped over to the kitchen to get the stove going. His hands began aching unbearably as heat finally penetrated the frozen layer of skin and, when he looked up, he saw Ellie's pained expression as she shook her hands.

'Hurts, doesn't it?'

'It's good. Means there's some circulation happening and nerves are waking up.' She nodded in satisfaction at the fire Jake was tending. 'I'll see if I can find us some dry clothes. My dad kept a trunk of stuff under the bed and it's a tin trunk so it should have kept the rats out.'

'Do you get snakes, too?'

'No snakes in New Zealand. Have you never been here before?'

'No.'

'I guess you were just passing by with the yacht race. Wasn't there a stop planned in Auckland?'

'Yeah. I was getting off then. I'm here for a job. That was why I talked Ben into giving me a lift on his yacht.'

'Ben? That's your friend who was on the life raft with you?'

'He's my brother. Twin brother.'

'Oh…'

The enormity of having to leave Ben behind and not trying to go back and get him was clearly registering.

'I…I'm sorry, Jake.'

'Yeah… Me, too.'

'It was a good life raft. There's still hope that he'll make it.'

Jake found himself staring at Ellie. It felt very odd—his gaze clinging to hers like this. As if he was pleading…

Desperately wanting to believe.

Begging her to prove herself trustworthy?

She was in the business of rescuing people who found themselves in dire situations so she should know what she was talking about.

'We weren't the only rescue team out there,' she told him quietly. 'There were other choppers. Planes. And there's other boats. Container ships as well as the coastguard. There's plenty of daylight left and…'

There was such compassion in her eyes and her body language. The way she was leaning towards him. Holding out one hand. If she'd been close enough, she'd be touching him right now.

He wished she was that close.

'And there are literally hundreds of islands on this part

of the coastline. All it needs is for a current to get him close to land and he'll be able to find shelter until the worst of the storm is over.'

Maybe it was the compassion he could see that did it. Or the comfort of the reassurance she was offering. Or maybe it was because of that longing that she had been close enough to underpin her words with human touch.

Whatever it was, Jake could pull back. Yes, she was offering him what he wanted more than anything in this moment. And the invitation to believe her was so sincere, but they were all like that, weren't they? Especially women.

He knew better than to trust.

'Yeah…right…' He wrenched his gaze free, turning back towards the fire and using a stick to poke at it. He didn't want to talk about Ben. He didn't want to show this stranger how he was really feeling. How *afraid* he was. Who knew what contacts she might have? What could turn up as a headline on some celebrity website?

The warmth Ellie had been getting from the stove seemed to have been shut off and the cold in her gut turned into a lead weight.

No wonder they'd been arguing about who got to be rescued first. Or that Jake had said he would have stayed if he'd been given the choice. She didn't even have a sibling and these men were twin brothers. She could imagine how close they were. As close as she'd dreamed of being with another living soul. Loving—and being loved—enough for one's own safety to not be the priority.

She would have gone back for Ben if it had been possible, but it hadn't been. At least she'd brought Jake to safety, but maybe, in the end, he wouldn't thank her for that. He obviously didn't want to talk about it. He was hunched over in front of the fire, looking very grim as he poked at the burning sticks, sending sparks flying and creating a new cloud of smoke. Fiercely shutting her out.

Was it the smoke in his eyes that made him rub at them with the heel of his hand? Even hunched up, she was aware again of what a big man he was. Intimidatingly big. She knew that trying to offer any further comfort would be unwelcome. She'd probably put her foot in it, too, the way she had when she'd tried to make some kind of joke about his obvious limp.

It had been the way Grandpa had brushed off any concern about his physical wellbeing.

It's nothing, chicken. Just the old war wound playing up.

But Jake was an American. Had she made a joke about some horrible injury he'd suffered in somewhere like Afghanistan? She'd been too flustered to think of a way to apologise without it seeming insincere. Or prying. There was something about this man that suggested he valued his privacy a lot more than most people.

So, once again, she simply avoided anything personal.

'I'll go and see if I can find us those dry clothes.'

By the time Ellie returned with an armload of clothes from the old tin trunk, the living area of the small house was already feeling a lot warmer.

'The trousers are pretty horrible, but we've scored with a couple of Swanndris.'

Jake looked up from where he was still crouched in front of the fire. He was shivering uncontrollably despite being so close to the heat. 'S-swan—what?'

'They're shirts. I'm wearing one.' Ellie dumped the pile she was holding onto the sofa, extracting a black-and-red-checked garment to hold out to Jake. 'New Zealand icon. A hundred percent wool. Farmers have relied on them for decades over here and they're the best thing for warmth. Even better, these ones are huge. Should fit you a treat.'

Neither her father or grandfather had been small men by any means. The shirt Ellie was wearing came well down over the baggy track pants she'd struggled into in the bedroom, but it was just as well they were so loose because they'd gone right over the sodden boots that had laces she couldn't manage to undo yet. And maybe it was better to leave them on. At least her ankle was splinted by the heavy leather and padding of her socks.

He took the shirt and nodded. 'Thanks.'

'Don't just stare at it. Put it on. No, hang on…' Ellie dived back into the pile. 'Here's a singlet that can go on first so it's not itchy.'

Getting changed into dry clothes was easier said than done. Ellie had found it enough of a struggle getting out of her wet clothes in the bedroom and she'd been wearing state-of-the-art gloves to protect her hands up until now. Jake's hands had been bare ever since he'd been plucked from the life raft and were still so cold there was no way he could manage the zipper of the heavy anorak he was wearing.

He fumbled several times, cursed softly and then stopped trying. Ellie dragged her gaze up from his fingers to his face and, for a long moment, they simply stared at each other.

The fire was crackling with some enthusiasm now. Adding enough light to the dark, stormy afternoon for her to get a good look at this man. He was big, broad shouldered and…and *wild* looking, with that long hair and the beard. His face was fierce looking anyway, with a nose that commanded attention and accentuated the shadowed eyes that had an almost hawk-like intensity.

The pull of something—an awareness that was deep

enough to be disturbing—made Ellie's mouth go dry. She tore her gaze away from those compelling eyes. They both knew she had no choice here.

'I'll help you,' she said.

Her voice sounded weird so she pressed her lips together and said nothing else as she started to help him undress. The scrape of the metal zip sounded curiously loud. He had layers underneath. A sodden woollen pullover and thermal gear beneath that.

And then there was skin. Rather a lot of skin covering the kind of torso that spoke of a great deal of physical effort.

Ripped. That was the only word for it.

Dark discs of nipples hardened by the cold decorated an almost hairless chest that seemed at odds with the amount of hair Jake favoured on his head and face.

And…dear Lord, there was a tattoo in the strangest place. A line of what looked like Chinese characters ran from his armpit to disappear into the waistband of his jeans.

It was discreet body art and it must have significance, but Ellie wasn't about to ask. She shouldn't even be looking. Just as well it got covered up as Jake pulled on the black singlet and then the thick woollen shirt. He managed to pop the button on his jeans but, again, the zipper was beyond the motor skills that had returned to his hands so far.

Ellie had undressed countless patients in her career. She'd cut through and removed clothing and exposed every inch of skin of people without the slightest personal reaction. Why did it have to be now that she was so aware of touching someone in such an intimate area? Why did she feel so uncomfortable she had to swallow hard and actually close her eyes for a heartbeat?

Like remembering her past when it should have been

totally obliterated by the adrenaline of being in real danger, maybe this was a sign that she was no longer fit for active service as a paramedic. Something like grief washed through Ellie at the thought and it was easy to turn that into a kind of anger. Impatience, anyway, to get the job over with.

'I'll do the zip,' she snapped. 'You should be able to manage the rest.'

She tried not to think of what her fingers were brushing. The zipper got stuck halfway down and she had to pull it back up and try again. A warmth that had nothing to do with the fire crept into her cheeks. As soon as she got the zipper down past where it had stuck, she dropped her hands as though the metal was red hot and she turned away as Jake hooked his thumbs into the waistband and started peeling the wet fabric from his skin.

She'd seen enough.

Too much.

Nobody had undressed Jake Logan without his invitation since he'd been about two years old and had kicked his nanny to demonstrate his desire for independence.

Except for when he'd been in the care of the army medics, of course, and then of the nurses in the military hospital back home. He'd flirted wickedly with those nurses, making a joke of the humiliation of being helpless.

He couldn't have flirted to save his life when Ellie had been struggling with that zipper. He'd been looking down at her bent head. The rope of black hair was still dripping wet, but the fronds that the wind had whipped free were starting to dry and they were softening the outlines of her face. Or they would have been if it wasn't set in such grim lines of determination.

She *really* didn't want to be touching him, did she? This

was an ordeal she was forcing herself to get through because she had no choice.

Like being unrecognised, this was an alien experience for a man almost bored by the way women threw themselves at him. Not a pleasant experience either, but it wasn't humiliation or even embarrassment that was so overwhelming. He couldn't begin to identify *what* it was he was feeling. He just knew that it was powerful enough to be disturbing.

Very disturbing.

The choice of trousers *was* embarrassing with the only pair he had any hope of fitting being shapeless track pants that didn't cover his ankles. At least the socks looked long and he could be grateful there were no paparazzi around.

'What will we do with the wet gear?'

Ellie had taken the lamp down from the hook on the ceiling and was pouring something from a plastic bottle into its base.

'We'll hang them over the chairs. They might be dry enough to get back into by the time we get rescued from here.'

'How long do you reckon that'll be?'

Ellie had the glass cover off the lamp now. She struck a match and held it to a wick. 'We had a lot of info coming in about the cyclone while we were in the air. The worst of it won't hit until early tomorrow, but it should blow through within about twelve hours.'

The flame caught and Ellie eased the glass cover back into place. She fiddled with an attachment to the base, pumping it gently, and suddenly the light increased to a glow that seemed like a spotlight focused on her. As she looked up and caught his gaze, a hint of a smile made her lips curve. 'It's going to get worse before it gets better, I'm afraid.'

Jake's mouth felt suddenly dry.

Even the hint of a smile transformed Ellie's face. Made it come alive.

She was an extraordinarily beautiful woman. He could actually feel something slamming shut in his chest. Or his head maybe.

Don't go there. Don't get sucked in. Even if she doesn't know who you are, it's not worth the risk.

Remember what happened last time.

But Ellie stretched to hang the lamp from its hook and the unbuttoned sleeves of her oversize shirt fell back to expose slim, olive-brown arms. Long, clever fingers made another adjustment to the base of the lamp.

Jake couldn't drag his gaze free.

Yeah…it probably *was* going to get worse before it got better.

But he could deal with it.

He *had* to.

CHAPTER FOUR

THE KEROSENE LAMP hissed and swayed gently in the draughts that were a soft echo of the fierce storm outside. The glow of light strengthened as day became night and shadows danced in the corners of the room as the light moved—a dark partner to the bright flicker of the flames in the open fireplace.

The room was warm enough for the wet clothing draped over the spindle-back chairs to be steaming gently and one end of the table was covered with a collection of items that had come from the pockets of Ellie's flight suit, like a bunch of keys, ruined ballpoint pens and an equally wet and useless mobile phone. Most importantly, there was a two-way radio that had been securely enclosed in a waterproof pouch.

Jake had been disappointed that they couldn't use it to listen and hear updates on the weather, but Ellie was more concerned about whether it was in working order. It didn't seem to be transmitting.

'Medic One to base—do you receive?'

A crackle of static and a beeping noise came from the device, but there was no answering voice. Ellie gave up after a few tries.

'We may be out of range or it could be atmospheric conditions. I'll turn it on in the morning and we might get communication about our rescue.'

The radio sat on the edge of the table now—a symbol of surviving this ordeal.

Except, for the moment, it didn't seem to be that much of an ordeal. They were safe and finally warm. And Ellie had discovered a store of tinned food in the bottom of a cupboard.

'Chilli baked beans, cheesy spaghetti, Irish stew, peas or tomatoes.' She held up each can to show Jake. 'As my guest, you get to choose. What do you fancy?'

'They all sound good. I don't think I've ever been this hungry in my life.'

'Hmm…' Ellie had almost forgotten what it felt like to really smile. 'That's not a bad idea. I'll see if I've got a pot that's big enough.'

The result of mixing the contents of all the chosen cans together was remarkably tasty. Or maybe she was just as hungry as Jake. Whatever the reason, sitting cross-legged in front of the fire, spooning the food from a bowl, Ellie decided that it was probably one of the most memorable meals she would ever eat.

'There's more in the pot if you're still hungry,' she told Jake.

'Maybe we should save it for tomorrow.'

'There's still more cans. My mother must have stocked up big time on their last trip.'

'When was that?'

'Six years ago. I didn't come on that trip because I was in the middle of my helicopter training.' Ellie stared into the fire. 'Who knew it would save my life?'

'How d'you mean?'

'Their yacht ran into trouble on the way home. Both my parents drowned.'

'Oh…I'm sorry.'

Ellie could see Jake put his plate down suddenly, as if his appetite had deserted him. She kicked herself mentally.

'No, *I'm* sorry. I didn't mean to remind you of…' Her voice trailed into silence. He didn't want to talk about Ben, did he? She didn't need to glance sideways at his bent head to remind her of that walled-off private area. It was none of her business, anyway.

But she heard Jake take a deep breath a moment later. And then he shook his head as he got to his feet. He shoved his hair behind his ears.

'You wouldn't have a rubber band or a piece of string or something, would you? My hair's going to drive me nuts if I don't tie it back.'

Ellie blinked. 'I can find something.' She couldn't help a personal question. 'Why do you wear it so long if it annoys you?'

'Not my choice. It's temporary. You could say it's a—a work thing.'

'Ohh…' Ellie was bemused. 'What are you—a male model?'

Jake's breath came out in a snort. 'Something like that.'

Ellie could well believe it. She'd seen that body. The dark wavy hair that almost brushed his shoulders would probably be wildly exciting for a lot of women, too, but the beard? No…it wouldn't do it for her.

She almost changed her mind as Jake used his fingers to rake his hair back properly from his face. Even with the beard hiding half his face, she had trouble dragging her gaze away from him.

'What? Have I got spaghetti on my face or something?'

'No…you just look…I don't know…different.'

Different but oddly familiar. Or was that simply a warning signal that something unconscious was recognising the magnetic pull this man seemed to have? Ellie turned away with a decisive enough head movement to make her aware of the heavy weight of her own hair. The loose bits had long since dried, but the braid was still wet.

'Here. Have this…' She pulled the elastic band from the end of her braid. 'I need to get my hair dry and it'll take all night if I leave it tied up.'

So Jake bound his hair back in a ponytail and Ellie unravelled hers and let it fall over her back with the ends brushing the wooden boards of the floor. Now it was Jake's turn to stare, apparently. She could feel the intensity of his gaze from where he was sitting on the sofa behind her.

Was it the hissing of the lamp or the crackle of the fire or was there some kind of other current in the air that Ellie could actually *feel* instead of hear? It had all the intensity of a bright light and the heat of a flame and something warned Ellie not to turn her head.

The current was coming from Jake.

She heard him clear his throat. As though he thought his speech might be hoarse if he didn't?

'Must have been tough, losing your parents like that. Have you got any brothers or sisters?'

'Nope.'

'Husband? Boyfriend? Significant other?'

'Nope.' Ellie felt her hackles rise. It was none of his business. He wasn't about to let her into personal areas. Why would he think she was willing to share?

'Sorry. Didn't mean to pry.' Jake's voice was flat. 'I just thought…it's going to be a long night and it might be kind of nice to get to know each other.'

Did that mean that if she was prepared to share, he might too? That she might even find out the significance of that intriguing tattoo, even?

'Fair enough.' But Ellie got to her feet. 'Let me find us some blankets and pillows first, if they're useable. And

I'll boil some water. We don't have milk, but there's probably a tin of cocoa or something around. We need a drink.'

It was some time before Ellie was satisfied they had all they needed for a while. The fire was well banked up with wood. They both had a blanket and a pillow and, by tacit consent, Jake would have the couch to try and sleep on while Ellie curled up in the armchair. Neither of them wanted to move any further away from the fire.

Exhaustion was taking over now. Her body ached all over and her injured ankle was throbbing badly despite the hastily applied strapping with a damp bandage that she'd found in one of her suit pockets when changing her clothes.

It had been one of the longest days of Ellie's life and the physical exertion had been draining enough without the added stress of the emotional side of it all. Not only the fear for her own safety but also the grief of knowing that the job was no longer enough to shield her from what she had run from.

Maybe part of it was renewed grief for the family she'd lost. Impossible for that not to be surfacing now that she'd finally come back to a place she'd been avoiding for that very reason.

And maybe that was what made her prepared to talk about it. About things she'd never had anyone to talk to about.

'I haven't been here since my parents died,' she told Jake. 'It was bad enough when we all came here after Grandpa died and I didn't want to come back knowing that I had no family left.' She sighed softly. 'I didn't have a boat anyway. I wasn't sure I wanted anything more to do with the sea.'

'Hard to get away from, I would think, when you live on an island.'

'Well—it's a big island, but you're right. The home I

grew up in is in Devonport in Auckland and it's right on the beach. I still live there. There's salt water in my family's blood, I reckon. That's why Grandpa took the job as the lighthouse-keeper on Half Moon Island.'

'The moon… Yeah, I heard you say something about that on the radio.'

'I recognised it from the air. I spent so much time there when I was little that it's like part of the family. That's a picture of it over there, on the wall.'

'I thought most lighthouses were automatic now.'

'They are. And Half Moon was automated long before I was born, but Grandpa couldn't bear to leave it behind. That's why he bought this patch of land and virtually lived here from when my dad was a teenager. I sailed up with them every school holiday until he died when I was seventeen. And then Mum, Dad and I still came at least a couple of times a year. Having Christmas here when all the pohutukawa trees are in full bloom is quite something. And we could still go over to Half Moon and explore. It's got an amazing amount of birdlife. It should be a national reserve.'

'Why isn't it?'

Ellie shrugged. 'Too remote, I guess. And it would be too expensive to run a pest eradication programme.'

She was so tired now, her eyes were drooping shut. That was enough of a foray into personal space, wasn't it?

Apparently not.

'I don't get it.' Jake's words broke a silence in which Ellie had been drifting closer to sleep.

'What?'

'Why someone like you is all alone.'

'Someone like me?' Ellie opened heavy lids and turned her head far enough to find Jake staring at her again.

'Yeah… Someone talented, incredibly brave…gorgeous…'

His words were doing something to her stomach. It felt like she'd swallowed one of the flames from the fireplace and it was tickling her with tendrils hot enough to be uncomfortable.

It made a response easy to find. 'Once burned, twice shy, you know?'

'Oh, I do know.' The words were laced with bitterness. 'What happened?'

'Same old story. Fell in love. Got betrayed. I won't bore you with the details, but it would have made a pretty good story line for a soap opera.'

The huff of sound that came from Jake managed to encompass both disgust and empathy. 'Good way to look at it, anyway.'

'How's that?'

'Like it's a movie and you can see the whole disaster up there on the big screen.'

A strangled sound of mirth escaped Ellie. 'And what would the humiliated, heartbroken heroine do in this movie?'

Jake's voice was soft. 'Pretty much what you've done. Got on with her life and turned herself into a real-life heroine.'

Ellie didn't want to hear any more of his praise. 'Life's not a movie,' she muttered.

'Helps to look at it like that sometimes, though.'

That woke Ellie up a little. Annoyed her, in fact. 'How does avoiding reality help exactly?'

'Because you see your life up on the screen and you're part of the audience. How would you feel if you were watching yourself giving up? Pulling the blankets over your head or crying in a corner? You wouldn't think it was worth watching any more, would you? Isn't it better to be cheering yourself on as you face the obstacles and overcome them?'

'Is that what you do?'

'Kind of, I suppose.' Ellie got the impression she was hearing something very personal here. 'Gets you through the tough bits.'

'The "fake it till you make it" school of thought?'

'Uh-uh.' The negative sound was very American. 'It's not fake. You're not pretending to be someone *else*. You're practising being the best person you can be, even if it feels like the skin doesn't quite fit yet.'

Had she annoyed him this time? The lapse into another silence suggested she had.

'So…' Ellie tried to keep her tone light. 'I'm guessing you're not married either?'

'Not anymore.'

It shouldn't make any difference to know he was single so why did her heart rate pick up a little?

'Used and abused, too, huh?'

'You said it.'

This time the silence felt like a door slamming. There was no point waiting for Jake to say anything else and his guard was up so firmly that Ellie wondered if she'd imagined that she'd been allowed briefly into a personal space. Instinct told her that if she pushed, that barrier would only get bigger.

She backed away. 'What's the happy ending going to be in the movie of my life, then? Do I get swept off my feet by the love of my life? Some gorgeous guy that I have no trouble trusting absolutely?'

'Of course.' There was a smile in Jake's voice that almost felt like praise. For not prying, perhaps?

She had to dismiss the fairy tale, though. 'That's why I don't watch movies. What's the point in escaping into fiction instead of facing reality?'

'If we couldn't hope for something better, life could be a pretty miserable business sometimes for a lot of folks.'

'I suppose.' Ellie snuggled deeper into her blanket and let her head sink into the pillow. 'Can't see it happening for me.'

'Me neither.'

The agreement felt like a connection. They were on the same page. And maybe what he'd said about playing a role had some merit. She could try faking it a bit herself.

'I'm happy with my reality,' she said. 'Why would I risk that happiness by hanging it on someone else? When it really boils down, the only person you can trust is yourself. Unless…' The words were sleepy now. Almost a murmur. 'Unless you've got a twin. That would be like having two of yourself.'

Jake said nothing and Ellie drifted closer to sleep, happy that they had got to know each other a little better. Had found a connection of sorts, albeit a negative one, in that relationships were currently a no-go area for both of them. Did that open the door, perhaps, to a friendship without the hidden agenda that always seemed to become a problem?

No. In those last moments before losing consciousness, Ellie's mind—and her body—insisted on remembering how it had felt to be so close to Jake's bare skin. To touch him. And just the thought of it meant she could still actually feel that sizzle that had been in the air when she'd felt him staring at her back.

There would be an agenda there all right, even if she didn't want it.

And it might not be just Jake's agenda.

It was a sudden change of temperature that woke Jake from a fitful, nightmare-plagued slumber. A slap of cold air on his face.

Sitting up to see over the back of the sofa, he found Ellie struggling to open the outside door.

'What's happened? What's *wrong?*'

'Nothing.' Ellie was wearing a heavy, oilskin coat. Her hair was still loose, but she had a woollen hat pulled down over her ears. 'I just need to go to the bathroom.'

'Are you crazy?' Now fully awake, Jake realised that all hell seemed to have broken out beyond the walls of their small shelter. The howling shriek of the wind was as unearthly as the weird half-light of the new day. Rain hammered at the tin roof and there was an ominous banging noise that suggested a piece of the roofing was coming loose.

Ignoring painfully stiff muscles and joints, he got to his feet and close to the window in time to see the meat safe give up any attempt to stay attached to the porch wall and the wind pick it up and send it bouncing into the trees.

'Wow…' Ellie sounded impressed by the force of the wind.

And she was planning to go out there? 'It's dangerous,' Jake growled.

'It's urgent,' Ellie said calmly. 'It's only a few steps. It's not as if I'm in danger of getting blown over a cliff or something.'

'There's branches flying everywhere. You could get hurt.' It was the sheer stupidity of what she was intending to do that was making Jake sound fierce. Or was it a sudden urge to protect this woman?

'You can get hurt crossing the road.'

She wasn't about to listen to him and who was he to tell her about assessing risk anyway? This woman dangled on thin wires underneath helicopters for a living, for goodness' sake.

'There's a pot of water on the stove,' Ellie told him. 'I'll be back by the time you've made us some cocoa.'

He could do that. He should do that instead of standing here by the window watching as Ellie bent almost double to force herself forward against the wind. It looked like she wasn't going to get the narrow door of the outhouse open against the wind, but he saw her wedge her boot inside a crack and then use her shoulder to force it open further.

Man…her strength was impressive, but her determination was downright intimidating.

Jake rubbed his eyes as he turned back to the stove. Not that he needed to be any more awake but there were still fragments of his nightmares that were swirling in his head.

Ellie—looking like a warrior princess with her long hair flowing in the wind behind her—pointing a finger at him and shouting.

Fake…fake…fake…

And Ben had been standing beside her. Equally accusing.

Play-acting… Just like Mom… You can't face reality.

But you're another me. I'm another you.

No. Jake prised the lid off the cocoa tin with the edge of a spoon. Ellie had been way off the mark with that sleepy observation. He and Ben had always been a unit, for sure—united against the outside world—but there were two distinct parts of that unit. They weren't the same person—not by a long shot.

Not even two halves of a whole. More like yin and yang. Very different but a perfect fit together.

And he'd never feel the same shape if Ben was gone.

But she hadn't been so far off the mark in suggesting that using a movie mode was sidestepping reality. Or Ben had been when he'd said pretty much the same thing in the life raft. Wasn't that pretty much how it had all started, even though he'd been far too young to realise what he was doing?

The water in the pot was boiling now. Ellie had been gone quite long enough so any second now she would burst back in through the door. Jake tipped water into the mugs, grateful for the need to focus and the distraction of the rich smell of chocolate. He could get on with surviving another day and banish the last of those disturbing dreams.

Especially the one where he hadn't been able to tell himself apart from his brother. When it was him who was lost on that unforgiving ocean. Tossed out of the life raft and dragged deeper and deeper under the weight of icy water. *Drowning…*

The explosive cracking noise from outside was more than enough to send that dream fragment into oblivion. It was enough to drain the blood from Jake's face. The whole house seemed to be shaking and the noise just got louder. One of the mugs toppled over and steaming liquid poured onto the floor, but Jake didn't notice. The light was changing. Getting darker. And then there was an impact that had all the force of an earthquake. The second mug crashed to the floor and shattered. A chair toppled. The kerosene lamp swung so violently the flame was extinguished.

The sound of any wind or rain felt like silence after that.

A very ominous silence.

Jake was already at the door, wrenching it open. He'd never shouted so loudly in his life.

'Ellie...'

CHAPTER FIVE

SHE FELT THE first shudders of the ground just as she tried to open the door of the outhouse again.

She heard the terrible cracking that could only mean one thing. A tree was coming down. A very large tree.

Was she about to get crushed? Trapped in what was little more than a wooden box?

This was more terrifying than being dragged through that wave like a fish on a line yesterday. At least she'd had a crew looking out for her and elements of the situation she could control herself. As she felt the outhouse being picked up with her still inside it and thrown through the air, Ellie was convinced she was about to die.

Did she imagine hearing someone calling her name?

A split second of sheer longing overwhelmed her. She wanted to be inside the beach house. With Jake's arms around her. Holding her tight. Keeping her safe.

The impact of hitting the ground shattered the old wooden boards around her, but instead of seeing daylight, Ellie found she was inside a layer of branches and the stiff leaves of a pohutukawa tree. A layer so thick it was hard to breathe. Miraculously, she didn't seem to be injured. Curling onto her knees, she started snapping small branches around her face and pushing them away to clear a space.

'Ellie...'

She definitely hadn't imagined it this time.

'I'm here, Jake.'

'I can't see you.'

'I'm under branches. I… *Ahh…*' Ellie groaned with the effort of trying to snap a bigger branch.

'Oh, God…are you *hurt?*'

The concern in his voice was enough to bring a lump to Ellie's throat. She might not have the backing of an experienced rescue team right now, but there *was* someone there who seemed to care whether or not she was okay.

She had to swallow hard before she could shout back. 'I don't think so. I'm just…stuck.'

'I'll get you out. Keep shouting so I know where you are.'

Ellie did keep shouting. She kept trying to find a way through herself, too, squeezing herself through smaller gaps and turning away from branches so big they would need a chainsaw to break them. She could hear the snapping of wood as Jake tried to create a path from the other side of the massive tree canopy.

It was dirty work and exhausting and Ellie could feel the scratches and bruises she was accumulating on her bare face and hands. Her hair kept getting caught and having to be painfully wrenched free. She was going to get it cut off when she got out of here, she decided.

If she got out of here.

The next desperate attempt to wriggle through a gap was badly judged. Ellie's leg got caught and trying to get free only wedged her foot further into a fork of thick branches. It was her injured foot that was caught, too, and even trying to pull it clear brought a sob of both frustration and pain from deep in her chest.

'I *knew* you were hurt.' After what had seemed an interminable amount of time, there was Jake's face only inches from her own. 'How bad is it?'

'It's just my ankle. From yesterday. But…it's wedged… I can't…'

'I can.' Jake crawled further into the mess of tangled tree and took hold of her foot. 'Sorry—this might hurt a bit.' He held onto her ankle and eased it out of the boot with a seesawing motion. Without her foot inside, it was easy enough to pull the boot free.

And then he was showing her which way to crawl after him.

'We'll go around the roots. The path's not so blocked that way.'

It was so wrong, seeing the massive trunk horizontal to the ground, with half the roots snapped off and taller than Jake's head. He had his arm around Ellie, taking most of her weight as he helped her move forward against wind that felt like a wall that kept shoving them viciously, but Ellie's cry, as they stumbled on the uneven, disrupted earth that had been beneath the tree, halted their progress. They were on the edge of a large hole and the earth was crumbling.

'I'll carry you.'

'No—it's not that. *Look…*' She had to shout to make herself heard. This was worse than it had been on the beach but not simply because of the weather.

Jake pulled strands of hair away from his eyes as he turned his head to where she was pointing.

'What *is* it? A rat?'

'It's a kiwi. A brown kiwi.' He wasn't to know how rare and precious this native bird was, but Ellie was too close to tears.

'Nothing we can do. It's been squashed. We've got to get inside or it'll be us next.'

But Ellie shook her head. 'There might be a nest. We've got to check.'

Jake was looking at her as if she was crazy. Could he see the tears that were now escaping? How important this was to her?

He stared at her for just a heartbeat longer. 'You stay here. What am I looking for?'

'A burrow. An egg…or a baby…'

Jake slipped as he stepped down into the hole and there he was on his hands and knees, with a cyclone raging around them, looking to rescue a small creature that could be in danger because it was important to Ellie.

He didn't even know what a kiwi was, so it couldn't matter to him.

He was doing this for *her*.

A piece of her heart felt like it was breaking away. Ready to offer to Jake? And then he was coming back—streaked with dirt and a trickle of blood on his forehead—with a huge, creamy egg in his hands. The wind was even louder now and Jake didn't bother trying to say anything.

He put the egg inside the boot that had come off Ellie's foot, shoved it into her hands and then kept one arm firmly around her body as he pulled them forward for the short distance back to the house.

'Let me look at that ankle.'

'No. I have to look at the egg first.'

What was it with this egg?

Okay, he'd heard of kiwis. It was what New Zealanders called themselves, wasn't it? Weird enough that they identified so strongly with some flightless bird, but was it that big a deal?

Had he really kept them both out there in such dangerous conditions because she was so worried that there might be an orphaned chick or egg?

Yeah… But he'd seen the tears, hadn't he? And coming from the bravest woman he'd ever met, they had been shocking.

Now the whole episode felt ridiculous. Jake ignored Ellie as she eased the egg out of the boot and examined it. He picked up a toppled chair and unhooked the lamp so that she could show him how to light it again. As the room brightened, however, her exclamation made him stop and join her at the table.

'Look at this.'

It was a hole at one end of the egg. Something was poking out of it.

'Must have got damaged when the tree came down. Shame.' Was Ellie going to start crying again and, if so, what would he do about it this time? Hold her in his arms?

But she was smiling. 'It's called an external pip. It's *hatching*.'

'No way…'

Even more astonishing was the way Ellie picked up the egg and sniffed at the hole.

'What *are* you doing?'

'I want to know how far along it is. Sometimes you can tell by the smell whether the chick's all sweaty and in trouble.'

'How on earth do you know that?'

'My granddad was passionate about birds. We looked after a lot of them on the island. And I volunteer, these days, at a captive rearing centre that's trying to save endangered kiwi. It's run by one of my best friends, Jillian. We look after eggs and chicks and then release them back into the wild.'

Okay. It was official now. Eleanor Sutton was the most

extraordinary woman Jake had ever met. He knew he was staring and probably looking vaguely starstruck.

Ellie simply shrugged. 'I've got a thing for nature, that's all. Enough Maori blood in me to revere the land. And our *taonga*. The treasure.'

Something fell into place. That gorgeous, olive skin and the impressive mane of black hair. The fighting spirit. It wasn't surprising in the least that Ellie was in some part descended from a warrior race.

But he had to stop staring at her so he stared at the egg instead. 'How long does it take to hatch?'

'Can be days but there's no way of knowing how long it's been already… Oh, look…'

The bump that had been protruding from the egg suddenly got longer. A piece of shell broke free and then he could see the head attached to the strange-looking beak. A tiny eye amongst wet-looking feathers.

In fascinated silence, they both perched on the edge of the spindle-backed chairs and watched as the chick struggled free.

It took a while and every so often they both raised their heads to make eye contact with each other. They were both witnesses to what seemed like a small miracle in the face of such destruction going on in the outside world. The shriek of the wind and the sound of the driving rain on the tin roof punctuated by the occasional bang of a branch hitting it was no more than a background at the moment. They were sharing the birth of something new and amazing.

Jake knew that whatever else happened in his life he would remember this. Ellie and the kiwi chick. New life. This was important. Momentous, even.

It was the strangest baby bird Jake had ever seen—totally out of proportion with a small head, long beak, distended belly and huge feet.

But Ellie was rapt. Her eyes were glowing. 'Congratulations, Dad.'

Jake snorted. If he'd felt ridiculous risking his life to save an egg, it was nothing compared to feeling parental pride over its hatching. And if he was the surrogate father, that made Ellie the mother. An almost wife scenario.

He glared at Ellie and she looked away quickly.

'We need to let it rest for fifteen minutes or so and then I can pick off any bits of shell and stuff. Then we need to keep it warm.'

'We need to check your ankle. And your face is a mess.'

Ellie's eyes widened, but she reached up and touched her face and then looked at her blood-streaked fingers.

'Soon. I need…' She twisted to look at what was draped over the back of the chair she was sitting on. 'Can you spare your thermal?'

'Sure.'

Ellie twisted the dry garment into a thick rope and then curled it into a circle, leaving a hollow in the centre. Very gently, she picked up the baby kiwi and placed it carefully into the hollow.

'They have a distended abdomen because of internalised yolk. It needs support so that it doesn't end up with splayed legs.' With a touch on the tip of its beak, so light it was no more than a thought, Ellie smiled. 'It needs a name, too.'

'I don't do baby names.' Jake turned away. 'I'll heat up some water so you can wash those scratches.'

'Pēpe,' he heard Ellie say softly behind him. 'It's Maori for baby.'

With Pēpe safely on his doughnut nest inside an old plastic container and close enough to the fire to keep warm, Ellie finally hobbled to the couch to check out the extent of her own injuries. Not that it mattered how bad her ankle felt or how awful her face must look. The miracle of the egg not only being viable but hatching was enough to make this whole ordeal worthwhile.

Her ankle certainly looked impressive, though. Her foot was so swollen her toes looked ridiculously small and the bruising down her ankle and along the sides of her foot was black and purple now.

Jake was horrified. Kneeling beside the sofa, he reached out to touch her foot.

'How bad does it feel?'

Ellie simply shrugged because right then she wasn't aware of any pain. All she could focus on was the feel of Jake's hands on her skin and how gentle they were as he traced the swelling and touched the tips of her toes.

'Can you feel that?'

Oh, yeah…

'Mmm. I've still got circulation.'

'Can you wriggle your toes?'

Yes. Ellie could.

'Can you press down against my hand?' He was cradling her foot on his fingers now.

Ellie actually grinned. 'Yes, Doctor. Oh… *Ouch.*' But she was still smiling. 'I'm sure it's only a sprain. I just need to strap it up again and rest it for a bit.'

'I'll strap it up.' Jake was rolling the dirty bandage he had helped her remove. 'Don't suppose you've got a dry one of these somewhere?'

'Hang it by the fire for a while. I won't try and walk until I've got my ankle wrapped up again.'

'I'll get the water. You can wash those scratches.'

Ellie nodded, but she was finally noticing how scratched Jake was himself, especially his hands. How hard had he worked to rescue her? And then she'd made him do more by sending him under the tree roots to look for the dead kiwi's nest.

How magic had it been, seeing the wonder of the chick hatching reflected in Jake's eyes every time she'd been able to look away from what they'd been watching?

And how gentle had he been in checking out her injuries?

Not that she was ready to put her trust in a man, but imagine if you *could* trust someone like Jake? So strong. Protective. Caring. Gentle…

So incredibly *male*…

She reached out to touch his arm as he got to his feet. 'I…I couldn't have got out of there by myself. And Pēpe would have died. Thank you…'

Was it intentional, the way he kept moving…escaping her touch? He looked down at her again and his mouth was twisted into a crooked smile.

A very endearing smile.

'Guess that makes us even, then,' he said gruffly. 'Equal partners?'

'Yeah…' Ellie was still caught by that smile. By the intensity of those dark eyes. Beneath all that hair, Jake Logan was an extraordinarily good-looking man.

He looked away first. 'So maybe next time you'll listen to me when I say something's dangerous.'

'Maybe…'

Outside, the storm still raged, but Ellie felt safe again.

More than safe. She felt cared for. By someone who had as much to give as she did. An ideal partner. There weren't many men who could match Ellie Sutton in terms of courage and resourcefulness. They had a lot in common, didn't they? Not only a spirit of adventure and the fortitude to deal with adversity but they'd both been burned by love. Not that Jake had shared any personal details about the marriage that didn't exist any longer, but that didn't break a sense of connection that only strengthened as the long day wore on.

Frequent checking of the baby bird created a shared pleasure that he seemed to be doing well.

'He's so fluffy now that he's dry,' Jake commented, crouched beside the container and staring into it intently.

'They're unusual feathers,' Ellie told him. 'Kiwis don't need to fly so they're more for warmth. More like hair than feathers.'

'How long until he can go back to the wild?'

'I'll take him to the centre back in Auckland. Jillian will want to put him in a brooder unit for a few weeks and, if he's healthy enough, he'll only need a few more weeks in a quarantine period. They can put a transponder on him and hopefully I can bring him back here. Or, even better, I might be able to release him on Half Moon Island. Grandpa would have been thrilled by that.'

'I'd love to see that. If I'm still in the country.'

Ellie wasn't sure how to respond to that. Give him her phone number? Ask him for his? Admit that she'd be keen to see him again? The ramifications were alarming.

'I'll have to see if it's even possible,' she said cautiously. 'There's lots of regulations.'

'Of course.'

Jake's expert bandaging of her ankle was something else that bound them into more of a team.

'I couldn't have done that better myself. You're not actually a doctor, are you? Or a medic?'

'I've learned a bit of first aid in my time. What with the army and stuff.'

So she'd been right. The limp was probably a legacy of being a soldier.

'Afghanistan?'

'Yep. A long time ago.'

And his tone told her that he still didn't want to talk about anything personal. Ellie got that. What was harder to get her head around was the intense curiosity she was developing. She had so many questions she wanted to ask. So much she wanted to know about this man. And it was more than mere curiosity, if she was honest with herself. This felt more like longing.

A longing to let go?

To trust again?

Maybe he wouldn't have to warn her about something dangerous.

Perhaps he *was* that something.

They slept for a while in the afternoon and by the time they woke it was obvious that the storm had eased considerably. There wasn't much daylight left, though, so perhaps they would be here for another night.

Ellie eased her legs off the couch as Jake stood up. They needed some more firewood if they had a second night to get through and it was past time to check on Pēpe again. Her first attempt to get to her feet failed, however, and she sat back down with a rush.

'Here...' Jake offered her a hand. 'Take it easy, though. That foot won't want much weight on it.'

He held out his other hand as Ellie started to rise and, a heartbeat later, she found herself on her feet, holding both Jake's hands.

And he wasn't letting go.

Ellie certainly couldn't let go first. For one thing her hands were encased by his and for another her body simply wouldn't cooperate. She couldn't even look away from his face. From a gaze that was holding hers with a look that made the rest the world cease to exist. Everything seemed to coalesce. Surviving the rescue, finding their way to shelter, being rescued herself and the bond that had grown and grown today, thanks to Jake's heroism in saving the egg. So many, powerful emotions.

His face was so close. She only had to lean a little and tilt her face up and her lips would meet his.

And, dear Lord…she could feel it happening and no alarm bells were going to halt the process, no matter how loudly they tried to sound.

She was so close now she could feel his breath on her lips and her eyes were drifting shut in anticipation of a kiss she wanted more than anything she could remember wanting in her life.

The sharp crackle of static from behind made her jump.

'Medic One, do you read? Ellie…are you there?'

CHAPTER SIX

A MOMENT HAD never been broken so decisively.

Jake froze. Ellie dived for the radio.

'Medic One receiving. Mike, is that you?'

Another crackle of static and Ellie's heart sank. Maybe she could receive but not transmit.

'...on our way. Can you...on the beach in twenty...?'

Ellie was used to filling in gaps in broken messages. *'Yes.'* Radio protocol was forgotten. 'We'll be there.' Aware of the intense focus of Jake, who was still standing as still as a stone, Ellie pushed the transmitting button again and held it down. 'Mike? Any news on...on the other man in the life raft?'

She held her breath through another burst of static. What if there was no news or—worse—bad news? Jake would be devastated and she would be the one who'd been the bearer of the news. He might shoot the messenger and she would never get as close to him again as she had a moment ago.

A curious wash of something like grief came from nowhere. Ellie could actually feel the sting of tears behind her eyes.

'...fine...' The unexpected word burst through the static. 'Washed onto island...taken to... Be in Auckland by the time you... Ellie, have you any idea who...?'

It didn't matter that the rest of the message was lost. Or

that Ellie still had tears in her eyes as she turned to Jake. He wouldn't notice anyway. She could see that he was shaking and he had a hand shielding his eyes as though he didn't want anyone to see whatever overwhelming emotion he was experiencing.

If she went to him and put her arms around him he would probably kiss her, Ellie realised. But would it be only because he needed an outlet for the joyous relief he was struggling to control?

But when he dropped his hand, his face looked haggard. 'I can't believe it,' he said hoarsely. 'I *won't* believe it…not until I see Ben again.'

'Let's move, then.' The switch of professionalism was easy to flick. Could still provide protection, even. Ellie didn't have time to indulge in any personal reactions. 'We need to change our clothes, put the fire out and get ourselves—and Pēpe—down to the beach. There's not enough daylight left to muck the crew around.'

The media were waiting.

No surprises there. It was enough of a story to have an elite yacht race decimated by the worst storm in decades and they had probably been earning their keep for the last couple of days editing and broadcasting film of dramatic rescues, interviews with survivors and heart-wrenching intrusions on the families of those killed or missing.

What a bonus to have an A-list celebrity as one of the survivors. The paparazzi would be fighting for the best spot to get a photograph that would earn big money. Any one of his favoured charities could be in for an enormous windfall when he chose the best offer for magazine coverage. And not only was Jake a survivor, there was a juicy glimpse into his family life thrown in. Coverage of the twin brother who'd successfully evaded any media spotlight until now because he hated the whole industry so much, thanks to what it had done to their mother. Their childhood.

The story would just keep growing legs, wouldn't it? A savvy journalist could delve into their background and rake over their father's reputation as an utterly ruthless businessman. Their mother's degeneration into reliance on prescription medication and alcohol, which had been her ultimate downfall.

Or had it?

He had to get to Ben. To talk to him.

The shouting from the gathered crowd as the helicopter landed took over from the noise of the slowing rotors as the doors were opened.

'Jake…'

'Mr Logan… This way…'

'Dr Jon… Code One…'

Good grief. Did someone think he would respond to the name of a character he played instead of his real name? It wasn't so stupid, though, was it? He almost turned towards the incessant flash of camera lights in that direction. Instead, he looked back to where Ellie was being helped from the helicopter. She was still clutching the container that held the baby kiwi and seemed to be arguing with her colleague over whether she was fit to walk on that ankle. Jake felt his lips twitching and suppressed a smile. Good luck to someone who wanted to make Ellie do something she didn't want to do.

But then she looked up and saw the media. She had to be hearing all the yelling of his name. She really hadn't had any idea of who he was, had she? No wonder she was looking so bewildered. The man beside her was grinning. He raised an arm to wave at the photographers and television crews. And then he was saying something to Ellie and she turned her head to stare at *him*.

She looked horrified.

Betrayed, even.

There was nothing he could do about it. People from his film production crew were here, too. The director and his PR manager were coming towards him and there was a black limousine with tinted windows waiting with its doors open on this side of the fence that was keeping the media at a respectable distance. An ambulance, with its back doors also open, was parked near the limousine.

'Jake… *Mate*…I can't tell you how good it is to see you. Let's get you to hospital for a check-up.'

'Don't need it,' Jake said.

'We do,' the director insisted. 'Insurance protocol.'

'Do you know where my brother is?'

'No. We do know he's okay, though. You can see him as soon as you've been given the all-clear.'

Ellie and her fellow paramedic were close now. The man had his arm around Ellie, supporting her as she limped. He couldn't hold her gaze. She seemed to lean into her companion, looking up as he spoke to them.

'Survivors have all been taken to The Cloud. Big building down at the Viaduct on the waterfront,' he told Jake. 'There's a medical team there and it's not far from the hospital if they decide you need attention. That's where we're taking Ellie—to the hospital.'

He kept moving, steering Ellie towards the ambulance. For a crazy moment Jake almost followed them—just to stay close to Ellie for a little longer. Who knew when or even if they would ever see each other again? He wanted…

He didn't know what he wanted. To try and explain why he hadn't told her who he was? To try and figure out if this guy she worked with was more than a colleague?

No. He did know what he wanted. What he had to do first.

'Take me to this cloud building,' he ordered his director. 'I'll do whatever I have to but not until I've seen Ben.'

'The media will be all over you.'

'I'll cope.'

'We've got a film crew tailing us.' Mike peered through the small windows at the back of the ambulance. 'You're famous, El.'

'I was just doing my job.' Ellie sat back on the stretcher, letting her head rest on the pillows. She closed her eyes, her breath escaping in a ragged sigh. 'I hope Dave's being careful, taking Pēpe to the centre.'

'He will be. He loves a challenge that's a bit different. You want some pain relief?'

'No. I'm fine.' Apart from feeling gutted without having any reasonable grounds.

The only sound for a moment was the rumble of the truck's engine.

'Did you really have no idea who he was?'

Her eyes snapped open. 'How could I? He didn't *tell* me.'

'Not even his name?'

'Well…yeah. He told me his name. It was just a name.'

Mike snorted. 'You've just spent more than twenty-four hours holed up with one of the most eligible males in the universe. Most girls would kill for an opportunity like that.

It was Ellie's turn to snort.

'*ER* used to be your favourite TV show. You must remember that French surgeon. What was his name? Pierre or something. And then the *Stitch in Time* series? Where that modern doctor keeps going through that portal and saving lives that change the course of history?'

Ellie shook her head. She hadn't seen it. And it had been

years since *ER* had been her entertainment fix. Jake would have been ten years younger and wouldn't have been disguised by far too much hair. She never knew the real names of actors anyway—she had enough trouble remembering the names of the characters they portrayed. But it made a horrible kind of sense.

No wonder Jake could act like a doctor. Gentle and caring and skillful. He'd learned how to pretend to *be* one, hadn't he?

'That's what he was coming to New Zealand for. To film the last bits of the movie they're making from the series. You wouldn't believe the coverage the E channel's been giving this disaster thanks to him being in it. And did you know that the other guy in the life raft was his brother? Not just a brother but his *twin?*'

'Yes. I did know that.'

Everybody would know that. Was that why Jake had revealed that much? And was the reason he'd been so shuttered about anything else personal because he knew it would be gold for the waiting media and he didn't trust her not to go and spill the beans?

The television crew had beaten the ambulance to the hospital. They were waiting for Ellie to come out of the back. A couple of photographers were there as well.

'Ms Sutton…how are you feeling?'

'What can you tell us about Jake Logan? Is he coming here as well?'

'You saved his life… How does he feel about that?'

'Ellie—over here. Slow down… We just need one shot.'

Ellie ducked her head behind Mike's arm. 'For heaven's sake,' she muttered. 'Just get me inside.'

The Cloud was an extraordinary building right on the waterfront of Auckland's harbour. Designed to accommodate up to five thousand people, it was long and low with an undulating white roof that had given it the unusual name. A perfect space to be catering for the huge numbers of people.

The Ultraswift-Round-the-World yacht race had come to a temporary halt due to Cyclone Lila. The boats that had made it safely to Auckland were all moored nearby and their crews were using The Cloud as their base as they had repairs done on their yachts and waited for the weather to settle. Families of those injured or still missing were here as well, and there were almost as many reporters as the race officials, crews and their supporters.

Jake was hustled through the crowd and allowed to ignore the press of attention. He was taken to a mezzanine level at the far end of the building that had been roped off to allow only authorised personnel. Up the stairs and in a private area of a large bar, Ben was waiting.

He had apparently refused to allow their reunion to be anything other than completely private and, as the two men held each other in a grip powerful enough to prevent a breath being taken and Jake felt the trickle of tears on his face, he had never been more thankful that the moment wasn't going to be shared with the world.

It was a long time before they broke apart enough to stare intently at each other.

'I thought I'd lost you.'

'Me, too.'

'I couldn't believe it. I *didn't* believe it until now. Are you okay?'

'Pretty good. Got a bit banged up and dislocated my knee. I'll be on crutches for a week or two. And I wouldn't mind sitting down again.'

There were comfortable chairs here. A small table had been provided with a cushion on it for Ben to keep his leg supported. A pair of elbow crutches lay on the floor beside the table. Apart from the splint on his knee, though, Ben didn't seem to have suffered a major injury.

'How did you do it? What happened after I got rescued? It felt like the worst moment in my life when I found out that the weather had got so bad they couldn't even *try* to get back to rescue you.'

Ben looked about as haggard as Jake was feeling. He was nodding and it looked as if he was swallowing hard before he could answer. 'And the worst moment of mine was thinking I'd never see you again.'

'So what happened?'

'Bit of a blur. Didn't think I was going to make it. Thought I was dead until I found myself being dragged up a beach.'

'Someone *found* you?'

'Wouldn't be here if they hadn't. And it wasn't just someone. It was a nurse who goes by the name of Smash 'em Mary.'

Jake had to grin. 'Sounds formidable.'

Something flickered in Ben's eyes but was gone before Jake could analyse it. 'She saved my life,' was all he said. 'And she was a nurse. If she hadn't put my knee back I'd be a lot worse off than I am now.'

'You got saved by a nurse.' Jake shook his head. 'And I got saved by a paramedic. A *girl* paramedic.'

Except that 'girl' was totally the wrong word. Courageous, determined...beautiful...Eleanor Sutton was a powerful woman. Compelling. And Jake was already...*missing* her? Not that he could begin to explain to Ben what had happened in the hours they'd been apart. It would have to wait until they had more time. Until Jake had had a chance to get his own head around what may well have been a life-changing incident. Best to ignore it for the moment.

'What happens now?'

'Guess I'll get the first flight I can back to the States. You?'

'I'll get on with what I was coming here for in the first place. There's a deadline on getting this film into the can.'

Ben nodded. 'We both need to get back into it. Put this disaster behind us.'

'Any word on *Rita*?'

'Doubt they'll even find any wreckage. She's gone.'

Just like her namesake. Rita Marlene. Their mother.

Jake closed his eyes and took a deep breath. 'What you said, Ben…it's not true. Mom didn't kill herself. It was an accident. That was the coroner's verdict.'

Ben was silent.

'It's *not* true,' Jake insisted. '*Is* it?'

'I wouldn't have said it if it wasn't true.'

'How do you know? Did you hide something? Like a *note?*'

Ben shook his head.

'So how do you know?' Jake's voice rose. 'You have to tell me. I've got a right to know.'

'I can't.'

'Can't…or *won't?*'

'Jake…' Ben held up his hands—a pleading gesture. 'Let it go. Please. It's so long ago it doesn't make any difference now.'

'Are you *kidding?* You can't say something like that and just leave it. If you've got some evidence and you've been hiding it all these years, you've been *lying* to me.'

'I haven't got any evidence. I just…*know*.'

'Jake?' It was his PR manager, Kirsty, who approached the men in their corner of this big space. 'Sorry to break in on the family reunion but we've got all the major TV networks queued up downstairs to talk to you. Adam's getting an ulcer, waiting for you to get a proper medical clearance. How long do you think you'll be?'

Jake glared at Ben. The joy of seeing his brother safe was being undermined by anger at not getting the answers he needed.

And there was fear there, too. Ben was the only person in the world he'd ever had complete faith in. Absolute trust.

He was looking completely shattered now. Instead of celebrating their joint survival, Jake had turned it into a confrontation that was something he'd never anticipated between them. Was he even ready to hear the truth?

And now they were being interrupted by the lifestyle that Ben deplored. The pursuit of fame that had always seemed more important to their mother than they had been. Play-acting. Sidestepping reality.

He could hear an echo of Ellie's voice in his head.

How does avoiding reality help exactly?

Maybe it didn't help but it was the only protection Jake knew.

Ben seemed to sense his train of thought. The softening in his eyes suggested that he understood. He gripped his brother's shoulder.

'Go, Jake. It's what you do. Your public needs you. *You* need them. We'll talk soon.' He even summoned a cheeky grin. 'And, hey…no amount of money could buy this kind of PR for the movie. You may as well milk it.'

'Amen,' said Kirsty. 'Come on, Jake. Pretty please… We'll set up a press conference so you only have to do it once. And while we're doing that, you can let the doctors check you out properly.'

X-rays had revealed no broken bones, but the ligament damage to Ellie's ankle meant that she needed a plaster cast for a couple of weeks at least. And complete rest. She was off active duty on the helicopter crew for the foreseeable future.

'I'm going to be bored out of my skull,' Ellie informed Mike, who had come back to hear the verdict and take her home.

'They'll find some light duties for you on base for a while.'

'Mmm.' Maybe fate was stepping in here, forcing her to take some time out and think about her future. Did she really want to give up on the part of her career that had meant so much to her for so long?

Right now, all Ellie wanted to do was to get home and eat something that hadn't come out of an ancient can. To call Jillian at the bird centre and get more information than Dave had passed on to Mike about the condition of the rescued baby kiwi. To sink into her own bed and sleep. A week or so should do the trick.

There was a slight problem with the plan, however.

'Where's my other boot?'

'You can't wear it with your foot in a cast.'

'No, but it had all the loose stuff from my pockets in it. I had to find a way to carry it all in a bit of a rush. My keys are in there.'

'You can't drive either.'

'My house key is on the same ring.'

'Haven't you got a spare?'

Ellie was too tired to be reasonable. 'I want my boot.'

'I'll ring the base. It might still be in the chopper.'

He ended his phone call a short time later. 'Dave reckons it went with some other clothing—to The Cloud.'

Ellie sighed. There had been a bundle of clothing. Jake had changed out of the horrendous trackpants and put his jeans back on, but either he'd run out of time or had become attached to his black-and-red-checked shirt because he had only put his coat on top and bundled his other belongings under an arm.

'Fine. That's on the way home, if you don't mind a quick detour.'

Mike's face lit up. 'And get a chance to rub shoulders with the rich and famous again? See you become world famous as the woman who rescued Jake Logan? I don't mind at all.'

'There'll be no rubbing shoulders,' Ellie warned. 'We get my boot and get out. I'm not in any mood to get interviewed.'

She had no intention of talking to Jake if she could avoid it. The shock of learning who he really was had more than one aspect that was making her cringe.

She'd made a joke about his limp. Ordered him to make himself useful. And had she really dismissed his whole career by suggesting that he might be a male *model?*

He hadn't enlightened her, though, had he?

And you didn't have to lie outright to be dishonest. You could lie by omission.

Arriving at their destination wearing their bright red flight-suits and with Ellie hopping on crutches should have attracted attention, but instead they slipped in virtually unnoticed. Everybody was crowded around an area that had been set up with a long table in front of a big screen.

Images of yachts and rescue scenes were providing a backdrop to a press conference. Jake sat centre stage, flanked by the man who'd met him at the helipad and others who were wearing lanyards and looked like race officials. Just under the mezzanine level of the building, there were people leaning over the balcony to watch as well and Ellie noticed she wasn't the only person on crutches here.

Jake's voice was clear and loud, not only because of the

lapel mike he was wearing but due to the rapt silence of an audience that was hanging on every word.

'…we thought that was it. And then we saw the chopper with the crewman on the end of the winch. Or should I say crewwoman?' Jake's headshake was slow and incredulous. 'I can't speak highly enough of the courage and skill of the New Zealand helicopter rescue service. You guys should be very, very proud of yourselves.'

Mike nudged Ellie, but she was heading purposefully towards someone on the edge of the crowd at the very front. A woman with blond hair and high heels, who was holding a clipboard. She'd been at the helipad with the other people who'd been waiting to whisk Jake off in that ridiculous limousine. Maybe she'd know where her boot was.

'Oh…you must be Ellie.' The woman's smile was very wide. 'I'm Kirsty. This is great. Can we get a shot of you and Jake together after this interview? I understand it was you that rescued Jake? That it was *your* beach house you used as shelter? And did you guys really watch a kiwi hatching? That's so *awesome*…'

Someone from the floor was asking a question about whether the race organisers were at fault for not postponing this leg of the race. One of the officials started explaining the cyclone's erratic path. A video clip of a weather map was now playing on the big screen.

Ellie looked at Kirsty's perfect hair and makeup. She might have been able to brush out the tangled mess of her own hair at the hospital and rebraid it but it was still filthy. And while the scratches and bruises on her face had been well cleaned, she didn't have a scrap of any makeup on to soften the effect.

'No,' she told Kirsty firmly. 'I look like I've been dragged through a hedge backwards.' It wasn't far from the truth, was it? If Jake had told people about Pēpe, maybe he'd also told them about saving her life by getting her out from under that tree? Wouldn't the media love that—to find that a movie star had morphed into a real live hero? But it felt like something private was being exploited.

'And I'm exhausted,' she added. 'I just want to find my boot and get home.'

'I had it sent to the front reception desk. I didn't know that you'd be coming to collect it in person. Are you sure I can't change your mind about a photo? Or a quick interview? There's a lot of people here who are super-keen to talk to you.'

The need for officials to deflect blame for the disaster the yacht race had become was still going on. Not needing to answer any questions for the moment, Jake was looking around the room. Ellie watched, using it as an excuse to ignore Kirsty's request even though she knew that she had to be very obvious, standing here on the edge of the crowd, not far from the end of the long table. Wearing bright red.

She was prepared for him to notice her.

What she wasn't prepared for was the effect of the eye contact.

For just a heartbeat, he held her gaze. Clung to it as though seeing her again was a huge relief. As if he'd been afraid of never seeing her again?

For just that infinitesimal fraction of time it felt like that moment when Ellie had known they were going to kiss. That the connection was far too strong to resist.

But then it was gone. So fast she could believe she had imagined it.

And Jake was interrupting the race official.

'There's no point in trying to blame anyone,' he said smoothly. 'It happened. Yacht racing is a risky business. I'd like to take this opportunity to say how devastated we all are that lives have been lost. And how incredibly grateful both my brother and myself are for being rescued. There's one person in particular that I will be grateful to for the rest of my life.'

'Who's that?' someone yelled.

Jake was smiling now. He stretched out a hand. 'Paramedic Eleanor Sutton. My real life heroine.'

Kirsty beamed, stepping aside slightly to allow Ellie to be seen more clearly.

Ellie cringed as cameras swung in her direction.

'They want you to join them.' Kirsty sounded excited now. 'Do you need some help?'

'No.' The word came out through gritted teeth. Jake had caught her gaze again as he'd stretched out that hand as an invitation to share his fame.

She must have imagined that connection she'd felt because it certainly wasn't there this time. This was Jake Logan the movie star looking at her and he wasn't the man she had rescued or shared the miracle of watching new life emerge with.

Couldn't anyone else see that he was only showing what he wanted the world to see?

That that warm smile and the over-the-top praise wasn't *real?*

She didn't know this man.

And she didn't want to. She had personal experience of a man who could make others believe whatever he wanted. An experience she would never repeat, thank you very much.

With nothing more than a dismissive shake of her head for Kirsty's benefit, Ellie turned and started moving.

She had to get out of there.

CHAPTER SEVEN

In the end, it was the rescue base manager, Gavin Smith, who gave the media at least some of what they wanted, providing details of the horrific day from the viewpoint of the emergency services and fielding some awkward questions from journalists.

'Is it normal practice to keep a victim on the end of a winch line like that? Isn't it incredibly dangerous?'

'The pros and cons of any emergency situation are something our crews are trained to weigh up. The chopper was already fully loaded. The only way to get the men out of the life raft was to try and transfer them to the closest land.'

'So why didn't they go back for Jacob Logan's brother?'

'Not only had weather conditions worsened, the condition of a patient on board was also critical. The risk to everybody involved was simply too great.'

'So they just got abandoned?'

'They weren't abandoned.' The base manager stayed perfectly calm. 'By a stroke of luck, the paramedic who was on the winch knew the area well. She knew that they could find shelter.'

'Why won't Eleanor Sutton talk to the media? Has she been told not to? What went on that needs to be kept so private?'

Gavin's bland expression made the question lose any

significance. 'As far as I'm concerned, there's nothing to tell. Our crew did their job under exceptionally trying circumstances. Successfully, I might add. If one of them chooses not to be in the public eye for doing that job, I'm more than happy to respect that. Perhaps you should too.'

It didn't appear that they were going to.

The phone had been ringing from the moment Ellie had got home. The offers to buy her story were starting to get ridiculous. Thousands of dollars turned into tens of thousands as the days passed and she continued to refuse an interview or photographs.

Maybe Jake had had good reason to keep so much personal information to himself. He wasn't to know that she was financially secure in a mortgage-free house she had inherited from her parents. Or that she'd been earning good money for years with no dependants to share it with. How many people would be tempted by an offer of such a windfall?

And wouldn't the gossip magazines love an account of what now seemed like a personal revelation about how Jake Logan saw movies as a means of coping with adverse life events?

About how he didn't see role-playing as being fake but as a chance to practise being the best version of himself he could be?

A tiny insight into how his mind worked, maybe, but it would be gold for these hungry journalists.

It was gold for Ellie, too. A small nugget that she had every intention of keeping entirely to herself, although she wasn't sure why it seemed so important. She'd probably never see him again so why should it matter what he thought of her?

Ellie had always been too trusting, and she had always

been utterly trustworthy herself. Deception was anathema to her. Okay, she'd been burnt too badly to ever be as trusting again, but she'd never sink to that level.

She was trustworthy.

If Jake had inadvertently trusted her with even the tiniest piece of something personal and she kept that information safe, at least he would know that her integrity was intact. That she could be trusted.

And that gave her the moral high ground, didn't it? Jake might wrap it up in words that made it sound almost acceptable, but acting was a form of deception. Fine for movies when people knew that the people on screen were only characters, but he'd proved he could do it in real life, too, with that polished performance for the media.

You'd never know whether he was being honest or acting.

Did he even know himself?

In the absence of any new material, magazines were using what they could find, and to her horror the picture that appeared all over the internet, newspapers and magazines was one that had been taken just after they'd landed. When she'd seen the media falling all over Jake and Mike had been telling her who he actually was. There was no mistaking the confusion and sense of betrayal on her face. Others were passing it off as no more than a bad photo and her expression was probably due to the pain of her injured ankle, but Ellie knew the truth. She now had a permanent reminder of exactly how she'd felt in learning Jake's real identity.

She had been deceived.

Again.

It shouldn't have come as such a surprise. Given her experience, it should be a lot easier to deal with than last time but, somehow, this was harder. Because she'd got to a point where she'd *wanted* to trust Jake?

For the first time since the devastating betrayal of a man she'd been about to marry, Ellie had been able to see that it might be possible to fall in love again.

To trust.

Such a hard-won step forward and she'd been shoved backwards again with what felt like a cruel blow.

Whatever. She had no choice but to deal with it and get on with her life.

The extent of the battering her body had taken and the exhaustion of both the rescue and its aftermath cushioned Ellie for several days, but then she began to feel like a prisoner in her own home.

In solitary confinement.

She was totally used to living on her own. Why did she suddenly feel so lonely?

The big windows of her living area had a stunning view of the beach and the distinctive shape of Rangitoto Island—an ancient volcano. Her father's telescope still had its position at one side of the French doors that led out to the balcony and Ellie had spent a lot of time watching the activity on the stretch of water that divided Auckland harbour from the open sea. It seemed like a good way to reconnect to her own life.

To forget about Jake Logan?

Except that the bleak landscape of Rangitoto made her think about the lush rainforest cover of Half Moon Island and long to see it again. The barrier that had been there ever since her parents had been tragically killed had been forced open. It wasn't just memories of her time with Jake that were haunting Ellie now. They were competing with memories of her parents and her beloved grandfather. Happy times in a place that was a part of her soul. People that were missing from her life and had taken such big pieces of her along with them.

Everyone knew that nothing was for ever but why had she had to lose every person she had ever truly loved?

No wonder she was feeling lonely.

The usual traffic of container ships, naval vessels and ferries had been noticeably interrupted by the fleet of racing yachts when the Ultraswift-Round-the-World race was started again a few days after the cyclone and by then Ellie had to accept that it was not going to be so easy to get Jake out of her head.

It was bad enough getting reports of the way he was still touching her real life.

The helicopter rescue trust had received an impressive donation that was labelled as anonymous but it was obvious it had come from one—or both—of the Logan brothers.

Jillian, at the bird-rearing centre, was almost speechless at the size of the donation the kiwi trust had received within days of Pēpe's arrival.

'I know it's anonymous,' she told Ellie, 'but it's a bit of coincidence, wouldn't you say?'

'Lots of people care about saving kiwis. Pēpe's famous now. He was on the news.'

'Not many people can afford to care to the tune of hundreds of thousands of dollars.'

'*That* much? Phew…' Ellie closed her eyes but it didn't shut out the pictures appearing in her head. If anything, it made them clearer. The way Jake had looked as they'd watched the baby bird hatching. The way he'd looked at *her* as they'd shared that unforgettable experience.

'I did an internet search on him,' Jillian confessed. 'He's seriously hot, isn't he?'

'Bit hairy for me.'

'Have a look at some of the older photos, then, where he's clean shaven. Like back in the day when he was on *ER*. Oh, *my…*'

Ellie had to laugh. It sounded like Jillian, who was in her early sixties and had several grandchildren, was busy fanning herself.

'Amazing he's still single,' Jillian continued. 'Or maybe not. That wife of his really did a number on him, didn't she?'

'I wouldn't know. I don't read that stuff and we didn't talk about anything personal.'

They'd come close, though, hadn't they? She could still hear the bitterness in Jake's voice when he'd answered her query about him being married.

Not anymore.

And she'd wanted to find out. It had been a personal challenge not to search the internet and devour every piece of information she could find. The curiosity was overpowering now.

'What did she do?'

'Only went and got herself up the duff by the leading man on her first movie. A part she only got because of her connection to Jake.'

'Oh…' Ellie was stunned.

How could any woman be that *stupid?* If she'd wanted a baby she couldn't have picked a better father than Jake. Impossible not to remember how protective he'd been in trying to stop her going out into that storm. The strength he'd shown in rescuing her. How gentle he'd been in that impressive examination of her injured ankle.

'And then she dropped the bombshell online so that the whole world knew before he did.'

'That's horrible,' Ellie said, but she was backing away fast from the onslaught of emotions she didn't want to try and handle. 'Jill—I've got to go, but it's great to know how well Pēpe's doing. I'll call you again soon.'

'Okay. Speaking of calling, has *he* called you?'

'No. Why would he?' To thank her again, perhaps? With the kind of polished speech he'd given the media? What if he offered *her* money as a gesture of gratitude—or apology?

'Someone from the film company rang to ask after Pēpe the other day. A woman called Kristy or something.'

'Kirsty?'

'That's it. She asked for your phone number. Said they'd tried to get it from your work, but they wouldn't hand out personal information. Anyway, I gave her your mobile number. Hope you don't mind.'

'My phone got wrecked. I haven't got around to replacing it yet.'

'Maybe you should get a new one. And talk to him if he rings. You've got a lot in common when you come to think about it.'

'Oh…right. Like he's a famous movie star and I'm a very ordinary mortal?'

'You're on the same page as far as your love lives go.'

Ellie's snort of laughter was not amused. 'Hardly. Guess I can be grateful that it was only my friends who found out how narrowly I escaped a bigamous marriage. Far more humiliating to have the whole world devouring every detail of your betrayal.'

She didn't want to talk about Michael and, this time, she was more successful in pleading a need to end the call. Having made a note to remind herself to sort out a new phone the next day, Ellie stared at the piece of paper and then screwed it up.

What would happen if her number worked again? Would she be waiting for it to ring? Be picking it up every five minutes to see if she'd received a message? Be disappointed if it rang and it wasn't Jake on the other end?

It would be better not to risk it. In fact, when she got a new phone she'd ask for a new number as well. It would be best to forget about Jacob Logan and the way he'd managed to stir up feelings that she'd thought she was immune to. Jake needed to be tucked into the past and largely forgotten. As Michael had been.

But everything conspired to remind her, even in the seclusion of her own home. Trying to put any weight on her foot would create a throb of pain that took her back to that awful moment of finding she had been unable to walk on the beach when they'd desperately needed to find the beach house. When Jake had scooped her up into his arms and carried her to safety.

Opening her pantry to look for something to eat, the sight of canned food would take her back to that extraordinary meal by the fire.

Just needing to go to the bathroom would remind her of that terrifying moment of the tree coming down. Of Jake screaming her name as if it would be the worst thing in the world if something bad had happened to her.

The nights were even worse. There was no protection to be found from the moments that she was forced to relive in her dreams. Helping Jake take his clothes off or that almost-kiss just before that radio message had come in was always the catalyst but her unconscious mind wouldn't leave it alone. The fantasy of what could have happened if they hadn't been so uncomfortable with the situation or interrupted was played out in glorious Technicolor with the added dimension of sensations Ellie had never realised could be so powerful. More than once, she woke to find her body still pulsing with a release that left…a kind of shame in its wake.

Here she was, a thirty-two-year-old woman, mooning after a celebrity like some starstruck teenager.

It had to end.

Ellie rang her boss. 'Smithie? I'm going nuts here. I might be stuck on the ground but I really need some work to do. Can we talk?'

Jake thought he looked more like a pirate than a nineteenth-century deckhand but that was okay. Fun, even. The baggy trousers weren't as bad as those old trackpants Ellie had given him to wear and they were tucked neatly into black leather boots that folded down at the top. The white shirt with its wide collar, laced opening and generous sleeves was a bit girlie but the waistcoat hid part of it and with some artfully applied smudges of grime and a rip or two it was quite acceptable.

He eyed himself in the mirror as the makeup technician started on his hair. Ellie certainly wouldn't think he was wearing his hair like this for a photo shoot as a male model, would she?

'What is that stuff?'

'Basically grease. We need that nice, dirty, dreadlocked vibe.'

'At least the bandanna hides most of it. Have to say I can't wait to get a proper haircut again.'

The makeup girl smiled at his reflection. 'I dunno… it kinda suits you. And I'm getting so used to it I almost didn't recognise you in that new article that's out.'

'Another article?' There'd been so many of them in the last few weeks that Jake didn't bother to look unless Kirsty insisted. He should be delighted that Ellie wasn't prepared to reveal anything about herself or her time with him, but perversely it was like a hurt silence that told him he'd done something wrong.

Because he hadn't trusted her?

'One of the local women's magazines. It's over there, by the wigs.'

He shouldn't have opened it. Why did they keep using that dreadful photograph of Ellie? The one where she'd clearly been told who it was that she'd rescued. When she'd realised that he had been less than honest with her. Where she looked not only as if she was in pain and exhausted but that she'd been betrayed somehow.

He'd wanted to try and explain. Of course he had. But she'd publicly turned her back on his invitation to share that press conference and she'd been unreachable ever since. Not that he'd been able to visit the rescue base where she worked in person. Or the bird sanctuary place that the baby kiwi had been taken to, but Kirsty had managed to find a phone number and he'd tried that repeatedly, only to get the message that the phone was either out of range or turned off.

How much clearer did Ellie have to make it that she didn't want anything more to do with him?

He should be over it by now. Well into the full-on work that was his career on set. They were on deadline here, with a release timed for the summer holiday season in the United States and a lot of editing, as well as special effects, that would have to be done before then. With practised focus, Jake dropped the magazine and stepped into the dark of predawn outside the caravan to begin his new day.

A good percentage of the movie was already in the can. The opening scenes with him being a surgeon with a tension-racked relationship in a high-paced American hospital before he stepped into the portal, and the ending when he was back there and trying to get to grips with normal life and able to repair the relationship thanks to what he'd faced centuries ago. There'd been scenes shot in London, too, where he'd started to grow his hair and beard to look the part as he got swept into employment on an immigrant ship.

They'd had to come to New Zealand to film the guts of the story, though, with the premise being that his medical knowledge would save the life of a woman who would go on to raise a child who would change history. A square-rigged sailing ship that was going to be wrecked just off the coast of the north island. A life-and-death struggle for survival in the wild land of a new colony. A love story that could never be consummated because that would have altered history, but the lessons learned meant that the real-time love story would come right.

Too ironic, really, given the experience Jake had been through before arriving on set. The media had jumped on that.

'How does it feel, having to be on a ship, given your recent brush with death?'

'Safe,' Jake had told them smoothly. 'Everything that happens here is carefully controlled. I doubt that we'll be doing any scenes at sea if there's another cyclone forecast.'

There was medical cover, too, in case anything untoward happened. An ambulance was always parked nearby, manned by volunteer officers from the nearest local town of Whitianga on the Coromandel Peninsula. One of them was a young woman, but thankfully she looked nothing like Ellie. It was bad enough having the emergency vehicle on site, reminding him every time of the unfortunate way they'd parted.

It was just as well the female lead didn't look anything like Ellie either. Amber was petite and redheaded, with skin so pale it was almost transparent. And her eyes were green, not that dark, chocolaty brown.

One of today's scenes was the first meeting of the deckhand and the immigrant girl during the arduous voyage in an overcrowded ship infested with lice, cockroaches and rats. He would be coming from a confrontation with a drunk and incompetent ship's-surgeon. She was out of the cramped, working-class cabins below deck to attend the funeral of a friend's baby who'd succumbed to typhoid fever.

That was an emotionally wrenching scene he was witness to, but being out on the water in the beautiful replica ship being used for filming was a pleasure. The sea was calm, the sunrise spectacular and the first scene of the day only needed one take.

The scene with the ship's surgeon didn't go so well. It was supposed to be a busy time for the crew, with sails being shifted to catch the wind while the argument was happening. Getting enough activity to ramp up the tension was difficult and by the third take people were tiring. During the filming, one of the extras managed to get tangled up in a rope as one of the huge sails was being lowered and he dislocated his shoulder.

It was Jake who helped carry the man to shore once the ship got back to the jetty, but the paramedic on duty wasn't qualified to administer IV pain relief. When she rang for backup, the only other ambulance in the area was out on a job.

'He'll have to be transported,' she informed the director.

He was already stressed about the hold-up in the day's filming. 'Call for a helicopter, then.'

But the closest rescue helicopter was attending a serious accident well north of Auckland and it would be over an hour before it would be available.

'I'll have to transport him myself,' the paramedic decided. 'At least I've got Entonox available.'

'How long will that take?'

'The closest hospital is in Thames. The round trip will

be at least two hours. Probably more like three, what with handing him over and roadworks and things.'

'Who's going to cover the set, then?' The director shook his head at the paramedic's expression. 'Nobody, obviously. That means we can't film.'

'Maybe one of the local doctors could come out for a bit.'

'We've got weeks of filming ahead of us. We can't afford this kind of hassle.' He looked over his shoulder towards the unfortunate extra, who was sitting on a stretcher in the back of the ambulance, Kirsty beside him, offering comfort. 'Go,' he ordered wearily. 'Get that poor guy sorted. I'm not going to make him wait.' He raised his voice. 'Kirsty? Can you come over here, please?'

'We'll have to hire independent medical cover,' was Kirsty's suggestion when she heard the tale of woe. 'Someone who's qualified to deal with any situation and give whatever treatment is needed until ground or air transport can get here. Someone who could live on site in the camping grounds with us and be available twenty-four seven.'

'How on earth are we going to find someone like that?'

'I don't know,' Kirsty admitted. 'But we do, at least, have a personal contact with the ambulance service, thanks to Jake.'

'I don't have contact, exactly,' Jake said. 'I haven't even spoken to Ellie since the rescue. The only contact was when I rang the base to see how she was a couple of weeks ago.'

It had been a last attempt to make some personal contact given that the mobile number had been such a failure. Had she really been unavailable or were her colleagues protecting her from a call from someone she didn't want to speak to?

'And how was she?'

'Getting over the ankle injury, apparently, but only on light duties. Her boss said something about her preparing teaching material. She wasn't on the base and she wouldn't be back on active duty for some time but she was fine.'

It had been a relief to know she hadn't been left with any lasting disability caused by the rescue of himself. Oddly disappointing to know that he'd have no more excuses to ask after her, though.

'Sounds perfect,' the director said. 'She's certainly qualified and not afraid of doing something different or challenging. Still got the number of her boss?'

'I have,' Kirsty said helpfully. 'His name's Smith.'

'Get him on the blower. We need to talk.'

Jake watched them walk away. It was highly unlikely that Ellie would want to take such an unusual job, even if it could be arranged, but the flare of something curiously like excitement told him that he hoped she would.

That he would get the chance to see her again.

To talk to her.

The feeling intensified as the day ticked on. Because they couldn't film without medical cover, there was too much time to think.

To feel bad that he had been less than honest with her about who he was. Had he really been worried that she might sell her story to the media? She hadn't breathed a word. She hadn't even taken the opportunity to bask in any glory associated with the dramatic rescue.

To feel frustrated, too, that he had never had the chance to try and explain anything. To apologise?

She hadn't believed him when he'd told her how acting could help you deal with real life. Maybe if she saw what really went on, she would see that it wasn't fake—not on an emotional level, anyway.

She might understand what he'd been trying to say when he'd told her something that he'd never told anybody else.

He had to admit that there was a longing there to have somebody who really understood. Ben understood his need for his career, but he still saw it all as play-acting. An escape from reality. He wasn't ever going to get close enough to the action to really get it because he hated the whole industry with such a passion.

And yet Ben had reaped the benefits of his twin's ability to act and make others believe in their early years. How often had he instigated a game that would take them away from what was happening around them?

Their lifestyle had had a veneer that was a dream to most people, but they didn't know what it was really like. A father rich enough to seemingly own half of Manhattan. A heartbreakingly beautiful mother who was loved by millions but desperately unhappy in her marriage to a bully who resented her fame.

Play-acting had been a way to escape the fights and misery and lingering bitterness. If he and Ben were pirates and they were being forced to walk the plank, the screaming row their parents were having could seem like nothing more than seagulls overhead and circling sharks below and the two small boys could poke them in the eyes and swim to safety.

All Ben could see in the industry of play-acting was the damage it had done to their mother. Their family. No wonder he hated it. And no wonder he was sticking to his unspoken vow of never repeating history. Had he ever got even as close to a woman as *he* was currently feeling about Ellie?

Ellie would probably agree wholeheartedly with Ben about the negative side of the movie industry, but...what if he could change her mind?

If someone like her could understand and maybe even approve of what he did, it could validate what he did for a living. Make him feel like he was contributing to making the world a better place.

Like Ellie did?

'That's a crazy idea.'

'A few weeks on the Coromandel Peninsula? In a nice little cabin in the camping grounds? Gorgeous weather. Probably still warm enough to swim and that would be as good for your ankle as the physiotherapy.'

'There's lots of people who'd jump at the opportunity. Why me?'

Gavin Smith grinned. 'I guess you proved yourself by saving the star of the movie once already. Maybe he asked for *you* personally.'

Why did her heart skip a beat like that? Her mouth suddenly feel unaccountably dry? Could that be true? More importantly, did she want it to be true?

Had she proved her trustworthiness by not saying anything to reporters? Did Jake realise, without knowing why, how hurt she was at having been deceived?

'I can't believe they can just click their fingers and get someone from the service who's that qualified just to sit around in case something happens.'

'New Zealand's getting a reputation as a great place to make movies. The government's keen to support the industry. The word's come from on high to provide the best we can.' Gavin raised his eyebrows encouragingly. 'That's you, Ellie.'

It was impossible not to imagine what it would be like to see Jake again. Their time together was too tangled in emotions that were partly due to the traumatic situation they'd been in. Maybe she'd get there and find that it had been nothing more than a reaction to the circumstances and that there wasn't any real attraction on either side.

And, if that was the case, maybe she could finally put the whole, disturbing episode behind her and get on with the rest of her life. It wouldn't be nibbling away at her peace of mind as it had done ever since she'd had that time with Jake.

Gavin was saying something about her being able to carry on with her current project of writing lectures about aeromedical transportation. About providing her with an extensive enough kit that she would be able to cope with any emergency with ease. That by the time she got back she'd be fully recovered and they could decide about what she wanted to do next in her career.

But all Ellie could think about was being close to Jake again. Would he look at her again the way he had in that moment before they'd almost kissed?

'Okay…' Her voice came out in a whisper. 'I'll do it.'

CHAPTER EIGHT

THE DRIVE FROM Auckland to the Coromandel township of Whitianga only took two and half hours, but it was enough time for Ellie to have a good think about how she was going to handle the moment when she and Jake met again.

It was ironic that she was joining a film crew and would be on set while a movie was being filmed because the only way she was going to be able to cope with this was to become something of an actress herself.

Well...she could hardly reveal to the world that she—an ordinary Kiwi girl—had some kind of mixed-up crush on a famous movie star, could she? How humiliating would that be?

And she had been humiliated before. She wasn't going there again.

Funny how Jake's words kept echoing in her head during that drive. And it was definitely motivating to imagine watching herself on the big screen here. Cheering herself on. Facing obstacles and overcoming them.

Practising being the best person she could be, even if it felt like the skin didn't fit yet.

She would be pleased to see him—as she would be to catch up on any of the patients she'd rescued during her career. Keen to do something so different. Excited, even, to be part of a totally new world.

She would realise that the crush was no more than the aftermath of an overly emotional situation and that there was nothing real to hang any fantasies on. She would re-affirm her faith that dealing with reality was preferable to trying to escape and then she would go back to her own life, with her head held high, to do exactly that.

The autumn weather was stunning as she wound her way through over the mountain range and through the small township of Tairua. Beneath a cloudless blue sky, the lush native forest looked cool and green and the glimpses of ocean a bottomless blue. The main holiday season was well over so Whitianga was quiet, but there was a buzz of excitement in the air that Ellie noticed when she stopped for a few supplies and directions to the camping grounds. That, and her uniform, earned her a curious glance from the shopkeeper.

'Someone been hurt again?'

'Again?' The pang of concern that it could be Jake came from nowhere and the way Ellie could feel her eyes widening was disturbing. She'd never make an actress if she couldn't keep her reactions under better control.

'Someone broke their arm a couple of days ago. Or was it their shoulder? Anyway...they had to stop filming for a day. Did you know they're doing a movie here? Have you seen the boat at the marina?'

'I did. It's beautiful.'

'They're going to do a shipwreck scene round at Cathedral Cove in the next week or two. There's places that people are allowed to go and watch.'

'Sounds fun.'

Her items were being slotted into a carrier bag. 'So no one else has been hurt, then?'

'Not that I know of.'

'But that's why you're here?'

'I'm here to give some first-aid cover.' Ellie practised the kind of smile she would use for a reporter, perhaps, who wanted information. 'Hopefully just as an insurance policy. Can you tell me where the local ambulance station is, too? I'll drop in and say hi on my way.'

She was here.

The SUV painted in ambulance insignia, with the beacon strip on its roof, stood out as clearly as if the lights had been flashing, when Jake emerged from the makeup caravan. The director, Steve, was obviously showing her around the camping ground, along with Kirsty and the camp manager.

Jake could feel his heart rate pick up. The kind of warmth in his chest that he'd only ever noticed when he saw his brother after a longer than usual period apart.

Relief, that's what it was. Mixed with joy. And...hope?

She looked very professional in a crisp, white shirt that had epaulettes and patches on the sleeves. Dark trousers and a belt that had things clipped to it, like a pair of shears and some sort of radio or phone. Her black boots were shining. So was the rope of neatly plaited hair that hung down her back.

Another image flashed into his head. Ellie, sitting in front of the fire, in shapeless trackpants and a checkered woollen shirt, her hair loose and tumbling as she raked her fingers through it.

He preferred that image...

He wished he wasn't in full costume and makeup himself because he was going to look as different to Ellie as she did to him and it felt...wrong.

She didn't even seem to recognise him as her gaze swept around and past where he was standing motionless. But then Steve spotted him.

'Here's someone you'll remember,' he heard the director say. 'Not that there's much time for a catch-up. I'm sorry. We're due to head down to the ship in a couple of minutes.'

'Jake…' Ellie's smile was wide and friendly. She was holding out her hand and when he caught it, the handshake was firm and brief. 'It's so good to see you again.' The smile was directed at the others in the group now. 'It's a bonus you don't often get in my job—catching up with the patients that get rescued.'

Jake blinked. He was a *patient?* Just one of the dozens—or possibly hundreds—that Ellie had rescued in her career?

'Great that you could come,' he heard himself saying. 'I didn't think we'd be lucky enough to get our first choice.' He was smiling, too. He wanted Ellie to know that he'd wanted it to be her. Had wanted to see her again.

'How could I say no?' The smile hadn't dimmed. In fact, it got wider. 'This is a once-in-a-lifetime opportunity for me. How many people get the chance to be part of what's no doubt going to be a blockbuster movie? I'm hoping you're all going to stay nice and safe and it'll work out as a holiday treat for me.'

'Hear! Hear!' Steve muttered.

'Not that I'm not fully equipped to deal with any emergency,' Ellie added hastily. 'My car is full to the brim with everything from sticky plasters to a portable ventilator.'

'And with your connection to the helicopter service, I'm sure we'd get priority treatment.' Kirsty nodded.

Ellie's smile faded only a notch. 'Doesn't work like that, I'm afraid. No preferential treatment because of who you are.'

Jake couldn't read the glance flicked in his direction, but it had been impersonal and there was something about the inflection in her words that struck a cool enough note to send a tiny shiver down his spine.

And then it hit him.

This wasn't Ellie talking. Not the *real* Ellie.

She was…*acting,* dammit. Saying the things that were presenting the image she'd chosen to present.

The way *he* had the last time they'd been breathing the same air, at that media conference in The Cloud? When he'd been putting all that warmth and gratitude into his pretty little speech about how good the New Zealand rescue services were and about one paramedic in particular? Had he really gushed on about his 'real-life heroine'?

This felt like a slap in the face. Payback.

But that wasn't Ellie either. Not the Ellie he remembered, anyway.

'Come on, Jake. Time to get to work.' Steve thumped him on the shoulder as he headed off. 'Kirsty will bring Ellie down to the set once she's had a look at her cabin and got herself sorted.'

With a nod at the women, Jake was happy to comply. Maybe it had been a mistake, getting Ellie here.

He certainly wasn't feeling any of that warmth or joy or hope of special moments to come anymore. The emotion he was left with after that little reunion was more like wariness. Dread, even, that Ellie might have more planned as some kind of revenge.

No. Someone as open and honest and caring as Ellie wouldn't even think like that. He knew her better than that.

Didn't he?

He'd seen straight through her.

And Ellie felt ashamed of herself.

The warmth in Jake's eyes when he'd seen her had been genuine, but Ellie had already been locked into her role as the caring and professional medic who just happened to have rescued one of the stars of this movie and she had been unable to find any middle ground between that image and the stupid, starstruck teenager with a crush she'd been scared of revealing.

She'd seen the moment he'd twigged that she was acting. Had seen his surprise and then the flash of something that had looked remarkably like hurt.

So now she felt bad.

It didn't take long for the camp manager to show her the tiny cabin that would be hers for the duration of her stay. Or to give her a bag of coins and explain about the showers.

'You get five minutes of hot water for one dollar. Just put another coin in if you need longer. The company's paying all those costs so I've got lots of coins available.'

Ellie nodded.

'The caterers have taken over the main kitchen areas and they've been putting on some amazing barbecues. You'll get well fed.'

'Excellent.' Ellie managed another smile but the churning sensation in her gut made her think she might never feel hungry again.

'Well, I won't hold you up. You probably can't wait to get down to the set and see what's going on. I'd kill for a chance to spend my day watching Jake Logan.' The middle-aged woman grinned at Ellie. 'If I was twenty years younger, he wouldn't stand a chance. Okay...make that thirty years. But you know what I'm saying?'

Ellie nodded politely.

'I'd be in a long queue, mind you. And it's not as if anything lasts in Tinseltown, but it would sure be fun for a while, wouldn't it?'

'Mmm.' Ellie couldn't manage to sound remotely enthusiastic. Of course Jake would have a queue of women happy to take their turn, even knowing how temporary that would be.

She wouldn't be joining any queue.

The camp manager gave up on having a girlie chat. 'Just knock on the office door, love, if you need anything.'

'Okay. Thank you.'

She wasn't in as much of a hurry to get to the set as the camp manager had assumed, however. She wasn't even sure if she wanted to be near Jake again so soon. She'd snuffed out the warmth she'd seen in his face in that reunion.

There was no use dressing it up as self-protection. The truth was she'd snubbed him and he'd known. Someone like Jake Logan didn't have to bother with people who snubbed him. He could just pick one of those willing women in the queue. If she never saw even a hint of that warmth again, she only had herself to blame.

That she'd made a bad mistake and that things could have gone very differently haunted Ellie for the rest of that first day.

Her nose was rubbed in it, in fact, by being allowed on the ship during the early evening to watch a sunset scene being filmed on the gentle roll of the open sea just outside the harbour.

A kiss scene between Jake and his stunningly beautiful leading lady, Amber.

Bad enough to have to watch it once but, for some reason, the director made them do it over and over again. And Ellie was forced to watch. Not only was she trapped on a ship but she couldn't even slip out of sight because the area of the deck not being used for the scene was so small that she and the other people watching were hemmed into a corner.

The clapboards came down again and again as another take began.

Ellie had to grit her teeth. She had no hope of controlling the stirring of feelings like longing. Envy, possibly. Just as well nothing had really happened between her and Jake. Imagine having to watch this if you were in a real relationship with one of them?

'Couldn't see what was wrong with the last one,' someone close to Ellie muttered.

A snort of mirth came from someone else. 'Maybe they're enjoying it too much.'

Jealousy was such a destructive emotion. She had no right to be edging dangerously close to feeling that herself. No right at all and she would be wise to remember that.

The director went in to talk to them at this point. He waved his arm, indicating the last of the glorious sunset gilding the water behind them and throwing the slopes of tree-covered land in the distance into soft silhouette. Maybe he said something about time being money and it was running out because Jake turned and took a couple of paces as if suppressing frustration.

'Places, please,' came the call for a new take. 'Picture is up.'

Jake turned back and it felt as if he'd known all along exactly where Ellie was standing.

For a long, long, moment he simply stared at her, his face completely expressionless.

And then the assistant director called for quiet, the sound crew confirmed they were ready and a now-familiar bark of 'Action!' was heard. The new take started and it felt to Ellie like she, along with the rest of the world, had been completely shut out.

Amber was his sole focus. Kissing her was something Jake couldn't avoid any more than taking his next breath. It was inevitable. As necessary to life as the oxygen around him.

The cameras were gliding in for a close-up, but Ellie felt like she was too close already. She could feel the intensity of every moment of that long, long kiss. Could feel Jake looking at Amber in exactly the way he'd looked at her in the moments before that radio message had interrupted them. She could actually *feel* his lips getting closer. Touching…

Dear Lord… How far did they go in a movie kiss? Were their tongues touching?

Desire was still there. She could feel it curling—almost exploding—deep in her own belly. Ellie didn't dare look at anyone near her in case they could see what she was feeling in her face. Not that she could look away from the kissing couple, anyway.

Until, finally, it was over.

'That's the one,' the director shouted. 'Thanks, guys. It was *perfect*.'

The caterers, once again, had done an impressive job with the barbecue dinner laid on for cast and crew when the day's filming was over. The array of meat and fish was complemented by numerous salads and fresh, crusty bread. Wine and beer were freely available at the table set up as a bar and clusters of people were enjoying the alfresco meal as stars glittered in an inky sky above.

Jake had used a handful of coins with the time it took to get rid of his makeup and hair product. Dressed in black jeans and a matching sweater, he set out to look for food.

And Ellie.

Time was a luxury because the meeting to watch the dailies of today's footage would be on before long and he needed to collect the next day's shooting schedule, but if he didn't do something about this, it was going to do his head in. For the first time in his life he'd felt self-conscious on set this evening. It was no wonder they'd had to do that kiss scene so many times. It had been impossible to get in the zone with Ellie standing there, *watching* him.

Either they needed to clear the air between them or he'd have to ask for her to be kept off set and he could imagine the awkward questions that might result from that request. It would, no doubt, get back to Ellie too, and that would only exacerbate any ill feeling that was there.

He spotted her, standing to one side of the large group of people, looking a little uncertain. She had changed out of her uniform and, like him, was wearing jeans. She might find that camisole top wasn't enough for the chill the evenings could offer later, but even as Jake had the thought he saw Ellie push her arms into the sleeves of an oversized cardigan that draped gracefully, like a kind of shawl. She might be feeling out of place here, but she still held herself tall, confident in her independence.

The cast and crew were predominantly male. Actors, stuntpeople, camera crews, sound technicians, the grip crew, the continuity guys and others. Yeah… There were a lot of men here and Ellie was a very beautiful young woman. She wouldn't be standing alone for long, that was for sure.

Snagging a bottle of lager and a glass of wine, Jake headed in her direction. He held the glass up as he got closer as if it could pass as a peace offering.

But Ellie shook her head. 'I might be out of uniform for the night but I'm on duty twenty-four seven,' she told him.

No chance that a drink might ease the atmosphere, then. 'Doesn't sound like much fun.'

Ellie's smile was bright. Too bright. 'I'm loving it so far,' she said. 'I've never been on a movie set before. Can't believe how lucky I am to score this gig. Guess I have you to thank for that?'

Jake said nothing. He was staring at her, but Ellie was looking around. At everyone except him.

'I didn't think you'd want to come,' he said quietly.

'Hey…' Her gaze brushed past his fleetingly. 'This is my chance. Who knows—the fame might rub off on me. Someone will spot me doing my job and Hollywood might be calling with a role for a paramedic in some upcoming movie.'

That did it. Jake's voice was quiet but cool. 'If you'd wanted fame, you could have had it in spades by now. You must have had any number of chances to get your picture in magazines and all over the internet by now. Why didn't you take them?'

That threw her. He managed to catch her gaze this time. And hold it. He could actually see the way she was searching for a new line. A plausible way of covering the real reason.

He almost smiled. She'd never make an actress, the way her feelings played out over her face like that. Unless she could tap into them, of course, and use them when she needed to. Like he did.

When he saw the softening in her eyes he knew that the real reason she hadn't acceded to the media's demands was because of…what was it…loyalty? To *him?*

What had he done to deserve that? Now was the time to thank her for respecting his privacy. To apologise. Explain and put things right. But even as he took a breath he could see Ellie's expression changing again. Getting distant. She had found something to hide behind.

'That would have been more like *shame* than fame,' she said. 'D'you think I wanted the whole world knowing what an idiot I was for not recognising you?'

Jake raised an eyebrow. 'I was in disguise.'

'You told me your *name*.'

'So? It's just a name. Have you ever done an internet search on yourself and found how many people in the world have the same name as you?'

'Fine.' But Ellie wasn't going to accept an excuse. 'Maybe I didn't want to come across as some uncultured slob who never watches movies.'

It was nowhere near the truth and Jake wasn't getting anywhere. Moving so fast Ellie had no time to prepare a defence, he discarded the drinks he was holding and grabbed her hand. Never mind if he missed seeing the dailies. He could catch up later. This was more important.

'Come with me,' he ordered.

She had no choice. It was lucky she'd been standing where she was, not only on the outskirts of the group but almost beside a track that Jake knew led to the beach. Intent on their meals and downtime, no one saw them slip away.

'What the—?' Ellie was resisting the firm grip on her hand and the way Jake was pulling her forward. 'Where are you taking me?'

'The beach.'

'Why?'

'We need to talk.' The words were clipped. 'Somewhere private.'

He felt her resistance ebb. By the time they reached the beach it almost felt like Ellie was happy to hold his hand, but it was harder going in the soft sand. When they got to the firmer sand close to where the gentle waves were slowly curling onto land, she gave a tug that made Jake let go.

'My shoes are full of sand.' She pulled off the canvas sneakers and emptied them but didn't put them back on. Instead, she rolled up her jeans as far as her knees and walked out far enough to let the foamy water cover her feet and ankles.

'Bit of sea water's just as good as a session of physio,' she said.

Jake closed his eyes and groaned. 'I didn't think. I'm sorry. There I was pulling you along that rough track and I didn't even ask how your ankle was.'

'It's fine. And this is nice. The water's delicious. You should try it.'

There was something different about Ellie's voice. She sounded more like the Ellie who Jake remembered.

And the suggestion sounded more like a peace offering than he'd managed with that unwanted glass of wine. Jake toed off his shoes, but he couldn't get his jeans any further than the swell of his calves. He walked into the water, anyway, uncaring when the first tiny wave soaked the denim.

For a while they simply walked together, listening to the wash of the sea. Smelling the fresh air and looking up at the deepening blanket of stars. The moon was rising now, but the pale light didn't dim the night sky.

And it was perfect. Even alone with his brother, Jake had never felt this...peaceful...in the company of another person. Able to be exactly who he was and know he would be accepted for that.

Liked, even?

Maybe. He had a bit of work to do first.

It was Jake who finally broke the silence. 'The sky never looked like this in New York. I grew up not even realising how many stars there are out there. I grew up without the chance to realise a lot of other important things, too.'

He waited out the hesitation in Ellie's response. 'Such as?'

'That who you are doesn't mean as much as *what* you are.'

Ellie stopped walking. Jake could feel her puzzled look behind him. He stopped too, and turned back.

'I grew up as Rita Marlene's kid,' he told her. 'That won't mean much to you but—'

'I know who she is,' Ellie interrupted him. 'Everybody knows who she is...*was*. She's up there with Brigitte Bardot and Marilyn Monroe. One of the world's most beautiful women.'

'And she was married to my father. Charles Logan. One of New York's most powerful men. There wasn't anybody who didn't want to get close to one or both of my parents. Getting their kids to get friendly with the Logan kids was a goldmine.'

Ellie said nothing but he could tell she was listening.

'I didn't mean to get into acting as a career,' he continued. 'I just sort of fell into it when Ben and I got back from Afghanistan. Well...after I got rehabilitated, that is. The opening was always there, thanks to who my mother was, and it seemed like a fun thing to try for a while. More fun than Ben was having, being responsible and getting into the family business anyway. So I took that part in *ER* and then it just snowballed.'

'Mmm...' Ellie was still standing there, letting the waves soak her ankles.

'What I'm trying to say, in a roundabout way, is that I didn't tell you who I was because I had the chance to be someone nobody else ever sees. *Myself*.'

The moon was bright enough for Jake to see Ellie's face so clearly he could swear her eyes were shining with unshed tears. He allowed his gaze to travel over her features. That glorious hair. The proud way she held her head. She was *such* a beautiful woman.

'I thought...I thought it was because you didn't trust me.'

'We were complete strangers,' he pointed out. 'Thrown together by extraordinary circumstances. We were trying to survive in what felt like the middle of nowhere and I was worried sick about Ben. Did *you* trust me?'

The hesitation was there again. 'Y-yes,' Ellie finally said. 'After you carried me along the beach like that? And after you rescued me from under that tree?' Her lips wobbled slightly. 'I…trusted you.'

'Past tense?' Maybe they were clearing the air here, but could they get back to what it had been like between them? It was only now that Jake realised how much he wanted that.

'I…' He could see the muscles in Ellie's throat working as she swallowed. 'I don't really let myself trust anyone these days.'

'Why not?'

The silence went on too long this time and Jake had no right to push. He could respect her need for privacy. It didn't need to stop him being honest.

'Not trusting you *was* part of it, I guess,' he admitted. 'But that was something I *did* learn as I grew up. A lesson that's only been hammered in a lot deeper in recent years. The only person I've ever been able to trust completely is my brother Ben.' Jake flinched as a higher wave splashed the back of his legs. Or was it because of the thought he couldn't repress? 'And I can't even trust Ben now.'

'Why not?'

He could have followed Ellie's lead and simply stayed silent, but he chose not to. 'Because he lied to me.'

'What about?'

Jake couldn't help looking around but they were alone on the beach. Two dark figures, late at night. They were probably virtually invisible.

'If I tell you,' he said softly, 'you'll know I'm trusting you. *Really* trusting you.'

And maybe this was the most sincere apology he could

offer. He saw Ellie nod, but he also saw her slight shiver. Anticipation? Or was she cold?

He held out his hand and this time she took it willingly. He led her up towards the softer sand that still held the warmth of the day's sun and, although he let go of her hand when they sat down, they were still sitting close enough to touch.

For a long time he couldn't find the words to start. It was too big and by telling it to someone else it was going to make it real. But Jake had forgotten how he'd met Ellie, hadn't he?

'I heard him yelling at you,' Ellie said quietly. 'When you were both arguing about who got to get rescued first. I heard him say "Why do you think she killed herself?" Is that what this is about?'

Jake's nod was jerky. 'I didn't know. I've always believed it was an accidental overdose.'

'Who was he talking about?'

'Our mother.'

'Oh...*Jake*...' This time it was Ellie who reached for *his* hand. 'That's horrible.'

'It's believable, though.' Jake's voice was raw. 'Looking back, I can see she was an alcoholic, but who wouldn't be, married to my father? He was a bully. A complete bastard, if I'm honest. And she was dependent on prescription meds. The media used to describe her as being "beautiful but fragile" and that hit the nail on the head. But...I thought she loved us. That she wouldn't choose to leave us alone with our father.'

'Of course she loved you.' Ellie's tone was fierce. 'But sometimes that's not enough. And sometimes people convince themselves that the ones they love will be better off without them, however wrong that is. How...how old were you?'

'Fourteen.'

'Young enough to still think it was somehow your fault.'

'Except I didn't. Because I didn't know it was suicide. Ben kept that to himself.'

'He loves you, too. He was protecting you.'

The words were simple.

And Jake could feel the truth of them. There was only a twenty-minute difference in age but Ben had always had the mindset of an older brother. The more responsible one. The more protective one.

Ben had been the one to spend a night in jail after one of their worst teenage pranks, hot-wiring the Lamborghini belonging to one of their father's guests and then crashing it. He himself had been safely out of the way, admitted to hospital overnight thanks to the concussion he'd suffered.

They'd never talked about that night either. Because it had been the next morning that their mother had been found dead?

And, while Jake had been the one with the more visible injury after that dreadful incident in Afghanistan, it had been Ben who'd really been traumatised. *He* had been unconscious after the bomb blast. He had no memory of it. Ben was the one who'd been in the midst of the carnage. Trying to keep his brother alive amidst the screams of dying children.

His brother had retreated into being even more responsible after that, finally—reluctantly—picking up the reins of their father's empire when the old man had been felled by a stroke, whereas *he* had just kept having fun. With easy access to the first rungs of a Hollywood career thanks to the legacy of their famous actress mother, his own talent at making others believe combined with what the glossy magazines called his raw sex appeal had ensured a meteoric rise to stardom.

The brothers had drifted apart in the intervening years and maybe he had been harbouring resentment about the way Ben viewed the movie industry. In the light of what he'd said about their mother, though, it was far more understandable.

Was there a way back?

It had taken Ellie to point out what should have been obvious all along. Maybe she was wise enough to have some other answers.

'Why can't he tell me that himself? *Talk* to me?'

'You'll have to ask him that yourself. But he's a bloke.' Ellie slanted him a look that was pure woman. 'You lot have trouble talking about feelings.'

'Yeah…'

'And speaking of feelings, I'm kind of hungry.'

'Me, too.'

'Shall we go back and see if there's any food left?'

'Sure.' Jake got to his feet and offered Ellie his hand to help her up. He held onto it for a moment longer. 'Friends again?' he asked softly. 'Am I forgiven?'

'Of course. And thank you for trusting me. I won't let you down.'

'I know that.'

He did. And the knowledge gave him the feeling of finding something very rare and precious.

Trust was a good foundation for friendship. Better than good. The fizzing sensation of unexpected happiness was magic. A bit like being drunk. Maybe that was why he opened his mouth and kept talking as they entered the darkness of the bush track that led back to the camping ground.

'I hope tomorrow's not such a long day. I couldn't believe how many times I stuffed up that last scene.'

Ellie's voice was a little tight. 'I heard the director say that it was perfect in the end, though.'

'You want to know why?'

They were almost back at the barbecue area. They could hear the sound of voices and laughter. Their private time was almost over.

And Ellie was looking up at him, her eyes wary.

'Why?'

'Because I stopped being aware that you were watching me.'

'I was putting you off?' Ellie sounded horrified. 'Maybe I shouldn't be on set, then.'

'No. It was good that you were there. That's how I got it right in the end.'

She was puzzled again now. Jake felt like he might be stepping over a precipice right now, but he'd gone this far. He couldn't stop now.

And maybe it was a cheesy thing to say and Ellie would think it was some kind of line, but Jake realised he'd been needing to do more than apologise. He needed to let Ellie know that the time they'd had together had been special. That he wished he *had* kissed her back in that beach house. Before she'd known who he was. When he'd just been being himself.

'I just had to take myself back in time a bit,' he said softly. 'I imagined that we'd never heard that radio message. And that Amber was you.'

Once again, Ellie had been stopped in her tracks by something Jake had said.

She didn't have the wash of sea water around her ankles this time and she wasn't at all puzzled by these words. There was no mistaking the meaning this time.

Jake was telling her that he'd wanted to kiss her when

he'd had the opportunity. As much as she had wanted him to?

He hadn't forgotten the moment anyway. Any more than she had.

Beyond Jake, she could see the lights and movement of the large group of people they were about to rejoin. She could smell the tantalising aroma of roasted meat, but her hunger for food had evaporated. Here, on this unlit track through the trees, she and Jake were still alone. Unseen.

On her first day on this job, Ellie had achieved what she'd hoped she might. Time with Jake Logan that had eliminated any sense of being deceived or betrayed.

Was she just being gullible, falling for that idea that she'd given him some kind of precious gift by allowing him to be simply himself and not a household name or the son of famous people?

How could she not believe it? Especially when he'd gone on to share what had gone wrong in his relationship with his brother. That was the kind of story a journalist would kill for and Jake had *trusted* her with that information.

That was enough to give her the closure she'd wanted, wasn't it? To turn that experience into something positive that she could remember with pleasure in years to come.

But…Jake was looking at her now, the way he had in all those secret fantasies she'd indulged in during some of the long nights in the last few weeks. As if every word he'd uttered this evening had come straight from the heart and she was special to him.

Special enough to want to be more than friends.

And, heaven help her, Ellie knew without a shadow of doubt in that moment that she was in love with Jake. She had been, ever since that moment he'd gone into the hole beneath the tree roots to rescue a kiwi egg for her. She might have buried the realisation because of what had come next, but she had nothing to bury it with now.

There it was. Newly hatched and exposed. Making Ellie feel vulnerable in a way she'd sworn never to let herself feel again. So vulnerable she could actually feel herself trembling. Had she really told him that she'd trusted him?

And meant it?

Yes… She'd not only reclaimed that step forward in her life, there was a part of her doing a victory dance on the new patch of ground.

Even if nothing was showing on her face, it was going to be a mission to try and disguise that trembling. Unless she said something about how cold it was getting?

She had to say something. She couldn't stand here all night staring at Jake as though the world had stopped spinning.

But it was Jake who moved. Stepping closer without breaking the eye contact that was holding Ellie prisoner.

That on-screen kiss must have been merely a practice session because this one was a thousand percent better. The way he touched her face with reverent fingers, still holding her gaze as if reading something printed on her soul. The infinite slowness with which he lowered his head. The sweet torture of his lips hovering so close to her own she could feel the warmth of them and a buzz of sensation that went through every cell of her body.

And then his fingers slid into her hair and cradled the back of her head as the whisper of touch danced and then settled. As her lips parted beneath his and she felt the first, intimate touch of his tongue, Ellie knew she was lost.

The world really had stopped spinning.

CHAPTER NINE

By TACIT AGREEMENT, no direct mention was made about whatever was growing between Ellie and Jake. They both knew it was there and it was getting bigger every day. Perhaps trying to confine it to words would put it at risk of being caged and stunt its growth. Or maybe, by acknowledging it, it would somehow make it visible to others. This was theirs alone and it was too fragile and precious to put at risk.

Keeping it secret became a game that only added excitement to the stakes as they went about the jobs they were paid to do. Jake had to spend hours in makeup and costume, learning his lines and filming scene after scene as the movie inched towards the major finale of the shipwreck. Ellie treated people for minor and sometimes moderate injuries and illnesses. A cameraman needed a night in hospital to check that his chest pain wasn't cardiac related. One of the catering crew got a nasty burn and someone else had an asthma attack that kept her busy for some time.

She'd never known that an ignition point of sexual tension could be stretched *so* far. One day led to another and then another where nothing happened other than an apparently innocent conversation over a meal, a lingering glance during the hours of a working day or, at best, a stolen moment of physical contact that was unlikely to arouse anyone's suspicion—like the brush of hands as Jake passed her a plate of food or a drink.

The movie's star didn't really need the skills of a highly qualified paramedic to tend to the small scratch he received after a fight scene. It wasn't very professional of Ellie either to spend quite so much time assessing and cleaning the insignificant wound but the time in the caravan set aside as an on-set clinic was as private as they'd been since that walk on the beach and that seemed so long ago it was getting shrouded in the same mists of fantasy that Ellie's dreams were.

As she used a piece of gauze to dry the skin on Jake's neck that she'd cleaned so thoroughly, the swiftness of his movement when he caught her wrist startled her.

'I'm going mad,' he said softly. 'I need some time with you. Away from this crowd. Or any of those nosy reporters.'

Oh…my… Ellie knew exactly what would happen if they were really alone again. Like they had been in the beach house.

Did she want that, too?

Oh…yeah… With every fibre of her being.

Even if a part of her knew perfectly well it couldn't last? That her world was so different from Jake's she knew she could never fit in and that, if she allowed herself to go any further down this alluring path, it had to end in tears?

Her tears?

But it was so easy to blot out the future and live in the moment. To view this interlude in her life as a one-off and that, if this was the only time she would ever have to be with Jake, it would be worth it. Yes. If the invitation was there, she could no more stop herself going down that path than stop breathing for a week.

The time it had taken to reach that conclusion had been

no more than the time it had taken Ellie to suck in a long breath, but it was enough for wariness to cloud Jake's eyes. He kept his voice low enough for no one to overhear, even if they were right outside the slightly open door of the caravan.

'Do you want that, too, Ellie? Is it only me that's going crazy, here? Would you rather—?'

Ellie stilled his words with her finger on his lips. She looked over her shoulder to ensure they were alone and then she used the tip of her finger to trace the outline of Jake's lips. When she felt the touch of his tongue against her fingertip she had to close her eyes. Stifle the tiny cry that escaped her own lips.

It was the only answer Jake needed.

'I'm overdue for a bit of down time. A day off. We could go somewhere. I've got a chopper available. We could go anywhere we liked.'

'Wouldn't it be rather obvious what we were doing?'

The media had been trying to link Jake romantically with Amber and it hadn't stuck. They'd have a field day if he took off to an unknown destination with the on-set paramedic, who just happened to be the mysterious woman he'd been confined in a remote cabin with for two days.

Unless…

'What if we went to visit Pēpe? That would be a legitimate reason to go somewhere together. A photo op for you, even. I'm sure Jillian would love the publicity that it would give the bird-rearing centre.'

'And then…?' Jake was smiling. He loved the idea. Excitement had Ellie's blood fizzing like champagne and a million butterflies were dancing in her stomach.

'If we've got the use of a chopper we could go anywhere.' She was on a roll here. 'We could buy some cans of spaghetti and restock the pantry at the beach house.'

You couldn't get more private than that. Especially if they sent the chopper away for an hour or three.

'You...' Jake was still holding the wrist he'd caught. He pulled Ellie's hand to his lips and pressed a kiss to the palm of her hand. '...are brilliant. I'll talk to Steve today. We're going to make this happen. Soon.'

'You almost done in there, Jake?' A crew member didn't bother knocking as he stuck his head in the door. 'Make-up's waiting to make you beautiful again.'

'All good.' Jake dropped Ellie's hand as if it was red hot. 'On my way.'

She hid her face by dropping to pick up the piece of gauze that had fallen, unnoticed, to the floor but looked up as Jake reached the door. The glance he sent over his shoulder said it all.

'Soon' couldn't be soon enough.

It was Kirsty who persuaded Steve that the publicity the visit would engender would make it more than worthwhile to give Jake a day off.

Unfortunately, she also insisted that she go too.

'I'm organising the coverage,' she told him. 'Setting up the interviews. I *have* to be there.'

'Look...' Jake tried to keep a note of desperation out of his voice. 'I was planning a little surprise for Ellie. The place we were when she rescued me is close to an island where her grandfather used to be the lighthouse keeper. I wanted to use the chopper to take her there to see it again. As a...a thank-you, I guess, for what she did for me. I hadn't planned on having a...a...'

'Chaperone?' Kirsty's glance was amused. And knowing.

'It's not like that.' Good grief... He was good at this acting lark. He could channel his frustration into injecting just the right note of irritation here to put Kirsty off the track. 'Would you want to swap your stilettos for trainers so you could go tramping around on an uninhabited island for a few hours, looking for native birds?'

'Heavens, no.' Kirsty was horrified. 'But I do need to do the media wrangling.' She raised an eyebrow. 'And wouldn't that make it seem more like what it is? Just a visit to somewhere that you both happen to have an interest in visiting?'

She was right. The more official it was, the less likely it would be that Ellie would start getting hounded by reporters or chased by the paparazzi. He had to protect her from that at all costs because, if anything was going to kill what was happening between them, it would be the relentless intrusion of the media and the way they could blow things up out of all proportion and offer their own twisted motivations for whatever was happening in a relationship. Ellie would hate that even more than Ben did and it would undoubtedly be a deal-breaker.

Maybe it could still work. He just had to come up with a way of making sure it did.

It was hard to tell whether Jillian was more thrilled by the attention the centre was receiving or by meeting Jake Logan. Everybody, including Kirsty, was delighted with how the morning went.

Jillian got to talk about the centre.

'Captive rearing centres like this are vital to the survival of our iconic native kiwis. Especially the endangered ones like Pēpe, who's a rare brown kiwi. Out in the wild, a chick has about a five percent chance of making it to adulthood. The ones we hatch and rear here have more like a sixty-five percent chance. We need support to do our work, though. We rely on public contributions as much as government funding.'

The small army of photographers and television crews loved the shots of Jake holding Pēpe. Having been told what a rare privilege it was, Jake was loving it too. His smile had camera shutters clicking madly and the reporter interviewing him couldn't help the occasional coo of appreciation.

'So he's due to be released soon? Will you want to be a part of that occasion, too?'

'If it's possible, I would consider it an honour.'

Ellie was more than happy to stay in the background. She was the link between the film star and the new poster bird for the centre and that was enough.

Having coached Jake on how to hold the bird by the legs with one hand so he wasn't in danger of being scratched and cradling the bird's body in the crook of his other arm, Jillian stood aside with her friend as they watched Jake being interviewed.

'You're right,' Jillian whispered. 'Too much hair.'

'He gets to cut it all off after they do the big shipwreck scene. He says he can't wait.'

'Does he, now?' Jillian's voice was a murmur. 'And what's with this threesome business on your day off? Did he have anything to say about that?'

'Apparently he has a plan.'

Something in her tone must have revealed more than Ellie had intended because Jillian's eyes widened.

'Oh...*my*...' she whispered. Then a shadow dimmed her smile. 'Be careful, won't you, hon?'

'Maybe I need to stop being so careful,' Ellie whispered back. 'This is too good to lose and...and I think I can trust him.'

'I hope so.' But there was concern in Jillian's eyes now. 'I don't want you getting hurt again.'

* * *

Ellie didn't know what Jake's plan was, any more than she knew what was in the basket that the caterers had given Jake to store in the helicopter. When they took off and headed north of Auckland after the visit to Pēpe, her heart sank. She assumed the basket was full of tinned food for the beach house and it looked as if Kirsty was coming with them. But as they got close the helicopter veered away from the shore and began to lose altitude.

'Oh, look…' Kirsty said. 'It's the lighthouse. And there's another house, too. Is that where we're going to land?'

Nobody answered her. Ellie was still too astonished to speak when the chopper touched down on the long grass of a small clearing between the lighthouse and the keeper's cottage. She didn't need the instruction to keep her head down as Jake helped her out but she did wonder why the engine wasn't being shut down. Jake followed her, carrying the basket and then he raised an arm and the helicopter took off again.

With Kirsty still inside it.

'He'll be back by four p.m.,' Jake told her. 'He's going to drop Kirsty off and refuel and have some lunch.' He raised the basket. 'This is our lunch. I hope the champagne's still cold.'

Ellie's jaw dropped. 'I thought it was full of cans of spaghetti.'

'Spaghetti's strictly for emergencies,' Jake told her. 'This was carefully planned.' His smile faded and he looked solemn. 'This is just for us, Ellie. Kirsty's job would be on the line if she said anything and the pilot's too well paid not to be trusted. We can restock the beach house another time.'

He was already planning another time? Ellie's joy—and her smile—expanded another notch. 'I can't believe I'm here. Standing on Half Moon Island. I haven't been here since…for ever. Are you sure it's okay? Did you check with the owners?'

'Owners? I thought it was government property.'

'I'm not sure now. It was put up for sale a few years ago, but I never heard whether anyone bought it.'

'It was for sale?'

Ellie smiled. 'A snip at only a few million. Pretty pricey for a holiday house with no amenities, don't you think?'

'And you didn't find out whether someone bought it?'

'I didn't want to know.'

'Why not?'

'I just didn't.' But, as her gaze was drawn back to her beloved lighthouse, she knew that wasn't enough of an answer. She'd never really thought about her reason herself but standing here was like being on a bridge to the past.

Old ground on one side. New ground on the other because Jake was there. The past and the future? For whatever reason, it felt important to say more.

'I guess it felt like it was ours. When Grandpa was the lighthouse keeper we knew the government owned it, but you couldn't put a face to anyone and they weren't going to change things and make it into a tourist resort or clear the bush for farming or something. It was ours. Part of our family. Where our roots were. If I knew it had been sold or—worse—the name of the person or people, it would stop being ours and I'd lose something precious. A part of my family when I'd already lost too much.'

Jake was nodding as if he understood, but he didn't say anything for a long time. He stood close beside her, looking up at the impressive height of the lighthouse. 'There's something magic about them, isn't there? Steeped in legends and with the history of dramatic shipwrecks swirling around the rocks they're guarding. Symbols of danger and safety at the same time.'

'Mmm...' A bit like Jake, then. How could she feel so safe in his company when she knew how dangerous it was to her heart?

The imaginary bridge beneath her feet was evaporating and the lines between her past and her future blurring, as if the magic of the lighthouse was drifting over her.

'Come with me.' She held out her hand. 'If the track hasn't disappeared, I can show you what used to be my favourite place.'

The track led down to the only point on the island where a boat could land, but they didn't need to go as far down as the dilapidated jetty. Halfway down the cliff you could still turn off and scramble to where massive boulders had shifted to form a kind of basin shape and pohutukawa trees grew almost sideways to provide shelter from the brisk sea breeze and dappled shade from a surprisingly hot autumn afternoon.

Directly under the lighthouse, they could see its shape through the canopy of leaves. Directly below them, waves crashed over more of the huge, volcanic boulders but the sound was muted, like the view of the lighthouse. This was a private spot in an already completely isolated place.

'This was where I always came when I was a kid,' Ellie said. 'When I wanted to be by myself.'

'You're not by yourself now.' Jake's eyes held a question.

'I'm where I want to be,' she said simply. Her heart was beating a tattoo inside her chest. 'With you.'

Jake dropped the basket and took a step closer to Ellie. Without taking his gaze from hers, he lifted his hand to touch her cheek and then cradled her chin as he tilted his head and brought his lips to hers.

Hints of the cool sea breeze kissed Ellie's skin as Jake

helped her out of her clothes. She could even taste the salt of it on Jake's skin as she got to kiss places she had only stolen a glimpse of before. She could still hear the sound of the waves below, but that sense faded, along with sight as her eyes drifted shut. Touch and taste were all that existed.

The touch of Jake's hands as he shaped her body as if imprinting it as quickly as possible on his memory cells. Learning the feel of her breasts and the silky skin of her inner thighs. She was doing the same thing. Too overwhelmed to do anything more than skate over what she wanted to learn so badly. The delicious dimples of his hardened nipples. The pulsing heat of his arousal. There would be time later for retracing these steps with the attention they deserved. Right now, a release from tension that had been building for far too long was what they both desperately needed.

And it was over too soon but they both knew it was only a beginning.

'Now we can take our time.' Jake smiled. 'We've got hours before our transport comes back.' His hand was still resting on her breast and the tiny circles he made with the tip of his little finger were enough to make her nipple hard again.

But Ellie wanted to touch, too. Turning on the blanket of the woollen Swanndri shirt Jake had insisted on wearing for the visit to Pēpe, she ran a fingertip down the intriguing tattoo.

'What does it say?'

'He who dares wins.'

Ellie liked that. She could use the mantra herself. And, in this moment, it seemed like a truth. She was daring here, allowing herself to fall in love again. To dream of a future. It even seemed possible that she could win Jake.

'And this?' Her fingertip had reached the end of the tattoo, just past the jut of hipbone. 'It's yin and yang, isn't it?'

'That's for being a twin. Ben has one too. He didn't go with the Chinese characters, though. Thought it was tacky thing to do.'

'I think it's beautiful.' Yin and yang. Two shapes that curved together to make a perfect circle. Two parts of a whole. Was that discordant jangle a hint of jealousy that it was his twin brother who was that close to Jake?

When *she* wanted to be?

Did something show on her face? Jake traced the outline of her cheek and jaw before pressing a soft kiss to her lips.

'You were wrong, you know.'

'What about?'

'About it being like having two of yourself, having a twin. We're very different. I don't think he even understands me. I'm not sure anyone does.'

Ellie's whisper felt like a promise. '*I'd* like to.'

His smile was a reward all by itself. 'I'd like you to.'

Ellie's fingers drifted sideways from where they'd been touching the symbol. She didn't want to talk about Jake's brother any more. This was *their* time. Hers and Jake's. Who knew when—or even if—they would ever get another time like this?

She felt Jake stir and harden beneath her hand and heard the way he caught his breath.

She was smiling as his mouth claimed hers again. Nobody else existed and this…this was paradise.

It was no surprise that there were reporters waiting to cover Jake's return to the camping ground, but he wasn't really prepared for it either. His heart sank as he saw the cameras. This wasn't good.

Maybe it had been a mistake to crack that bottle of champagne on the flight back from Half Moon Island.

More likely, it had been too hard to hide the glow that

their time together in the privacy of the island had left shining in their faces and the loose-limbed relaxation of their bodies. Laughter came too easily and it seemed physically impossible not to hold eye contact for a heartbeat longer than was socially acceptable if they were just friends. And he was still holding the hand he had taken to help Ellie alight from the helicopter.

He dropped it hastily. 'I'll deal with this,' he said. 'Just head off to your own cabin as though this afternoon never happened.'

Ellie managed a very creditable casual wave as she turned away before they got too close to the waiting photographers and she raised her voice so that her words could be clearly heard.

'Thanks, Jake. It's been fun. And I'll keep in touch about how Pēpe's doing.'

Nice try but Jake could sense the expectation ahead of him. These guys knew they were onto something.

'Had a nice afternoon, Jake?'

'Where did you take Ms Sutton?'

'You're looking happy, mate. You're not going to deny that there's something going on between you two, are you?'

Jake considered trying to silence the barrage of questions with a filthy look but he knew that would be tantamount to admitting he had something he wanted to hide. So, instead, he grinned at the cameras.

'No story here, sorry. I've been bird watching, that's all. And soaking up some of the stunning scenery this country's got to offer.'

'*With* Ellie Sutton.'

Jake's head shake was amused. Dismissive. 'Of course. She's got just as much of a vested interest in how our baby kiwi is doing as I have.'

'She's very different from your ex-wife, isn't she? Couldn't be more different.'

'Exactly.' Fear about Ellie running because of media interference in their lives was getting harder to contain. He had to put them off. 'Not my type, as you've so kindly pointed out. Yes, we visited the bird-rearing centre together. And, yes, we had lunch, but you're all wasting your time. It means absolutely nothing.'

His smile became more relaxed as he saw two reporters exchange disappointed looks. One had to have a last try.

'You were holding her hand.'

'As any gentleman would, helping a lady alight from a helicopter. Now, if you'll excuse me, I've got things to do. I'm sure you do, too. There's a lot that's going to be happening in the next day or two.'

'It's weather-dependent, isn't it? Shooting the shipwreck scene?'

'Yes. But I believe the forecast isn't too bad. Check the press release. Or talk to Kirsty. I'll talk to you again soon, yeah?'

Jake walked away, confident that he'd put them off the scent.

That he'd protected Ellie, at least for now.

But it wouldn't last, would it? At some point, if he wanted to keep Ellie in his life, it would have to be made public.

Jake had no idea what would happen then.

What he did have a very clear idea of, however, was that he *did* absolutely want to keep Ellie in his life.

And it was looking more and more like he might want that for ever.

The weather wasn't as good as expected over the next couple of days and the sea swell was too big to make filming close to shore safe. Camera crews were dispatched to get some good footage of the wild surf at Cathedral Cove that could be used later and there was some editing work, production meetings and rehearsals going on that Jake was involved with, but there wasn't much for Ellie to do.

She tried to use her time productively and got out her laptop to work on some of the lecture material she was writing on aeromedical transportation, but the world of academia and even front-line rescue work seemed very distant. It wasn't long before she was checking in with the local meteorological website for both the short-and long-range weather forecasts. She almost hoped the weather would stay uncooperative because when the final scenes had been done, this interlude in her life would be over, and what would happen then between her and Jake?

He'd go back to the United States. Move on to his next movie project.

Email for a while, perhaps. Talk on the phone occasionally?

And then the contact would fade and all she'd have left would be memories of time spent with the most remarkable man she'd ever met.

Finding herself doodling a yin and yang design in her notebook made Ellie sigh and drop her pen. She clicked out of the page of weather charts and found herself on the home page of the news service she favoured. The pop-up box of hot topics was one she never normally took any notice of, but Jake's name jumped out, along with the words '...denies new romance...'

It only took a tiny movement of her hand to click on the link and there it was—a photograph of her and Jake with their hands linked, laughing as they ducked and ran from the private helicopter.

Looking, for all the world, like a couple in love.

Jacob Logan categorically denies any love interest with the mysterious paramedic who's not dishing on the time she shared with the star recently in the wake of rescuing him so dramatically. Could it be that he's protesting too much? Judge for yourself.

The triangular 'play' button on the video clip was also only a click away. And there was Jake, smiling confidently.

'...not my type, as you've so kindly pointed out. Yes, we visited the bird-rearing centre together. And, yes, we had lunch, but you're all wasting your time. It means absolutely nothing.'

How believable was that dismissive tone? That amused smile that said they were all barking up a totally ridiculous tree?

It wasn't true. He was just saying that to protect her from the media. To keep what they had private. But, even knowing that, it was still so...convincing. And weren't the best lies the ones that were a version of the truth?

Echoes of things that had unwillingly embedded themselves in her brain floated to the surface. Like what the camp manager had said. *It's not as if anything lasts in Tinseltown...*

And Jill—her most trusted friend—had had her doubts, hadn't she? *Be careful...I don't want you getting hurt again...*

The echoes became a chant until a new thought rocked Ellie. They'd been so careful to keep things secret, but was that really because it was something special and private? Or was it because it actually wasn't important? Because it meant absolutely *nothing?*

Stunned, Ellie slowly closed the lid of her laptop. She sat there, in her cabin, for a long, long time, trying to make sense of the emotional roller-coaster she'd been on ever since she'd met Jake.

She'd believed in the connection they'd made at the start, only to have it dismissed with the distant way Jake had treated her at that first press conference.

She'd totally believed him during that heartfelt conversation on the beach and...yes, she'd been insanely flattered that he'd pretended he'd been kissing her instead of Amber when he'd filmed that *perfect* scene.

Jake could never know how much it had meant to tell him that she trusted him, and that *had* been the truth.

Or had she been acting herself without realising it? Trying on that new skin that would allow her to be the best person she could be? It had felt so good, too.

She'd willingly gone along with the game of ramping up the sexual tension, but now she'd swooped down to a new low on the roller-coaster and the skin was too tight.

It felt like it was ripping in places.

Bleeding.

What if this was all just a game to someone who could make people believe whatever he wanted to make them believe?

And she was just as gullible as she'd always been?

CHAPTER TEN

He hadn't seen Ellie for hours.

When the afternoon wore on into the evening, everybody gathered for a meal. Standing beside Steve as they joined the queue to help themselves to steak and salad, Jake took another look around.

'Seen Ellie today?'

Steve shook his head. 'Things were quiet. She said she needed some time to work on lecture notes or something. She's probably in her cabin.'

'Might let her know it's time for dinner.' Jake abandoned his empty plate and slipped away.

Something about how quiet this part of the camping ground was made Jake frown. Or maybe it was the closed look of the cabin he knew was Ellie's. The door was shut. The curtains on the small window were drawn. He knocked on the door with a sense of foreboding that only increased sharply when he saw her face.

'What's wrong?'

'Nothing.' Her voice was tight. '*Absolutely* nothing, in fact.'

Good grief...had she been *crying?*

'Ellie...' Jake gave the door a push, but Ellie was pushing back, keeping it only slightly ajar.

She was clearly upset about something. Her words, and

their tone, repeated themselves in his head. *Absolutely* nothing.

Oh, no… Had someone printed what he'd said in dismissing any suspicion of their relationship? Had she *believed* it? How could she? It was too ridiculous for words.

'Let me in.' It was a command, not a request, and Jake emphasised his intent by a shove at the door that Ellie couldn't prevent.

'Someone might see you.'

'I couldn't give a damn.' Jake pushed the door shut behind him with his foot. 'We need to talk. This is about what I said to those reporters about our day together, isn't it?'

She didn't say anything. She didn't need to.

'You *believed* it?'

That hurt, dammit.

'I didn't want to believe it.' The rawness in Ellie's voice only added to his own hurt. 'It was the *last* thing I wanted to believe but you're *so* good at lying.'

'Acting.' The word was a defensive snap. 'For both our sakes. You should have known that's what I was doing. I thought—*hoped*—you knew me better than that. That you would know I was trying to protect you.'

'By *lying?*'

He couldn't win, could he? The pain of being labelled a liar and untrustworthy was gathering heat and morphing into anger.

'What did you want me to say, Ellie? That I'd just had the most incredible afternoon of my life, making love to the woman I'm head over heels in love with?'

Her jaw dropped and she went a shade paler. No wonder. He was almost shouting, which wasn't exactly a romantic way to tell someone how you felt about them, but he had to try and make her understand.

'Can you imagine what that would have unleashed?

Do you want the whole world pointing out how different our lives are? What the odds are that it could never work? Dredging up all the sordid drama of my last marriage? Finding people they could pay to reveal details of your past?'

Yes. She was beginning to understand. He could see the flicker of fear in her eyes. His voice softened.

'I know you have things you'd rather keep hidden and I respect that. I'm not going to ask you what they are because I know you'll tell me when you're ready to. When you trust me enough.'

'I *want* to trust you, Jake. I do…but…'

Her voice trailed into silence but she wanted to believe him and maybe that was enough. All he needed to do was chase the last of that uncertainty from her eyes. What he said next might be the most important lines of his life.

'I want that day to have a chance to get here,' he said slowly. 'I want…'

What did he want?

So much. A future that included Ellie. The longing was so fierce that it made the prospect of failure terrifying.

Words deserted Jake. This was too big to try and put into words because he might get it wrong. What could he say that might help Ellie see the same future he could?

Future…

Suddenly the words were there. Jake swallowed hard and stepped closer to Ellie without breaking their eye contact by so much as a blink.

'I can see the future in your eyes,' he said softly. '*My* future. Without you, it's not going to happen and…and you can't begin to know how much that scares me…'

There was more he should say but the words vanished as swiftly as they had come. He'd hit a kind of verbal wall and it felt jarring. Had he said the wrong thing?

No. From the way Ellie's gaze was softening, his words had hit the right note. He could close the gap between them now and kiss her and everything would be okay.

Except that Ellie shifted her head back a fraction. Enough to stop his movement.

'You don't need to lie to protect me, Jake,' she said. 'I can look after myself. And—if this *is* real, it can't stay hidden for ever, can it?'

'No.' Jake touched her lips softly with his own. 'And I don't want it to. But let's just get through the next few days and get this filming finished before the world goes crazy.'

The next kiss made it feel like it should. Made Jake feel like they were back on Half Moon Island and the whole world was right there in his arms.

'Does anyone know where you are?'

'Only Steve. He won't say anything.'

'So you could stay for a while?'

'Oh, yeah…' It was becoming such a familiar pleasure, scooping Ellie into his arms and taking her somewhere.

And taking her to bed was the best possible place.

Cathedral Cove was a perfect location for what would be the most dramatic scenes of this movie. The marine reserve area was only accessible by boat or on foot, which led to some major logistical issues for the huge crew, but the setting was a jewel in a country already renowned for its unbeatable scenery. With a backdrop of sheer limestone cliffs topped with ancient pohutukawa trees, the cove was named for the spectacular archway rock formation that linked its two beaches.

The frame of the archway, with the sinking ship in the sea beyond would be used for the scene in which Jake saved Amber's life and ensured that history would stay the same. First he had to persuade her to jump off the ship, keep her afloat in the waves despite the dead weight of her long dress and petticoats and then carry her through the surf and onto the safety of the beach.

Everybody was hoping a single take would be enough, especially Ellie, who'd had to carry all the gear she might need to the scene in a backpack. There were rescue boats available and she had lots of foil blankets in case of hypothermia but it was going to be a long and tense day.

No amount of anxiety or tension could undermine how happy she felt, though. Jake had told her he was in love with her—albeit in a roundabout way—with what he could have told those reporters. The time he'd spent with her last night had told her more than any words could anyway, and soon—when these final scenes were in the can—he would stop trying to hide anything and then she could really trust that this was, in fact, *real*. That she and Jake had a future together.

Her heart was in her mouth as she watched Jake jump from the tilted ship. Why wasn't he using a stunt double, like Amber was? Boats stayed near enough to help if needed during the difficult swim and then they had to reposition everyone to do the bit where an exhausted Jake staggered through the shallower surf to carry the heroine to safety.

Just like he'd carried her when they'd still been strangers.

She could remember the comfort of being encircled by those strong arms and being carried to safety. She'd thought later how amazing it would be to be able to trust someone as protective and caring as Jake.

And she was so nearly there. As scary as it was, she was ready to trust him completely with her heart. With her life. To banish for ever those warning whispers in the back of her mind.

She was close enough to hear every word of the final beach scene to be filmed. To be so proud of Jake as he played his role to perfection—using modern medical resuscitation procedures to save the life of someone who would have died if this had really been back in the eighteenth century.

The portal that would take him back to the present day was within the ancient stone archway and the heart-wrenching scene where Jake had to leave the woman he thought he loved but could never be with was gripping.

Especially that last kiss.

Was he still pretending that Amber was *her?* Ellie was having trouble hiding a tender smile as she watched. And listened. She could certainly pretend that she was the one being kissed and, yes...it did make her feel uncomfortable, watching Jake kiss another woman, but she'd have to get used to this, wouldn't she? She had to remind herself that he was only acting here. When he was with her, it was *real.*

Jake was holding Amber in his arms now. The cameras moved in for a close-up.

'I can see the future in your eyes,' he said softly. '*My* future. Without you, it's not going to happen and...and you can't begin to know how much that scares me...'

The smile on Ellie's lips died. Those words he'd said to her that had finally won her fragile trust had been nothing more than lines in a script, written by someone else. A rehearsal for an upcoming scene.

She felt faint. Dizzy and sick.

A huge cheer went up from cast and crew as the director signalled that this was a wrap and filming was over. Even if she'd wanted to, she couldn't have got near Jake in the midst of the congratulatory buzz and the chaos of moving all the people and gear from this location.

But that was fine.

Because she *didn't* want to get near him. Not before she'd got her head around this. Before she knew how on earth she was going to handle what felt like a kind of death.

There was nothing like the buzz of a wrap party.

The hard work was over, at least for the cast and crew. There was still a lot to do, of course, and Jake would be very busy for the next few weeks because he wanted to be involved with the post-production work. Thank goodness Steve had contracted some brilliant New Zealand musicians to write and record the score, and this country was beginning to lead the world in special effects. It gave him a reason to stay here for some time. Enough time, hopefully, for he and Ellie to figure out how they were going to make things work. To nurture their newborn love and make it strong enough to withstand the pressures that would inevitably come.

Jake's heart sank when he saw Ellie finally arrive but stay on the outskirts of the exuberant gathering. She looked tired and less than happy despite the smiles with which she was greeting the people she'd come to know. She wasn't enjoying being with them and that was a worry. These people were his colleagues. The faces might change from movie to movie, but the feeling of camaraderie was always the same. By the time they got to the end of a big production like this, having coped with all the hassles and hiccups, there was a real sense of being comrades-in-arms. A family.

It took a while for him for fight his way to where Ellie was standing.

'It's over, babe. Real life can resume.' He couldn't wipe the grin off his face. 'As soon as we're back in Auckland, I'm heading straight for the barber shop. You won't know me.'

'Yeah…' Ellie's smile looked brittle. 'It *is* over.'

Someone thumped Jake on the shoulder as they went past. 'Well done, Doctor.' They laughed. 'Another life saved.'

Jake ignored them. He was staring at Ellie, trying to make the connection that should automatically be there when he looked into her eyes.

But it wasn't. It was like shutters were down and there was no way he could see past them.

'I'm all packed,' Ellie said. 'I'm heading home as soon as I've said goodbye to everyone.'

Jake simply stared. Bewildered. Demanding an explanation for the inexplicable. Why was Ellie raining on his parade like this? Okay, they'd hit a speed bump yesterday but they'd sorted all that last night, hadn't they?

More than sorted it, as far as he'd been aware.

'I thought you'd been honest with me last night.' Ellie's voice was dangerously quiet. 'I actually believed what you said about the future, but you were just practising your lines, weren't you? "*I can see the future in your eyes.*"' The mimicking of his voice was painful. '"*My future.*"'

Oh…*God…* He *had* used those lines. Because he'd been lost for words and that bit of his script in the back of his head had happened to be just what he'd wanted to say. No wonder the words had come so easily. Why hadn't he realised why they'd suddenly jarred?

He must have looked as horrified as he was feeling. The look Ellie gave him dripped with pity.

'You didn't even notice, did you? I don't think you even know the difference between reality and fiction. It's all fake, isn't it?'

'No…' But Jake could hear echoes of the accusations Ben had levelled at him so many times.

'Do *you* even know who *you* really are, Jake Logan?'

'Of course I do. And so do you. You know me better than anyone, Ellie. You know more about who I am now than even Ben does.'

His tone was fierce enough for someone approaching them to take a second glance and turn away hurriedly.

'But I can't *trust* you.' The words were clearly being torn from a painful place.

'Don't do this.' Jake cast a desperate look over his shoulder. How could the party be still going in full swing when the bottom was falling out of his world? He had no idea how he could fix this.

If he could fix it.

And a tiny voice in the back of his head was asking him if he even wanted to if it was going to be this difficult.

'You said I'd tell you what I'd been hiding when I was ready to. Well...I'm ready.'

'When you trusted me enough, I said.'

'What comes first, do you think? Trust...or love?' Ellie didn't wait for an answer. 'I grew up with my parents and my grandfather—people I loved with all my heart and trusted without ever having to question it.'

He could see the muscles move in her throat as she swallowed hard. 'When you lose someone you love that much you lose a part of your soul and I...I lost everyone I had.'

He wanted to touch Ellie. To try and comfort her. To let her know that she still had someone. *Him*. But Jake knew that she wouldn't welcome the touch. She had more she wanted to say.

'It took a long, long time before I was ready to risk that kind of pain again. To love again. But I finally did. I met Michael and I fell in love. We dated for about two years and when he asked me to marry him, I was happy to say yes.'

Her tone was almost conversational. 'I already had the house with the picket fence but I was so ready for the husband who would be the father of my babies. The wedding was all planned. He travelled a lot with his consultancy work, but he promised me that we'd make it work. I just had to trust him.'

Jake knew this story was not going to end well. The sinking feeling he'd had when he'd first seen Ellie this evening was getting rapidly stronger.

She had an odd smile curling her lips now. There was no hint of genuine amusement in it.

'I guess I'm lucky that his wife and three kids didn't turn up at the church in that bit where they ask if anyone knows any reason why someone can't be lawfully wed. He left his phone behind one day when he went out to the shops to get some milk and for some reason I picked it up and answered it when it rang. His wife thought I was a colleague who was attending some conference with him. She asked me to pass on the message that he needed to remember to pick up the birthday cake for their daughter on his way home.'

Jake was stunned. 'He wasn't really going to go through with a bigamous marriage, was he?'

Ellie shrugged. 'That's not the point, is it, Jake? The point is that I trusted him. Believed everything he told me. I'm willing to bet that his wife believed everything he told her, too—all the lies that covered the time he spent with me.' She turned her head enough to break their eye contact. 'I loved him and I trusted him and when I lost him I realised I'd lost another part of me. On top of all the other parts I'd already lost. And I knew there wasn't enough of me left to risk that again because if I lost any more there might be nothing left.'

He could see the slow tears tracing the side of her nose and the tremble in her voice was heartbreaking. 'I knew I'd never be able to trust another man like that, but then

I went and fell in love with you. Of all the people in the world, I had to pick an award-winning actor.'

She looked back and Jake had never seen so much pain in anyone's eyes. He couldn't hope to make this better. It was too big.

But he had to try.

'So you're going to throw away what we've found together? Because I made the stupid mistake of saying something that was in my head thanks to a script? Because I couldn't think of a better way to say it myself?'

That tiny voice in his head was there again. Man, she's got issues, it said, but it's not your job to try and fix her. Maybe nobody can. And if she's prepared to throw it away this easily it can't mean that much to her anyway.

'What we had wasn't real. Any more than my "engagement" was real. It's all a fantasy. You're watching yourself on a big screen all the time, Jake—whether you're aware of it or not. It's the way you live your life, but I can't live like that. I don't have a script and I don't want one.'

Not being able to help soothe the pain of someone he cared about this much felt like an epic failure. Jake wasn't up to the task and it made him feel inadequate. As useless at keeping a woman happy as—God help him—his father had been?

What had he done that was *so* wrong? All he'd tried to do was love Ellie. And keep her safe. She wasn't the only one with trust issues and wasn't she doing pretty much what she thought he'd done to her? Offering something precious, only to snatch it away again?

This wasn't fair, but it *was* happening and now fear kicked in. He was going to lose Ellie and there was no way this scene could end well.

Fear and frustration were easy to twist into anger, but was he going to harness that anger to fight for this? For *them?*

'I can never, ever know whether you're for real or whether you're acting because I've been there before. Michael may not have been a famous actor, but he was as good at pretending as you are.' She seemed to get taller as she straightened her spine. 'I can't ever trust you and without trust there's nothing. Nothing worth fighting for anyway.'

She wasn't going to fight, then. So why should he?

'You're right,' she said softly. 'It's over. *Really* over.'

This time, when she turned her head, she began to walk away as well. But she had one last parting shot to send over her shoulder.

'Reality isn't that bad, Jake. Maybe you could try it one day.'

CHAPTER ELEVEN

Nothing worth fighting for.

The words were a mantra now. Part of him agreed wholeheartedly. The part that wanted to argue just needed to be reminded that it took two to tango and if one of them didn't think it was worth fighting for, it was pointless for the other to batter themselves to bits in the name of a hopeless cause.

There were elements of drama queen in it as well that reminded Jake disturbingly of his mother's reaction to life. Blowing things out of proportion. Overreacting. Making grand gestures. Did her suicide have anything to do with trying to turn real life into a scripted drama? A grand gesture gone wrong?

Maybe he'd finally find out.

Ben was unexpectedly in the country and they'd arranged to meet in Auckland after Jake's busy day of setting up the post-production work he was really looking forward to.

Had been looking forward to, anyway.

The creativity that came with the editing and sound and special effects were more satisfying than acting in many ways. Jake had been seeing his future moving in this direction for a while now and he'd viewed the next few weeks as the highlight of this whole project.

Even more so, given that it would have provided extra time with Ellie.

But Ellie was gone and her cutting last words had fuelled an anger that he was trying to hang onto because it made her disappearance from his life easier to handle.

Or not.

He couldn't keep her out of his head. No matter how hard he tried to concentrate, it seemed like every few minutes something would sift through a tiny gap in the barrier. Images of her face—the way it changed and softened with that special smile that he knew was only for him. The tone of her voice—and her laughter. The way the connection between them had made him feel…like that moment they'd looked at each other when Pēpe had been hatching.

Even Steve noticed that he wasn't entirely present in some of those meetings.

'You don't like the music?'

'I love it.'

'Could've fooled me. And the workshop for special effects? It's going to be fantastic, don't you think?'

'Absolutely.'

Steve just gave him a look. Shook his head and moved off to talk with the crowd of technical wizards they were pulling together.

No wonder he wasn't in the best of moods when he walked down to the bar he'd heard of near the Viaduct to meet Ben. It was late. He was tired.

Tired of the silent battle going on in his head.

And his heart.

He missed Ellie…

She was no drama queen like his mother. You couldn't get more real than Ellie. She didn't have a script and she didn't want one.

She thought he was fake. And here he was about to spend time with his brother, who also thought he was fake.

It was important to see him, though. If there was some way they could resolve the lingering tension between them, at least he'd have someone back in his life who meant the world to him.

He wouldn't continue feeling so…so *lonely*.

It had been weeks since the brothers had seen each other and initially it was too much like a rerun of their reunion after the rescue. Huge relief at seeing the other was okay but there was an undercurrent that was swirling over rocks that weren't very far below the surface. Weird to feel nervous about talking to Ben but Jake felt his heart skip a beat as the small talk faded. Jake needed to find a way to steer the conversation towards what really mattered.

'I gather you're not here just to see me?'

'That's why I'm here in Auckland.'

'That's not what I meant. Why come to New Zealand?'

'I brought Mary home.'

'Mary?'

'The girl who saved my life. She came to New York, but she was ill so I brought her home.'

The words were stark. The sentences bald enough for Jake to know there was a lot being left unsaid. But they were still too far apart. He needed to tread carefully if he wanted to get as close as they had once been. Close enough to really talk about the biggest rock in that undercurrent?

'So now you're heading back?'

'Yes. Tomorrow.'

'How ill is she?'

'She's okay now.'

'And you're not getting involved any further?'

'I brought her home. In the company jet.'

Jake couldn't suppress a soft snort. He knew what was happening here. The control Ben was trying to exert over himself. That he was trying to protect himself. Surely it was enough that one of them was dealing with the dark side of emotional involvement with a woman right now. Maybe Ben needed a push to wake up and smell the roses before it was too late for both of them.

'That's involvement?' The words came out more harshly than he'd intended.

'Cut it with the snide, Jake.'

'I'm not snide,' he said, on an inward sigh. 'I'm worried.'

'She'll be fine.'

'I'm worried about you.'

'Why on earth…?' He could see the way Ben's eyes widened. *He* was the big brother. He was the one who got to be worried.

'I've met a woman, too, Ben,' he said. 'Same as you, it's the woman who plucked me out of the sea. Only, unlike you, I'm in it up to my neck and…well, it's not going so well right about now.'

Talk about an understatement. Why had he said that anyway? It wasn't 'not going so well'. It was *over*. And he didn't even want to try and fight that decision.

Or maybe he did. Maybe even sorting things out with his brother wasn't going to make that lonely place disappear. Man…this was confusing. And how could he begin to try and explain that to Ben when his brother's expression suggested that he couldn't be bothered with another one of Jake's dramas. He even held up a hand as if to ward off any more information.

'You don't need to tell me. Of course it's not going well. But there's no need to talk about it—I'll be reading about it in the glossies soon enough. Maybe it's time you grew up, Jake. Marriages and happy endings belong in one of your movies. They're not the real world. Not for us, that's for sure. You've already tried and failed. You play-acted the perfect husband last time. Wasn't that enough?'

Ben was angry. Fed up with him, or was there something else bothering him even more? Jake was pretty sure there was more to this reaction than the embarrassing publicity that had come in the wake of his failed celebrity marriage. Had he really believed he was in love then? Had Ben been able to see something he hadn't?

'You think I was acting?'

'You've acted all your life—just like our mother. You don't know what's real and what's not.'

And there was Ellie's voice in his head yet again.

You're watching yourself on a big screen all the time, Jake—whether you're aware of it or not.

It wasn't true.

'I wasn't acting the first time round,' he told Ben. It was the truth. He'd believed he'd been in love, but he hadn't really known the meaning of the word, had he? 'Believe it or not, I thought it was real. But now...I'm sure not acting this time. Ellie's different. She's one in a million. This is a million miles from one failed marriage.'

Ben looked really angry now. He jerked himself to his feet. 'Then you're even more of a fool than I thought. One in a million—just like the last one. And the next one and the one after that?'

The sarcasm in his brother's tone was enough to push Jake's buttons. He didn't know Ellie. He had no idea that he was dismissing the most amazing woman on the planet. He pushed himself to his feet, his fists clenched.

'Will you cut it out?' They were getting noticed. The bar might be empty of punters but the barman was watching them carefully. 'Ellie *is* different, Ben. And we're not… we're not our parents, Ben.'

'What's that supposed to mean?'

'Just that. We're our own people.' Jake took a deep breath. 'You finally let it out, didn't you? In the life raft when you said I wouldn't know reality if it bit me. That I was just like Mom. You told me she'd killed herself and you think I'm on the same path. Heading for self-destruction because I can't pick what's real or deal with it.'

'I don't…' Ben's face was agonised. He couldn't find the words.

'Yeah, you do. It's gutted me knowing that Mom's death was suicide, but it's gutted me even more that you've kept it to yourself all these years. You've been protecting me, but you didn't have to. You've been protecting yourself and that's even worse.'

Ben shook his head. 'This isn't making any sense.'

'Maybe it's not.' Jake wasn't sure of what he was trying to say either, but the words kept spilling out. 'But this girl you brought all the way to New Zealand. Mary. She went all the way to the States to see *you?*'

'So…what?'

'I'm not even beginning to guess what that was all about,' Jake continued, 'but I don't have to guess because it doesn't make any difference. No matter who she is, no matter what she's done, no matter what she means to you, you'll never open yourself up. Because if you do, you'll have to open yourself up to the whole mess that was our mom. Our family. And Mom killed herself. Finally, I'm seeing why you're so damned afraid.'

'I'm not afraid.' A knee-jerk response. Defensive.

'If you're not afraid of relationships, then why assume that whatever I have going on with Ellie will inevitably be another disaster for the glossies to gloat over?' He turned away. 'Well, maybe it is a disaster, but at least I'm involved. I know I'm capable of loving. I'm not running away, like you.'

'Oh, for…' Ben was barely controlling his anger now. 'I'm not *running away* from anything.'

'It looks that way to me. You run. You hide. Just like you've been hiding from me all these years by not telling me the truth. Shall we go there, Ben? Talk about it properly? Or do you want to run away from that, too?'

Despair and anger were a curdled mess in his gut. Things were going so wrong here and he couldn't stop it. They were standing here in this deserted bar and staring at each other. If they'd still been ten years old one of them would have thrown a punch by now. Or twenty years old.

Maybe they still would.

The moment could have gone either way, but Jake could see so many things in Ben's face. Fear that what he was saying might be true? Sadness that they were so far apart? A willingness to try and put things right?

It wasn't going to happen, though. Not yet.

'I need to go.' Ben's tone was final.

'Of course you do.' Jake's anger was draining away, leaving a horrible empty feeling in his gut. 'People talk about emotions, you run. You've spent our lives accusing me of being like Mom every time I showed emotion. Play-acting. Yeah, okay…maybe some of it was, but not all of it. I'm trying to figure it out at last. Maybe the real is worth fighting for. The real is even worth hurting for.'

It sounded good to say it out loud.

Right.

'Yeah, well, good luck with that.' It was Ben who was being snide this time. 'What did you say—that things aren't going well between you and this new woman? Amazing. I stand amazed.'

'Get out of here before I slug you,' Jake snapped. He didn't need Ben echoing the other voice in his head. The one that was trying to persuade him to let it go. To let Ellie go. That it *wasn't* worth fighting for.

As if on cue, Ben's phone started ringing.

Someone wanted to talk to Ben. Mary?

What if it had been Ellie ringing *him* right now? Would he want to answer it?

The strength of his affirmation went a long way towards sorting his current confusion.

'Maybe you should get that,' he growled. 'Maybe it's Mary.'

'It's work.' But Ben clearly wanted to answer the call.

'There you go, then.' Jake turned away. 'I don't know why you're not taking it. Work's always been your place to hide, hasn't it, big brother? Why should anything I say make it any different?'

Well…

That had gone well.

Not.

He'd had a few beers with Ben in the bar, but that was a long time ago now. Needing to burn off some of the anger and frustration, Jake had taken a long route back to his hotel to try to walk it off.

All he'd succeeded in burning off had been any mellowing effect the beers might have had. Maybe he needed something stronger. Just as well the minibar in his room was well stocked.

The first Scotch didn't even touch sides. He could, at least, taste the second. The third ended up sitting in its glass on the coffee table in front of him as Jake tipped his head back with a groan of frustration. He went to push his hair back but the barber had dealt with the long locks today and there were no tangles to provide the welcome distraction of pain. He rubbed at his chin. Clean shaven now. He'd been looking forward to getting rid of that beard.

Looking forward to finding out what it would feel like to kiss Ellie without it. Hoping she'd love the change and be attracted to him all over again with that same passion they'd discovered between them.

Maybe he did need that third Scotch after all.

What was going so wrong in his life?

He'd lost Ellie.

It felt like he might have really lost Ben this time, too.

Sleep wasn't an option but sitting here for hour after hour, trying to make sense of the downward spiral his personal life was taking, wasn't either. By 2:00 a.m. he'd had enough. He punched in the number of Ben's phone, only to get an engaged signal. Who was he talking to at 2:00 a.m.?

This Mary maybe?

More likely to be someone in New York.

Whatever. Jake dropped the phone and closed his eyes. If he didn't catch at least a few hours' sleep, he'd have trouble keeping up with the hectic schedule tomorrow would bring. And if he couldn't keep up with the play, he might as well kiss goodbye any ambitions he had to move into a directing and editing role in the near future.

Things were bad enough already. He really couldn't afford to let his life spin any more out of control right now.

'I wish I could help, hon. I hate seeing you so sad.'

'It's helping being here, Jill. I love this place.'

Ellie was spending the afternoon at the bird-rearing centre. There was always plenty for a knowledgeable volunteer to do. The brooder pens needed to be wiped down and the peat moss dug over and checked for moisture content. Food for the older chicks needed preparation by mincing the beef heart to mix with shredded fruit and vegetables. If she was lucky, she would get to help weigh chicks or to sit quietly to observe and record their behaviour. A real treat would be helping to feed a chick, but there weren't any that needed that kind of assistance today. Maybe next time.

It *was* helping. Being here and being with one of her closest friends.

'How's the lecture writing going?'

'Okay, I guess.' Ellie put gloves on to push raw meat through the mincer. 'I've just finished one on the physiological effects of altitude. Tomorrow I'll get stuck into the biodynamics of flight. And I'm spending some time on base, getting images of aeromedical equipment. I'm keeping busy.'

'Are you enjoying it?'

'Honestly?' Ellie looked up as she moved to get a set of scales to start weighing portions of the minced beef. 'I don't think I'm cut out for an academic life. It's kind of lonely...and boring.'

'It'll be better when you're actually teaching it instead of writing about it.'

'Maybe.' Ellie was really trying hard to be optimistic but being less than honest with someone she trusted felt wrong. 'I'm not sure I'm cut out for being in a classroom, day in, day out, either. You know what they say? Those that can—do, those that can't—teach...'

'Nonsense.' Jillian emphasised her contradiction by turning on the food processor to shred some carrots. She threw Ellie a speculative glance when she turned it off again.

'Can you really not go back to active duty? Your ankle's fine now, isn't it?'

'My back isn't. That injury I had years ago was always going to limit my time on the choppers. It's time to be careful if I want to be walking properly when I'm old and gray.'

'You miss it, don't you?'

'Yeah...' But active duty as a paramedic wasn't the only thing Ellie was missing. Not by a long shot.

'You could go back on the road, then.'

Ellie shook her head. 'If I want to stay in the ambulance service, I'll either have to teach or I'll get put behind a desk as some kind of manager.' The dismal prospect made her throat feel tight. Or maybe that was due to the never-ending ache of what else she was missing.

Jake...

She tried to smile at Jillian. 'Maybe I'll just come and work for you instead.'

'Cool. We won't be able to pay you, but you'd be most welcome.'

Turning on the taps to wash some feeding bowls, Ellie had to blink hard. She needed to get over herself. There must be dozens of people who'd love the chance to do the kind of work she had the skills to do now. Like teach... or manage.

The problem was, she'd had a taste of things that were so much more exciting. Even if she knew she was lucky to have had that taste and there was no way to have it again, there was no easy way back to reality.

In her working life *or* her love life.

Jillian handed her one of the feed bowls when everything had been weighed and charted. 'That's Pēpe's. You get to feed him. He's your baby.'

The squeeze around Ellie's heart was a physical pain. He wasn't just hers, he was Jake's too. She'd never again be able to look at as much as a picture of a kiwi without thinking of him. Without the pain of knowing that she'd lost something precious. Not really fair when she lived in a country that had made the bird its national icon.

Except she hadn't lost it, had she?

It had never really been there. Just an illusion on her part and play-acting on Jake's.

If it had been real, she would have heard from him by now. How many days would it take before she gave up and started getting over him?

Right now it felt like there wouldn't be enough days in the rest of her life for that to happen.

She needed to try harder.

'Have you had any luck getting through the red tape for Pēpe's release? Did you find out who owns Half Moon Island now?'

'I'm working on it.' Jillian tapped the side of her nose. 'I have contacts. Give me a bit more time and I'll get it sorted.'

Ellie nodded. She managed a genuine smile this time.

A bit more time. Perhaps that *was* all that was needed. For Pēpe's release and for her own return to happiness.

The headache Jake had the next morning was entirely self-inflicted. The weariness was bone deep, but at least the combination of physical and emotional suffering made him feel like he might have finally hit rock bottom.

Did that mean the only way might be up?

It was during a meeting with sound technology experts that a moment of clarity hit. He wasn't the only person present who was dubious about what was being planned to emphasise the crashing of surf against rocks during the shipwreck scene and the music that would accompany it.

Steve was frowning. 'Isn't it a bit over the top?'

'It'll work,' the sound guy said. 'Trust us.'

And there was Ellie's voice in his head yet again.

Without trust there's nothing.

The echo stayed with Jake for the rest of the day. It got louder when he didn't have to focus on work and was trying to kill the last of his headache and fatigue with a brutal workout in the hotel gymnasium.

Lack of trust was what had blown them apart.

It was what was still wrong between himself and Ben.

With a towel knotted loosely around his hips, Jake caught his reflection in the locker-room mirrors as he walked back from the showers. His tattoo was such a part of his body these days he barely registered its presence unless it had to be masked for a scene. Or when someone asked about it. Like Ellie had.

It was actually possible to still feel the light touch of her fingers as she'd traced the characters. To hear his own voice as he'd explained their meaning.

He who dares wins.

Jake's step slowed. His gaze lifted to stare into his own eyes.

Did he dare?

Could he win what he wanted most?

The answer was suddenly crystal clear. He had no other choice but to try his best, because if he didn't, he would be haunted by what-ifs for the rest of his life.

But how?

Again, the answer seemed obvious. He would ask someone who might know. Someone whose advice he could trust.

This time, Ben answered his phone straight away. 'Jake… Hey, man! I'm glad you rang. I—'

'I need help,' Jake interrupted. He couldn't afford the distraction of any small talk. This was too important. 'I've done something and I don't know how to fix it. How to get Ellie to trust me again.'

She had every reason not to trust him. He'd proclaimed publicly that their relationship meant absolutely nothing and then he'd compounded the situation by using lines that had meant nothing because they were no more than part of a rehearsed script.

The silence on the other end of the line was startled. Jake rushed to fill it.

'I lied, Ben. I told the media that Ellie meant nothing to me.'

'Well…of course you did. They would have destroyed any privacy you could have had for the foreseeable future. You were protecting her.'

'That's what I thought. But what it's really done is destroy the trust that was there. And that's what matters most, isn't it? It's what's gone wrong between us, too.'

The silence was heavier this time. He could imagine Ben closing his eyes or starting to pace as he tried to figure out what to say to that.

'I understand that's why you lied about Mom,' Jake said quietly. 'To protect *me*. And it's okay. I *get* that and…and I still love you, man. It's why I knew you'd understand. Why you can help me out here.'

'It's not that simple.' The words were almost a sigh. 'I wasn't lying to protect you. I was trying to protect myself, I guess. I was…hiding—like you accused me of doing—and…I can't do that any more. I've…' He sounded choked now. 'I've learned something today. Something *huge*… and—'

Again Jake interrupted his brother. 'I don't understand. How were you trying to protect yourself?'

He didn't try and fill the silence this time. He simply waited it out.

'It was my fault.'

The incredulous huff came out almost like a snort of laughter. 'Are you *kidding* me?'

'You weren't there, Jake. You were in hospital, remember? And I was in jail for the night.'

'The car conversion incident. Of course I remember.' Jake couldn't help a wry smile. 'A highlight in the disreputable adolescence of the wild Logan boys.'

'Things were bad at home when I got out. Mom had a black eye and she was hysterical. She kept crying. Telling me how sorry she was. Telling me I had to look after you.'

'Sounds like Mom.' That sadness was never going to go away completely. Jake sighed. 'Was Dad responsible for the black eye or did she get drunk and fall over?'

'I'm pretty sure it was Dad.'

'Bastard.'

'You said it.'

'Even so, Mom was being a drama queen. That's the way she always reacted to stuff.'

'No. She was telling me she was going to kill herself. I could have done something, Jake, and I didn't. And I was too ashamed to tell anyone. That's why the coroner ruled it had been an accidental overdose. Because I was hiding and not telling the truth.

The expletive Jake used dismissed any credence the statement had.

'You were *fourteen*. A kid. Even if it *was* a cry for help, she couldn't have expected you to recognise it, let alone know what to do about it.'

'You don't...blame me, then?'

'The only thing I'd blame you for is hiding it from me. Not telling me right from the start.'

'You were so gutted. I couldn't make it worse. I...love you, too, bro.'

Jake wished he was close enough to give Ben a hug. 'And let's agree to leave the bad stuff behind, okay? No more thinking the past is going to shape the future. We might be Charles Logan's sons but we're *nothing* like him.

You were wrong when you said that happy endings only belong in one of my movies. They can happen for real.'

'I know.' Ben sounded choked up. Good grief...was that a *sniffle* Jake heard?

'No more hiding,' he ordered, trying to keep his tone light. 'Put the truth out there and live with it. The people who love you will understand.'

'You're right.' Yep. Ben certainly sounded more emotional than Jake had ever heard him sound. 'I've done that, Jake. With Mary—the woman I'll love till the day I die. You're not going to believe this but...I'm getting married. Not only getting married but I'm going to be a father.'

'Holy heck...'

'I *can* do it. Love. Family. The whole shebang. So can you. Get the truth out there and see what happens. *Trust*.'

The truth?

The truth was that Jake loved Ellie and didn't want to spend another minute without her in his life if it could be helped.

There was still the small problem of finding a way to tell her.

Of even getting her to agree to see him. He might not be responsible for the way her trust in men had been shattered in the past but he'd still have to pick up those pieces as well as the contribution he'd made.

The route from the hotel gymnasium to his room took Jake past the reception desk and a souvenir shop, the window of which had a display of cute, fluffy, soft toy kiwis.

Jake stopped in his tracks, staring through the window.

Then he pulled out his phone and hit a number on his speed dial.

'Kirsty? How's it going in Queenstown? You having

a good break?' He listened for only a moment. 'Can you do me a big favour? As soon as you hang up, text me the number for the woman who runs the bird-rearing centre we took the baby kiwi to. Jillian? I need to talk to her.'

CHAPTER TWELVE

For a moment Jillian hesitated before dialling the number she needed.

Was she doing the right thing—interfering in her friend's life like this? Jake had been very convincing, of course, but wasn't that part of why Ellie didn't believe she could trust him anymore—because he was capable of making people believe whatever he wanted them to believe?

No. It wasn't just that she was prepared to believe the best of people. Or that she didn't have the kind of tragedies and disappointments that Ellie had had in her life that made it harder for her to trust. This was a time when the wisdom of years counted. When you could see the big picture and more than a glimmer of hope that someone you loved so much might be able to find the happiness she deserved.

Waiting for the call to be answered, Jillian deliberately put a big smile on her face so that her voice wouldn't give away the secret she'd been keeping for days now. She'd be able to sound no more than excited.

'Ellie...I've got news.'

'Hi, Jill. Is it good news?'

'Sure is.' Jillian's smile widened. 'I've managed to track down the new owners of Half Moon Island. And we've got permission to release Pēpe there.'

'Oh...that's *fantastic* news. When?'

'As soon as it can be arranged. I'm onto it…but…' Jillian took a deep breath. 'Hang onto your hat, hon. That's not all.'

'Oh?'

'The new owners are really excited by the idea. So excited they're planning to turn Half Moon into an official bird sanctuary.'

She could hear Ellie's gasp. 'Have they got any idea how much that would *cost?*'

'I get the impression they're not short of funds. What they *are* short of, though, is expertise. They need to find someone who could set it up and keep it running. I said I might know someone who could be interested.'

There was a stunned silence on the other end of the line. And then Ellie's voice was no more than a whisper.

'You mean *me*…? Oh, Jill…That might be exactly what I need in my life right now.' Her voice grew stronger. 'Have you met the owners? Who are they? What are they like?'

'You can find out for yourself. I suggested that we meet for a drink. They're pretty busy, but are you free late on Thursday night? Say nine p.m.? I'm thinking somewhere local for you. One of those gorgeous little café bars in Devonport?'

'I'm free. Of course I'm free. Oh…I can't believe this is happening. Am I dreaming?'

Jillian laughed. 'No. You're not dreaming and neither am I but— I've got to go, hon. I think we've got a new arrival coming in. See you Thursday.'

Ending the call, Jillian looked through the window of her quiet office into an equally quiet area outside. Nobody was arriving, but she hadn't been sure how much longer she could keep the lid on her secret.

She closed her eyes. Her part was over.

It was up to Jake now.

And Ellie could still make her own choices. It wasn't really interfering, was it?

Just helping.

The timing was perfect.

Ellie had been dreading Thursday night ever since that invitation had arrived in the mail a few days ago.

An invitation to a private screening of the first cut of Jake's movie. There was still a lot of work to do, but the production crew was ready to get a feel for the whole movie and not just sections, and they wanted a big screen so they'd hired a small theatre. The venue was top secret so that there was no chance of anyone from the media sneaking in or someone trying to pirate the footage. Anyone who wanted to attend would have to ring Kirsty on the day to find out the location and time.

Ellie had been circling the problem, torn between a longing to see Jake again—even if it was only on a big screen—and not wanting to take such a huge step backwards in the programme of 'getting over Jake.'

Now she didn't have to fight the battle. Meeting the new owners of Half Moon Island and discussing what could be an entirely new future for herself was not only the sensible thing to do—it was the first time since things had ended with Jake that Ellie was feeling hopeful that life could still be good.

What did you wear to a meeting that might be such a huge turning point in life? Someone who was serious about bird conservation and was prepared to live in isolation on a tiny island wouldn't be interested in dressing up to the nines and they were only meeting in a casual bar, but Ellie still wanted to present herself well.

She'd lost weight recently so her jeans looked pretty good, especially since it was cool enough in the evenings now to tuck them into long boots. Something for warmth was needed over her pretty top but when Ellie pulled out her favourite long shawl cardigan, she had to fight back sudden tears.

This was the cardigan she'd worn on that first night on set. When she'd gone for that walk on the beach with Jake and he'd shared secrets with her because he trusted her.

The night he'd kissed her and she'd known there was no point in trying to deny that she was in love with him.

The soft wool felt warm and comforting as she buried her face in it. Could she bear to wear it again? This might be the real test. If she could wear an item of clothing that almost had the smell of Jake on it and still step forward into a new future she would know that everything would be all right. That she could survive.

By the time she'd stepped off this particular ride on her emotional roller-coaster, Ellie was running late. With no time to braid her hair, she simply brushed it, grabbed her bag and headed out to meet Jillian. At least the meeting point was within easy walking distance.

'Which bar are we going to?' she asked, having greeted her friend.

'Come with me. It's not far.'

Ellie knew this area like the back of her hand, but she had no idea where they were going as Jillian ducked down a side street, into a driveway and past a row of rubbish bins to a very unassuming wooden doorway. Oddly, a man who looked like a bouncer was standing outside. Even more oddly, he gave Jillian a nod and opened the door that led into a long, narrow and very dark corridor.

'Where on *earth* are you taking me?'

'Shhh...' Jillian held a warning finger against her lips and Ellie was startled enough to fall silent.

And then she heard them. Voices. And one of those

voices was someone she knew so well that the sound entered every cell in her body and took her breath away.

Jake's voice. So loud and clear it could only be a recording.

She would have stopped in her tracks. Turned around and fled even, but Jillian was blocking any escape route. Urging her forward. And suddenly Ellie found herself in the back of the small theatre, having come through a curtain screening one of the emergency exits.

And now she couldn't have moved even if Jillian had tried to force her. The screen was huge and it was filled with Jake's face. The room was resonating to the sound of his voice. It was the first time Ellie had seen him on a big screen and the effect was totally overwhelming. She shrank back into the folds of the curtain, trying desperately to get a grip on such a larger-than-life experience. To cope with the wash of such an overwhelming rush of emotion.

The comfortable, plush seats of the theatre were full of people, but they were all riveted by what was happening on screen. Apparently nobody had seen Jillian and Ellie sneak in and while she was appalled at how her evening had been hijacked, there was nothing she could do for the moment. And they were standing near the back. It would be possible to slip out before the lights came back on and nobody would even have to know she'd been here. It wouldn't be for very long either, because they'd come in quite close to the end.

Jake was busy saving Amber. How had they managed to get such good close-up footage of him making the dangerous jump off the ship into the sea with Amber in his arms, without revealing that it was a stunt double he was carrying?

Watching him walk out of the surf with those wet clothes clinging to his body was almost too much. Ellie's hands clutched a fold of the velvet curtain beside her and crushed it into her palm.

The cardigan wasn't the real test of her resolve, was it? Not even close. *This* was going to be the real test. Having to listen to Jake say those lines again. The lines he'd deceived her with. Ellie steeled herself and willed them to happen because they would hurt all over again and they'd make her angry and get rid of any doubts she might be harbouring that she'd done the right thing in walking away.

And it was so much clearer. Not just bigger. The cameras had gone in for a very close shot as Jake was speaking and it was a perspective that she couldn't possibly have had, seeing it in real life.

Dear Lord…she actually got to see the very pores of his skin and every minute twitch of muscles as he spoke the lines. To see right into his eyes. Those beautiful, dark gray eyes.

Except…something felt wrong.

Ellie had the curious sensation that her body was simply vanishing as she concentrated so hard on the screen, trying to figure out what was so discordant between what she was registering on screen and what was happening in her head. It was almost as if she was floating…getting closer and closer to the screen and those enormous eyes.

And then, with a blinding thump, well after the lines had finished and the scene was racing forward as Jake stepped through the portal and back to real time, she realised exactly what it was.

What was missing.

Jake's eyes hadn't looked anything like that when he'd said those words to her. They'd been so much more…alive.

Genuine?

Ellie was gripping the curtain again, but this time it

was to help her stay on her feet because the realisation was enough to make her feel dizzy.

Okay…the lines *were* part of a script and Jake had rehearsed them enough to have them well tucked into his memory so that he could produce them perfectly on screen.

But he had been acting when he'd used those lines in the movie.

He *hadn't* been acting when he'd said them to her. He'd meant every single word.

He *could* see his future in her eyes.

And he *had* been scared.

And what had she done when he'd made himself so vulnerable? She'd hit back and thrown everything away.

Any thoughts of escaping before Jake could see that she was here drained away. This might be the last chance she ever had to say something to the man she had loved and lost.

Still loved.

The very least she could try and do was to apologise. She owed it to Jake to let him know that he hadn't deserved the way she had treated him. Not that she would expect a mere apology to put things right but surely it would be better for both of them to make at least a kind of peace with which to move forward?

She was here.

He'd seen the two women slip in through the emergency exit because he'd been watching for it. He'd barely focused on the majority of the movie until then. It was even harder to try now.

Despite the darkness of the theatre, there had been more than enough light coming from the screen to reveal that Ellie's hair was flowing loose and Jake's hands itched to bury themselves in that cascade of silk again. And she was wearing *that* cardigan. The one she'd worn that evening when they'd paddled in the sea. When he'd known he was with someone he felt totally safe with.

But if focusing on the movie was hard then, he knew it would be nothing compared to having to watch *that* scene. He would never be able to watch that without cringing. It was all too easy to put himself in Ellie's place and imagine how she must have felt, learning that his apparently heartfelt declaration had been nothing more than rehearsed lines.

It was so hard not to turn his head again, but if Ellie knew that he knew she was here, she might simply vanish again and he wouldn't have the chance to say what he wanted to say so much. He could only hope that she wouldn't see all this as being stage-managed. Fake. That maybe she would understand that desperate times called for desperate measures.

The clapping and cheering of all the people still involved with the movie, or staying on in New Zealand to have a holiday, faded as the massive curtains settled back into place in front of the screen and Steve stepped up onto the stage to say how happy he was with the way the movie had come together and thank everyone for all their hard work.

'Drinks and supper will be served in a few minutes,' he finished, 'but I know you're all waiting to hear a few words from the star of the show. So here's Jake…'

He'd never been this nervous giving a speech in public. His heart had never thumped this hard or his mouth been this dry. Jake didn't dare look to see if Ellie was still there, shrouded by the curtain. Not yet anyway.

'Obviously, I want to echo Steve's thanks to you all,' he began. 'It's not only a great movie but I've had the best time of my life making it. Acting's the best job in the world because—for a while—you get to play—to live the fantasies that most people can only dream about.'

He swallowed hard. 'Maybe the lines between reality and fantasy get a bit blurred now and then, but I want you to know that *I* know what's real.' He took a deep breath and allowed his head to turn slowly until he was looking straight at Ellie.

'What's worth fighting for.'

Her gasp was involuntary.

He had to have known she was there all along for his gaze to find her so unerringly as he said those words. She hadn't been able to take her eyes off him. He looked so different, with his hair short and only a dark shadowing on his jaw as a faded echo of that beard. She wanted to bury her fingers in his hair. Stroke the outline of that strong jaw and then leave kisses in the trail her fingers had made.

Shocked out of where her thoughts had been drifting, Ellie tried to cling to that gaze but Jake looked away. Let his gaze rove over everybody present.

'It's been a real privilege to spend time in New Zealand and I have to say I've fallen in love with kiwis. One in particular anyway.'

Ellie's head was spinning. Was he talking about Pēpe? Or *her?* And why on earth was he doing this in public?

A somewhat panicked scan of the theatre reassured Ellie that she knew most of the people here and that she could feel safe as part of the family that the cast and crew of the movie represented, but this was still a huge step into a space between something private and something that would be on display for the whole world. Jake couldn't know that what he was saying wasn't going to be leaked to the media.

And this was...*real*.

With her new-found ability to see the difference, Ellie could read Jake's body language and hear it in the tone of his voice. It felt like she had suddenly become fluent in a new language.

She could speak Jake.

And fear had been replaced by trust.

He might be an amazing actor but Ellie could see the difference between the acting and reality now. So clearly, even a tiny flashback to the lines he'd given the media about their relationship meaning nothing made her cringe inwardly. How could she have believed—even for an instant—in something that was such obvious acting?

Did other people ever find a connection like this? On a level so deep that it felt like something vital in her very soul could see its own reflection in Jake's?

To love someone this much was terrifying.

Especially when she couldn't know where this was going or what Jake was going to say next.

Those words only confused her even more.

'I have a new project,' Jake said. 'I want to give this kiwi a home. Security for the rest of her life. Love.'

Jillian nudged Ellie and leaned close to whisper. 'Did I tell you that the feather test results came through? Pēpe's a girl.'

No. She hadn't passed on the news. He was talking about the baby bird, then. So why was her heart thumping so hard and so fast that Ellie thought she might pass out?

'This special kiwi has given me a new direction,' Jake continued. 'As some of you know, I've been looking at taking my career in a new direction. The Logan brothers' company funds wildlife projects and I intend to start filming and fronting documentaries about them. To try and do my bit, I guess, to make the world a slightly better place.'

The clapping was appreciative and encouraging, but

Ellie couldn't join in. Her hands wouldn't move. Her body was frozen. She had that odd, floaty feeling again.

'Acting has taught me a great deal,' Jake told everybody then. 'And maybe I've learned that the most important lesson is the value of *not* acting. Of being able to be myself.'

He was looking at Ellie again. So intently that other heads began to turn as well, but it didn't matter. The only thing that mattered was the next thing that Jake was going to say.

'And I've heard tell that you don't go looking for the person you want to live with for the rest of your life.' His voice was soft but it still carried in a silence that felt as if everybody in the theatre was holding their breath. 'You go looking for the person you can't live without.'

Everybody was staring at Ellie now.

What had she said to him that time? That if this was real then other people would have to find out some time?

This was that time. She couldn't be the only person here who could feel the electricity in this room. A current that was adding a delicious kind of buzz to that floating sensation.

'I've found that person,' Jake said, raw emotion making his voice a little hoarse. 'My kiwi.'

The trust being put on public display was breathtaking. From a man who'd been humiliated in public by a woman before, it was courageous to say the least. He couldn't know whether he was safe. He'd put his vulnerability into her hands once before and she'd trampled on it. Not only was he prepared to trust her again—in front of all these people and potentially in front of the whole world—he was trusting what they had found between them.

That connection. And a love that was strong enough to last the distance.

The rest of their lives.

Was Jake the person *she* couldn't live without?

Oh…there was absolutely no doubt about that.

Suddenly Ellie's body could move again, although her legs felt distinctly wobbly. She didn't have to think about where to move because there was only one direction she could possibly go.

Judging by the crescendo of applause and cheering as she floated towards the stage to join Jake, everybody else thought exactly the same thing.

They belonged together.

It was surprisingly easy to escape the champagne supper after the first wave of congratulations had been made.

Using the same emergency exit that Jillian had tricked Ellie into entering the theatre by, Jake took her out into the night to walk down to a tiny beach near the marina where the moonlight filled the sea with flashing diamonds of light.

Not that they could compete with the flash of the diamond Jake produced from his pocket.

'You can change it if you don't like it.' He smiled. 'But I couldn't ask you to marry me without having something to put on your finger.'

'I love it,' Ellie said. 'I love *you*. I think I have, ever since you carried me along that beach into the teeth of a cyclone.'

'And I think I started to fall in love with you when you gave me your hair tie.'

Ellie made a face. 'Wasn't much of a gift.'

'But I already knew how brave and amazing you were. When I saw you sitting there in front of the fire with that glorious hair all free—like it is now…' Jake's fingers wove themselves into her hair. 'That was when I realised you were incredibly beautiful as well. I might not have known it then, but I was already lost.'

'And I should have known I was lost when you went down into the hole to rescue Pēpe just for me.'

There was no more talking for some time then. They sat, side by side on the top of a rock wall, sharing magically tender kisses under the moonlight.

'I've missed you so much,' Jake whispered. 'It's only been days but I feel like I've wasted half my life.'

'Me, too.'

'We'll never let that happen again. Wherever we need to go, let's do it together. Even if we have to drag half a dozen kids with us to a hut in a wildlife park in Africa or a lighthouse in a bird sanctuary on Half Moon Island.'

Ellie's jaw dropped. 'Oh…*no.* I totally forgot. I was supposed to be meeting the new owners of Half Moon Island tonight. Or was that just a trick of Jill's to get me to the theatre?'

'It wasn't and you have.'

Ellie laughed. 'Fire that scriptwriter,' she said. 'I didn't understand a word of that.'

The flash in Jake's eyes was fierce. 'It's not a script,' he said. 'And it never will be, between us. Even if the words happen to be the same. This…this is as *real* as it gets. The truth and nothing but the truth, okay?'

Ellie could only nod. Her heart was so full it hurt.

'Always.' Her smile wobbled. 'But I still didn't understand.'

'Jill's been a rock,' Jake told her. 'She knew how I felt about you and she gave me hope. She also put me in touch with some other people. The paperwork's not through yet, but you've met the new owner of Half Moon Island. It's me. Us.'

The gift was priceless. Because of the memories. Because it was already a part of her soul.

'And...and you're serious about turning it into a sanctuary?'

'Couldn't be more serious. And not just a sanctuary for birds. I'm hoping it will be a sanctuary for us, too. We could do up the cottage, couldn't we? Put in a proper helipad and boat ramp and go there whenever we need time just for ourselves? A place that couldn't be more private?'

To always be able to go back to the first place they'd made love? Blessed by the memories of the other people in her life that she had loved and been loved by? Ellie couldn't stop the tears filling her eyes and her chest being too tight to speak, but it didn't matter. She could simply kiss Jake until she found her voice again.

'That would be...just perfect.'

'You know what else would be perfect?'

'What?'

'If we could get married there.'

EPILOGUE

IT *WAS* THE perfect place for a wedding.

Okay, the logistics had been a bit challenging, but they were getting used to that now, after months of ferrying tradesmen and materials to the tiny island. But given that it was a ceremony half the world seemed to want to watch and that the stars of this particular scene wanted to keep it as private as possible, the isolated venue couldn't have been better.

They weren't shutting the world out completely. The important people in their lives were here. An off-duty rescue helicopter, which had brought Dave and Mike and Smithie and their partners, was sharing the helipad with the sleek black machine that Ellie intended to learn to fly herself because Jake had claimed the captain's duties for their yacht.

There was company for that yacht down at the new jetty, too. Steve and Kirsty and others from the movie crowd had come by boat and Ben and his new wife, Mary, had been excited to try out their new yacht—a gorgeous replacement for the one wrecked in that long-ago storm.

As she took a last peep through the window of the cottage, Ellie could see the brothers standing side by side outside the white, open-sided marquee that had been erected on the newly mown grass beneath the lighthouse. They weren't identical twins, but they were equally tall and gorgeous-looking and they were wearing the same elegant gray suits with the flash of red from the posy of pohutukawa flowers in their buttonholes.

She saw them exchange a glance and smile at each other. She saw Ben squeeze his brother's shoulder as Jake cast a hopeful look towards the doorway through which his bride would emerge. He had to shade his eyes against the glare of the summer sunshine. The marquee had been an insurance policy against helicopters and cameras with telephoto lenses, but the shade it provided was going to be a bonus on this stunning day with its clear blue sky and calm seas.

The conditions couldn't be more different from when Ellie had first met Jake. And Ben, come to think of it, when the brothers had been fighting over who was going to be rescued first.

Who could have dreamed that that storm would have changed the futures of both the Logan brothers? Not only because they'd both found new happiness and life partners but because, in the end, the rift between them had been healed and they were now closer than ever.

She saw the brothers turn and enter the shade beneath the marquee. They would all be waiting for the bride and matron of honour to arrive now.

'You look gorgeous. I don't think I've ever seen you wearing a dress, but that is absolutely perfect on you.'

'Thanks, Jill.' Ellie smoothed the raw silk of the sheath dress that fitted like a glove until it flared out from knee level. How long would it take Jake to see the private message in the beadwork on the bodice and cap sleeves? Subtle shades of white and cream in the tiny pearl beads had lent themselves to a discreet repeating pattern.

Yin and yang. Two halves creating a whole.

Not just for twins.

For herself and Jake now.

She picked up her bouquet. The main flush of red blooms from New Zealand's native Christmas tree was well over, but they flowered a little later out here on Half Moon Island and it hadn't been hard to find enough to accompany the white roses. More of the feathery red flowers were clipped into the twist of hair that was supposed to make Ellie's loose hair behave in the sea breeze.

Jillian's youngest granddaughter, Charlotte, was holding a basket of red and white rose petals.

'Can we go now?' she begged. 'I want to throw the petals.'

Jillian smiled at Ellie. 'You ready, hon?'

'I can't wait. I'll be right behind you.'

Jillian took Charlotte's hand and moved towards the door. 'Don't start throwing until we're under the tent. We don't want to run out of petals, do we?'

Stepping outside, Ellie looked up at the lighthouse.

Tears blurred her eyes for a heartbeat as she gathered the memories of her family around her.

'I so wish you were all here,' she whispered. 'Grandpa and Mum and Dad—I hope you know how happy I am. And how much we love this place. We're going to take such good care of it, I promise.'

Jake had seen this lighthouse as a symbol of both danger and safety.

Ellie could only see the safety. A strong, silent sentinel that was always going to be there to help bring people home safely.

Gathering her skirt in her hands, Ellie moved towards the marquee.

She was going home.

Because that was where the heart was, wasn't it?

It wouldn't matter where in the world she and Jake were, she would always be home because she would be with the man she would love for the rest of her life.

She paused again before she stepped onto the trail of rose petals Charlotte had created to lead her through the centre of the intimate gathering.

Just for a moment.

So that she could bask in the expression on Jake's face when he saw her. The admiration. The love. The promise…

And then she walked forward. Past smiling faces and murmurs of appreciation. Past where Mary was sitting with the cocoons that held her and Ben's newborn twins.

Tears threatened to blur her vision again then. She would never forget the look in Jake's eyes when he'd met his tiny niece and nephew for the first time a couple of days ago.

He'd caught her gaze and held it and she'd seen the same kind of wonder she'd seen when they'd been watching Pēpe hatch. And more…she'd seen his hopes and dreams for their own future family. She'd seen the love that would be there for all of them.

For ever.

That look was there again as she reached his side, handing her bouquet to Jillian so that she could link hands with Jake in front of the celebrant.

For a long, long moment, however, they could only look at each other.

Sharing vows in public was merely a formality. Those vows had already been made and were locked in place for ever. Their hopes and dreams were the same.

And it would happen.

Sooner than Jake might expect.

Later, when everyone had gone, they could go back to their secret place. Even more special now because it was where the burrow had been made for Pēpe's new home, it had been used more than once to share their love.

It would be the perfect place to tell him that he was going to become a father.

* * * * *

THE BILLIONAIRE'S NANNY

BY

MELISSA McCLONE

With a degree in mechanical engineering from Stanford University, the last thing **Melissa McClone** ever thought she would be doing was writing romance novels. But analyzing engines for a major US airline just couldn't compete with her happily-ever-afters. When she isn't writing, caring for her three young children or doing laundry, Melissa loves to curl up on the couch with a cup of tea, her cats and a good book. She enjoys watching home decorating shows to get ideas for her house—a 1939 cottage that is *slowly* being renovated. Melissa lives in Lake Oswego, Oregon, with her own real-life-hero husband, two daughters, a son, two lovable but oh-so-spoiled indoor cats and a no-longer-stray outdoor kitty that has decided to call the garage home.

Melissa loves to hear from her readers. You can write to her at PO Box 63, Lake Oswego, OR 97034, USA, or contact her via her website, www.melissamcclone.com.

To the authors, readers and friends
who helped me save Miss Mousie, a foster cat,
who now has a forever home with us.

Special thanks to Sarah for sparking an idea
about a nanny heroine, and Lisa Hayden,
Terri Reed and Teresa Morgan.

Chapter One

"Mmmeorrrrrooooowwwrrrrreeee."

The cat's mournful they-left-me-here-to-die wail grated on Emma Markwell's frazzled nerves. She wiped her sticky palms on her serviceable knee-length gray skirt. Her gaze dropped to the cat carrier on the floor of the small airport catering to corporate and private planes in Hillsboro, Oregon. "I know you don't want to be here. Me, either. But we'll be on our way to Haley's Bay soon."

Blossom hissed. The sound echoed across the waiting area.

Emma's shoulders were hunched, as if she could hide from the people looking at her. But with the slasher movie sounds spewing from the she devil in the cat carrier, no one would ignore them now.

Perspiration dampened the back of Emma's neck. The brown plait of French braid felt heavy and sticky. If she wasn't careful, anxiety might create a perspiration crisis before she set foot on the private jet. Not good. She wanted to meet her new boss, Atticus Jackson "AJ" Cole, looking professional—a perfect temporary personal assistant—not show up on his plane smelly and wet.

So what if she hadn't flown in five years, two months and seventeen days? The flight to AJ's hometown in Washington, where the Columbia River met the Pacific Ocean, would be short. Time to pull herself together. Blossom, too. Emma peered into the crate.

The eight-year-old orange tabby's backside greeted her. The cat's tail trembled.

Poor kitty. Last night, Blossom's first at Emma's studio apartment in southeast Portland, hadn't gone well. The foster cat had shredded two rolls of toilet paper. Now the cat stared at the crate wall as if she were in a time-out. Adjusting to a new environment was difficult when you were alone in the world. Emma had been old enough to understand what being a foster kid meant and learned to adapt, unlike this frightened feline.

She reached toward the carrier's door. Sixteen years without any family to rely on and six years being a nanny made her an expert caretaker, no matter what the age or species of her charge. "Hey, no worries. I won't let anything happen to you. Promise."

The cat responded with a banshee yowl. Three men in business suits glared. A woman pressed her lips together and narrowed her gaze.

Emma rubbed her fingertips along the strand of fake pearls hanging over the neckline of her pink short-sleeved sweater set. She leaned closer to the crate's door. "You might not agree, but traveling with me is your best option. Otherwise, you'd be stuck in a metal cage at a vet's office while they repair the shelter. Kitten season means foster homes are full of little ones. I called each and every person on the foster list to see if they had room."

None did. With such short notice, no pet sitter was available. That meant Blossom was coming along with Emma.

Traveling was difficult for animals, but especially cats. Still, the shelter director thought flying by a private jet and staying with Emma, who Blossom tolerated unlike the other shelter volunteers, would be less stressful than being crated at a clinic.

A name sounded over the PA system. Not Emma's. Her relief was palpable.

A man with salt-and-pepper hair and a black messenger bag swung over his shoulder walked toward the door.

"Not our turn, Blossom."

Thank goodness. Emma glanced around the waiting area full of orange upholstered chairs. People sat, working on tablets or laptops. Others stood, talking or texting on cell phones. No one looked nervous about flying. She hoped she didn't. She crossed her fingers.

Always appear cool and confident even if you're not, an instructor had told the class at the Rose City Nanny Academy. Emma lived by those words whether she was rushing bleeding or sick kids to the ER, speaking about a child's behavior on behalf of a parent with a school principal or giving statements in custody battles. Today should be no different. Not should, would.

A security guard passed in front of her. A chain jiggled from his belt loop.

Blossom hissed.

"Stupid cat," he muttered, walking away with a disapproving look.

"Stop acting like a grumpy diva," Emma said to the cat. Blossom's antisocial behavior had kept her from being shown at any of the Portland Paws Rescue's adoption events. However, the cat did better one-on-one. "No one wants an unfriendly kitty. And you don't want to spend the rest of your life at the cattery. Being in a forever home with a loving family would be so much better for you."

She dreamed of owning a home and having a family herself. She would take care of her own house and children, not be an employee who never quite fit in or belonged. Someday…

Libby Hansen's catchy ringtone sounded.

Emma grabbed her phone and hit Answer, eager to talk to her best friend recovering in a New York hospital. "How are you?"

"I could be better."

Her pulse accelerated. "Complications from the ruptured appendix?"

"I wish." Libby's voice sounded dry, scratchy. "A smokin' hot resident made rounds today. He didn't give me a second glance. All he cared about was reading my chart."

Emma released the breath she'd been holding. "He was wowed speechless by your beauty."

"I look like a zombie from a high school kid's horror movie project. Enough about me. You're at the airport, right?"

"I'm here with Blossom." Libby and her parents were Emma's final foster family, the closest thing she had to living relatives. She would take Libby's place as a personal assistant for the next five days, even fly, to give her friend the rest and recovery time she needed. "Attila hasn't arrived yet."

Libby sucked in a breath. "Don't you dare call AJ that to his face."

Emma hadn't met Libby's boss, but the nickname fit the

photographs she'd seen of AJ. Over six feet with a beard, he looked more like a conquering warrior than computer geek turned billionaire. Libby described her boss as gorgeous. The guy might be attractive with a hot body, but Emma had never been a fan of tall, dark and dangerous men with facial hair. "You call him Attila."

"Only when I'm hungry or PMSing or overworked."

Libby sounded exhausted. But recovering from emergency surgery while on a business trip to the East Coast would wear a person out. "So that leaves what? Two days a month?"

"Ha. Ha. AJ's a good boss who pays me extremely well."

"A good boss does not wake you up in the middle of the night to order flowers for his woman du jour. Or make you spend Christmas on an airplane instead of with your family. Or put his interview on CNBC ahead of your abdominal pains. All that money he pays you is worthless if you're dead."

"Hey, I'm very much alive."

No thanks to Mr. Atticus Jackson Cole. The what-ifs surrounding Libby's appendix turned Emma's stomach into enough knots to make a Boy Scout proud. "I'm thankful you're alive."

"I'm thankful you're filling in for me on such short notice." Libby, who focused on what her boss might need before he realized he needed something, didn't miss a beat. Even when connected to an IV and on painkillers. "Did you have a shot of tequila?"

"It's still morning."

"Remember what happened when we flew to Mexico?"

"Of course." Flying for the first time on a spring break trip to Puerto Vallarta had nearly turned into a one-way trip. Boarding a plane…no big deal. Accelerating along the runway…no big deal. Feeling weightless when the wheels lifted off the tarmac… Emma tapped her toe, a race-walk patter catching up to her marathon-run pulse. "Well, except for the flight home. You got me so drunk I passed out before the plane left the gate."

"I did that on purpose, and my plan worked. You didn't throw up. Go down a shot. For medicinal purposes. You need to settle your nerves for the flight."

Getting drunk at ten in the morning on the first day of a new job wasn't an option today. Emma would have to tough out the flight without alcohol. She'd survived worse, right? "My nerves are fine."

"Your voice sounds an octave higher."

"Bad connection."

"I hope so, because AJ's jet just landed."

The phone slid from Emma's sweat-slicked hand. She tightened her grip. "How do you know that?"

"I'm paid to know these things." Libby's words had a sharp edge, the way she sounded when handling a rare mishap. "But don't worry. The majority of your work will be party planning. But you might have to remind AJ that he's on vacation."

Libby's new tone and her old tales told Emma that caring for a dozen kids in training pants running with open pots of finger paints might be easier than assisting one billionaire while he tried to relax on a trip to his hometown. "I can't believe I'm going to be doing your job."

"You're perfect. You've dealt with angst-ridden teens, tweens with horrible attitudes, tantrum-throwing kindergartners, pampered preschoolers and toddlers with death wishes. You can handle anything, including AJ."

"I don't know about that." Emma watched a little girl carrying a stuffed dog and her mother talking into a cell phone walk into the restroom. "A bachelor billionaire with no kids doesn't need me."

"AJ needs you." Certainty filled Libby's voice. "Don't let his type A personality get to you. Billionaires aren't that different from toddlers except they know how to use silverware and occasional manners. Sometimes. Trust me, they need direction and supervision."

"You'd think he could pull together his grandmother's birthday party."

"AJ doesn't make his own dinner reservations," Libby said matter-of-factly. "Arranging his grandmother's soiree on his own is out of the question."

Emma's insides twisted. "Soiree sounds fancier than a party."

"Semantics. Stop worrying. You threw a spectacular birthday party for the twins."

Abbie and Annie. Cute six-year-old twins Emma had cared for the past year.

Trey Lundberg. Their handsome, widowed father who was about as perfect as a dad could be.

A weight pressed against Emma's chest. She'd stopped working for Trey three months ago. He'd made his personal interest in her clear and suggested they go out without the girls. Everything Emma wanted—a family of her own and the house with the white picket fence—had been within her grasp. But something had felt off. The idea of a ready-made family appealed to her, but Trey was still grieving the loss of his wife. Any feelings he had for Emma couldn't be real. Not that soon after burying the mother of his children. The more Emma had thought about going after her dreams with Trey, the more wrong doing so had felt. So she quit.

She shifted the phone to her other ear. "The twins were easy. They're little."

"AJ's grandmother is little. Barely five feet tall from what I've heard."

Emma sighed. "Libby."

"What? You have all the skills needed for my job. I could never do yours because of the crud and ick factor."

True. Libby didn't do crud or ick. She moved ten feet away from people who sneezed. She used two napkins during meals. She carried hand sanitizer at all times.

Emma never minded the messes kids made. Holding tissues during nose blowing. Wiping jelly spots off Abbie's cheeks. Helping Annie change her sheets before anyone noticed her wet bed.

A lump formed in Emma's throat, pressed upward. No regrets. She couldn't work for the Lundbergs when she didn't have the same feelings for Trey as he had for her. She'd helped find her replacement, trained the new nanny and told the girls to call if they needed anything...anytime.

A wistful, but not unexpected, sigh escaped. She wanted to find that special someone who would take care of her the way she took care of everybody else. Too bad happily-ever-after endings happened only in storybooks, not real life.

Emma cleared her throat. "The cruddy stuff isn't so bad. There's lots of fun to be had on the playground, believe it or not."

Except on the swings. She hated swings.

"I'll take your word for it," Libby said.

Emma's name sounded over the PA system. Every muscle group bunched, including ones she'd never met. Her stomach jangled, a mix of worry and trepidation.

She'd ridden enough elevators and carnival rides to know her tummy's reaction to weightlessness. Antigravity was her proven enemy, its falling sensation her greatest fear.

She blew out a puff of air. "Time to go."

"Good luck, not that you need it."

She swallowed. "Thanks."

"Have a good flight."

The line disconnected.

Emma tucked her phone into her tote bag, hand trembling. She swung the leather strap over her shoulder then picked up the cat carrier. "Here we go, Blossom."

The cat's snarl sounded like a combination of moan, hiss and spit. An omen of things to come? Emma hoped not.

The jet taxied on the tarmac in Hillsboro, Oregon. Except for a slight movement of AJ's tablet on the table in front of his seat and a glance out the window, he wouldn't have realized they'd landed. Not surprising. His flight crew consisted of top-notch, former military pilots. AJ never worried what was happening in the cockpit. But he was worried about the stranger, a nanny with a cat, who would be his assistant for the next five days. AJ rubbed his chin.

Emma is my best friend. She's smart and conscientious. A hard worker. She doesn't like to fly, but trust me. She's the perfect person, the only person, to take my place while you're in Haley's Bay.

Libby had been his personal assistant for two years. He had no reason to doubt her. Relying on her recommendation made more sense than yanking an employee away from other duties or hiring an untested temp from a service. A nanny should be able to follow directions, entertain his brother Ellis's kids at their grandmother's birthday party and, most importantly, deal with AJ's family. He wasn't a fan of cats, but he hoped the feline would be a distraction. The more attention his family gave the cat, the less they would give AJ. A win-win situation for all involved. Mostly him.

Dad wouldn't say much, if anything, unless forced to talk by Mom. The man would never forgive AJ for leaving Haley's Bay and the family business after graduating from college. The fact that he'd bailed out the fishing company during the economic downturn had only made his father resent AJ more. As if he'd had any other choice.

What was he supposed to do? See his family bankrupt and out of work, especially Ellis with a wife and two kids? No way. AJ had the means. Not helping would have been worse. Unthinkable.

He would never apologize to his father or anyone in his family for choosing to make billions with a computer instead of breaking his back working on a boat. AJ regretted nothing. He doubted his dad could say the same thing, if Jack Cole ever decided to talk to his oldest son again.

AJ wasn't sure how his four younger brothers would react to his being home. Only Grady, the youngest of the family, kept in touch. At least AJ wouldn't have to worry about the female members of the Cole family.

The Cole women would welcome him home with smiles and hugs. His grandmother, mom and two sisters called, texted, Skyped and visited him as much as they could. Though the four would likely be butting their noses into his life and asking much too personal questions while he was there. His stomach tightened.

Why had he wanted to come back? Oh, yeah. His grandmother's eightieth birthday.

An alarm sounded. The buzzing filled the cabin and made him glance at his tablet.

A message illuminated the screen. Conference Call—Marketing Department. Libby must have set his clock when he said goodbye at the hospital. The woman was the definition of *competent,* vital to his success for keeping his life running smoothly.

If only Libby were here with him. Damn appendix. Striking her down in New York. He balled his hands. AJ couldn't believe Libby had hidden her condition from him until it was almost too late. A foolish move, but one done out of loyalty to him. She knew how much he relied upon her. Or had until leaving him stuck with a nanny from Portland, Oregon.

If AJ didn't know better, he would think his father planned this. But nothing, not a hospitalized assistant or a cat-carrying nanny, would stop AJ from showing his family how far he'd come. Nothing was going to stop him from making a triumphant return to Haley's Bay.

Nothing at all.

Emma stepped outside the terminal, a sunny August sky overhead. Flying was safer during good weather, right?

But the roar of engines weighted her feet like chimney bricks.

For Libby. Step by dragged step, Emma crossed the tarmac toward a new-looking jet. Her heart pounded in her throat.

For Libby. Emma clasped the jet's railing. Her legs trembled—*don't stumble*—and she forced herself to climb the short staircase, one step, then another, followed by two more.

For Libby. Emma stepped into the plane. The hair on the back of her neck and arms prickled, ramrod straight beneath her sweater.

Noise from planes taking off and landing faded. Air-conditioning cooled her skin. The jet's interior muted tones exuded calm comfort. The plush carpet and cushioned chairs were a hundred and eighty degrees different from flying on a packed 737 with zero legroom and no empty seats. This time might be different.

"Welcome aboard, Miss Markwell." An attractive woman with long blond hair, a light blue blouse and navy slacks greeted her with a bright, white-tooth smile. "I'm Camille. I'll be your flight attendant today."

"Hi, I'm Emma." She forced a first impression smile and raised the cat carrier, welcoming the distraction. "Is there a place this should go?"

"I have the perfect spot." Camille took the carrier. "What's your cat's name?"

"Not my cat. She's a foster. Long story. But her name is Blossom. Thank you."

Camille peered into the carrier. "Hello, Blossom."

The cat's growl, a hair-raising, guttural sound, made Emma cringe.

Eyes wide, the flight attendant drew back. Her at-your-service smile faltered. She lifted the carrier away from her body as if radioactive waste filled the inside, then tipped her head to her left. "AJ's in the cabin."

"Thank you."

Emma passed between two forward-facing leather-covered captain's chairs. Each seat contained a television screen and game controller. The understated look was more luxurious man cave than flashy flaunt of wealth.

The next row faced backward. Someone with a head of thick brown hair occupied the seat to her left.

Attila. Atticus. AJ. This had to be him.

Libby thought the world of her boss, when she wasn't complaining about AJ. She described him as exacting. "Workaholic" was how Emma imagined him, based on how many hours he kept Libby working. And prompt. Libby said he would fire a manager if a project went over schedule, break up with a woman if she arrived late for a date and eviscerate a chef if forced to wait between courses.

Not everything Emma had heard about AJ Cole was awful. He paid employees well, was a philanthropist and doted on his grandmother, who visited him in Seattle at least once a month. The guy couldn't be all bad if he was throwing his grandma an eightieth birthday party—make that a soiree.

Voices sounded. Three or four.

Emma didn't see anyone else on board. She stepped closer.

The brown-haired man sat with a tablet in front of him. Three other faces appeared on the screen. One, a woman, spoke about branding.

Emma glanced from the tablet to her temporary boss. Whoa. A six-foot-plus mass of male hotness sat in the seat. A guy with no beard.

She blinked. Refocused. Still hot. Definitely AJ. She recognized his intense green eyes from the photographs.

Yum. Libby called her boss a nice piece of eye candy, but now that Emma was standing next to AJ Cole, he seemed more like a five-pound box of gourmet chocolates. Mouthwateringly delicious.

His gray suit jacket, expertly tailored, accentuated straight, wide shoulders. Unruly brown hair, curly at the ends, fringed the starched collar of his white dress shirt. His ruggedly handsome features fit perfectly together, making her heart accelerate like a car on a racetrack.

His smoldering gaze met hers.

Her throat tightened. She wished he hadn't shaved his beard so she wouldn't find him attractive. Then again, she still might. A photograph couldn't capture the 3-D version of the living, breathing man.

He motioned with his finger to the seat facing him. A small table separated the two chairs.

Emma removed the tote bag strap from her shoulder and sat. She ignored the conversation from the conference chat, not wanting to eavesdrop. She pressed each button to see what it did. Peering inside the pouch on the side of her seat, she saw a barf bag. She hoped she wouldn't need it.

The decibel level of the conference call rose. Voices talked over one another. Not quite a debate, but a lively discussion.

Her gaze fell on AJ's face. Talk about stunning. He laughed at a joke, softening the planes, angles and lines of his face. She focused on his mouth, zeroed in on his lips. Bet he was a good kisser.

What in the world was she doing? Thinking? AJ wasn't only her boss. He was also Libby's boss.

Emma looked at her lap. The seat belt ends lay on either side of her. She fastened the buckle and tightened the strap, as if the pressure could squeeze out her nonsensical thoughts before she embarrassed Libby and herself.

So what if the real-life AJ Cole was more attractive than his photographs? He was her boss, not a random guy she could flirt with at Starbucks then breeze out the door without a look back. Besides, he wasn't her type. She preferred a family man. Not a guy who, according to Libby, hadn't visited his family in ten years.

"Don't do that." AJ's hard tone made Emma jump. "If any of you disturb Libby while I'm away, you won't have a job when I return. Understood?"

Not so bad. Emma hadn't expected him to stick up for Libby.

"See you on Monday," he added.

The words *Don't bother me* were implied.

He tucked his tablet into the side pocket of his seat. "Emma Markwell."

His deep voice flowed through her veins like warm maple syrup. She fought the urge to melt into her seat. "Hello, Mr. Cole. It's nice to meet you."

His critical gaze ran the length of her, scrutinizing, as if she were a line of bad computer code wreaking havoc with his program. *This* was the man she expected minus the gorgeous face and athletic physique.

"Libby tells me you're a Martha Stewart–Mary Poppins mash-up, able to master home, hearth and heathen children."

"I don't have anything magical to pull out of my tote bag, but I do have a few modern-day equivalents for tricks and can spell supercalifragilisticexpialidocious backward." Something she'd learned being the nanny of a gifted child one summer.

"So you have no magic, but you brought a homeless cat."

His eyes were flat, no glint of humor or spark of amusement. Was this the intimidator Libby told Emma to ignore?

"Libby assured me that bringing Blossom was acceptable." Emma's voice sounded hoarse. She cleared her throat.

"If it was a problem I would have hired you a cat sitter." He shrugged off his suit jacket, tossed it onto the seat across the aisle, then buckled his seat belt. "My niece, nephew and cousins' children will play with the cat. Just keep the beast away from me."

"Allergic?"

"No."

Camille picked up the jacket, glanced at the seat belts fastened across their laps, then headed to the front of the jet.

The silence made Emma bristle, reminding her of the impending takeoff. She needed to distract herself. "Not a fan of cats?"

His lips narrowed, reducing their kissability factor by 70 percent. Not that she would ever kiss him.

"If you must know, they're pampered, vile creatures. I don't see the appeal."

His good looks had sparked an initial attraction, but his fire-extinguishing personality was making sure no flames erupted. She, as his employee, should let his words drop and discuss what her job responsibilities would be. But the cat lover in her couldn't do that. Nor could the friend in her, either. His lack of warmth and understanding he displayed with the cat probably also translated to his over-working Libby to the point of her almost dying.

"Blossom is not a pampered cat, Mr. Cole. Her owner died. The family didn't want to be bothered so surrendered the cat to an animal control facility in California. She ended up on a kill list. The shelter I volunteer for in Portland stepped in to rescue her. Blossom lived with thirty-five other cats until the space flooded yesterday. She had to come with me as a foster or spend the next week in a metal cage at a vet's office."

"Not pampered." He sounded more amused than irritated. "I stand corrected."

"Thank you for admitting that."

"I hear a 'but' coming."

Libby had said AJ didn't like being wrong. Emma didn't want to annoy him or upset him, but she had more to say. She scraped her teeth across her lower lip. "I've said too much."

"Perhaps, but I'd like to know."

Libby had told Emma to do what he requested without

asking too many questions. But this probably wasn't what her friend meant.

"Go on," he urged.

"Well…I'm sorry, but you're wrong about cats. They're intelligent, independent and inquisitive. They're amazing pets and have made innumerable people happier for their company."

His eyes widened, then narrowed. He pressed his steepled hands against his lips.

Uh-oh. He didn't seem to like her answer. "Remember, you wanted to know," she reminded.

"I did." He lowered his hands. "Are you as passionate about the children you care for as felines?"

"Yes."

"Do you express your views with their parents as you have with me?"

Emma wasn't about to lie. She raised her chin. "If warranted."

"What is their response?"

"In one case, I was let go."

"Fired for speaking your mind?"

"I wasn't hired to spout my opinions," she admitted. "But by that point, the only reason I hadn't quit was the children. I was staying on for their sake."

A closed-mouth smile curved his lips. "Lucky kids to have you on their side."

He didn't sound upset. That surprised her. "I do my best, but I expect kids to behave, so maybe they aren't so lucky to have me."

"What happens if they don't behave?"

"Depends on the child. Some kids need to talk it through. Be heard. Others don't understand why they act out." Emma's ability to read people had helped her survive in one foster home after another, but she couldn't read Mr.

Cole. A billionaire shouldn't be interested in her job as a nanny. Maybe one of his colleagues needed to hire child care. "With certain children, more tangible consequences like a time-out or chores are necessary. But I prefer using kindness and a loving hand if at all possible."

"What will my consequence be?"

"Yours?"

"If I misbehave."

Playful images of how he might misbehave flitted through her mind. Unwelcome ones. Ones that made her cheeks burn. "I…I'm your personal assistant. Not your nanny."

"If you were my nanny."

Emma would have to resign due to naughty thoughts. Wrong answer. She cupped the side of her neck with her palm, shaken by her reaction to the sudden change in him. Her skin didn't feel warm to the touch. Maybe only her cheeks were red. But a blush was too much. "Mr. Cole—"

"AJ." His smile, full of sex appeal and devilish charm, stole her breath. "We're going to be working together for the next five days. Putting on a birthday party and surrounded by my family. Humor me, Emma."

Her name rolled off his tongue and heated her insides twenty degrees. A flame reignited deep within her. So not good. And 100 percent unacceptable.

Get a grip. AJ wasn't flirting. A rich, gorgeous man would never be attracted to a simple, unremarkable nanny. More likely he was testing her. Libby had mentioned something about AJ's tests.

A test Emma could handle. She'd been a good student, mostly As, a few Bs. But she'd grown up since then. Emma straightened, book-on-top-of-her-head posture. She had no doubt she would pass this test with an A-plus no matter what Attila threw at her.

She looked across the table at him. Awareness of the man's good looks and power shivered through her. At least she hoped she would pass his test.

Chapter Two

What was Emma thinking? Of course she would pass any test her new boss threw at her. She stared at AJ, seated across from her, noting the devilish smile on his face.

"What would I do if you misbehaved?" She tilted her head to the right and made a stern face, something she rarely used with children. "I'd start by talking to you."

"I'm not a big talker." His mouth quirked, a sexy slant of his lips she tried to ignore. "I prefer action to words."

Libby hadn't called her boss a player, but implied as much. Emma could tell he knew the rules of the game and how to break them. Especially when the game was business. "I imagine you know exactly when you're behaving badly."

"That's part of the fun."

No doubt. "A time-out wouldn't work with you."

"I'd only get into more trouble if I had time to think."

Or he might come up with a way to make another few million dollars. "Then I would do something else."

He leaned forward, a movement full of swagger though he was sitting. "What?"

Emma took her time answering. She studied his hair, lowered her gaze to his intensely focused eyes, followed his straight nose to those sensual lips, then dropped to his strong jaw and square chin. Handsome, yes, but calculating. She made her own assessment of what might mean the most to him. "I'd take away your electronics."

His model-worthy jaw dropped. "What?"

A satisfied smile tugged at the corners of her mouth. Her answer surprised him. Good. "I'd confiscate your cell phone, computer, tablet. That might teach you a lesson."

"Sounds a bit harsh."

"Not if it's for your own good."

He rubbed his chin. "Then I'd better behave."

"Yes, you should." His bank account didn't impress Emma. He didn't, either. Not much anyway. "Don't make me go all Supernanny or Nanny McPhee on you."

The plane lurched.

Here we go. Emma gripped the seat arms and glanced out the window. A small single-propeller aircraft taxied in front of them.

"Please prepare for takeoff," a male voice announced from overhead speakers.

Must be the pilot. Her gaze traveled to AJ. He looked blurry. The rest of the cabin, too. She adjusted her glasses, blinked, but her vision remained fuzzy, the air surrounding her hazy and white.

"Emma?"

She squinted, trying to bring his face and body into focus. "Yes."

"You're pale. Libby told me you don't like flying."

Emma didn't blame her friend for warning her boss.

"It's the moment the wheels lift off that gets to me the most, but I should be okay."

Please let me be okay. The engines revved, louder and louder.

No big deal. She dug her fingers into the butter-soft leather. Pressed her feet against the floor. Leaned her head against the seat.

No big deal. The jet bolted forward, as if released from a slingshot, accelerating down the runway. Dread crept through her stomach and hardened into stone, an uncomfortable heaviness settling in. She burned again, her skin, her insides, immune to the blasts of cool air.

No big deal. Emma squeezed her eyes shut. Darkness didn't keep the sickening, familiar sensation of weightlessness at bay. The moment the wheels lifted, her stomach plummeted to her toes, then boomeranged to her throat.

Memories bombarded her. The choking smell of smoke. The scorching heat of the flames. The terrifying screams of her brother.

Nausea rose inside her like the jet climbing in the sky. She opened her eyes. "Oh, no."

AJ's hands rested on his thighs. "What?"

Emma's stomach constricted. Her mouth watered. She reached into the seat pocket. "I'm going to be sick."

Damn. AJ stared at Emma, who held on to a white barf bag as if it were the Holy Grail. He pushed himself forward in his seat, difficult to do facing backward and strapped in with the plane climbing, but he'd achieved the impossible before.

He reached for her, uncertain how to help, but needing to do something. "Emma."

She raised her left hand, an almost imperceptible movement he took to mean "not now." He didn't blame her, but sitting here unable to do anything brought back a dreaded sense of helplessness, of uselessness. He remembered being out on the water with his father during a storm. More than once AJ figured they would have to abandon ship. More than once he thought they would die. More than once he vowed to do something different with his life if they survived.

You'll never amount to anything if you leave Haley's Bay.

His father's words pounded through AJ's head like high tide against the harbor rocks. He'd spent the past ten years proving his dad wrong. In spades.

Except AJ's private jet, fifteen-hundred employees and a net worth of eleven billion were irrelevant at the moment. None of those things could help Emma.

Her greenish complexion worsened. Her white-knuckled fingers, clutching the barf bag, trembled.

The plane continued climbing. If he unbuckled, he might end up on top of Emma. Better to wait until the plane leveled.

The least he could do was give her privacy. Not easy in this confined space, but he glanced out the window.

Tendrils of fluffy white clouds floated in the blue sky. A good day for flying, unless you suffered airsickness.

A moan filled the cabin.

The cat's stop-they're-torturing-me cry irritated AJ. Who was he kidding? Everything about felines, especially how much bandwidth people wasted posting "cute" cat pictures on the internet, bugged him. He wanted the cat to be a distraction when they reached Haley's Bay, not during the flight. AJ drummed his fingers against the armrest.

Emma's retching stopped. The cat kept howling. He suppressed a groan.

AJ wanted to start his day over. Nothing about his trip

was turning out as expected. He wanted to make a triumphant return to Haley's Bay. He wanted everything to go smoothly during his five-day stay. He wanted Libby with her anal-retentive organizing skills accompanying him, not some…nanny. He'd joked with Emma to see her response and glimpse her social skills.

What in the world was he going to do with an uptight, vomiting Mary Poppins? Libby had warned him about Emma's problem with flying. If he'd known her issue involved bodily fluids, he would have asked his chauffeur Charlie to drive Emma to Haley's Bay instead. A car ride would have been easier on her, on AJ, on the annoying cat.

He flexed his fingers. Libby's brain must have been foggy after her appendectomy. He didn't understand why she thought her best friend was the perfect person to take her place. Emma might be good with kids. She hadn't been bad at bantering. But she didn't seem up for the rigors of the job. Or his family.

Something clicked. The sound came from Emma's direction. He glanced her way.

She held on to the barf bag with one hand and a wipe with the other. Her hands shook. Her face looked deathly white.

AJ's chest tightened. He needed to do something. "I'll call Camille."

"I'm fine." Emma's words sounded strangled. She stared at her lap.

"You need help."

She gave a slight shake of her head, washed her face, then tossed the wipe into the barf bag. "I'm doing better."

Emma removed another wipe from her bag and cleaned her hands. No hesitation, no wasted movement, no hunching her shoulders trying to disappear.

"You're doing great under the circumstances," he said.

Her self-sufficiency and resiliency intrigued AJ. She was no damsel in distress waiting to be rescued by a handsome prince. Not that he was a prince. More like a black knight or the devil himself, according to his father. "But please let Camille assist you. That's her job."

"My job is to assist you, not cause anyone extra work."

AJ studied the woman. Emma Markwell was not unattractive, in spite of her pallor. He would call her… unfinished, an artist's sketch on a piece of canvas waiting to be painted. Her braided hair accentuated her heart-shaped face and clear complexion. Smart-girl glasses hid a pair of wide-set bluish-gray eyes and rested on a straight, pert nose. Tight lines hovered at the corner of her full lips.

Of course they did. She'd thrown up breakfast. But the way she handled herself impressed him. AJ had judged her too quickly and she was earning his respect now. He'd gotten seasick on a boat when he was younger and not handled himself nearly as well. Maybe she was up for the job.

A woman who dressed practically would be a refreshing change from stilettos and tight pencil skirts. The nanny was pretty. If Emma unbraided her brown hair and wore makeup to highlight her cheekbones and lips, she could be beautiful. She lacked the sophistication and worldliness of most women he knew, but a nanny didn't need to dress to impress and show off flawless beauty. He imagined that Emma's fresh young face and prim appearance earned her more jobs than looking like a sexy supermodel. She might not be a high-flying businesswoman, actress or socialite, but she reminded him of the women in his family—down-to-earth, practical, strong. So far she'd been less nosy than his grandmother, mom or sisters. He hoped Emma's lack of interest in his personal life continued.

She tucked another wipe into the airsickness bag, folded the ends, then secured the flap with wired tabs.

Competent and capable. Resilient with an underlying toughness. Those traits would serve her well.

He wondered if she'd been disappointed by someone she loved. Perhaps someone she'd trusted had failed her. AJ's skill at assessing staff had been key to his success, and he understood her qualities from his own experience. Setbacks made you stronger, if you didn't allow them to win. And he knew how to help her. By putting what she needed within reach.

"It's obvious you're fine, but is there anything Camille can bring you? A glass of water? Ginger ale?"

Pink tinged Emma's cheeks, the blush bringing much-needed color to her face. "No, thanks. The plane's no longer climbing. I'm going to go to the lavatory and put myself back together."

She sounded confident, but she hadn't looked him in the eye since being sick. She might not be as in control as she appeared. "The bathroom is at the front of the jet."

Emma's gaze met his. Her vulnerability would have knocked him flat on his ass if he were standing. She was twenty-six, the same age as Libby, but Emma looked younger, like a naive college freshman away from home for the first time.

A protective instinct welled inside him. "Em…"

"Thank you, Mr. Cole."

Her polite tone jerked him back to reality. She didn't want pity. But he wasn't offering that.

She unbuckled her seat belt. He did the same. "Don't feel bad. Libby warned me you didn't like flying. I'm assuming she spoke with Camille about adding airsickness bags to the seats."

"I appreciate Libby's foresight. She's a good friend who

knows me well. I'll do my best to fill her shoes. In spite of the past few minutes, I'm up to the task." Emma stood. She placed the strap of her large purse over her shoulder and held on to the barf bag. "Now if you'll excuse me."

AJ jumped to his feet. She walked past him toward the front of the plane. His gaze followed, zeroing in on the sway of her hips and the purse bouncing against her thigh. Nice. Feminine. Sexy.

Whoa. What was he thinking? He didn't want anything to do with Emma except to comfort and reassure her. He considered employees assets, efficient resources, not playthings. Besides, she reminded him of the girls back in Haley's Bay, rather than the glamorous women he dated in Seattle, San Francisco or wherever else he might be working. The next-door neighbor types weren't the kind of women he was attracted to now. Not that he found Emma...okay, he found her attractive, which surprised him.

With a towel in hand, Camille stood next to his seat. "Emma said she was sick."

"Yes, but remarkably neat about it."

Camille checked the seat and floor anyway. "Libby was right."

"She usually is." He glanced toward the front of the plane. "Make sure Emma is okay."

"Of course."

The cat screeched.

Camille shook her head. "Not your typical uneventful flight."

"No."

Things might not be uneventful until AJ was back home in Seattle. Five days. Five days until his visit would be over. Five days until he would say goodbye to Haley's Bay for another decade. He couldn't wait.

* * *

Emma couldn't wait to get off this airplane. Hitting rock bottom less than fifteen minutes after meeting a new boss had to be a record. But at least things couldn't get worse.

Unless the plane crashed.

She returned her toothbrush to her toiletry bag. Given her luck so far this morning, that was a distinct possibility. But the odds against crashing after throwing up had to be astronomical, right?

Surveying her reflection in the mirror, she tucked stray strands back into her braid. Her Goth-white complexion had disappeared. Good. She would rather look human than like a vampire wannabe.

She pinched her cheeks to give them more color. Reapplying the makeup she'd wiped off was beyond her. But she looked better, passable, no longer green.

She straightened her glasses, wanting to present a confident, unflappable air. Mr. Cole never needed to know she was dying of embarrassment. Neither did Camille, who kept knocking every minute and a half to see if Emma needed help. She opened the lavatory door.

Blossom's ear-hurting screeches could wake the dead, officially starting the zombie apocalypse.

Emma followed the racket.

The cat faced forward, screaming her lungs out as if doing her best T. rex impersonation.

Emma knelt in front of the cat carrier. "Shhhh. I know you don't like this, but we're almost there."

Blossom barked, sounding more like an ankle-biting dog than a pissed-off feline.

"Your cat doesn't sound happy."

Emma felt AJ's presence—a potent mix of heat, strength and confidence—behind her. "Blossom doesn't like to fly, either."

"You look good as new."

She glanced over her shoulder, her gaze at crotch level. Lingering on his zipper. Her cheeks burned. No need for pinching cheeks or makeup now. She looked up at him. "I am. Flying doesn't really get to me. Taking off is the culprit. The weightlessness."

"Your stomach can't handle the feeling."

"Nope." And the flashbacks nearly did her in each time, but nobody needed to know about those. "The landing will be a breeze. But I'm guessing Blossom won't quiet down until she's out of her carrier."

AJ kneeled. The left side of his body brushed hers, sending sparks shooting across her skin. The scent of his aftershave, something musky with a touch of spice, enveloped her.

She sucked in a breath. *Oh, boy.* He smelled so good, fresh, like the first spring day after months of dreary winter rain.

He peered into the carrier. "What's its name again?"

"Blossom. *Her* name is Blossom."

He tapped on the carrier. "Be quiet, Blossom."

"Cat's don't respond to—"

The cat stopped meowing. Blossom rubbed her head against the carrier door.

He stuck his finger through the grating and touched the cat. "Don't respond to what?"

"Logic."

Blossom, however, didn't make another noise. She soaked up the attention. Purred. Unbelievable. The cat hadn't purred at the shelter or at Emma's apartment. At least not that any of the volunteers had noticed. Yet this guy, a non-cat-lover guy, had the feline purring like a generator. "Blossom likes you."

"She likes the attention."

"Attention from you. This is the first time I've heard her purr."

AJ yanked his hand away, plastered his arm against his side. "I'm not a fan of cats. She wouldn't like me."

Tell that to Blossom. The cat pressed against the crate door, fur squishing through the grating. She stared up at AJ as if he were her sun, stars and moon.

Thanks to AJ Cole, Blossom had transformed from she devil to sweetheart. Emma grinned, something she never expected to do after getting sick in front of her new boss. "She does like you."

AJ's gaze bounced from the cat to Emma. "The cat needed someone to tell her what was expected."

"Cats do what they want."

"Perhaps the cat needed to have a higher bar set for its behavior."

He didn't use Blossom's name, but the feline didn't seem to mind. She was trying to get out of the cage and closer to AJ. "Perhaps. But this gives me hope."

"Hope?"

"That Blossom will find her forever home. There's been concern she might be unadoptable. She doesn't seem to like many people."

He looked at Blossom, but he didn't touch her. Much to the cat's dismay. "I don't know anything about cats, but she seems fine to me. Not so annoying now that she's quiet."

Camille approached. She handed AJ a glass with a straw sticking out. "Your protein shake."

"Thanks." His fingers circled the glass.

The flight attendant handed a small juice-sized glass to Emma. "A little ginger ale for you."

"Thank you," Emma said.

"We'll be landing soon." Camille motioned to the back of the plane. "Please return to your seats."

Emma did and buckled her seat belt. The engines whirred. She waited for Blossom to meow, but the cat remained quiet.

AJ sat across from her. Sipped from the straw. "You okay?"

She nodded.

"If you feel bad again, Camille restocked the side pocket."

Two more airsickness bags were inside. "Thanks, but I've never had trouble during landings." At least not the one Emma remembered.

"We're beginning our descent into Haley's Bay," the pilot announced. "Please remain seated."

She gripped the armrests, a combination of anticipation of wanting to be on the ground and apprehension over what the rest of the week would hold.

AJ stared at her over the rim of his glass, his eyes full of concern. "The pilot's very good."

"You don't have to reassure me."

His gaze narrowed, darkened. "Why not?"

"It's not your job."

"I get to write my job description. One benefit of being the boss."

"Do you like being the boss?"

He stiffened. Stared into his drink. Toyed with the straw.

"No one's asked me that. People assume..." He shifted in his seat. "But yes, of course. What's not to love?"

He was bluffing, hiding something, like a child who said swim lessons were fun when dunking his head under water terrified him. What other secrets was AJ hiding?

None of Emma's business. She didn't need to go looking for AJ Cole's demons. She had enough of her own. But she hoped this vacation went well for him because the only thing worse than having no family would be having a family that didn't get along. Best to make sure she knew what AJ needed from her.

She removed a half-inch binder and a mechanical pencil from her tote bag. "Libby sent me your tentative itinerary. Any changes to today's schedule I should know about?"

He waved his hand, as if brushing aside Emma's question. "Relax until we land."

"Let's confirm today's agenda first." She adjusted her glasses. "Then I'll relax."

AJ took another sip of his drink. "Read what's on your list."

"Lunch with your grandmother while I arrange meetings with the party rental company and florist and check into the Broughton Inn. A conference call at two, another one at three, followed by an interview at four with a technology blogger. Then you have a break until dinner with your family at seven."

"Easy afternoon."

"Three calls on the first afternoon of your vacation sounds more like you're working."

He raised a brow, as if surprised by her words. Guess Libby didn't speak to him like that. Well, Emma wasn't like her best friend. Not even close.

"This is a light day." He placed his empty glass on the table between them. "I've limited what's on my schedule."

Emma guessed she had a different definition of limited from his. "If there aren't any changes—"

"There is one."

She readied her pencil.

A muscle ticked at his jaw.

She leaned forward. "What?"

"We're staying at my grandmother's house. It'll be easier with the party planning, and my grandma thought it would be better for the cat."

Disappointment shot through Emma. She'd been a live-in nanny so she knew what staying at someone's house as an employee meant. But the arrangement made sense, even without the cat factored in. She pasted on a smile. "That's generous of your grandmother."

He leaned back against his seat, but his gaze never left her. "My grandmother loves playing hostess. She's thrilled I'm bringing company, not to mention a cat."

The noise level of the engines changed. She clasped her hands together. "I'm sure your grandmother's more excited to have you staying with her. Ten years is a long time to be away."

"What has Libby told you?"

"Not much." A glance out the window told Emma the plane was descending. "I know you're throwing your grandmother an eightieth birthday party. Very nice of you to do."

"Just holding up my end of a deal."

Emma looked back at him. "Excuse me?"

His gaze, warm and clear, met hers. "When I was eight, I wanted a space-alien birthday party. My dad said no, so my grandma offered to throw me a party if I agreed to do the same for her when she turned eighty. We shook on it."

Emma tried to picture AJ as a boy, but looking past the handsome man sitting across from her was impossible. "You remembered that after all these years?"

"No." He half laughed. The charming sound sent a brush of tingles across Emma's tummy. "My grandma did. She reminded me in February."

She rubbed her stomach. Maybe she was feeling the aftereffects of being sick earlier. "Still nice of you."

"She's my grandma. I wasn't about to say no."

"Would you be returning to Haley's Bay if it weren't her birthday?"

"Probably not, which she knows." Affection filled his gaze. "My grandmother's a sly one. But I'm on my way so she's happy. I want the party to go smoothly. That's what I'm counting on you for, Emma."

She wrote the words "anticipate and prevent problems" in her binder. "Yes, Mr. Cole."

"AJ."

The man had seen her vomit. The only other people to see her do that were her parents, God rest their souls, and Libby. "AJ."

He smiled. She smiled back. The moment lingered. Filled her with heat. She looked at her binder. "Anything else I should know?"

"My family is big and crazy and loud." AJ sounded amused, not annoyed. "I have four brothers—Ellis, Flynn, Declan and Grady—and two sisters—Bailey and Camden. Not to mention my sister-in-law, Risa, and more aunts, uncles and cousins than I can count."

"That is a big family."

"The single Cole men will hit on you because you're new in town and their reputations haven't been sullied yet. They've done that in the past. You're under no obligation to them, and let me know if they annoy you." AJ's dark eyes and serious tone told Emma he wasn't joking. "What you do on your own time is none of my business, but don't let your actions affect your ability to get the job done."

His words irritated her. Okay, he didn't know her, but she wasn't about to sleep around because good-looking guys were giving her attention. She imagined his brothers were attractive, AJ in multiples, like the Hemsworth brothers. That could be dangerous. To her job and her heart. She jotted a note in the margin. "Stay away from Cole males."

"I'll keep my distance."

A lopsided grin formed. "Smart."

She hated the way her body responded to his compliment. "It's been my experience that business and pleasure don't mix well."

"Mine, too."

At least they agreed on something.

"But business has to be fun," AJ added. "All work and no play…"

"Would be boring." Emma recalled Libby's description of the Cole corporate headquarters in Seattle with a game arcade, gym, massages, errand service, and free meals, snacks and drinks at the employee cafeterias. *Fun* seemed to be the operative word at his company. Not surprising given that he developed a photography-based blogging platform and created a social media gaming site for friends to compete. "I wouldn't last long as a nanny if I didn't play. Having fun means everything to children."

"What about you?"

"I like to have fun."

He drummed his fingers against the chair arm. "What do you do for fun?"

"Play tag, dress-up, bicycle, hunt for treasure, bake, board games, and go to the Oregon Zoo, the children's museum or OMSI."

His fingers stilled. "I meant what do *you* do when you're not being a nanny."

"Oh. Sorry. I like to read, watch movies, hike, volunteer at an animal rescue center."

"Quiet pleasures."

"It's not always quiet at the rescue shelter, but the noise is different there. I love being a nanny. The children are wonderful, but they're loud and full of energy and want your undivided attention. A little quiet is nice."

"Alone time is fun for you."

She bit back a smile. AJ wasn't grilling her, but he seemed to want to know more about her. She would have expected a billionaire to brag and make sure the conversation centered around him. Not that she knew any billionaires, but she'd worked for a millionaire. "Escaping inside a dark theater with a bucket of popcorn, a soda, a box of candy and no one to take to the bathroom at the best part of a movie is the definition of superfun."

"There's a theater in Haley's Bay."

"Thanks, but I doubt you'll be screaming and tugging on my shirt to get attention all day long."

"No screaming." He winked. "And I've found persuading a woman to take off her shirt works better than tugging."

"I'm surprised you have to persuade them." The man's smile could charm a snake out of its skin. "I assumed women flashed you, like at Mardi Gras."

"Only in my dreams." With a wry grin, he settled back in his seat. "But they're very nice dreams."

"I imagine so."

"What do you dream about, Emma?"

"I… Um, a lot of things."

"Like what?"

She fiddled with her seat belt. "Cats. Children. Family."

"Nanny things?"

A lump the size of a Super Ball burned in Emma's throat. She swallowed, kept her smile from wavering and looked AJ straight in the eyes. "Yes, nanny things."

Cat lover things. Mommy things. Wife things. Things a man who had a family, albeit an estranged one, would never understand. Things she dreamed about. Things she wanted…desperately.

Chapter Three

Charlie, AJ's chauffeur for three years, cut five minutes off the drive from the minuscule airport to Haley's Bay. AJ rubbed his thumb against his fingertips.

He liked being on time. He preferred arriving early. Charlie was doing his job, getting AJ to his destination as quickly as possible. But this once, he wouldn't have minded being late.

Still, he didn't lower the glass panel and tell Charlie to slow down. Not until AJ had a reason, one beyond his wanting to prolong the inevitable.

Music played from the speakers. Stock quotes ran across the bottom of a television screen. The bar called to him, but he needed to be stone-cold sober when he faced his family. AJ glanced at Emma, seated next to him, the cat carrier at her feet.

She stared out the window. Her serious expression—dare he say dour—took prim and proper to the next level.

So different from how she'd been right before landing. Her sense of humor had disappeared. Her smile, too.

She might be upset over getting sick earlier. She might be nervous about her new job. Or she might be acting the way she always did. Whatever the reason, she was his employee, his responsibility. The least he could do was help her relax after a rough flight and coax a smile out of her. "Let's take a detour. Check out a lighthouse or two."

Her lips twisted. "You're expected at your grandmother's house."

"I wouldn't be a gracious host if I didn't show you the sights."

"You're not my host," she countered. "You're my boss."

Being her employer was easy to forget. Libby had hired Emma. "I don't mind playing tour guide."

Her nose crinkled. "You have a schedule—"

"Subject to change."

"True, but as your personal assistant I'm supposed to keep you on schedule."

"True, but you're also supposed to do what I ask."

"Even if doing so isn't in your best interest? I mean, you haven't been home in ten years. Your grandmother might be peeking out the window waiting for you to arrive."

He pictured Grandma doing that. "I'll concede the point."

"Thank you."

"You're welcome."

His gaze met Emma's. She removed her glasses to blow on the right lens. Pretty blue eyes surrounded by long, thick lashes. He hadn't noticed her eyelashes before. "Does your grandmother do the same when you visit?"

"My grandparents are dead." Emma put on her glasses and stared out the window. "Looks like we're here."

A wooden sign on the side of the two-lane road welcomed visitors to Haley's Bay. The sign was new. The churning in AJ's stomach wasn't.

After a decade, the town had likely changed. In that same time, his life had also changed. His family's opinion of him might never change. That could take a century. Or longer.

The last time he was home his family had tried to shame him into staying in Haley's Bay. That wouldn't happen again, but something else might. He wanted to be prepared. "One of your responsibilities is running interference for me."

"What do you mean?"

"If I find myself in a difficult situation, I may need you to get me out of it by texting or calling or physically interrupting me."

She smiled at the sleeping cat before looking up at him. "Afraid you might run into old girlfriends who might want to rekindle the flame?"

"That isn't likely to happen." His high school sweetheart and ex-fiancée, Natalie, had dumped him and married one of his closest friends. AJ had been devastated, but recovered. A good lesson learned—immediate gratification was more important than loyalty to some people. "But there will be people around. My family, too."

Emma eyed him warily. "Family?"

He nodded once. "Libby and I have a code word. If I text or say the word, she knows to take action."

Emma removed her notepad from her bag. "What's the code word?"

"Top secret."

"If I don't know what to listen for, I'm not going to be able to help you."

He rubbed his chin. "We need our own word. Something obscure, but not too random."

Emma tapped her pen against her notepad. "How about…lighthouse?"

AJ mulled over the suggestion. Ten letters would be a bear to text, but the word could be worked into a conversation without sounding like a non sequitur.

"That'll work." Satisfaction flowed through him. The word played perfectly into his plans. "To make sure we remember the code word, we'll visit one now."

"No need. I'll remember."

"A few hours spent sightseeing won't make a difference."

"What's really going on?" She studied him. "You remind me of a kid trying to put off going to the doctor's for a shot."

His jaw tensed. "I'm not scared of needles."

"You're scared of something."

Emma's insight made him squirm. She had zero qualms pinpointing and commenting on what was going on in his head, trying to fix what was upsetting him. He was used to having people try to fix things for him, but not with nurturing concern, as if she really cared. AJ didn't like it.

"I'm not scared of anything." The words flowed quickly, one after the other without any breaks. Not like him. But then again, he was back in Haley's Bay. That changed everything. "Okay, that's not quite true. The threat of an EMP, electronic magnetic pulse, making every electrical device obsolete has given me nightmares."

"You're not scared about coming home?"

"Nope." Damn. He sounded like a kid, a scared little kid trying to put on a good front, and Emma seemed to know that. "I lived here for eighteen years. I might be a little on edge, but that's because I haven't been here in a while."

"Ten years is a long time."

"I've been busy." A stupid excuse, but she didn't need

to know the real reasons. "But I'm free now. Let's take in a few sights on our way. This is my first vacation in over a year."

Emma's not-going-to-happen-on-my-watch shake of her head stopped him cold. "You'll have a free block of time after your calls this afternoon," she said. "Plenty of time to see the sights over the next five days."

Her friendly tone, as though she was using extra patience for her recalcitrant charge, made him feel like an idiot for bringing this up again. He must be back in his hometown. He'd felt like the village idiot living here.

Emma leaned toward the limousine window. The shift of position brought a whiff of her citrus shampoo—grapefruit or maybe lemon. The fresh scent appealed to him like the nanny.

"Wow." She pressed closer to the glass. "This place is beautiful."

He followed her gaze to the sparkling expanse of water and the heart of the town hugging the shoreline. Pride welled. Foolish, irrepressible pride he buried in a no-nonsense response. "The town hugs the waterfront. Most of the shops and restaurants are on Bay Street near the harbor."

"Is Haley's Bay named after an original settler?"

"Yes." AJ didn't know if she was making conversation or wanted to know the answer. Given her occupation, he'd guess the latter. She seemed the type to pay attention and ask questions of white-haired docents leading museum tours. He wouldn't mind taking her through a couple of the historic sites around here. "Haley was a trader who anchored in the bay during his voyages. That's according to the Lewis and Clark expedition. The bay was renamed Baker Bay, after a British merchant, but the original town name stuck."

"You know your history."

Her praise made him sit taller. A stupid reaction, but returning to his hometown was a stupid move. He should have thrown a royal extravaganza for his grandmother on his turf, in Seattle. Rented the Space Needle. Staged a massive fireworks display. But she'd wanted the party here in the town where she'd been born and lived her entire life.

"I learned Washington state history in school, but the old folks around here bring the past alive, especially the fishermen. They love sharing every legend about Haley's Bay."

"I'm usually the one telling stories. I'd love to hear some tales."

The excitement in her voice made him want to offer to introduce her around. Talk about a stupid move. She would be more welcome here than him. But something about Emma made AJ want to help her. Maybe he was feeling sorry for her after the rough flight, but he didn't like it. She worked for him, not the other way around.

"Make friends with the locals," he suggested. "You'll hear them all."

"Must have been fun growing up here."

"When I was a little kid." He studied the buildings—stores and cafés he didn't recognize—along the inland side of Bay Road. Maybe that would take his mind off the woman sitting next to him. A wrought iron wind vane of a sailboat faced west. On the sidewalk, two people walked hand in hand. An unleashed golden retriever trotted next to them. "Not so much when I became a teenager."

"It's a charming town."

"If you like small and boring."

"I do." She stared across him. Her lips parted, spreading into a wide grin that made him want to smile. "Look at the boats."

Sailboat masts teetered on the harbor. Flags fluttered in

the breeze. Empty moorings meant most boats had headed out to sea for the day. “Fishing used to support this town. Now I hear the biggest catch is tourists. A couple of my brothers take them deep sea fishing.”

That must kill his dad, who believed the only way to make money was building boats and catching fish. He’d called tourists “barnacles” and a few other choice words he wouldn’t say in front of his wife or mother.

With her eager gaze, Emma looked like a tourist herself. All she needed was a camera, sunglasses and a guidebook. “I could see coming here for vacation.”

He’d taken days off work, but he couldn’t relax here. Still, talking about Haley’s Bay with Emma wasn’t so bad. Being so aware of her movements and expressions, however, was making him uncomfortable. He focused on the town’s geography. “Cape Disappointment is next door with campsites, yurts and hiking trails. There’s the Lewis and Clark Interpretive Center. Long Beach is a coastal resort community to the northwest and Astoria, Oregon, is south across the Columbia River. I guess if I hadn’t grown up here…”

“You’d come for fun.”

“I might.” AJ tried hard not to think of this place. “But I always thought of Haley’s Bay as the place I couldn’t wait to leave when I went to college.”

“Back east, right?”

Libby must have prepped Emma with his background info. He assumed only the basics. All he knew about Emma was that she’d been in the foster care system before moving in with Libby and her parents during high school. “MIT.”

“Boston must have been a big change with the crowds and skyscrapers.”

“My first week it took me three days to fall asleep because of the noise, but I loved living there. Compared to a city, this place is dead."

"You might view your hometown differently now that you're an adult." Emma pointed to the Captain's Café, a multistory restaurant complete with weathered front, crow's nest, anchor and captain's wheel. "Do they have good food?"

"I've never seen the place." He searched his memory for what had been there before. The doughnut shop, no… that wasn't right. "That used to be Stu's Sandwich Shop, a hole-in-the-wall storefront. But no one could top their pastrami on rye."

"I love a good Reuben."

AJ imagined her biting into a big sandwich, a dab of Thousand Island on the corner of her mouth. He wouldn't mind licking it off and tasting more than the dressing.

Whoa. Where had that come from? He didn't lick, let alone kiss, employees.

And she was his employee. Smart. Observant with journalist-writing-a-travel-piece insights, opinions and questions. Qualities he searched for when hiring staff. The other things he looked for were initiative and loyalty. Always, after what he'd gone through in Haley's Bay, loyalty.

She gestured to the passing scenery, giving him another whiff of her shampoo. "What other places are new?"

Ignoring how good she smelled, he took in the street, noting the differences from his memory to reality. "The Coffee Shack, Donut Heaven, Bert's Hardware, the Bay Mercantile Store and the barbershop were here before, but the building facades are updated. The Candy Cave, the Buried Treasure and Raging Waters are new. They appear more for tourists than locals. But I'll bet the new store owners have the same small-town mentality as everyone else."

"That so-called mentality is part of the appeal."

Her odd—almost disapproving?—expression jabbed at him. Libby wasn't a yes-person, but if her opinion differed from his she wasn't vocal like Emma. The nanny had no problem speaking up. He wasn't used to people doing so and wasn't sure if he liked it or not. "The mentality is difficult to take growing up."

"You feel that way, but many people didn't grow up in a small town. They want to experience what that's like. That's why tourists like visiting. Haley's Bay has to be a popular destination or we'd see the effects of a downturned economy, empty businesses and for lease signs in the windows."

Interesting. A nanny with a keen sense of business. She wasn't a carbon copy of Libby, and that was surprisingly okay. He leaned toward Emma, wanting to know more about her. "What was your major in college?"

"I didn't go to college." Not an ounce of regret sounded in her voice. She raised her chin with a hint of pride and determination, two more traits that appealed to him. "I attended a thirty-month nanny certification program in Portland. But I loved my economics class in high school. I like to read and stay up on current events. Nannies are a child's second teacher, after their parents. I aim to enhance a child's natural interests."

Initiative in the flesh, plus confidence and curiosity. All packaged as a prim, proper, mousy nanny who had a pretty smile when she let it show. Emma would work out nicely. The more she dealt with, the more he could retreat.

"You might not like your hometown, but I love the quaint shops and cafés." She rested her head against the back of the seat, her shoulder brushing his. "Quintessential Pacific Northwest coastal town."

Her wistful, romantic tone annoyed him. So did the tingle racing down his arm from where she'd touched him. "Forest and water, Emma. Please. Don't get all rose-tinted on me, okay? This is Hicksville and being here held me back, badly. I never would have amounted to anything if I'd stayed in Haley's Bay. This place was suffocating."

The words rushed from his mouth before he could stop them. He'd never said these thoughts before. Weird. He was more careful and reserved around strangers. Around people he knew, too.

She tilted her head, attention fixed on him. Her focus unsettled him. He was used to being deferred to. Most bosses were. Emma must not have gotten the memo.

Of course she hadn't. She consulted with parents and left when they didn't agree. A free agent unused to following the chain of command. Like him when he'd started his business. How unexpected.

"What?" he asked finally.

"You..." She pursed her lips, full and unglossed.

He prepared for a lecture. Wanted to hear what she had to say if she didn't drag on for more than a minute or so.

"...couldn't have done a better job at getting away and making something of yourself."

The praise filled him with unexpected warmth. Most people complimented him, but AJ never knew if they meant the words or were trying to suck up to him. Emma didn't seem to be the kind of person to belong in that second group. "Thanks. There's more—"

She nodded to him, as if encouraging him to continue. "More what?"

Damn. AJ balled one of his hands. He didn't know why he kept telling Emma things. He didn't let his guard down around anyone, friend or employee. Fresh-smelling hair and pretty smile aside.

"More I want to do. Places to visit." Not what he intended to say, but the words were true and the perfect way to change the subject. "Are there places you'd like to travel?"

"Anywhere."

"In the world?"

She nodded. "The farthest from Portland I've been is Puerto Vallarta. It's hard to get around the flying."

"You flew today."

"To help Libby." Emma's gaze returned to the view out the window. The limousine followed the road along the bay toward his grandmother's house. "I should have suggested driving myself and meeting you here, but I was so worried about Libby I wasn't thinking straight."

He knew the feeling being with Emma. "When it's time for you to return to Portland, my driver will take you home."

She glanced around the limousine, taking in the multiple screens, leather seats, bar. "This is your, um, car."

AJ nodded. "Charlie drove down from Seattle this morning. I never intended on flying to Haley's Bay, but I didn't want to leave Libby alone in New York. She's too valuable to me. If I'd known she hadn't been feeling well before we'd left on the trip, I never would have taken her along, but she hid her abdominal pains until they became acute. I waited for her mother to arrive, made sure she was settled and comfortable, then flew here with a couple stops along the way."

"Oh."

The surprise in the one word spoke volumes. Emma Markwell had thought the worst of him. She wasn't the only one, especially here in Haley's Bay. "You assumed I left Libby in the hospital alone."

"Maybe."

"That means yes."

Emma stared up at him through her eyeglasses, her cheeks red and a contrite look on her face. "It's nice to know you didn't. Leave Libby, that is."

Not a full compliment, but better than being slammed for something he didn't do. Still, he liked the idea of making Emma squirm since she'd done the same to him. "You're backpedaling."

"Not really."

"I'm a nice guy."

Emma raised an arched brow. "Are you always nice?"

Damn. "I try to be."

"Trying doesn't always work."

"No, but I can tell myself I didn't set out to be a jerk."

"Is this something you tell yourself often?" she teased.

Her sense of humor had returned. She would need every funny bone with his family. "You'll be able to answer that question on Sunday."

"That sounds like I should be worried."

"Maybe."

Emma laughed. "Guess I deserve that."

The limousine pulled to a stop. The engine turned off.

AJ glanced to his right. His grandmother's Victorian stood peacock-blue and proud across a lawn of manicured grass and blooming flower beds. His heart beat like a halyard on a mast. "We're here."

"Wow. Your grandmother's home is perfect. Even with the water right here, the house is what shines."

He recognized the awe in Emma's voice. A familiar sense of reverence—of home—brought an unexpected smile to his face. "The house has been in our family for generations."

Emma's eyes widened. "That's a long time to stay in one place."

"Coles have lived in Haley's Bay since the Civil War."

Her gaze bounced from the house to him. "The house isn't that old."

"My great grandfather bought the house ninety years ago. He liked the view of the bay."

"Let me guess, he was a fisherman."

"And boat builder."

Emma looked over her shoulder at the bay. She took her time, allowed her gaze to absorb what she saw. "Lovely."

The dreamy haze in her eyes and a soft smile on her face made her lovely, too. He shook the thought from his head. "The view from the second floor is better. You can see the harbor."

Charlie opened the door.

AJ motioned for Emma to go first.

She slung her bag over her shoulder and clasped the plastic handle on the cat carrier. Moving toward the open door, she looked like she might topple out of the car. He didn't need her to get hurt. One personal assistant in the hospital was enough.

He took the carrier from her. "I've got the cat."

Her gaze met his then she looked away. "Thank you."

AJ followed her out and stood on the sidewalk. Vividly painted terra-cotta flowerpots full of colorful pink, purple and yellow blossoms sat on each step leading to the wraparound porch. His sister Bailey's creations, he was sure, the sight comforting as his grandma's crocheted afghans. He only hoped his dad wasn't part of the welcoming committee.

AJ gestured to the steps. "After you."

Halfway up, Emma stopped. "There's a swing."

The breathless quality to her voice surprised him. He peered around her to see the white slotted-back, two-person bench hanging from thick silver chains. "Looks like my grandmother replaced her old swing. She used to love to drink tea out here and watch the boats. Guess she still does."

"We had a swing." Emma took the last two stairs. "Boy, did we abuse that thing. My mom got so mad at us."

A bright, toothpaste-ad smile lit up her face.

AJ's chest tightened. Emma looked so lighthearted and happy. She should smile more.

He joined her on the porch. "Us?"

Something—not panic, perhaps surprise—flashed in her eyes. "My, um, older brother."

"My younger brothers and I played on Grandma's old swing all the time. Had to fix it more than once after climbing and hanging off the chains." He set the cat carrier on the porch. "We used to stand on the backrest and swing to see how high we could go. We also jumped off the seat to see if we could clear the porch rail and bushes."

She leaned over the rail as if estimating the distance down to the lawn. "Sounds dangerous."

He bit back a laugh. "You sound like a nanny."

"Occupational hazard." Her amused gaze met his. "But you can't tell me no one got hurt."

He pointed under his chin. "I have a scar to show for the fun we had. My youngest brother, Grady, has two."

"Your poor grandmother."

"She didn't mind. Now our mom—"

The front door opened.

"You're here." His grandma stood in the doorway. She wore a pair of light blue pants and a white peasant blouse. All five feet of short gray curls and sharp blue eyes barreled toward him like a stampeding water buffalo, albeit a baby one. "You're finally home."

Not his home. He lived in Seattle. But the excitement in her voice reminded AJ that this visit wasn't about him.

AJ hugged his grandmother. Her rose-scented perfume

smelled sweeter than when she'd visited him in Seattle. "It's not like you gave me a choice, Grandma."

She tsked, stepped back and assessed him from head to toe. "I like the long hair, but you need the ends trimmed. Go visit Monty at the barbershop. He'll fix you right up."

AJ shook his head. "Nice to see you, too, Grandma."

Emma laughed under her breath.

"Grandmother." He motioned to his new assistant, who stood with a patient smile on her face and her arm half-extended toward his grandmother. "I'd like you to meet—"

"Is he here?" A high-pitched female voice called from inside the house. "Grandmother Cole? Is he?"

"AJ is here." Grandma leaned closer, lowering her voice. "Risa has been waiting for you to arrive all morning. Her youngest sister is here, too. And she can't wait to meet the illustrious and incredibly wealthy AJ Cole."

Danger-up-ahead infused his grandmother's tone. His gut clenched. He'd heard about his sister-in-law's matchmaking from his sister Bailey. Two brothers and his youngest sister, Camden, had been targeted over the holidays last year, making Thanksgiving and Christmas dinners uncomfortable. "I thought her sister lived far away."

"Hawaii," Grandma said. "But I suppose meeting a billionaire was worth the expense of a trip to the mainland."

Crap. AJ blew out a puff of air. Matchmaking friends and relatives were as bad as a case of chicken pox. Enough women wanted a piece of his bank account. He didn't need an in-law giving one of her sisters a push or inside access to him. On a rare vacation. That he already dreaded. This was not-not-not going to happen.

Grandma shook Emma's hand. "You're Libby?"

"Emma," she said. "Emma Markwell."

Grandma's white eyebrows drew together. Her surprised gaze shot from Emma to him. "I thought your assistant was coming with you."

"Emma is my—"

"AJ." Risa exited the house, her blond ponytail bouncing in the back and a wide smile on her face. She wore a pair of black yoga pants, two pink fitted T-shirts and tennis shoes. "Welcome back to Haley's Bay."

AJ hugged her. She was thin and pretty, a first grade teacher turned stay-at-home mom. They'd met in Seattle a few times, but never with his brother Ellis present. "Nice to see you. How are the kids?"

"Growing so fast I feel old. They'll be by tonight to see their long-lost uncle. But right now there's someone I want you to meet." Risa pointed to the front door where a twentysomething woman with long blond hair struck a sexy pose. "This is my little sister Madison. She lives in Hawaii."

"Hello, AJ." The woman's husky voice sounded like she needed an inhaler. He wouldn't be surprised given the skintight, oh-so-short cocktail dress she wore. Her outfit, complete with stiletto heels showing off toned long legs, was more appropriate for a hip dance club than lunch at his grandmother's house. The two sisters resembled each other, but Madison's looks were harder edged, hyperathletic compared to stay-at-home, happily married Risa. "Nice to meet you. I've heard so much about you."

AJ knew nothing about Madison. He hadn't been at Risa and Ellis's wedding, though AJ had paid for the reception, his gift to his brother. But one glance told AJ what this sex kitten was offering. Beauty up front, claws in his back. "All good, I hope."

She batted her eyelashes and leaned into the doorway, giving him a flash of her black lace bra. "Of course."

"I can't believe the two of you are in Haley's Bay at the

same time. I thought you could show Madison around. The town has changed a bit since you've been here last, but you can have fun exploring together." Risa's gaze flew between her sister and him so fast he thought she might end up with whiplash. "You have lots in common."

Madison nodded, reminding him of a bobblehead doll. "I love computers."

Right. He'd bet anything she loved the attention she got through Facebook and Instagram by posting selfies snapped in the mirror, posing as though she was a supermodel. AJ pressed his lips together.

"You'll have a good time with Madison," Risa encouraged.

AJ had no doubt about that. But he also knew Madison's type. She might claim to want only a casual fling or relationship, but the I-will-stop-at-nothing-to-win-the-lotto-jackpot-standing-in-front-of-me look in the woman's green eyes gave her away.

AJ inched closer to Emma, who remained quiet with a pleasant smile on her face. He wanted to stay far, far away from Madison. Oh, he'd dated women like her. Casually for a good time. She was his type—a go-getter. But when those women tried to sink their fingernails into him, he disentangled himself. That made Madison more than just an inconvenience because she was his sister-in-law's sister. He had enough family trouble without adding more. If he wasn't careful, Risa's misguided matchmaking could ruin not only his vacation in Haley's Bay, but also his grandmother's birthday. "Sounds fun, but I'm going to be busy planning Grandma's birthday."

"Not that busy," Risa countered, much to Madison's delight. His sister-in-law motioned to Emma. "You brought your assistant to do most of the work. Libby, isn't it?"

Emma's smile didn't waver. "I'm Emma."

The two sisters exchanged a confused glance. Madison frowned.

If only he could keep the woman frowning. Okay, not really. This wasn't personal. Ordinarily he'd be up for hanging with Madison. But he couldn't under the circumstances.

AJ's gaze jumped from Emma to Madison. Two women couldn't be more different. Emma might not be drop-dead sexy in a hot dress, but she was pretty with her girl-next-door looks and practical outfit. Emma wasn't on the hunt for a rich husband so she could live a life of luxury. She worked hard caring for other people's children, taking in homeless cats and helping out her best friend. Some men might want a Madison on their arms. He had, but Emma was the type of woman to bring home to meet the family.

The thought gave AJ an idea, a bad, stupid idea. Nah, he couldn't do that.

With a pointed stare at Emma, Risa's arched brows lifted. "And you're..."

Emma kept smiling. "I'm AJ's—"

"Girlfriend," AJ interrupted, realizing stupid or not, he had no other choice. "Emma is my girlfriend."

One beat. Two. He waited for God to strike him down for lying. Nothing. The Big Man must understand. Desperate times, desperate measures. He stole a glance at Emma.

She looked pained but held her smile in place. Atta girl. Team AJ all the way.

His gaze pleaded, begged her to play along. "Emma is a fan of lighthouses. This trip is the perfect opportunity for her to check them out and meet the family."

He hoped she remembered the code word. If not...

"AJ's girlfriend!" His grandmother hugged Emma. "I'm sorry I assumed you were his assistant. How long have you been dating?"

He bit the inside of his mouth. "I..."

"Not long," Emma finished for him. The way a helpful personal assistant would. Or a girlfriend. "But it feels like—"

"Forever," AJ said.

Even Madison sighed.

The lines on Grandma's forehead deepened. "Why didn't you introduce us when I visited last month?"

"I live in Portland," Emma said, thankfully keeping the charade going.

He nodded. "A long-distance relationship."

"Well, this is simply wonderful." Grandma clapped, then pointed to the cat carrier. "I must admit I didn't know what to think when AJ said there'd be a cat coming, but I figured it was none of my business. What's your cat's name, Emma?"

Emma's smile was more saccharine than sugar. "Blossom. She's a foster cat, but if everything works out as we hope, she'll soon belong to AJ."

What? The scheming, quick-thinking minx. Blackmail. Unbelievable.

He would adopt that pathetic feline over his dead body. But if Emma didn't play along with this charade, he might find himself in an early grave. He was a firm believer in quid pro quo. He pasted on an aspartame smile. "That's right."

Grandma's gaze narrowed. She eyed him suspiciously. "But you don't like cats."

Damn. He took a quick breath, hoping for the right words to say. "I didn't. But that's before I started dating a crazy cat lady."

Emma stiffened then moved closer. Wrapped her hand around his arm. Pinched him.

Ouch.

She waved her fingers. "That would be me. Crazy about cats and lighthouses."

Risa and Madison sized up and glared at Emma. If looks could kill, the two sisters would be behind bars and he'd be hitting up a temp agency to find a new assistant. Time to put an end to Madison's flirting.

AJ removed himself from Emma's hand, then placed his arm around her. Her muscles tensed beneath his palm. But he was more interested in her thin waist and the curve of her hips hidden by her clothes. His pulse kicked up. His temperature spiked. "And I'm crazy about you."

More likely just crazy. All he could think about doing was pulling her closer and kissing her hard on the lips.

Don't make me go all Supernanny or Nanny McPhee on you.

AJ had a feeling kissing Emma might be worth whatever trouble he got into and any punishment she might dish out. Even taking away his electronics.

Chapter Four

Forget the code word. AJ had lost his mind. Eccentric or certifiably insane? That was the question Emma needed to answer before this crazy idea of his went any further. Well, once they were alone. Until then she would act like a dutiful employee. Make that, um, girlfriend.

She followed Mrs. Cole—AJ's grandmother—up the stately Victorian's wide staircase trying not to burst out laughing. Emma Markwell the girlfriend of a hot internet billionaire? Yeah, right. No way could they pull this off. Okay, maybe he could, but not her.

Agreeing to be in a fake relationship with her temporary boss was not going to end well. The logistics of staying in the same house with him were bad enough, but Libby's reaction when she found out about the charade… That would not be pretty.

Emma expected yelling, followed by the silent treatment. Her insides twisted. She loved Libby like a sister.

Upsetting her best friend was not an option. Keeping quiet about the situation was key.

No one outside of Haley's Bay and the Cole family could know about the so-called dating. Now or after the fact. If, and it was a big if, Emma didn't put a stop to the entire thing before someone else called them on the relationship farce. No one, including Libby, would ever believe AJ Cole would date a boring, quiet nanny, let alone take her home to meet his estranged family.

Emma's stomach hurt with an icky, sinking feeling. Not even the scent of lemons and wood polish eased her discomfort. The pewter-framed family photographs covering the walls pressed home all the ways she didn't belong here.

She recognized AJ in several of the pictures. A younger AJ, bearded and happy. He was going to be upset when this lie exploded in his face. Of course it was his fault, but she sympathized with the guy over his sister-in-law's not-so-subtle matchmaking. The fix-up vibe had been strong out on the porch. AJ must be deluged with desiring women.

That would make her unusual in his world. The antithesis to a woman like Madison. Though the pretty woman earned points for being able to walk in such high heels. No way Emma could wear those without ending up face-first on the ground.

Mrs. Cole's thin, veined hand ran along the carved mahogany banister. She glanced over her shoulder at Emma. "How did you meet my grandson?"

"Through Libby." The muscles around Emma's mouth hurt from forcing a smile, but she assumed a girlfriend would look happy while on vacation with her *boyfriend.* Her stomach churned. She was a horrible liar, something AJ would have known if he had mentioned his idea to her first rather than telling her at the same time as everyone one else. She touched her tummy, trying to calm the nausea. "She's been my best friend since freshman year of high school."

That much was true. Emma didn't want to think about pertinent details such as the fact that she and AJ had met only a couple hours ago and he was paying her for her services and…

"Bet Libby gets a big bonus from my grandson for introducing you," Mrs. Cole said.

"Let's hope so." Unless Emma screwed this up. Highly likely. She'd dated, but never seriously and never a rich and powerful man such as AJ Cole. Playing make-believe with children was one thing. She could be a princess, queen, fairy godmother, pirate and ninja with the best of them. Being a pretend girlfriend would take acting abilities she didn't possess. Since this had been AJ's idea, maybe he wouldn't hold her failures against Libby. Emma crossed her fingers. "Libby works hard every day. She deserves a bonus and a raise."

"My employees are well-compensated," AJ said behind Emma. "A happy, satisfied staff makes for a more productive work environment."

If that was his goal, he was failing. Big-time. Emma was not happy or satisfied. She was peeved at being put into the position of lying to his family and friends. She glanced over her shoulder.

AJ's lips pressed together in a thin line. His dark brows furrowed, yet gratitude shone in his eyes. He mouthed the words *thank you,* surprising her.

"I was going to put you in bedrooms down the hall from each other, but that was before I knew you were dating." Mrs. Cole stood on the landing. "There's no reason you can't share a room."

"You don't have to do that." The words rushed from Emma's mouth, matching the panic coursing through her.

Her gaze bounced between AJ and his grandmother. "I mean… This is your house. Separate bedrooms are fine."

Preferred. Emma rubbed her hands together, her blood pressure spiraling with each passing second. Sharing a bedroom was not an option. She clenched her teeth and glared at AJ, trying to signal that they were fighting and not getting along. A couple on the outs wouldn't be forced to stay in the same room.

He gave her a smoldering look, as though he was so hot for her his clothes were singed.

Darn the man. He was having fun with this. Her temper rose. How dare he get her into this situation and now make it worse? If he thought this was a great way to get her into bed he had another think coming. She pursed her lips and crossed her arms over her chest.

"Now, now." Mrs. Cole's blue eyes twinkled. She winked, a mischievous grin on her face. "I may be old, but I remember being young once. You only have five days together. Enjoy your vacation and each other."

So. Not. Good. Emma inhaled but she couldn't get enough oxygen to fill her lungs. Any minute she was going to hyperventilate. Her gaze implored AJ to do something.

"That's generous and sweet of you," AJ said to his grandmother. "But Emma and I don't want to make you uncomfortable."

Finally! Emma nodded, hoping she didn't look like a battery-operated bobblehead. But that was what she felt like trying to get her agreement across to his grandmother.

"You don't have to worry, dears." Mrs. Cole patted AJ's arm. "This is better than you sneaking around at night. Trust me, you won't be fooling anyone. Especially your old grandma. Besides, it's about time this house saw some action."

Heat flooded Emma's face. She wanted the floor to open up so she could disappear. "Please, Mrs. Cole—"

"Lilah. Mrs. Cole was my mother-in-law. Nothing I did was good enough for that woman." She gave Emma's shoulder a squeeze, but the touch did nothing to calm her tap-dancing nerves. "Technology makes keeping in touch easier these days, but long-distance relationships are still difficult. Make the most of your time together."

The woman emphasized the last word.

Together. So not happening. Emma bit her lip.

"This is your room." Lilah stepped through a doorway. She motioned to the wood-paned windows on the opposite wall. "I love the view of the harbor. I used to stand there and watch for AJ's grandfather's boat to come in."

"That's sweet." Or would be if Emma would see past the queen-size four-poster bed covered with a white comforter and fluffy lace trimmed pillows. A romantic bed. A bed for lovers. Not a boss and his employee. The pillow-sized lump in her throat threatened to choke her.

"The room has its own bathroom," Lilah said. "I took the liberty of putting a litter box in there for the cat."

"Thank you." A real smile tugged at the corners of Emma's mouth. She wished she had a grandmother like Lilah. Emma didn't remember hers. "Blossom and I appreciate that."

Lilah peered through the grate. "The cat must be cramped after being stuck in the crate so long."

AJ placed the carrier on the floor, then opened the gate. Blossom dashed out. The ball of orange disappeared under the bed.

"Blossom needs time to adjust to her new surroundings. That's how cats are. Let me show you the room." Lilah pointed out the bathroom, a closet with built-in dresser and fireplace. "You should be comfortable here."

Maybe if on a honeymoon. Goose bumps covered Emma's skin. She rubbed her hands over her arms. The bedroom was oh so romantic, the kind you might find in a quaint B and B. Not the place she wanted to spend the night with AJ. A total stranger.

Emma forced the word *thanks* from her dry mouth. She didn't dare say anything directly to AJ's grandmother and appear rude. The woman had been gracious, kind and… um, progressive.

"We'll be very comfortable, thank you, Grandma." AJ escorted Lilah toward the door. "Charlie will bring up our luggage. We'll get settled, then see you downstairs."

Mischief danced in his grandmother's eyes. She sashayed out the doorway with the grace of a chorus-line dancer. "Don't rush on my part."

The innuendo was clear. The older woman had given them the thumbs-up to have sex before lunch.

Emma bit back a groan. She wanted to be anywhere but here. Her cheeks warmed. Who was she kidding? Her skinned burned like glowing barbecue charcoals.

AJ closed the door. "I—"

"I quit."

His mouth dropped open. He pressed his lips together, then adjusted the cuff of his dress shirt. "You promised Libby you'd take her place."

"As your assistant. Not your…" Emma couldn't say the word aloud. She squeezed the back of her tight neck. "I realize you got caught in some bizarre matchmaking situation out on the porch, and I went along because of Libby, but this is ridiculous. You're a grown man. A billionaire, for goodness' sake. You should be able to handle a scheming woman without resorting to an impossible charade. I don't like lying to your grandmother. I don't see how you can, either. She's so sweet and really cares about you."

"I'm doing this for my grandmother," he said. "If we're not dating, I'm going to have to reject Madison and call Risa on her misguided matchmaking attempt. That's going to make for an awkward time and ruin my grandmother's birthday party."

"No." Emma held up her hands, palms facing him. "This is way beyond what I was asked to do as your personal assistant. Fix it with your family or I walk."

"You don't have to walk. Everything will be okay."

"How so?" Her voice cracked. She didn't appreciate that his voice remained calm. "Your grandmother thinks we're about to make mad passionate love."

"She's…romantic. Indulge her."

Every muscle tightened. Emma glared. "No way. Not going to happen."

"I'm not asking you to have sex with me. Just pretend we're together. We've committed to the ruse. I can't do this without you."

"No one is going to believe we're a couple."

"My grandmother believes. Risa and Madison, too."

Emma bit her lip, unconvinced.

"I'll find a way to make this work so you're not horribly uncomfortable," AJ added. "Please. I need your help."

He sounded sincere. He'd said *please,* emphasizing the word. But something held her back. Okay, a lot of things. "I don't know. I feel really weird about this."

"Me, too." He brushed his hand through his thick hair. "This goes way beyond what a person should ask of someone they met a couple hours ago, but think about Libby. She's your best friend. I know you'd do anything for her or you wouldn't be here now. By Sunday, you and I will be friends, too, and this won't seem as weird then."

Emma eyed him warily. "You and me, friends?"

AJ nodded. "You're the only person who tells me exactly what they're thinking."

"That's not always a good thing."

"No, not always. It's refreshing to be with someone so open and honest," he admitted. "I'll be honest with you. I panicked with Risa and Madison. I got us into this mess, but I need you to get me through it."

Emma felt trapped. No matter what she decided, she would have regrets. Sure, she could walk away, but she'd agreed to help Libby. Emma hadn't spoken up when AJ introduced her as his girlfriend and led his family to believe they were dating. She bore some responsibility here. Not as much as AJ, but some. She took a breath, then another. "You're used to getting what you want."

His easy smile curled her toes. She promptly uncurled them.

"Pretty much." He sounded amused. "I can afford most things, but I like to believe it's because I want only rational things."

"My being your girlfriend is not rational."

"True. That's more of a necessity."

"I'm a raft of cotton in your sea of cashmere."

"I like cotton. Practical and soft. Low maintenance. Perfect for everyday wear."

The slight change in his tone and way he leaned forward to get closer irritated Emma. She pursed her lips, hoping she looked haughty rather than pouty with duck lips. "Flattery will get you nowhere."

"Not flattery. Honesty."

She chewed the inside of her mouth, not wanting to buy his words, but having a difficult time not believing him. "If I do this favor for you, I expect a few things in return."

"What?"

"More vacation time for Libby. She's so dedicated and

devoted to you, she put her job ahead of her health. She needs more balance in her life, not working nonstop."

"I count on Libby."

"She's not much good to you sick or dead."

A beat passed, then another. "Okay, Libby gets more vacation time."

"With no contact from you during that time. That includes texts."

His mouth twisted. "Fine. What else?"

"I would like you to make a large donation to the Portland Paws Rescue Shelter. They need their plumbing replaced so they can reopen. They are a 501(c)(3) nonprofit so your donation will be tax-deductible."

"How much?"

"Fifty thousand dollars."

"You think you're worth that much."

"I have no idea, but you might think I'm worth that much or you wouldn't have introduced me as your girlfriend because you were afraid of another woman."

A sheepish look crossed his face. "Not afraid. Concerned over the consequences of what might happen."

"Afraid."

He opened his mouth, then closed it. "Fine. Contact my CPA today and tell him to have a check delivered."

"Just like that?"

He nodded once.

Billionaire, she remembered. Fifty thousand might seem like a lottery jackpot to her, but AJ lived in a different world. "There's one more thing."

"Money for you?"

"A home for Blossom. You know people. Find her a forever home."

A muscle ticked at his jaw. His lips drew tight. "That's—"

"The last thing I want." She stared down her nose at

him for emphasis, hoping with her glasses she didn't look cross-eyed.

He swore under his breath.

Emma didn't expect him to be happy, but now he knew what being trapped in an awkward position felt like. "If you'd rather not—"

"I'll find the damn cat a home."

"Not any home. A forever home. One that will love Blossom the way she deserves to be loved and take care of her."

"This is going to cost me another fifty grand." He looked at the rumpled bed skirt where Blossom had disappeared. "Maybe more."

"Libby said you made the Forbes 400 this year. You can afford it."

Emma wasn't sure where her bravado came from, but what was he going to do? Fire her?

"Anything else you want?" he asked.

"That's all."

"Nothing for yourself?"

"Helping Libby, the shelter and Blossom is all I want."

AJ studied her, his mouth slanted and his eyes narrowed.

"What?" she asked.

"Nothing." He gaze traveled from her to the empty cat carrier to the bed, then returned to Emma. "You have a deal."

She blew out a puff of air.

He grinned. "You thought I'd say no."

"I was hoping."

"Is this the nanny or the personal assistant or Emma talking?"

"All three." Emma was about to apologize, but realized he'd put her in this situation. If her behavior wasn't quite up to the Rose City Nanny Academy's standards, oh, well, she was doing her best. "Bringing a real girlfriend would have been cheaper."

"True." He looked away, making her wonder what kind of women he dated. Not nannies like her. "But we'll make this work. We don't have a choice."

Emma remembered this was his first time home in a while. "I'm here to make sure your vacation and the birthday party go well. I'll do my best to play your girlfriend, but that doesn't mean I'll be able to pull off the act. I'm still uncomfortable sharing a room with you. Nothing is going to change that."

"I understand and I'm grateful for your going along with this. Who knows, this might be fun."

She made a face.

"Or maybe not," he quipped. "I'll try to come up with another accommodation option, but until then you don't have to share a bed with me. I'm fine sleeping on the floor and you'll have to be flexible about us sharing a room."

The word brought up all kind of images of the two of them being *flexible* together. Unwelcome images that made her want to fan herself. Not good. Having a billionaire she was supposed to take care of end up with a stiff back while planning and hosting a birthday party wouldn't be good, either. "What if someone walks in and sees you sleeping on the floor?"

"I could say you kicked me out of the bed for eating cookies or snoring."

"I'd still hear you snoring if we're sharing a room."

"We'll have to think of something that makes sense."

"I don't think that's possible since none of this makes sense." She thought for a moment, not liking the option coming to her. "We're both adults. We could share the bed if we put a wall of pillows between us. Or one of us can sleep on top of the sheet and the other underneath it."

Amusement gleamed in his eyes. "Excellent idea. You must have experience being someone's pretend girlfriend."

Heat rose up her neck and settled in her face. Tomato-red, no doubt. She didn't like how AJ kept making her blush.

"No," she said. "But I'm a nanny. Sometimes siblings don't want to share a bed or aren't getting along during naptime. I know all the tricks."

"Then this shouldn't be a problem."

"Maybe not for you, but this is way outside my comfort zone. I'm old-fashioned."

"Old-fashioned in what way?"

Emma fought the urge to shrug. She shouldn't have brought this up. "A few ways."

"Let me guess. You don't call men or ask them out. Wait until you're in a committed relationship to have sex. Expect men to pay when you go out."

Oh, boy. Two out of three. Though his definition of a committed relationship might be different from hers. "Yes, yes and no. I'm fine paying or splitting the check. Otherwise dates can get expensive fast and that's not fair."

"While you're my girlfriend, I pick up the tab. I'm sure it'll be a helluva lot cheaper than $50K and finding your cat a home."

"Should be. I don't eat *that* much."

Laughter, deep and rich, wrapped around her like strong, comforting arms. The sense of security and belonging nearly overwhelmed her. She took a step toward the window.

"We'll make this work, Emma."

"If you say so." Her gaze rested on his smiling lips. Nice lips. She wondered how he tasted. Uh, no, she didn't. "I realize that in public and in front of your family we must act as if we're in a relationship. But any other time..."

"Under any other circumstance, I would never date an employee. We may need to act romantic around my family, but you have nothing to worry about when we're alone."

She stared at the carpet, feeling as appealing as a slice of moldy bread. But she wanted him to leave her alone. If not, she wouldn't be complaining about sharing a room. She lifted her chin and looked straight at him. "Thank you."

"We'll get through this."

The way his voice softened gave her chills. His gaze lingered, practically caressed. Every nerve ending tingled. What was going on?

Not trusting her voice, Emma nodded. She hoped AJ was right about getting through this because she wasn't sure about anything at the moment. Especially herself. And him.

An hour later, with the fake smile he'd perfected for use during interviews and business meetings, AJ sat at the dining room table with his grandmother, his mother, Marianne, Risa, Madison and Emma. His siblings and father would be joining them for dinner.

The reprieve from the entire family would give AJ and Emma much-needed time to practice their couple-ness. Things were not going well, but he wasn't giving up. Visible trouble in paradise would encourage Madison's attention and Grandma's advice, neither welcome.

AJ swung his arm around the back of Emma's chair. A friendly gesture, not the slightest bit intimate. He didn't want his pretend girlfriend joining the cat under the bed.

Emma stiffened, her back ramrod straight. She didn't

glance his way, but scooted forward, putting distance between her back and his hand.

If she didn't loosen up, the gig would be up before dessert. He still couldn't believe she'd agreed to help him out with this enormous favor. He wanted to cut her some slack, but they were on display with his family watching.

He appreciated what she was doing. The way she'd leveraged what she did out of him for others, not herself, impressed him. He hadn't been in this kind of partnership since his early days when he needed venture capital for his start-up. He liked the feeling of having a partner, or rather, in this situation, a partner in crime.

If only she'd stop acting as if she were on a bad first date. The first date part was technically true, but he needed her to act interested. Most women didn't have a problem with that. Then again, Emma wasn't like the women he normally dated. He shouldn't treat her like one of them. He leaned toward her. "Would you like another serving of chicken pot pie, honey?"

Her startled gaze met his. "Um, no thanks. I've had seconds."

Across the table, Madison picked at her quarter-sized portion without eating a bite. "Might as well have thirds. Nannies must use a lot of energy running after kids all day."

Emma nodded.

AJ didn't appreciate Madison's I'm-better-than-you tone. He toyed with the end of Emma's braid. "I appreciate a woman with a healthy appetite and curves. Emma needs her energy for me, not just kids."

The gratitude in her eyes made his pulse increase. His stomach tightened.

"Beeeep. Goal rate met," AJ's watch announced. He blinked and hit the reset button. Normally that only hap-

pened when he'd reached the target range during a cardiac workout. That was odd.

Madison took a bite off her plate.

"I have apple pie for dessert," Grandma announced. "It's AJ's favorite."

"Mine, too," Emma said.

Grandma pushed back in her chair. "Glad to hear it. So many people are into cake pops and cupcakes these days. But pie is down-home goodness. Takes skill to perfect the crust."

His mom's forehead wrinkled. She still looked to be in her early forties except for some silver in her brunette hair and the lines at the corner of her eyes. "I thought you went to the bakery this morning."

"I did, but the baker had to get it right," Grandma stood. "I'm assuming everyone wants a scoop of vanilla ice cream loaded on top?"

Emma nodded. "Please."

"Me, too." Madison inched forward in her chair until she was nearly pressed against the dining room table. "I love pie and ice cream."

His mother stood. "I'll help you serve up dessert."

"Wonderful." Grandma kept her gaze on Emma for some reason. "We'll be back in a flash."

Risa wiped her mouth with her napkin, then stared pointedly at Emma. "A long-distance relationship must be difficult."

"Seattle is a short train ride from Portland," Emma said.

AJ tried not to grimace. He hadn't ridden a train since college. "I have a jet, too."

Emma smiled, seeming to relax for the first time during the meal. "True, but I love the train. Much more cost-efficient than wasting the crew's time and all that fuel jetting me around."

He scooted closer, so close he could smell the citrusy scent of her shampoo. He took another sniff. Better than any expensive perfume. "I know you prefer the train, but the jet's faster. That gives me more time with you."

The lines around Madison's mouth deepened. "I don't get it. Nannies can work anywhere. Why don't you move to Seattle?"

A valid question. AJ tried to come up with a logical explanation why Emma wouldn't be living closer to him.

"I may be moving to Seattle," she said to his surprise. "I recently finished an assignment with a family. I'm currently working temporary babysitting jobs until I figure out what to do next."

"Just say the word and I'll have a moving crew at your apartment to pack up your stuff." He knew this was the perfect opportunity to let Risa and Madison see that the two of them were *serious*. "I have plenty of room at my house."

"I know there's room." Emma didn't miss a beat. Nor did she blush. Progress? He hoped so. "But I'd like to have a secure a job before I make any definite plans."

"You don't have to work," he said.

A wistful expression formed on Madison's face.

"I want to work," Emma said, making him wonder if she ever took the easy way out. Something told him unlikely.

"The offer stands if you change your mind." AJ knew this conversation was nothing more than a show for his sister-in-law and her younger sister. Yet he could rattle off a handful of reasons why a move to Seattle made sense for Emma. Starting with a higher salary due to being in a larger city, living closer to Libby and ending with—not him—the cat.

"Thanks." She looked at Risa and Madison. "Sorry for bringing this up in front of you."

"It's fine," Madison said. "You must have a lot of catching up to do."

"Don't mind us." Risa's sounded genuine. "We're family. It's nice knowing what's going on with AJ beyond what we read on the internet."

"I'm only a phone call, text or email away if you'd like to find out for yourself," he countered.

"True, but so are we," Risa said. "Flynn manages to keep in touch even when he's deployed. The last time he was in Afghanistan, he and Ellis kept in close contact. The kids were always asking when they can Skype with Uncle Flynn. They still ask."

"Flynn's amazing. Always has been. The Cole family's personal superhero."

AJ hadn't meant for his sarcasm to be so thick. He appreciated his brother's service to this country, but AJ didn't get why everyone applauded his brother's enlisting in the military at age seventeen, while AJ's leaving to attend a top university was considered traitorous. Pursuing dreams outside of fishing and boat building should work both ways. Especially since each of Ellis and Risa's children had trust funds to cover their education costs through doctorate degrees.

Madison straightened, her face brightening. "Is Flynn going to be at the birthday party?"

"No," Risa said. "He's off somewhere again. Never know where."

"That's too bad." AJ hadn't spoken with Flynn in…a long time. Ten, no, twelve years. "Libby mailed him an invitation, but he's never been one to RSVP."

Risa pinned him with a stare. "Family shouldn't be required to RSVP."

Silence descended over the table. Even Risa was getting on him now.

"I wonder what's taking so long with the pie. The ice cream's going to melt." Emma scooted back in her chair, breaking the tension in the air. "Let's see if your mom and grandmother need help."

Emma didn't wait for an answer. She headed into the kitchen without a glance back to see if he was following.

He was, nipping at her heels, grateful she'd helped him escape Risa and Madison. He'd forgotten that saying anything against Flynn was forbidden in the family. AJ was in the doghouse before even seeing his father. This was not looking good. If Emma and he couldn't pull off being a happy couple, he'd be worse off than when he left ten years ago. He only hoped his grandmother and her birthday party wouldn't be the ones who suffered.

Chapter Five

After AJ's conference calls and interview had been completed, Emma walked along the shoreline with him at her side. A breeze carried the briny scent of the sea and toyed with the ends of AJ's hair, making him look way too sexy strolling on the rocky beach in his dress shirt, trousers and leather shoes. Temporary bosses and fake boyfriends shouldn't be so utterly attractive.

She should be enjoying this break from his watchful family, but being near him increased her anxiety. The man put her on edge with his constant devising and revising of strategies. She didn't need experience in mergers and acquisitions to know lunch had not gone well. Maybe he was going to fire her for being such a rotten girlfriend. Being fired would be welcomed, appreciated even.

"What do you think so far?" AJ asked.

Walking alone with him on the beach was harder than faking a relationship publicly. He was so focused on success that relaxing was impossible. His family's Victorian stood on a bluff in the distance, a beacon to the Cole men after a day on the sea. "Haley's Bay is lovely, and Lilah's house is spectacular."

"True, but I want to know how you thought lunch went."

Of course he did. AJ was worked up over his family. The dynamics were becoming clearer to her, but she wondered if he truly cared what his family thought of him or if the only thing that mattered to him was his grandmother. He hadn't seemed to put much effort into healing the rifts between them. "Not well. Being a girlfriend doesn't come naturally to me."

"You pulled out a win with the moving to Seattle talk."

"That's because I was telling the truth." The truth mattered. When she was a kid, her mother had dragged her brother back into a convenience store after he'd walked out with a pack of gum in his pocket. He'd been only eight, but their mom had made him apologize and pay for the gum with change from his piggy bank.

Little life lessons like that were all she had left of her family. Every physical reminder of her parents and brother had been destroyed in the house fire. Her memories kept fading so she wrote what she remembered in a journal.

She picked up a shell, then rubbed her fingers over the ridges on the outside. "I talked to Libby about moving to Seattle before she left for New York. She's been after me to move now that I'm no longer working for a family..."

"Your salary will be higher. No state income tax. Several tech companies, including mine, provide employee perks ranging from in-house day care centers to take-home dinners for our employees. If you decide you want to try the business world, you could work in the day care center, be an admin, support the development team. Whatever you wanted to try."

"Libby's suggested I do that." And went as far as typing up and submitting Emma's résumé to the day care manager. Not that a job was guaranteed, or that she would take one if offered. "But I was born and raised in Portland. I've never lived anywhere else. Libby's parents are there. Friends. The nanny agency. Families."

Families Emma had worked for. Families whose children had grown up, moved on and forgotten their nanny. Her chest tightened.

"Move back to Oregon if you don't like Washington."

She shrugged, but the last thing she felt was indifference. She'd left so many things behind over the years—foster families, schools, clients, children. She longed for a time when things would be stable. Hers. If she left…

The rocks gave way to damp sand. She glanced back. A trail of footsteps remained behind her and AJ.

Maybe a change of scenery would be good. Something different. A place to make a new start. Put down roots instead of always feeling transitory. "Did you consider moving back to Haley's Bay after you graduated college?"

"Never." The word burst from AJ's mouth. He rubbed his lips together. "But my situation's different. I felt if I returned I would constantly have to prove myself and live with my family second-guessing me all the time. They don't care what I'm able to do for them, give them. None of that matters. You saw how Risa reacted when we talked about Flynn."

Emma nodded, though Risa hadn't been the only one to react. AJ had been on the defensive, and Emma doubted he realized that. He had set opinions about his family, similar to what he said they had about him. Maybe that was how families acted toward one another after you grew up, though Libby's parents had always been warm and supportive.

"My father will be worse," AJ continued. "Flynn's a hero for leaving. I'm a jerk."

For a man who had enough money to do whatever he wanted, the bitterness seeping into AJ's tone surprised her. But ten years of ignoring issues and not talking could harden the softest of hearts. She never thought she'd feel sorry for AJ Cole, and now she did. He needed to let go, put the past behind him and move on. She hoped he could do that. For his own sake. "You're the oldest, right?"

"Yes. Flynn's third, behind Ellis. Bailey's next, followed by Declan and Camden, the twins, then Grady. He's twenty-two. The youngest."

"What's the age difference between you and Grady?"

"Ten years."

"Your mother must be a patient woman."

"She is. I'm not sure how she managed all of us, though Grandma helped. My dad's only fifty-seven, but he's patriarchal like my grandfather. Never pitched in around the house or changed a diaper. Only yard work—men's work—or tinkering with the cars. Fishing and paying the bills, too."

"That explains it."

"What?"

"The reason your father was…is…upset at you for not following in his footsteps. He, and by his example, your entire family, had expectations about what you, the oldest son, would do with your life."

"That's—" AJ rubbed the back of his neck. "Maybe."

Emma appreciated that he considered the possibility. "Younger siblings don't feel as much pressure. I've seen parents go crazy with everything from elementary school grades to recreational soccer when it comes to their first-born children."

"That makes sense, but it sucks for us oldest."

She smiled. "Depends. The oldest child in the families I've worked for are often overachievers. Intelligent. Mature for their age. Excellent qualities to possess."

"If they don't cave from the pressure."

She grinned. "Well, some have been more neurotic than their younger siblings, but not all."

"So now I'm not only eccentric and insane, but neurotic."

"You said it, not me."

He winked. "You said the first two. The third was implied."

"Implied for children under my care. I'm not your nanny."

"I don't need a nanny, but I do need a girlfriend." He laced his fingers with hers, causing her entire limb to crackle with electricity and tingle so much so she had to remember to breathe. "Time we acted like a real couple."

Every nerve ending stood at attention, buzzing like a broken electrical cable. She glanced around, searching for his motivation to do this. Water. Sand. Rocks. Birds. "No one is around."

"Exactly."

She stared at the horizon, not wanting to meet his gaze. Afraid of…she didn't know what, but AJ made her uncomfortable. His confidence, his strength, his wealth intimidated her. Two people couldn't be more different. "You're not making any sense."

Emma pulled her arm away, but he didn't let go. A rough patch of skin rubbed against one finger. A callus. Not something she would have expected on a computer geek's hands. And then she remembered. He hadn't grown up indoors sitting behind a monitor and keyboard. AJ had the hands of a laborer, a boat builder and fisherman. "Please let go. There's no reason for us to hold hands if no one else is here."

He didn't release her hand and stroked her skin with his thumb. Physical awareness shot through her, sending her pulse rate and temperature climbing. "If you can't be comfortable with me close to you, touching you, we'll never be able to pull this off with an audience."

Darn. She bit on the inside of her cheek, trying to distract herself from the good feelings his touch brought. "Okay, I see your point." Even if she didn't like it.

"So we're good?"

"For now."

She concentrated on her steps. All she needed to do to make this a stellar day was stumble and fall.

"Is this so bad?" he asked.

"No." Her hand snuggled against his larger one, their fingers laced together in a way that felt natural, not awkward. Though she'd die before admitting that. "Holding hands is part of my job description."

He raised an eyebrow.

"As a nanny," she clarified. "Though this is different from the last time I held hands with a guy."

"Should your pretend boyfriend be jealous?"

"Well, Ewan's collection of superhero action figures is to die for," she teased.

AJ's eyes widened. "Action figures? How old is Ewan?"

"Four. Cute as can be, too. Drives all the girls at preschool crazy with his big blue eyes and blond hair. He's going to be a real ladies' man once he outgrows his infatuation with men in tights, masks and capes."

"Sounds like I've got some tough competition." AJ rubbed his chin with his free hand. "But I'd wager my collection of sports cars beats his action figures."

"Depends on if you'll let me drive one or not. Ewan shares his."

"I only have the limo with me."

"Too bad." She liked his sense of humor. Talking with him like this was easy. Fun. "But you've got one thing in your favor."

He winked. "Only one, huh?"

"So far." She bit back a smile, trying to act serious, when all wanted to do was laugh. "Ewan's hands were sticky no matter how many times I asked him to wash them. Yours aren't. That's an improvement."

He swung his arm higher and hers, attached to his hand, followed along. "This is about as kidlike as I get. Unless you count liking saltwater taffy. And that does make your hands sticky if you're not careful."

"Well, if you want to know the truth, sports cars are cooler than action figures."

"I can't imagine being a nanny, or a parent for that matter. Sticky hands, fights and demands. I want results ASAP. You said it talking about my mom. Raising kids takes patience I don't possess. Even a pet who didn't do what I wanted would annoy me."

"I imagine being a CEO is like raising kids times a thousand. Fights and demands among staff. Appeasing stockholders. The constant need to innovate and be efficient. All those employees and budgets, not to mention stockholders."

He glanced off to his left. "Then we're even."

AJ must be kidding. She half laughed. "If you mean we're both human living on this planet, then yes, we're even. Other than that..."

With a tug against her hand, AJ spun Emma around like a ballroom dancer, until she stopped in front of him. He stared down at her with a mischievous gaze.

"What's going on?" she asked.

"If we're really going to sell being a couple, there's something else we need to practice…kissing."

Her heart slammed against her chest. "You want to kiss me now?"

"Practicing holding hands worked. Practicing kissing seems the next logical step."

"There's nothing logical about this." The space between them, less than a foot, buzzed with energy. A strange combination of anticipation and nervousness buzzed through her. "But a kiss would probably make your grandmother happy."

"Exactly. So you're game?"

"For one brief practice kiss, yes."

"That's all I'm asking for."

AJ leaned toward her. Emma met him halfway.

His lips touched hers. *Soft,* that was her first thought. *Warm with a hint of salt* was her second. The taste, not exactly sweet, but yummy.

Her eyelids closed.

Remember, he's not your boyfriend.

The truth was easy to forget. The kiss felt as real as the pebbles beneath her shoes, but much, *much* nicer.

AJ wrapped an arm around her, bringing her closer, bridging what little space separated them. He deepened the kiss. His lips moved over hers, sending pleasurable sensations into places she didn't know existed.

Not real. Logic tried to stop her from feeling oh, so good and desired. *It's pretend. That's the only reason he's kissing you. For practice. Like holding hands.*

But the kiss felt real. Her lips thought the kiss was real. Her body reacted as if this was for real. Too much for a practice kiss. She opened her mouth to tell him that and his tongue slipped into her mouth, taking the action as an invitation to visit, explore, taste, tease.

Oh, wow. She gripped his shirt. A good thing his arm was around her or she might sink to the sand. Her knees turned to taffy, barely supporting her. Triumph, that AJ was into kissing her for more than just practice, mixed with panic, because practice kissing a gorgeous billionaire was a bad idea for her sense of balance. Wow, the man could kiss.

His hand moved up her back, sending another wave of tingles. Her temperature spiraled, matching the desire building within. She arched to deepen the kiss. She wanted more, so much more. If the man hadn't made billions programming social media sites, he would make at least a million with his kisses.

A red light flashed in her mind. Caution, danger. This time, Emma recognized the warning, knew she needed to act.

Stop. Stop. Stop. This time logic wasn't shouting, but common sense. With her heart pounding in her ears, drowning out everything around her, telling her to keep kissing him, she knew that was exactly what she needed to do.

She dragged her mouth away from his, but her lips continued tingling and the rest of her body, as well. The confusion in AJ's eyes matched the way she felt.

"So this is why you went on a walk," a man off to her left yelled across the rocks. "Didn't want to make out at Grandma's."

Another man laughed. "Not too late to book a room at the B and B or inn."

Emma's face, no doubt flushed from kissing, burned hotter. She glanced to the side to see two good-looking, incredibly fit men walking toward her. The kind of hot guys who worked out at those industrial gyms in Portland tossing beer kegs and pushing huge tires. Both men were tall, maybe taller than AJ, and had dark hair like him though different styles. Their casual dress, athletic swagger and curious smiles directed at her and AJ spelled trouble. She remembered his warning and knew who the two must be. "Your brothers."

"Declan and Grady."

"Did you know they were here?"

"No or I wouldn't have let you stop kissing me."

Feminine pride rushed through her. AJ had taken the practice kiss further not for show but because he enjoyed kissing her.

"We may need to practice some more," he said.

For a practice kiss, her reactions hadn't been faked. His kiss had sent her pulse sprinting toward the finish line, her temperature into a feverish zone and her heart rate into ninety-minute Zumba intensity level. Emma needed to dive into the bay to unmuddle her mudkiss-confused head and body. "I think we're good."

One sexy brother with a scruff of whiskers, hair tied back and clear hazel eyes hooked his thumb through a belt loop. "You not only come home for the first time in ten years, but bring a pretty woman. Trying to show us up again, bro?"

Emma liked having a hot guy compliment her, but she remembered AJ's warning about his brother. This one must be a natural-born maneuverer like AJ. She would have to be careful around all the Cole men.

AJ pulled her against him, close enough to hear the sounds of his breathing, uneven like hers. The kiss or nerves? She wouldn't expect him to be worried, but then again with her as his so-called girlfriend, he might be concerned how she would act in front of his brothers. The least she could do was try. She hadn't at lunch. Not really.

Emma placed her hand on his chest, staring at her fingers to keep her gaze from straying to his lips. His heart beat rapidly beneath her palm. She looked up.

AJ's surprised gaze met hers.

She forced a smile. "Aren't you going to introduce me, sweetie?"

The word sounded strange coming from her lips given she wasn't talking about someone under the age of ten, but she didn't allow her smile to falter or her hand to move or her feet to take ten steps back. Because she wanted to do all three. She wanted to run far, far away from Haley's Bay and pretend she'd never heard of the place, because if she didn't run she would want to kiss her pretend boyfriend on the lips again.

"These are two of my brothers, Declan and Grady. This is my girlfriend, Emma." AJ held her possessively, his hand on her waist, making her feel as though she not only was dating him, but also belonged. She liked the unfamiliar feeling very much. "Thought she should meet the family in case it's another ten years until we come back."

Both men's eyes widened. They must have picked up on his use of the word *we,* too. She had to give AJ credit. The man knew what to say to get his point across.

Grady, wearing a navy T-shirt with the words Port of Haley's Bay printed across his chest, stood next to them and touched AJ's shoulder. His eyes were the same green as AJ's, but he had his mother's smile. "Happy you're home. I'd hug you, but you've got your arms full. Not that I blame you. I'd rather hold her than hug me, too."

The men's gazes raked over Emma, making her feel like a fish hanging from the end of a pole with a hook through her cheek. Was she good enough to keep or should they toss her back into the water?

Not that she cared, not much. Being on display wasn't the most comfortable feeling, but more was going on than just her being introduced as their brother's girl. She loosened her hand from AJ's, then slipped her arm around his back. He tensed for a nanosecond before relaxing and pulling her even closer.

"Hello." She worked hard to keep her smile in place. "I'm Emma Markwell."

Declan's scruffy grin widened. "I'm Declan. It's so nice to meet you, Emma."

The charm in his voice matched the curiosity in his gaze. Confidence must be a family trait. Declan oozed self-assurance and sex appeal.

"You're one of the twins," she said.

"That's right," Declan said. "My sister Camden is four minutes and twenty-eight seconds older. You'd think it was forty years. But I can do more pull-ups than her. We're about even with push-ups."

The affection for his twin sister loosened Emma's bunched shoulder muscles. She would never remember all these people. Not without seeing them and putting faces with names. "I'm sure you could do more pull-ups and push-ups than me using only one hand."

Declan sidled up to her, his salt-of-the-earth scent appealing at a gut level. These Cole brothers must drive the women of Haley's Bay crazy. "I'd be happy to help you with your technique. A few lessons and you'd be good to go."

"Back off." AJ's firm voice reminded her of his conference call on the jet. "I warned Emma that you bozos hit on any woman new to Haley's Bay. Remember she's taken."

AJ's jealousy surprised and intrigued her. He had the

boyfriend acting down. Her turn to get in on the action. Emma ran her fingertip along his jawline. "Guess I should have let you put that ring on my finger after all."

He brushed his lips across hers, long enough to make her want more. "Damn straight, but you will."

An image of an engagement ring flashed in her mind. A thrill trembled through her even though she knew AJ wasn't serious.

"Ring, huh?" Declan asked. "Mom mentioned you two might be moving in together, but this takes things to another level."

"And leaves Madison for us." Grady stepped forward. His bright smile and straight white teeth belonged in a toothpaste ad. "So glad you're here, Emma. It's great to see my big brother settling down with a real woman, not some lollipop head with extensive plastic surgery. No offense, bro."

"None taken," AJ said. "Emma is as real as they come."

She wasn't sure what to say. "Thank you, I think."

"It's a compliment," AJ assured her. "And one of the reasons I brought you home. To show them that what they see on tabloids and read on the internet isn't always the truth."

Except in AJ's case, Emma knew he dated actresses, models and socialites. Never for long, much to his dates' chagrin. That was why so many spilled their billionaire dating woes to the media, at least according to Libby. Why have a pity party for one when you could invite everyone in line at the grocery store to join in for a few minutes?

"Mom and Grandma are surprised," Grady said.

"Us, too," Declan admitted. "But in a good way. Dad's reaction will be interesting. Not because of you, Emma, but our father has some preconceived notions about AJ and his life."

"What my brother's trying to say is don't let my father's negativity bother you." AJ's defensive tone returned.

"Dad's…" Declan shook his head. "Who knows how he'll act. Ten years is a long time."

"It'll be fine," Grady said. "Dad's mellowed."

Declan shot his younger brother a sideward glance.

"A little," Grady added.

Tension emanated from AJ. She gave him a half hug. That was what a supportive girlfriend would do. At least she hoped so. "I look forward to meeting him and the entire family."

"The feeling's mutual." A dimple appeared on Grady's left cheek. The guy really was cute. Young, but she wondered if this was how AJ looked when he was in his early twenties. "We never thought AJ would settle down again."

Again? Interesting. Libby had never mentioned a woman from AJ's past, but Emma reminded herself his personal life was none of her business. "Your brother is an amazing man. He goes after what he wants."

"I do, and I have what I want." AJ brushed his lips across her neck, sending tingles zipping through her. The guy seemed to enjoy playing the boyfriend role and taking advantage of their deal in front of his brothers.

"Thank you." She might be a nanny from Portland, Oregon, but his words made Emma feel like the most desirable supermodel in the world. But she resented having him be the one to make her feel that way. If she'd wanted to play house, she could have done that for real with Trey, getting an instant family in the process, but she didn't want to be a fill-in wife for a widower who was lonely and desperate to find a mother for his girls. Not after years spent in the foster system with so many different families.

Someday, Emma would find what she was looking for—a man who loved her unconditionally. She would finally have her own family. Until then she'd bide her time. And as long as she was in Haley's Bay, she'd pretend to be head over heels in love with AJ Cole. But right now she needed a break from the charade. She had a feeling tonight would be harder than lunch and this. "I should check on Blossom."

"I'll go with you," AJ said.

She ran her hand along his arm. "Thanks, but stay here and catch up with your brothers for a few minutes. We'll have plenty of time together."

She didn't wait for an answer, but walked in the opposite direction back toward the Victorian.

"Not your usual type." Declan's voice carried.

Emma slowed her steps to hear AJ's reply, then changed her mind, accelerating as if she were at the start of a 5K race. Whatever AJ said to his brothers didn't matter. His words would be a lie, no more real than their kiss a few minutes ago.

And that bothered her. When he asked what she wanted for herself, she should have said money. The cost of therapy when she returned to Portland or enrollment in a diet center after she overdid the sweets was going to be expensive. But she hadn't. She would have to rely on her nanny skills to keep her wits about her and survive the next five days with AJ Cole.

Chapter Six

"Not your usual type."

Declan's words hung in the air, punctuated by the cry of a seabird overhead. Tension thickened. AJ didn't mind if his taste in women was the issue, but he didn't like the way his brother insinuated something was wrong with Emma. Emma, whose spicy kisses surprised the hell out of AJ and made him want another taste of her. His hands balled. "You haven't seen me in ten years and that's all you have to say?"

"Thought talking about your girlfriend would be better than asking you to buy me a new truck or a house." Declan lifted one shoulder in a casual gesture. "But what the hell do I know? It's not like you haven't been generous with mysterious items showing up in the driveway or unexpected deposits in our bank accounts, but if you're making a list: black, king cab, 4x4, and a three-bedroom, two baths with an ocean view will do. Fenced yard would be good. Someone to scoop up my dog's crap would be nice, too. That gets old."

Declan's humor and wry grin evaporated the tension. AJ would like to do more for his family and had, until a cease and desist letter arrived from the only legal counsel in Haley's Bay, his cousin Tyler, telling AJ his gifts to family members were no longer necessary or welcome. He flexed his fingers. "You're wasting your charm and talents earning a living on the water. You'd be a natural in sales."

"Like I said, what do I know?"

"I'll take a truck and a house, too, if you're playing Santa in August," Grady piped up, the same way he used to do when he was little and trying to be heard.

And like then, AJ ignored the youngest one. Grady would get his turn soon enough. "Good to see you again, Dec."

Declan embraced him, the familiar scent of sweat, salt and fish bringing back a rush of memories. "Been way too long, bro."

A lump lodged in AJ throat, burned like a hot coal. His brother's embrace and warmth were welcome but hurt in a way AJ hadn't expected. Declan was seven years younger, more a shadow and pest than a buddy growing up. Now he was a man. AJ had missed a lot during his exodus. He stepped back, took a hard look at his brother. "You're no longer a scrawny kid."

Declan rocked back on his heels, raised his chin. "Taller than you."

"You are." AJ tried not to feel weird about that. He'd always been the oldest, the smartest, the tallest.

"I'm taller than both of you. And stronger." Grady's chest puffed. His biceps showed beneath the sleeves of his T-shirt. "I can finally kick all of your butts after years of being called the baby. Except Camden's since Dad would kill me if I ever fought a girl."

"Woman," AJ and Declan said at the same time.

"Jinx, you owe me a Coke," Declan teased the way they had when they were kids.

Joking around with his brothers was something AJ missed. Nowadays he was never sure if people were laughing at his jokes because they were funny or because they wanted something from him.

"Being taller and working out can't change your birth order," Declan continued. "You'll always be the baby, even now that Mom and Dad have grandkids."

Grady frowned. "That sucks."

"Live with it," Declan joked. "Though you might earn a little respect now that you're wearing a badge."

"Badge?" AJ asked.

Grady's green eyes twinkled. "Surprise! I told you I had news."

"Not exactly," AJ corrected. "You texted about applying for a new job, but nothing more."

"It's true." Pride filled Declan's voice. "Our baby brother is Haley's Bay's newest police officer."

"One day I'm going to be chief," Grady said with the same enthusiasm he showed on Christmas morning about his gifts from Santa. "Just watch and see."

"When did this happen?" AJ asked.

"Just finished the academy. My degree in criminology helped. Thanks for covering the tuition."

"My part was easy. Congrats." Shaking Grady's hand, AJ wondered what their father thought of this, but didn't want to ruin the moment by bringing up their dad. "Things have changed around here."

"Some things," Declan agreed. "Not others."

AJ wondered which group his father would belong in, most likely the latter. "Well done, Grady."

"Thanks," he said. "So far it's been great. Ladies love

a man in uniform. Especially the tourists. My cell phone contact list is going to be full of pretty women."

"Remember what I told you." Declan motioned to AJ. "Don't settle down with just one. Loose and carefree is the only way to be until you're over thirty and old like AJ."

"Gee, thanks," AJ said.

"Anytime, bro." Declan slapped his arm. "So how long has Emma had you whipped?"

AJ gritted his teeth. That was the last thing he'd been since Natalie broke off their engagement when he was at college and married his friend Craig.

"From the moment we met." Not a lie, because the day they met was the day they started "dating." No one needed to know that was today. "Speaking of Emma, I should get back to the house and see how she's doing."

Maybe AJ could get her to practice another kiss or stage a kiss in front of his family. He still couldn't believe the way she'd kissed him back. He wondered what else he would discover about the nanny.

AJ turned and walked toward the house. His brothers fell in step on either side of him.

"Emma seems nice." Grady scooped up a rock and tossed it into the water. "A little young."

"She's older than you," AJ said. "Twenty-six."

"Still robbing the cradle," Grady teased.

AJ didn't respond.

"Emma's too short to be a model so she must be an actress," Declan said.

"She's a nanny."

Declan made a face. "I thought you only dated actresses and supermodels. That's who you're always pictured with online."

Interesting. His brother had kept up with AJ's private life. He hadn't expected that. Nor thought about doing the same thing in return. "The paparazzi catch me with those dates, but I go out with all kinds of women."

Declan eyed him warily. "You and Emma aren't exclusive, but are talking moving in together?"

"And rings," Grady added. "Sounds weird if you ask me."

Damn. AJ's neck tightened. He needed to be more careful and think like a boyfriend. But he hadn't seriously dated a woman in a very long time.

"We're exclusive. I was talking before I met Emma." Which had only been a few hours ago. Comical almost. Another slipup wouldn't be so funny. "She might not be famous, but she's exactly what I need."

Another woman might use this situation to her advantage, but something about Emma, something that had nothing to do with her friendship with Libby, told AJ he could trust the nanny, even though he trusted few people. He kicked a rock with the toe of his leather shoe.

Emma's willingness to go along with being his girlfriend even though she had doubts showed him she thought of others before herself. A woman who would sell this story to a tabloid would not care about her friend's work schedule or an animal rescue group or a foster cat.

He stopped on the opposite side of the road from their grandmother's house. Cars he didn't recognize were parked in front of the limousine. Noise came from inside the house. He hoped Emma was okay. "Full house."

"Mom was on the phone inviting others when we headed out to find you. I'm not sure she believed you'd really show up." Declan's voice held a bitter edge.

"Don't blame me." Nothing had been worth defying the old man until now. AJ would do anything for his grandmother. "You heard what Dad said about my not coming back unless I planned to take over the business."

"Right," Declan said. "Like you were always so awesome listening to Dad."

"I sure wouldn't have ignored my brother for ten years just because Dad said to."

"Not fair."

"The girls and Grady remained neutral. You could have, too." Losing his oldest brothers had been hard on AJ. "Seattle isn't that far away."

"You can't change the past. Clean slate starting now." Grady stepped off the curb, his cop mediation skills already in use. "Come on. Grandma's probably put out appetizers. I could go for a stuffed mushroom. I'm starving."

He jogged across the street with a bounce to his step.

AJ stepped onto the road. He remembered how his little brother loved to play cops and robbers when he was younger, except Grady wanted to be the bad guy. "He's really a police officer?"

"Hard to believe, I know." Declan shook his head. "Grady always got into so much trouble I figured he'd end up behind bars, but as soon as he showed interest in police work Dad told him to go for it."

AJ's jaw dropped. "That's…"

"Shocked the hell out of me, too. But Dad said fishing isn't for everyone. Especially when Grady would rather be in the water than on a boat."

"Are you talking about our father or some alien being who took over his body?"

"Dad's a tad bit more open-minded these days. You'll see."

AJ wasn't sure he would. Nothing he did had ever been good enough for their father. High grades and test scores hadn't been important. Winning a prestigious science competition had earned him a snicker, not praise. Getting seasick during rough waters brought nothing but scorn.

"I will warn you, though," Declan continued. "Dad still thinks you made a mistake leaving and should return to Haley's Bay."

"Thought he would."

"He can be hardheaded."

"Doesn't matter if his head's made of concrete. My business, my life, is in Seattle."

"Your family is here. I'm not buying it. You could move your business to Bora Bora if you liked. But then again I don't really know you anymore."

Which is why AJ had never been back until now. No one in his family understood who he was or respected his work. Moving a multibillion-dollar corporation was not as easy as buying a nice piece of property on the bluff.

He knew returning was a mistake. The question was how big a mistake would coming back to Haley's Bay for his grandmother turn out to be.

At the house, Emma checked on Blossom, still under the bed, kicked off her shoes and called the two party vendors to set up appointments for tomorrow. She sat on the edge of the bed, grateful for a moment alone.

"Emma, we need your help."

She recognized Lilah's voice, slipped on her shoes and made her way to the kitchen. "What do you need?"

"Be a dear and slice the garlic bread, please," Lilah said. "There are eight loaves."

With a cutting board underneath the first loaf and a serrated knife in hand, Emma stood at the counter and set to work. Music played from the living room. People came in and out of the kitchen, introducing themselves in a flurry of words and busyness.

Two loaves later, a satisfied feeling settled in the center of Emma's chest. She'd never been part of a large family. Both her parents were only children. Libby was an only child until Emma moved in during high school. She'd never cared for more than three children at a time, unless at a party.

She'd wondered what being part of a large family would be like. Today, she was getting a glimpse and loved what she saw.

"Cut a few slices in half for the kids." Marianne, AJ's mother, stirred a huge pot of marinara sauce simmering on the stove. Her brown shoulder-length bob hairstyle suited her casual floral print shirt, jean skirt and sandals. Her arms constantly moved, if not stirring then accentuating her words with her hands or hugging a child who popped into the kitchen. She exuded warmth and friendliness. "They never eat a whole piece. And with all these extra people who showed up we might not have enough."

Lilah tossed a gigantic bowl of fresh baby greens with her homemade poppy-seed dressing. She waved off her daughter-in-law's concern with the tongs. "I've been doing these big dinners for decades. We'll have plenty of food."

"Everything smells delicious." Emma sliced the third loaf, still warm from the oven. AJ's sisters, Bailey and Camden, were in the dining room where dinner would be served buffet-style, the only way to feed a crowd, according to Lilah. Risa and Madison were off having pedicures, but Risa's kids were running around somewhere. Her husband, Ellis, too. "It's nice of you to throw this welcome-home party so people can see AJ."

"Easier to have people over once then having them come each night. Haley's Bay is a wonderful place to live, but like all small towns, people are curious, especially when anything changes."

"AJ's been away a long time."

"True, but they also want to meet you."

The knife slipped and crashed against the cutting board. Emma picked it up, reminding herself to be more careful. "Why me?"

"To see if you're anything like Natalie, his ex-fiancée." Lilah spoke as if she were talking about some girl he'd taken to a homecoming dance, not wanted to marry. "You're not. She was…"

"Mom," Marianne said, her voice rising at the end of what suddenly became a two-syllable word.

"I was just going to say Natalie was impatient, wanting to get married so badly she broke up with AJ to marry Craig Steele. But her loss is your gain."

Emma continued slicing the bread, unsure what to say. She was trying to digest that AJ had been dumped by his fiancée for another man, and also that he'd been engaged. Maybe he wasn't quite the player she thought if he'd been serious enough about a woman to propose. She'd never been close to that herself. Truth was, she rarely dated these days, a combination of her job and wanting quiet time when she wasn't working. The Cole family had a totally false impression of her, thanks to AJ, and the less she said the better.

But she enjoyed being here, surrounded by these loud, happy people. Strangers, yes, but the love they showed each other warmed her heart and reaffirmed what she wanted most of all—a family.

Kids darted in and out, grabbing handfuls of chips from a basket and cans of soda from the refrigerator, laughter bubbling from their lips. Crumbs fell to the floor but no one seemed to mind.

"Don't run with food in your mouth," Marianne shouted after three young boys bolting from the kitchen. She stared lovingly after them, then stirred the sauce with a wooden spoon. "I remember when they couldn't crawl and now they won't sit still. The family keeps getting bigger and older."

"Older and better." Lilah wiped her hands on the front of her Kiss the Chef apron. "Do you have a big family, Emma?"

Her throat tightened with a familiar sense of loss and regret, but her emotions remained under control and no tears stung her eyes. She might not have a family to call her own, but she could live vicariously, even if she didn't belong here. "No, but it's fun to see yours."

Family, as defined by the Coles, included cousins twice removed, neighbors who moved away three years ago and the butcher who provided the Italian sausage for tonight's pasta dinner. A crazy, loud bunch, coming and going like the kids. Emma had no idea where everyone would sit, but Lilah said she had a plan.

The woman might be going on eighty, though she was as sharp and mobile as someone twenty years younger. The contented smile on her lined face spoke of family and love. "I am blessed and very happy you and AJ are here."

A warm and fuzzy sensation cascaded to Emma's toenails. "Me, too."

She meant that, even if she did feel odd misleading them about her relationship with AJ. However she'd gotten here, she was grateful and enjoying herself tonight. "Thank you."

"Yes, thanks, Grandma." The rich sound of AJ's voice sent Emma's pulse skittering. "It's great Emma's getting a chance to meet everyone right away."

Before she could respond, strong arms wrapped around Emma's waist and pulled her against him. She went willingly, reminding herself this display was strictly for show.

The scent of him surrounded her. He smelled so good, better than the chocolate cupcakes Bailey had baked for dessert. Emma forced herself not to take another sniff, even though she wanted one. Going around smelling her boss would not be a smart move, or professional.

His warm breath tickled her neck. Tingles shot down her spine. Real ones like she'd felt when he kissed her. Lips brushed the right side of her cheek. She used every bit of strength not to turn her head so he'd kiss her on the lips.

PDA wasn't her thing, but what was going on had nothing to do with a public display of affection and everything to do with convincing his family she and AJ were seriously dating.

Lilah beamed at her eldest grandson. "Emma's been a big help. Knows her way around a kitchen."

"That's part of her job," AJ said.

The lines around his grandmother's mouth deepened, matching the concern in her eyes. "Cooking for the man you love is a pleasure. You make Emma sound like one of your employees."

AJ's startled gaze flew to Emma's. He opened his mouth to speak, but she cut him off. "One of my responsibilities as a nanny is to cook for the children I care for. That's what AJ meant."

Lilah returned to the salad, seemingly satisfied with Emma's explanation.

Crisis averted, for now.

The Coles were trying to figure out what was going on with her and AJ's relationship. That much was clear. She didn't want his family asking too many questions—ones they couldn't easily answer. That would cause friction and might tip off the charade.

AJ cuddled closer to her. Gratitude or show or a combination of both? Emma didn't want to know, because having him so close felt wonderful. Sensation danced across her skin. She raised the bread knife. "Be careful pulling me too close, I'm armed and dangerous."

"That's true whether you have a weapon in hand or not." AJ nuzzled against her neck, making her inhale sharply. He was one to talk. If she'd been in the process of slicing garlic bread, she would have lost a fingertip. She set the knife on the cutting board.

"I'll take my chances," he added, then kissed her neck again.

Tingles erupted. Heat pulsed through her veins.

Not real. Not real. Not real. Maybe if she kept telling herself the kisses didn't mean anything she could ignore the ways her body reacted to him.

"You really came back." The deep male voice sounded surprised and his words edged with something else, something unwelcoming. "Didn't think you would."

AJ's body tensed, his fingers tightening around her. "I'm throwing Grandma a birthday party, Dad. Couldn't do that from Seattle."

AJ's voice sounded strong, but the underlying hurt was unmistakable. Emma wanted to hold him tight and kiss away his pain. She covered AJ's hands with hers, a sign of her support and solidarity.

A man with tanned, weathered skin and salt-and-pepper hair stood in the kitchen doorway. He was tall like AJ, mid-fifties, and the resemblance between father and son was strong. The man's eyes narrowed, zeroing in on her and AJ's locked hands. "I see you brought company."

"Not company," Lilah said. "His girlfriend."

"Emma, this is Jack Cole, AJ's dad." Marianne's smile no longer seemed natural. "Jack, this is Emma Markwell. She's from Portland."

"I thought AJ lived in Seattle."

"I do," he said. "Emma lives in Portland."

"That makes no sense." The man's expression cast a dark shadow on the playful party atmosphere. "How can you be serious with someone who lives in a different state? Didn't you learn your lesson with Natalie about long-distance relationships?"

AJ inhaled sharply. Emma wanted to shake Mr. Cole for acting the way he was and AJ for letting the rift remain strong after ten years. The two men had no idea how lucky they were to still be able to say hi, whether either wanted to say another word or not. She would give anything for five more minutes with her parents and brother. Words wouldn't be necessary. A hug would mean everything.

"Hello, Mr. Cole." Emma used her cheery voice. The one that worked magic when kids weren't feeling well or parents were stressed. AJ's father had the same intense stare as his son, but Emma couldn't allow herself to be intimidated. She needed to be strong for AJ, as his assistant and his girlfriend. "It's nice to meet you. Did you have a good day out in the water? That's what my mom always said to my dad after a day of fly-fishing in the Metolius River."

"A very good day." He studied her the way his sons had out by the bay. "Do you fish?"

"Not in a very long time." Fishing was something her dad loved to do. The family tagged along. She hadn't gone after his death. "But I enjoy eating fish."

"That keeps us in business." Mr. Cole grinned, the smile transforming his rugged face into a handsome one, much like AJ's. "When I heard AJ brought home a woman, I figured she'd hate fish or be a vegan."

"Not a vegan. I love cheese and burgers. Not to mention whipped cream and milk shakes."

"Then you're staying at the right place. My mother loves

to cook with butter. Warn your arteries. Comfort food is her specialty."

"It is." Lilah shooed her hands at her son. "Now get out of here so we can finish getting dinner on the table."

"I need something first. "Mr. Cole snagged a kiss from Marianne. "Now I can leave you ladies alone."

His wife swatted his bottom. "Have the kids wash their hands."

With a nod, Mr. Cole exited the kitchen.

AJ exhaled. "I suppose not making sense is a step up from being a complete moron."

"Give your dad a chance," Marianne said. "He's trying."

AJ's chin jutted forward. "I'm here, aren't I?"

"Yes, and you should be with your father and brothers, catching up with them." Lilah motioned to the doorway. "Get out there."

"But Emma—"

"I have garlic bread to slice," she said. "Go visit with your family."

AJ didn't move, but kept hold on her. "I want to visit with you."

The man was used to getting what he wanted. Not this time. "We'll see each other during dinner."

Lilah gave him a nudge. "You heard your woman, go. We won't spill any family secrets that will scare her away."

"But those are the ones I want to hear," Emma teased.

AJ made a face. "Grandma..."

"Out." Lilah gave him a shove. "Before I decide I want a *My Little Pony*–themed birthday party."

He gave Emma a don't-make-me-go look. Too bad if he wanted to stay in the kitchen; this was for his own good.

"I'll be fine." She leaned closer as if to nibble on his earlobe. Emma had solved many problems on the playground. The situation between Jack and AJ Cole was more complicated than children not wanting to share the swings or take turns on the slide, but she wouldn't give up without at least trying to help father and son talk, if not reconcile.

"And so will you," she whispered.

Chapter Seven

Four hours later, AJ disentangled himself from Madison in the sunroom, leaving her in the capable hands of Declan and Grady. AJ didn't care which one she ended up with as long as she left *him* alone. What part of his having a serious girlfriend didn't she understand?

He had to admit he'd rather spend time with Madison than his dad. AJ had been upset at Emma for making him leave the kitchen, but his father hadn't said another word to him all evening. At this rate, AJ would survive his time in Haley's Bay without too many battle scars.

He wanted to find Emma, to thank her for making him see that his dad wasn't so scary after all these years. AJ should have known that, but her push had been good for him. He checked the kitchen, living room, backyard and front porch. No sign of her. He pulled out his cell phone and called the number Libby had programmed into his contact list before he left New York. No answer.

The last time he'd seen Emma had been two hours ago. She'd been helping his sisters with the dishes. She could be back in Portland by now. His heart tripped. No, she wouldn't have left, would she? His pulse rate accelerating with his steps, AJ made a beeline for the stairs.

On the second floor, the door to the guest room was ajar. AJ stepped inside. "Emma?"

Something banged near the bed. "Ouch. I'm here."

Relief was palpable, except he didn't see her. Though he noticed a smoke detector sitting on the dresser that hadn't been there before. Guess the nanny brought her own. "Where?"

"Under the bed."

He'd been joking about her joining Blossom. "What are you doing under there?"

"Blossom won't eat."

Dedicated didn't begin to describe Emma. AJ walked into the room. Two panty-hose-clad legs and feet stuck out from underneath the bed. Nice legs. "The cat might not be hungry."

"Cats need to eat regularly. If they go too long without food they can develop fatty liver syndrome." Emma groaned, then scooted farther under the bed. "Come on, Blossom. Stop being a diva kitty and eat."

"Blossom will eat when she's ready."

"I'd feel better if she ate now."

Emma wiggled farther under the bed, sending her skirt up another two inches. He tugged on his now too-tight shirt collar. He was going to have to open a window to cool down the room. "Want help?"

"I don't think you'd fit."

"Probably not." But based on kissing her and holding her, they might fit nicely together. He shook the appealing thought from his head. "I can move the bed."

"Why didn't I think of that?" She scooted backward, the hem of her skirt riding even higher.

Look away. Now.

He moved to the foot of the bed where he didn't have a view that would embarrass Emma. He wished he could blame his leering on one beer too many, but he'd drunk only two and didn't feel the slightest bit buzzed.

Emma stood. She smoothed her skirt back in place, straightened her sweater and adjusted her glasses. "Sounds like the party's still going strong. Why are you up here?"

"I couldn't find you. I called your cell phone, but no answer."

"Sorry. I turned off the ringer before I boarded your jet and forgot to turn it back on after we arrived."

"I need to be able to get in touch with you at all times."

"I'm here now." She grabbed a pad of paper off the nightstand. "What do you need?"

"Excuse me?"

"You called me." She readied her pencil. "You must have wanted something."

You. But he couldn't say that. Nor could he tell her that of all the people in the house, many related to him by blood, she was the only one helping him adjust to being home. Libby and he knew each other better but could never pull this fake dating off. They'd talk work and sync schedules and kissing her would be far too uncomfortable. She would never give him advice because that wasn't her job. Emma didn't know him, but kissing her was a pleasure, her advice was sound.

AJ searched his brain for a task that would make sense. "On the flight you mentioned phone calls that needed to be made."

"Done. When I returned to the house from our walk." She tapped her pencil against the edge of the pad. "I spoke with your CPA about the donation to the shelter, and I've scheduled two meetings for tomorrow. Anything else?"

She was efficient. "No."

"Then let's get Blossom out from under the bed."

Damn. He'd forgotten about the cat. But the dark circles under Emma's eyes told him she needed to sleep, not waste more time cajoling a cat. "Where's the food?"

She pointed to a small stainless steel bowl on the floor. "I took that under the bed with me, but Blossom wasn't interested. She skipped lunch, too. I decided to try dry food instead of canned this time."

"Sounds like the cat is figuring if she holds out she might get something more palatable." He picked up the bowl and shook it once. "Dinner."

"I've tried shaking, calling, sticking the food under the bed. Blossom wouldn't budge."

AJ wasn't about to kowtow to a cat. "Give her a chance."

Less than a minute later, the cat's nose poked out from under the bed skirt. Whiskers twitched.

"I don't believe it," Emma said.

He waved the food in front of the cat's nose, then placed the bowl three feet away to draw out the cat. Time to eat."

Blossom's head appeared. Her wide green-eyed gaze bounced from him to Emma, then back to him. The cat cautiously made her way from under the bed, step by careful step, her eyes never straying from the bowl. She sniffed the contents, then ate.

Emma's mouth formed a perfect *O.* If someone other than the cat had been around, he would have stolen another kiss.

"I've been trying for over an hour to get her to eat," Emma said. "You waltz in here, shake the bowl and call her. Now she's chowing down. I don't get it."

"Why should Blossom eat when she can get your attention and make you crawl under the bed to keep her company?"

"I'm an idiot, and you're a cat whisperer."

"You're compassionate," he countered. "I know nothing about cats, but I know behavior. I have a couple coders who are divas. Brilliant programmers, but that kind of personality needs firm handling. The same as Blossom."

The cat glanced up at hearing her name, then returned to her dinner, as if she hadn't eaten in days. Given her weight and appearance, he knew she was well fed.

"You're welcome to manage Blossom anytime you'd like." Emma touched the top of her head. That must have been what banged against the box spring. "She's got me wrapped around her paw."

He should be so lucky. "Let's hope she doesn't abuse the privilege. Head hurting?"

"It's just a little bump."

"You hit hard. Show me where."

Emma stared up at him, above the rim of her glasses. "You don't have to manage me. I'm as far from a diva as you can get."

"True." Genuineness was part of her appeal, another reason this dating game must be difficult for her. AJ had to bluff through business deals all the time. She was clearly a rookie at deception and that, above all, made him comfortable. "From what I've seen, you're a model team player. A hard worker who pitches in where needed with no concern about herself. Now show me the bump."

"Yes, Coach." She pointed to a spot on the top of her head. "Right here."

He gently touched the spot.

She winced.

AJ pulled his hand away. "Sorry."

"It's okay. Just a little tender."

He brought his hand back, more carefully this time. Her hair, still pulled back in a braid, was soft against his fingertips. "A slight goose egg."

"Told you I'll be fine."

"Ice—"

"Would have your grandmother in here fussing over me."

That wouldn't be so bad. An audience would give them a reason to act like a couple, something they hadn't done much of tonight since they'd been apart. "If it were me or the cat or one of the kids who were running around, you'd be the one fussing."

She shrugged, but the sheepish look on her face told AJ he was correct. The long day seemed to be weighing on Emma. She deserved a little TLC. "Change into your pajamas and I'll get the ice."

"I'll be fine."

"Yes, but ice will help the swelling. You'll feel better." He brushed a strand of hair that had fallen out of her braid off her face. His hand lingered on her soft hair. "Let someone take care of you for once."

"It's not necessary."

"Many things aren't necessary, but we still do them out of respect or desire."

"Or duty." Her face flushed a dark pink. So sweet.

"I've never been great with that one." He was operating off the first two options. If he didn't move away from her now, he would kiss her. He'd promised her they wouldn't touch without an audience. Practicing by the water had been pushing the rules. He couldn't keep that up without being disrespectful. But his feet remained glued to the rug, his gaze locked on hers. Was that longing he glimpsed in her eyes?

Something bumped against his leg. Once, twice. He

looked at the floor. Blossom was squeezing between their feet.

"Still hungry, kitty?" Emma stepped back, breaking the connection between them, and kneeled. The cat nuzzled against her hand. Purred. "She's so content. I've never seen her act like this."

The cat rubbed against his legs, leaving orange fur on his pant leg. He hoped Haley's Bay had a competent dry cleaner, otherwise Charlie would be driving to Long Beach or across the Columbia to Astoria. "She's happy to be in a home. That's all."

AJ should be happy the cat kept him from kissing Emma, but he wasn't. Not really. *That* was a problem. Keeping a firm grip on his libido had always been essential for keeping himself—and his company—out of trouble. "I'll be right back with the ice."

Emma scrubbed her face, flossed, brushed her teeth, put on moisturizer, unbraided her hair and changed into a pair of sleep shorts and a camisole in less than seven minutes. Not quite a record, but she wanted to be under the covers before AJ returned.

She stared at the queen-size bed, knowing she'd have to share it soon. "I can do this."

Blossom jumped onto the bed, circled around a pillow then lay on her back, exposing her tummy for belly rubs. Emma obliged. "Make yourself comfy, why don't you? I hope it's that easy for me."

The cat meowed.

"You like AJ so much you sleep with him."

"I'm not sleeping with the cat."

Emma jumped. Her hand covered her chest. "Don't be all ninja around me."

He closed the door behind him. "I didn't realize I was stealthy."

"My heart's pounding."

"Other women have experienced the same phenomenon around me. My ninja skills had nothing to do with their reaction."

The man was too charming for her own good. Rules and boundaries were in order. "Please knock or announce your presence the next time."

"Will a 'Honey, I'm home' work?"

Having fun and playing around would be easy to do, but self-preservation told her no. "An 'I'm back. Are you decent?' will suffice."

His gaze raked over her, a slow appraisal that sent heat rushing through her veins. "If I was your boyfriend, I'd say you're much better than decent."

"But you're not."

"Right. So I'll just do what you ask next time."

"Thanks." And she'd dream he was her boyfriend.

Something sparked in the air. Emma felt exposed. She crossed her arms over her chest, wishing she'd packed flannel pajamas even though it was summer. Staying in the same room was not going to work. Not at all. Sleep would be impossible with AJ Cole lying beside her. "I—"

"I brought the ice." He held up a Baggie full of ice wrapped in a dish towel, but his intentions didn't look friendly. They looked lethal.

"Well done." Her voice cracked. She tried to remember the last time she felt this way about a man. Umm…never? Forget her aching head. She needed the ice to cool down.

A knock sounded. "How is Emma's head?"

Oh, no. Lilah. Emma's muscles tightened.

"Just a minute," AJ yelled.

That would work for about thirty seconds. "What do we do?" she whispered.

He kicked off his shoes and pointed to the bed.

This was one way to get her into bed without her putting up a fight or a wall of pillows. She hopped under the covers, settling next to Blossom.

AJ followed so he was on his side, facing Emma with Blossom on the pillow to his left. He held the ice pack against Emma's head then twirled a strand of hair with his free hand. "Come in, Grandma."

The door opened. Lilah stood with a glass of water and a container of painkillers. "I thought Emma might need more than ice."

"Thanks," AJ said.

Lilah moved closer to the bed. "How are you, dear?"

"Feeling silly that I hit my head."

"It happens." Lilah's gaze traveled from the messed-up bed coverings to AJ's shoes lying haphazardly on the floor. "I hope my grandson is taking care of you."

"He's making a big fuss out of a little bump."

"Let him fuss. Shows how smitten he is."

Emma liked the word *smitten.* Too bad it didn't have anything to do with AJ's motivations in caring for her. "He spoils me."

"I see that," Lilah said.

"You deserve to be spoiled." AJ kissed her quickly, a brush of his lips across hers. "Taking care of Emma is my favorite job."

Her gaze met his. Time seemed to stop for a moment.

"Where's Emma?" Grady entered the room, a beer in one hand and a cupcake in the other. "I had first aid training at the academy."

Marianne followed. She held up a white bottle of pills.

"I have ibuprofen. Do you think we should call Doc Hunter?"

Lilah clapped her hands together. "Oh, yes, let's call him. He makes house calls. He's also single, in his early thirties. Maybe Bailey or Camden will want to date and marry him."

Grady groaned. He ate the rest of the cupcake and set his beer on the nightstand. "You need to let people find their own dates and spouses, Grandma."

"Some need a little push," Lilah said. "That's all I'm doing. A shove here or a nudge there."

"No doctors needed." Grady stood over Emma. "I've got this under control."

AJ sighed. "You hurt her, I hurt you. Got it?"

Grady nodded, but seemed confused. "Pupils are equal. Do you feel nauseous or weak?"

Emma did, but the feelings had nothing to do with her head. She wasn't used to being the center of attention, but that was nothing compared to having AJ so close. The way he played with her hair and touched her played havoc with her insides. Butterflies revolted in her stomach to the point she thought she might be sick. "I'm—"

"Fine," AJ answered for her. "She has a goose egg, but I got ice. A couple painkillers and a good night's sleep, Emma will be good as new."

Grady winked. "If you let her sleep."

Emma fought the urge to cringe, but she had no doubt color was creeping up her neck.

Marianne clucked her tongue.

Lilah laughed. "They hardly see each other. Sleep will be overrated while they're here."

Emma's cheeks burned. Libby's parents had never discussed sex, let alone joked about it in front of everybody.

Grady looked closer at her head. "There's blood."

AJ moved closer. "I didn't see any. Where?"

"Right here." Grady pointed, both men hovering over her, but Emma couldn't see what they were looking at. "The wound is clotting so no need for stitches. You must have hit hard. What were you doing?"

Emma glanced up at AJ, unsure if he wanted her to tell the truth. She assumed most billionaires' girlfriends wouldn't be crawling under the bed and that might lead to more questions.

"Never mind. I think I know." Grady looked over her with wicked laughter in his eyes. "If you get sick to your stomach or the headache gets worse, go to the hospital. You might have a concussion."

"I didn't hit that hard," she said.

"You still want to be careful." Grady looked at AJ. "If she starts acting different, see a doctor. Wake her up every couple of hours to check for changes in mental status and don't leave her alone for the next day or so."

"I can manage that."

Lilah nodded. "I'll provide backup."

Grady lifted a pocket-size reference book from his pocket and flipped to the back. "Oh, yeah. Avoid the pain meds if you can. They'll mask the intensity of the headache. Call the doctor if it's bad."

"I've got this." AJ caressed Emma's chin with his fingertip. "I'm happy to spend the next twenty-four hours right here."

That wasn't going to happen. Especially when she liked him being so close to her right now. For show, she reminded herself. But that didn't explain the tingles a brush of his hand brought. Or how his playing with the ends of her hair made her feel special. Emma sat up. "The appointments tomorrow..."

AJ placed two fingers against her lips, a gentle touch that made her ache for a kiss. "Let's see how you feel first."

"Looks like we're done here. Emma needs quiet and to rest." Marianne motioned Grady out of the room. "We'll say your good-nights to everyone. They can see you around town and at the birthday party."

"Thanks, Mom," AJ said. "And thanks, Grady. You're going to be a decent cop."

Grady grinned. "Already am."

"Well, good night." Lilah walked toward the door. "We'll leave you two alone. But let me know if you need anything."

Emma held her breath until the door closed, leaving her and AJ alone. She exhaled. Then burst out laughing. "That was..."

"Unbelievable," he finished for her. "At least only three of them came up."

"Grady brought his own refreshments."

"At least they weren't here long." AJ rested his head on his bent arm.

"I feel so silly. It's a little bump on the head. No need for any of you to fuss over me."

"People are worried."

"Not people, your family. That's very nice of them." She relaxed against the pillows. "Their worry is an extension of what they're feeling for you. They seem to link me with your being here, and for that gift they're all grateful. Even your dad."

"I wouldn't go that far."

"It's true." She wasn't going to let this go, even if common sense and a pounding head told her she should. "They care about you, AJ. They really do."

He froze. The only sound was the beating of her heart.

"Everyone was nice to me tonight," she continued. "But

all of them wanted to talk about one thing…you. Your family and friends miss you so much."

"Right. That's why I get only form letters at Christmas and printed birth announcements that find their way to my office when a new family member arrives. Trust me. They do fine without me."

He sounded like a rejected boy. "I understand you're hurt, but did you contact any of them?"

He drew back. "Excuse me?"

"Since you left Haley's Bay, who do you still talk with?"

"Grady. Bailey and Camden. Mom and Grandma. Occasionally Risa. That's pretty much it."

"Why is that?"

"They're the ones who make an effort."

"And how about you?" Emma wasn't challenging him. She wanted to help. AJ didn't seem to have thought this mess through.

"Everyone knows how to reach me."

"You're a billionaire. I can't call your corporate headquarters and be transferred directly to you."

"Ten years ago, I was a kid out of college. I was reachable. Hell, I was desperate for a call."

"I'm guessing so were your brothers and father. I'm sure you had their numbers memorized. You probably still do. Boy, you Cole men seem like a stubborn lot."

AJ smiled. "Determined, is what my grandmother says."

"Fine, so you were all determined not to have a relationship with each other. And you succeeded. But what have you gained?"

AJ didn't say anything. He rolled onto his back and drew a deep breath. "We didn't have anything to talk about. If I stayed, there were conditions I couldn't live with. If I left, I lost their respect. Not only my father, but my three oldest brothers who backed him. There was nothing *to* be gained. It was a no-win situation."

"So you all lost. But it's not permanent, right? They're here. You're here. You can fix this. I'll bet you've fixed much worse."

"Maybe."

She couldn't decipher his voice. She didn't know him, but somehow she felt "in" this. He'd dragged her into this. She'd try to be useful. "When you left town, did you just leave, or were their words exchanged with your brothers?"

"I don't remember."

"I doubt that." The way he huffed was adorable. As a mover and shaker of the tech world she could tell he wasn't used to being called to task. But she respected his willingness to think in a new way. She felt safe because he wasn't going to fire her. He needed her more than she needed him. "What did you say?"

"Not much. I may have said a few things about people who wanted to be stuck in a dead-end town their entire lives. Who wouldn't?"

"You were young, but you need to make nice."

"Huh?"

"Mend bridges, extend the olive branch, whatever other cliché you can think of. You never know what might happen."

"Trying to make nice could make things worse."

"Maybe, but expecting bad things to come from good is no way to live. What have you got to lose?"

"I'm not here for my family. I'm here to plan my grandmother's birthday."

"I'm here to do the planning work. You're here to say yes to the details and pay the bills," she clarified. "But only you can reach out to your family and friends now that you're back in Haley's Bay. You need to do that for their sakes and your own."

"Why should I listen to someone I just met with a bump on her head who could have a concussion?"

"Because it's good advice and I'm guessing if Libby were here she'd say the same thing."

"You and Libby are nothing alike."

"I know I can't fill her shoes—"

"I meant that as a compliment, Emma." He adjusted the ice pack on her head. "Libby is a great personal assistant. The best. But she has never spoken to me the way you have. I appreciate hearing what you have to say. You're the first person besides my mom and grandmother who doesn't hold back."

"That's me." Emma giggled. "Honest to a fault."

His smile was mischievous, intriguing. "I'll give you a pass for today."

"Thanks." She stifled a yawn.

"You're tired."

"A little," she admitted. "Go back to the party. I'll rest."

He set the alarm on his phone. "You heard what Grady said. Can't leave you alone. I need to wake you every two hours."

"You'll be exhausted in the morning."

"So will you. We can both sleep in."

Her eyelids felt heavy. She struggled to keep them open. "I'm supposed to be taking care of you."

"You are. Better than anyone's taken care of me in a long time."

Emma could say the exact same thing about him. Maybe they would come out of this as friends. She snuggled against the pillow. "There's something else I've figured out that's in your favor besides your sports car collection and not having sticky hands."

"What's that?" He covered her with a quilt.

"You're a really nice guy, AJ Cole."

"Thanks, but don't let anyone know." His conspiratorial tone amused her. "It'll ruin people's image of me around here."

"You don't want people to know you're nice?"

"Hell, no. They might expect me back next year."

She laughed. That made her head hurt more. "Heaven forbid you step foot in Haley's Bay again before another decade passes."

"If you knew—"

"I'm figuring it out." She adjusted the ice pack on her head. "When I met your dad, I could imagine how Maria in *The Sound of Music* must have felt the first time she met Captain von Trapp. Talk about intimidating. But you don't have to be the same guy who left here ten years ago."

"I'm not. I didn't have a clue back then."

"And now?"

"You think I'm still clueless."

"What I think doesn't matter, but the past will influence the present without us realizing it."

"That's what you think I'm doing."

"I'm trying to get you to understand if you're doing it or not," she explained. "I didn't know you ten years ago. I've known you for about twelve hours so I have no idea if you are or aren't. Only you know that."

"Do you ever turn off the nurturing nanny part?"

"What are you talking about?"

"That's what I thought." He gave her shoulder a squeeze. "Sleep. You've got two hours then we can talk again."

She couldn't wait.

Chapter Eight

Rays of light streamed through the bedroom window, but AJ didn't need the sun or an alarm clock to wake him this morning. He'd barely slept due to checking Emma every two hours, but it hadn't been a chore. A few minutes of pillow talk, then watching her fall asleep with the moon casting shadows on her pretty face, was worth being tired today.

AJ made multimillion-dollar business decisions daily and turned an idea into a successful company worth billions, but others did everything for him, from handling his bills to cooking his food. He hadn't run an errand, written a check or purchased a gift since his company went public. Even before that, staff members had taken over doing the basic things in his life, things he'd never thought twice about doing himself before. His time had become too valuable to be spent standing in line at the deli or vacuuming his living room rug.

Watching over Emma was a novelty. The feeling of satisfaction had nothing to do with profits and good PR. Maybe he should add an element of service to his charitable foundation's work in addition to writing checks and grants.

He lay on his side, looking at Emma. Her glasses sat on the nightstand. She slept with one arm under the covers and one the outside. Long, wavy strands of brown hair spread across her white pillowcase. A few reached all the way to his.

Earlier her lips had been parted, filling his mind with possibilities. Now the slight curve to her mouth intrigued him. What was she dreaming about? Cats and kids? A man? Maybe him?

Yeah, right. AJ smiled at the truth. His money didn't impress Emma. Nothing about him seemed to impress her except his family. What he'd previously considered his most obvious liability were those who didn't believe in him. Yet Emma seemed to bridge that gap and not choose sides. Impossible.

Still, AJ liked her. Blossom liked Emma, too.

The cat slept between them. She rested her head and one paw on Emma's arm. The cat's tail was against him, but AJ wasn't about to move the feline. Disturbing the cat might wake Emma. He wasn't going to do it. If he were a cat, he would prefer using Emma as a pillow, too.

He gave Blossom a rub, her orange fur soft against his fingers, the way he knew Emma's hair would feel, though hers was longer. He'd given his word about not touching her so he hadn't except for a nudge on the shoulder during the 3:00 a.m. wake-up.

Blossom purred, the sound comforting and surprisingly not unwelcome. Kinda cute. Maybe cats weren't that bad. At least this one.

Emma stirred. She blinked open her eyes, then rolled to face him without disturbing Blossom. "Good morning."

"How's your head feel?" he asked.

"Better." Her smile brightened not only her face, but also the room. "Thanks for waking me up through the night. I'm sorry you had to do that."

"Not a problem." And it wasn't. If an employee or someone he knew were sick or injured, Libby sent flowers, balloons or a fruit arrangement from him without asking. Emma was different. He hadn't wanted to pass her off to someone in his family. Waking up a person every two hours wasn't that hard, and helping Emma was a good way to repay her for what she was doing for him. "Go back to sleep. I'll bring you breakfast."

She carefully moved Blossom's head off her arm, then sat. The covers fell to Emma's waist, giving him a nice view of her bare arms and chest. She wasn't wearing a bra.

He forced his gaze to the cat, who was stretching after having her pillow removed.

Emma looked at the nightstand, picked up her glasses and put them on. "Thanks, but I have meetings at ten and one. I need to get ready."

"Your work ethic impresses me." One more thing to add to the growing list. "But don't push yourself. Reschedule the meetings and rest."

"No way."

"Excuse me?"

"I'm not rescheduling. The party is on Saturday night." She rubbed the top of her head. "I'm fine."

He couldn't believe she'd told him *no way*. Employees never spoke to him like that. Then again, he'd never had a discussion with an employee while in bed and wearing pajamas that outlined beautiful curves.

"The bump's almost gone." She leaned over, her breasts

jiggling and making him forget what they were talking about. "Feel it."

He did, wishing he were feeling something else instead. "You're right. The bump's much smaller this morning.

"Don't sound so disappointed." Her voice held a nanny edge rather than the sex kitten tones he preferred when in bed, but then again this was her job. "I'm not going to be an excuse you use to avoid your family."

"That's not what I'm doing." Avoiding his family hadn't entered AJ's mind. He wanted to spend more time with Emma alone, preferably in bed. Talk about crazy. What were they going to do? Play Words With Friends? Maybe he bumped his head and hadn't realized he was the one with an injury. Nothing else would explain his desire to play hooky from life with her. "You heard what Grady said."

"I did, but I'm okay. Really. You, however, look tired and a little dazed," Emma continued. "Rest while I'm out."

He bolted upright, sending Blossom to her feet. "You're not going to the meetings alone."

"I won't be alone. Charlie can accompany me."

"I'm going."

Her slanted mouth was a new look, but the way her gaze narrowed was familiar. She would let him have it in three…two…one…

"You wouldn't be going if Libby were here. You wouldn't go if your family didn't think I was your girlfriend." She pursed her lips. "I'm still your personal assistant and have a job to do. Let me do it."

He liked when she spoke her mind. "What kind of boyfriend would dump an entire birthday party on your lap? Especially when she hurt her head."

"A typical one. Most guys aren't event planners."

"But my family will think—"

"You said you didn't care what they thought."

AJ didn't want to care what his family thought. He told himself he didn't care, but a part of him still did. A big part, unfortunately. He didn't know why.

"You said you only came back to Haley's Bay for your grandmother."

"I did, but I want my grandmother to know I put some thought into this and didn't leave all the details to Libby and you."

His words didn't ring true. Not to him. No doubt Emma would see right through them. Because until this moment, he'd planned on letting her handle everything while he was here, from the party to his family. He didn't know what had changed or why he was fighting Emma on this. He'd known her for a day, but she'd earned his trust and could make independent decisions.

"You're here," she continued. "That's more than enough for Lilah. Enjoy your vacation. Spend more time with your grandmother and family. Relax."

"I'm going."

Emma toyed with the quilt, her fingers working back and forth along the edge. She didn't look nervous, but something was on her mind.

"What?" he asked.

She released the blanket and stared at Blossom, sleeping at the foot of the bed. "It's…nothing."

The way her eyes clouded told him the opposite. She wanted to say something. "Come on."

"If you want to go to the meetings, go. It's not my place to stop you. You're the boss."

"I am." Except he didn't feel in charge around Emma and that bothered him. Being in Haley's Bay was messing with him. He hoped things would be back to normal today. "We'll formulate our plans for the day over breakfast."

"Okay, but I'm getting dressed first. I'm not used to working in my jammies."

"Me, either. Not sure they'd pass as office chic."

"You could be the trendsetter."

"The company has a casual dress code, but pajamas would be pushing it."

"Even for you?"

"Especially for me. Though if there's ever a day I telecommute, I'll have to make it a PJ day."

"Until you have a video chat to attend."

"Shirt and tie and pajama bottoms." He played along, liking that she was smiling again. "No one would ever know."

"I'm sure telecommuters have lots of 'no one ever knew' stories. Especially before video calls became the rage," she said. "I cared for three children one summer. Their mother liked to have conference calls while taking bubble baths. Claimed the acoustics were better in the master bathroom."

"I never knew acoustics were so important."

"I think she liked the idea of being naked in the tub and no one on the call knowing."

He wouldn't mind seeing Emma naked in a tub. No bubbles required. Water wouldn't even be necessary. He grinned at the image forming in his mind. "I'll have to listen more carefully the next time I'm on a call."

"Don't be too distracted."

"Never. Well, unless I hear splashing."

With a smile, Emma gave a slight shake of her head. "Good thing you don't have to worry about being distracted by me. I'm taking a shower so no splashing."

The thought of her undressing to take a shower was definitely distracting. He hadn't slept with a woman in a while. As in having sex, not for concussion checks or a fake relationship. Something about his "usual type" had lost its appeal. Declan hadn't been far off. AJ was ready for a change, though he'd never have an affair with an employee. A man could dream, though, and Emma…

She crawled out of bed, giving him a full view of her in her pajamas, a camisole and coordinating shorts. No panty hose.

…had the sexiest legs this side of the Cascades. Long, firm, the perfect amount of muscle. Man, she'd look great in a pair of heels and a short cocktail dress. "You're a runner."

Lines creased her forehead. "I jog. Only once or twice a week. I do run after children. That amuses them to no end."

"If you want to jog here, there are trails."

"Thanks, but I didn't think there'd be much downtime so didn't pack my running shoes or clothes." She picked up Blossom from the bed. "I'm going to take her with me in case she needs to use the litter box."

Lucky cat. Though seeing Emma in the shower with water streaming down her body would be wasted on the feline. "I'll see what's going on with my grandmother and touch base with Charlie about the meetings."

"I texted him today's itinerary last night." Emma cradled Blossom like a baby. "Charlie will be here at nine-forty. That gives us an hour and a half to get ready and have breakfast."

Too bad they weren't a real couple because AJ knew exactly how he'd want to fill that time—an hour in bed sans jammies followed by a shower for two. His groin tightened. Now that would be a perfect morning.

Thinking about Emma, dressed or undressed, turned him on and made this faux dating thing work. It was also making him crazy in the presence of her barely clothed, hardworking, likes-to-jog, unpampered body.

What was happening to him? The damn cat wasn't annoying him as much. He brushed his hand through his hair. Once Emma finished in the bathroom, he needed a shower. A cold one.

Emma walked out of the ten o'clock meeting at the party rental place in Astoria, Oregon, with an odd feeling in her gut, one that had nothing to do with the man at her side. Oh, being near AJ brought tingles and knots, butterflies and chills, but those were good feelings. Unexpected, unwelcome, but okay. What she felt now was more…not foreboding, but troubling.

Charlie opened the door. She slid into the limo, feeling more comfortable inside the fancy car than yesterday. The air-conditioning soothed. The coast stayed cool, even during the summer months, but the meeting had sent her blood pressure spiraling and her temperature soaring.

AJ followed her into the car. His bare leg touched hers for a nanosecond. Long enough to make her catch her breath. Blossom's sleeping between them last night had been a blessing. Waking to find herself spooning him would have been as much a nightmare as a pleasure. At least they wouldn't be forced to pretend to be dating here.

The door slammed. A minute later, the limo pulled onto the highway, heading north toward the Columbia River and Haley's Bay, Washington.

AJ leaned back against the seat, then stretched out his legs. He looked liked a guy on vacation in his blue shorts, green-and-white-striped polo shirt and flip-flops. "Tony seems a little laid back. More interested in surfing than the party rental business."

"So laid back he's flat on the sand at the beach." The

last thing she wanted to do was send AJ back into business mode, but this was too important not to deal with now. "We need to find another vendor to supply the tent, tables, chairs and dance floor for the party. Tony seems like a nice guy, but he's going to flake on us come Saturday."

AJ straightened. "We have a signed contract."

"Not everyone treats a contract the same way."

"You didn't mention any concerns during the meeting."

Emma appreciated how AJ let her handle the meeting. He must be a good boss, not one who micromanages his staff.

"I wanted to hear what Tony had to say. I was trying to give him the benefit of the doubt, but what he said increased my worries."

"What worries are those?"

"I researched the vendors Libby selected, and checked the most recent reviews. Tony's parents retired. He took over their business a week after Libby negotiated the contract with his father," Emma explained. "Tony's been a no-show for events five times in the past month. Your grandmother's party is the only thing listed on the upcoming event whiteboard. And his phone didn't ring once while we were there."

"I hadn't noticed."

"Libby gave me a list of things to look for with vendors. She's more experienced with event planning and knows what can go wrong. That's why she wanted me to meet with each in person." Emma might not have taken on a party of this scale, but she trusted her instincts. "I'm concerned we're going to find ourselves scrambling if Tony doesn't show up the day of the party. That's why I suggest we hire another vendor. You'll lose your deposit with Tony's company, but have peace of mind of knowing we'll have the supplies we need the day of the party."

"Sounds like a good plan. I don't want anything to go wrong with the party. Do you have someone else in mind to hire?"

Emma nodded. "Libby spoke with four different vendors before deciding on Tony's parents. I have the names and numbers. She did her homework, and until the change in management, made the right choice, especially since Tony's parents know Lilah. I'll find out if her second choice is available."

"Call now." AJ smoothly launched into CEO mode, and she noticed the change in his expression. Hard. A little ruthless. Nothing like the guy she'd woken up with a couple hours ago, who sang her 'NSync songs every two hours to keep her upbeat about the concussion checks. "They can email the contract. I've got a hot spot and wireless printer here in the car."

"That's convenient."

"Some issues are time sensitive. I need to work on the road."

"No wonder you need a vacation. But it's still hard to turn off the CEO, isn't it?"

He shifted positions. "Sometimes, but I'm trying."

Harder than tough decisions to make and firing people must pressure AJ to always be "on." He needed to be the smartest one in the room, the director of the action. His following her to the meeting, that was about her ridiculous twenty-four-hour watch, nothing else. Other than attending, he deferred to her. That made her warm with pride. Emma pulled out her notebook and cell phone. She made the phone call.

Ten minutes later, she gave another party rental place AJ's credit card number, then disconnected. "All set. Contract is being emailed. I'll have Charlie drive me up there later to drop it off so I can meet them."

"Charlie will drive us there."

She knew better than to argue the point. "Fine."

"We have nearly two hours until the one o'clock appointment. Time for some R & R."

"You deserve it," she said.

"Not for me. You."

"I don't understand."

"It's time for you to see Haley's Bay. We can have lunch and walk around town." He flashed her the same charming grin she'd woken up to this morning and made her heart bump. "What do you say?"

Spending more time with AJ without working on the party wasn't the smartest move. But they did have time, and she wanted to see the town. This was also one way to make sure he relaxed. "Sounds great."

The limo pulled to a stop in the harbor's small parking lot. Charlie opened the door, but AJ was the one who took her hand to help her out of the car. "Ready to see Haley's Bay?"

"Yes."

Emma knew he disliked his hometown, no doubt blaming the conflict with his dad and what happened with his ex-fiancée. But AJ didn't look miserable here. He'd smiled last night. He was smiling now. Maybe she'd been correct. Maybe he was letting the past interfere too much. Hating Haley's Bay could be his defense mechanism.

"Anything in particular you don't want to miss?" he asked.

"The candy store. Your sister Bailey told me they have the best saltwater taffy around."

"Taffy equals sticky hands."

"I have wet wipes in my tote bag."

"Then I'll have some, too." He held her hand. "Not sticky now."

She looked down at her hand in his. "What…?"

"This is a small town. My brother is a cop. My dad and brothers might have come in early. Who knows what my two sisters are up to. Not to mention my mom, grandmother, cousins and friends."

The charade. She'd forgotten for a moment and thought he was really holding her hand. Silly.

"Okay." Emma didn't mind. She liked holding his hands. More than she should. She also liked kissing but that was a little too real. "Let me put on my pretend girlfriend persona."

Maybe if she kept her self separate from the role-playing, things would be easier to handle and not so confusing, especially the kissing part.

He squeezed her hand. "I'm ready to be the perfect fake boyfriend."

The longing in her heart for a relationship with a real boyfriend nearly overwhelmed her. Visions of candlelit dinners and making out on a bench by the water swam before her eyes. Where had that come from? Her dates had always trended toward the pizza-and-bowling combo, and the nice-but-not-memorable category. Emma pasted on a smile and tilted her head toward the line of shops across the street. "Let's explore Haley's Bay."

An hour later, AJ held open the door of the seafood café where he and Emma had eaten lunch—salmon coated in a rice flour batter and waffle-cut French fries. Not the fish and chips he'd grown up eating, but tasty. The best part of the lunch, though, had been talking with Emma. She was closemouthed about her life before meeting Libby but he knew Emma had had a far rougher beginning than him, and was drawn to Haley's Bay for its picturesque beauty and curb appeal.

"Admit it," Emma said on the way out the door. "This town isn't purgatory on earth."

Compared to whatever she'd faced that put her into the foster care system, Haley's Bay must seem perfect. AJ knew better—small towns were not judgment-free zones—but he didn't care enough to correct her because he couldn't stop smiling. She made him, in a word, *happy,* a way he wasn't used to feeling. Oh, he was content. He had a good life, but *happy?* That wasn't a word he'd use to describe himself.

But he was having his best day in forever. Better than his last merger. Better than his last million-dollar fund-raiser. Funny considering the most exciting thing they'd done was have a souped-up seafood combo and fire a lazy party guy who reinforced AJ's belief that inheriting a company made you less invested than if you'd been a founder.

He joined Emma on the wood-slatted sidewalk. The sun was high in the blue sky. A nice wind off the water turned the weather vanes on top of shops. "I may have exaggerated."

She peered into the window of the souvenir shop next door. "If this is purgatory, I'm in."

"You didn't grow up here."

"I wish I had. Especially now that I know you give full-ride scholarships to any honor roll student who gets accepted into a four-year university. That's so generous of you. Obviously all the people who came to the table are grateful."

"I have a foundation. The money needs to be given away. Kids who live in towns like this don't always have the means to attend college."

She turned away from the display of seashells, beach towels and sun hats. "Kids like you."

Her gaze pierced deep inside him, as if she could see

straight to his soul. He looked away. "I earned a full ride. If I hadn't, I'd have wound up at the local two-year college or not gone at all. I don't want others to find themselves in the same position."

The soft smile on her face filled him with warmth. She pointed to his heart. "This town will always be a part of you. Right here. Welcome home, Atticus Jackson Cole."

His throat tightened. Something about this woman made him feel things he'd either forgotten or never known. He was a computer programmer. Code, he understood. Logic ruled his world. Emotion played a minor role, except, as Emma discovered, when it came to Haley's Bay and his family.

AJ didn't understand. How could she read him when he was so practiced in not giving his thoughts away? Her ability bothered him, left him feeling exposed. He knew exactly what would soothe him. "The candy shop is up ahead. Let's try some of that taffy Bailey told you about."

He opened the door for Emma then followed her inside. A counter with a glass display case of chocolates and other candies was on the left hand side. On the opposite wall, a built-in shelf unit held clear buckets full of different flavored saltwater taffy. A popcorn popper and cotton candy machine sat in the rear of the shop.

Emma glanced at the delicious looking chocolates. "The smell alone is going to add three inches to my hips, but what's that saying? You only live once. Who knows if I'll ever be back? Might as well take home a few souvenirs."

"Choose whatever you want," he said. "My treat."

"Not to scare you, but I have a huge sweet tooth."

"Huge I can afford. Ginormous I might have to limit you."

She smiled.

He smiled back, feeling a comfortable connection with her once again.

"Welcome to the Candy Cave," a familiar-sounding voice said from behind swinging doors. A woman appeared in a white shirt, white pants and pink apron. Blond hair was pulled back into a bun and covered with a hairnet. "I was in the back checking a fresh batch of fudge. Would you like a sample?"

"I'd love a taste," Emma said. "Thanks."

AJ did a double take. No, it couldn't be her. He blinked then took another look. His muscles bunched. He used to think Natalie Farmer, captain of the cheer squad and homecoming queen, was beautiful with her soulful brown eyes, ivory complexion and long blond hair. But her eyes looked tired and weary. Her features were tight, almost pinched, and her ruddy skin made her look older than thirty-four. "Natalie?"

The woman froze. Color drained from her face. Her mouth gaped. "AJ. You're back."

He nodded, not trusting his voice. He hadn't seen her since Christmas break of his freshman year of college. By the time he returned in June, she'd married Craig Steele, one of AJ's best friends. He waited for the anger over their betrayal to hit.

"Hello." Emma greeted Natalie warmly. "I'm Emma Markwell."

Natalie's narrowed gaze flew to AJ. "A friend of yours?"

"My girlfriend." The words came naturally. He wasn't upset. He didn't feel anything for the woman who broke his heart. No emotion, no attraction, no regrets. A shocking but sweet surprise. "Emma, this is Natalie. We went to high school together."

"Nice to meet you," Emma said.

Ignoring her, Natalie's lips thinned. "Has your billionaire brain forgotten we were more than high school classmates?"

"Natalie and I were once engaged, but she married someone else," AJ said, amazed by his indifference. "How is Craig doing?"

"I wouldn't know. We've been separated since June. That's why I'm working here. But our kids tell me he's doing well." Natalie's eyes gleamed. "He's met someone else."

Emma shifted her weight between her feet, then dragged her teeth over her lower lip. "I'm going to look at the taffy."

She moved to the wall of buckets on the right side of the store. Far enough to give him and Natalie a little space, but the store wasn't large enough to provide much privacy. Emma playing the gracious employee irritated him. She shouldn't have moved away, but stayed next to him acting like the upset, affronted girlfriend.

Natalie cleared her throat. She waited with an expectant look on her face.

AJ didn't know what he was supposed to say. "I'm sorry, Nat."

"Me, too." She glanced over at Emma. "Your girlfriend seems nice."

"She is."

"Young."

He knew Emma could hear every word. "Yes."

"I don't see a ring."

Natalie sounded harsh, bitter. The bouncy girl who floated through life like a princess on a parade float had completely disappeared. Maybe she hadn't really been that way. "Like you said, she's young. No rush."

"I shouldn't have rushed. I should have waited. I'm… sorry. If I could do it all over again—"

"It's in the past, Nat. There aren't any do-overs."

"What about second chances?" Natalie asked.

He couldn't believe she wanted to rekindle their romance. "It's been a long time since we knew each other."

"We were in love once," she said in a low voice. "Who knows what might happen this time?"

He knew, because he might have been in love with her, but she hadn't been in love with him. A woman in love and wearing a man's engagement ring wouldn't have started dating others because she was lonely. Natalie hadn't left AJ for another man. She'd been in love with getting married and AJ had fit the groom mold until his going away to school threatened her timetable. Nat's solution? Replace the groom.

To think he'd let her haunt him for so long. Stupid.

What I think doesn't matter, but the past will influence the present without us realizing it.

Emma was right again. She could teach Mary Poppins a thing or two. He bit back a smile. "I can't."

Natalie inclined her head toward the taffy display. "Because of her."

Holding a paper bag, Emma studied the labels on the buckets of taffy. AJ knew the difference between the two women in that instant. Emma seemed to like the person he was while Natalie had liked the person she wanted him to be. A big freaking difference. She'd made her choices, but AJ felt sorry for Natalie. "I hope things work out with you and Craig."

For their kids' sake, AJ thought to himself.

Executives and employees at his company had gone through divorce. He wouldn't wish that pain on anyone, including Natalie and Craig.

"Thanks, you never know what might happen." Natalie sighed. "Emma's a lucky woman."

"I'm the lucky one."

And he was. In a pretend relationship or a real one, Emma would go out of her way to help a friend or a stranger. She would never break her word or promise the way Natalie had.

Time to put this chapter of his life behind him and move on. He had one person to thank for that—Emma.

Chapter Nine

"The florist is a five-minute walk from here."

"We have fifteen minutes until our appointment. Plenty of time. I want to tell you an idea I had about Lilah's party theme," Emma said to AJ, walking next to him toward the harbor. He didn't look upset from seeing his ex. If anything, he looked satisfied, with a smile on his face and a bounce to his step. That seemed an odd reaction to bumping into the woman who supposedly broke his heart. Declan had implied Natalie had been part of the reason AJ avoided town. If so, that particular concern seemed to have been laid to rest. Very strange.

"Have you tried a piece of taffy yet?" AJ asked.

She carried a small bag from the Candy Cave, but she didn't feel like munching on the taffy they'd purchased. "No, I'm still full from lunch. Would you like one?"

"Later."

Questions about Natalie Steele rattled around Emma's

brain. The woman was pretty, tall and model thin, exactly the kind of woman a man like AJ would date. Though Natalie didn't seem to be living a happily ever after in Haley's Bay. Emma respected AJ for stuffing cash into the tip jar while Natalie rang up their candy purchase. The nickname Attila didn't fit him at all.

Tourists crowded the sidewalk, forcing her to separate from AJ. She let a woman pushing a double stroller pass. He waited for Emma to catch up to him. "You're about to chew your bottom lip to pieces. What's on your mind?"

She ran her tongue across her lower lip. Oops, he was right. Except… "Your personal life is none of my business."

"That's never stopped you before."

"You don't sound upset about that."

"I'm not." He shortened his stride to match hers. "So spill."

She laughed at the term. "I don't have anything to, um, *spill.*"

"But you have questions. I'm assuming they're about Nat."

"Yes." Meeting Natalie hadn't made Emma feel inadequate—nothing she could do about her average height and being a little curvy—but seeing the woman with AJ put the relationship charade into much-needed perspective. Time to put a blaring, neon-colored emphasis on the *pretend* part of being AJ's fake girlfriend. When Emma was with him, talking to him as though they'd known each other forever, pretending slipped her mind. She couldn't let that happen again. *Not real.* She needed the words tattooed as a reminder. "Seeing Natalie like that was unexpected. Are you okay?" Emma asked finally.

"Yes."

"Are you going to see her again?"

"What?"

No. No. No. She hadn't meant to ask that question even if she was dying to know the answer. "It's just…Natalie mentioned being separated from her husband. If you still have feelings for her—"

"I don't."

"You were engaged."

"A long time ago. I was eighteen. Young. Stupid. In love. Bought into the fairy tale."

Emma's relief was palpable, something she didn't understand. "And now?"

"Even if I was interested in her, which I'm not, Natalie's separated from her husband, not divorced. I don't mess around with married women."

"Another rule, like how you don't fool around with employees."

A beat passed. Then another. "Not a rule per se, but common sense to avoid complications, lawsuits and jealous estranged husbands."

"That makes sense."

"Glad you think so." Amusement danced in his eyes. "By the way, you were right."

"What about?"

"Letting the past influence the present. I thought I was still upset at Natalie, but once I saw her I realized I wasn't. If anything, I felt sorry for her. Things turned out for the best, even if I didn't think so at the time."

"That's great. I'm glad you bumped into her."

"Me, too. I never thought I'd be saying that."

A tall man caught her eye. Jack Cole stood across the street from the harbor, his eyes locked on her and AJ. The hard set of Jack's jaw and thinned lips reminded her of a sculpture. No warmth or life in the etched stone. "Now all you need to do is work through things with your father."

AJ slowed his pace. "That's not going to happen."

"You didn't become the man you are by giving up."

"Giving up implies I want something from my father. I don't. Not anymore. Just like Natalie. Over it."

"Hmm. Well, that's good to know. Then again, your father's standing at the end of the block. Perhaps you could test how much you don't care by asking his opinion on your last business venture. Unless seeing your dad right after Natalie—"

AJ kissed Emma on the lips. Hard. A kiss full of longing and desire.

Awareness thrummed through her body. Everything on her mind disappeared. All she could think about was AJ. All she could feel was his mouth moving against hers. Fireworks exploded inside her, but she didn't think twice about getting burned. She arched against him, wanting to be closer.

His kisses were like oxygen, necessary for life. She pressed harder against his lips. More, she wanted more. He pulled away from her, ending the kiss, leaving Emma gasping for a breath of air and not sure what had just happened.

"I told you I'm fine." He waved to his dad with his free hand. "Never been better."

That made one of them. Emma blinked, took in her surroundings, forced herself to breathe. She was in big trouble.

Forget pretend kisses. That one had been real. Who was she kidding? They'd all been real to her, even the practice one by the water.

Uh-oh. She wiped her mouth, as if she could wipe away the tingles and the memory of his kiss.

"Come on. We have a couple minutes before our meeting." AJ pulled on her arm. "I'm not interested in your experiment, but let's see what my dad wants."

Emma followed, her actions more robotic than human. Confusion made her brain feel like mush, the same way AJ's kisses turned her insides to goo. She noticed the frown on Mr. Cole's face. "He doesn't look happy."

"That's his here-comes-AJ face." He didn't let go of her hand; if anything, he held on tighter. "Hey, Dad. What's going on?"

"Tony Mannion called me. Says you canceled the rental agreement for your grandmother's birthday."

Emma released AJ's hand and stepped forward. "I'm the one who wanted to hire a new vendor, Mr. Cole."

"I agreed with Emma." AJ stood next to her, put his arm around her shoulder and drew her against him. "It was the right decision."

"We've been friends with the Mannion family for years." Mr. Cole's cheeks reddened. "Hell, I taught Tony how to fish. Call him back and tell him you made a mistake before his parents find out."

"No," AJ said.

Emma slipped her arm around his waist in support. AJ's ignoring his dad's opinion would only make things worse. She tried to send relaxing, peacemaking vibes by rubbing her fingers up his spine, but his back was stiff and proud due to his father, magic fingers or not.

Mr. Cole blinked. "What did you say?"

"I'm not going to do that." AJ's voice sounded strong, but not defensive. "Grandma's birthday is too important to leave anything up to chance."

Mr. Cole's nostrils flared. "His parents—"

"Are RVing their way through British Columbia." The way AJ squared his shoulders. He was in this fight to win, but Emma hated that she was the one who caused the argument. "I doubt they have any idea Tony is ruining the business they built over the years. Not that it matters since you never listen to me."

Jack Cole looked at her. "Do you know what's going on?"

She nodded. "Since Tony's parents turned over the business to him, he's been a no-show at several events. The recent reviews from customers are all negative. Meeting with him this morning confirmed my fears so I suggested we hire another vendor."

"Who'd you go with?"

"A company in Long Beach," she answered.

"Guy Schrader?"

"Yes. We're dropping the contract off this afternoon."

The lines on Mr. Cole's face relaxed. He rocked back on his heels. "Known Guy for years. Good choice. He won't let you down. Good catch on Tony. I'll see if I can get in touch with his parents and set things right there." Mr. Cole glanced at his wristwatch. "I need to get back to the boat. See you at Bailey's tonight for dinner."

With that, he turned and crossed the street, making traffic stop for him, as if Jack Cole owned the town.

"He's a little...gruff," she said.

AJ barked out a laugh. "That's one way to put it. But don't let my father get to you."

"I won't."

"Good." He stared down at her with tenderness in his eyes. "It may be hard for your optimistic view on life to handle, but people don't change."

"I wouldn't say that." Emma had seen the physical similarities between the two men last night, but they shared many of the same personality traits, too. She wondered if AJ knew he was as stubborn, or that she was no optimist, but now wasn't the time to bring any of that up. "He agreed with the new vendor."

"Your new vendor, not mine."

"He doesn't know which one of us picked Guy Schrader. Your dad would assume it was you, not me."

"Maybe."

"Not maybe." She raised his hand and kissed the top of it. "You let go of the anger over Natalie. It felt great, right? Imagine how light you'd feel if you let go of this battle with your dad. Called a truce. You'd float. I'd have to hold on to make sure you wouldn't sail away on me."

AJ touched her face. "Total nutty-in-the-head optimist. If you were an analyst, I'd have to fire you for all the money you'd lose. But in a nanny—I like it."

"I can't be a pessimist. I work with kids," she said with a smile. "I'm supposed to be teaching them, but the truth is I learn so much from them. They get over hurts in five minutes, and make up after fights that same day."

His grin made her think of kids, her kids, ones with his clear green eyes and bright smile. Like her brother, the last time they'd been happy together. A child with AJ would bring that kind of joy back to her life. A family, her own people to love forever. She swallowed, wanting the images erased from her mind. Her brother was gone, soon AJ and his family would be gone, and she'd be alone as she'd been since the fire. Like living with Libby for her last three years of school, this was temporary. Not real. A fantasy.

"We'd better get to the florist." He held on to her hand again. "Did you hear me mention we're expected at Bailey's tonight?"

"Another family dinner?"

"Immediate family only. Bailey's house isn't big enough to hold aunts, uncles and cousins, too."

That sounded like the best kind of problem to have—

too many family members to fit in your house. Although acting the part of AJ's besotted girlfriend wasn't too bad a problem to have, either. Pretending had transformed into an absolute pleasure today. She just had to remember what was real and what wasn't.

"So what was your idea for a party theme?" AJ asked.

"Welcome to the house that AJ bought."

"Very funny, sis." Following Emma into the house, AJ handed Bailey the bouquet of flowers Emma had picked out after their meeting with the florist. The bright-colored flowers would go well with his sister's little cottage surrounded by a white picket fence and flowers growing in pots and containers and even the basket of an old rusted bicycle. "These are for you."

"They are lovely." Bailey sniffed the blossoms, her long ringlet-curled copper hair falling across her face. "Thank you, Emma."

"They're from AJ," she corrected.

"You must be a good influence, because I can't remember the last time AJ bought something on his own," Bailey teased with a smile that reminded him of Grandma.

AJ looked around. "Nice place."

"I have you to thank for that." Bailey kissed his cheek. "I know you thought I was crazy for wanting this foreclosure."

"I'm impressed. You've done an incredible job remodeling." He pointed to a painted textile hanging on the wall. "I like that."

Bailey nodded, sending long earrings clinking against the necklaces she wore. "Thanks. I'm still trying to decide if more blue is needed."

"Looks good to me," he said.

"Says my big brother who thinks anything I make is

brilliant and finds computer code sexy." Bailey gave him a hug. "But thank you. And just so you know, you're not allowed to buy it."

Emma looked around at the artwork covering the brightly painted walls and built-in shelves. "You created all of this?"

"Guilty as charged." Bailey looked at her pieces the way a mother stared at her children. "AJ convinced me I was wasting my talents as a short-order cook and should pursue art instead."

"Art's been my sister's passion for as long as I remember. When she was little, she'd paint rocks and seashells and sell them to tourists," he added, so proud of what Bailey had accomplished. "She made a great omelet, but her heart was in the studio, not the kitchen."

"I still make a great omelet," Bailey joked. "And my rocks and shells are for sale at the souvenir shop. But I'm much happier as an artist than I ever was as a cook."

"Well, whatever you're making in the kitchen smells delicious. It's obvious you have many talents and gifts." Sincerity rang clear in Emma's compliment. The wide smile on Bailey's face told AJ that his sister heard it, too. "I'm really impressed."

"Thanks." Bailey spun toward the other wall, where a metallic sculpture sat, sending her flowing skirt outward and the bangles on her arms clanking against one another. She'd always dressed bohemian-style, even when she was a little girl. "That's my newest creation. I rotate items between a gallery at the Broughton Inn here in Haley's Bay and one in Seattle. But a piece's first stop is my house. I want to make sure each work gets the thumbs-up from my brother's discriminating eyes. As you know AJ's into art."

"I didn't know that." Emma's eyes widened. She must have realized her lapse. "I mean..."

Standing behind Emma, AJ wrapped his arms around her. He placed his cheek against hers. "What Emma means is when we're together the last thing on our minds is hanging out in an art gallery."

"I don't blame you." Bailey sounded wistful. She hadn't had much luck in the romance department, but wouldn't go into details. "Long-distance dating must be tough."

He nodded. "But worth it."

Emma looked up at him through a half moon of thick dark eyelashes. "Definitely."

His heart bumped. What was going on? He tried to let go, but doing so was taking so much effort. His body seemed on autopilot, ignoring captain's orders and drawing closer to the sea nymph. His fingers cupped her hips from behind as though they were beckoned and possessive. She swayed, warm under his touch, and he imagined the skin under the skirt. Lifting the skirt.

He jerked away, such an idiot. Emma was not going to lift her skirt for a temporary boyfriend. And AJ was not going to lift the skirt of a temporary employee, despite luscious hips and their warm sway and his idiocy.

"Next time you're in Seattle, make him take you to his art gallery," Bailey said, glancing oddly at AJ, likely noticing his jerking away from Emma as though the woman had whacked him with a hot poker.

He gave his sister a weak smile. He'd never felt so foolish in his life. Emma's body held him captive.

Her smile looked forced, as well. "I, um, will."

Pretending was getting harder, not easier. He hated putting Emma through this. Only a couple more days… "Where is everyone?"

"Backyard." Bailey led them past the dining room, into the small kitchen where the delicious aromas made his hungry mouth water, toward the open back door. "Not enough space in here. Fortunately Mother Nature cooperated. Ellis, Risa, the kids and Madison arrived a few minutes ago. Grady should be here shortly with Camden."

Emma touched the white-tiled backsplash. "You have a lovely home."

"Thanks. I dreamed about owning this cottage for years. When I saw the foreclosure sign I nearly hyperventilated."

"Now the house is yours," AJ said.

Bailey grimaced. "Not quite mine yet."

He sighed. They'd been through this for the past two years. "You don't have to pay me back."

"I know I don't." Bailey looked at Emma. "But my big brother doesn't understand that I *want* to pay him back. A zero-interest loan is enough of a gift."

He shook his head. "My sister is stubborn like our father."

"She's not the only one," Emma muttered.

Bailey laughed. "You've got that right. It's a trait we've all inherited. Some more than others."

"What's that supposed to mean?" AJ asked.

Emma rose up on her tiptoes and kissed his cheek. "It means you're more like your father than you realize, but that's part of what makes you lovable."

Warmth flooded AJ, and likely spread a goofy grin across his face. Damned if this woman's opinion hadn't become his be-all and end-all. She thought he was lovable. He felt like Rudolph dancing his red-nosed reindeer self in circles after Clarice told him he was cute.

Good thing none of AJ's business rivals—or Libby—were around to see he'd gone totally, raving bonkers. Only his family was here, and he could avoid them another ten years or so. Easily. Especially without Emma pushing him to make nice.

* * *

Stupid. Stupid. Stupid. Emma couldn't believe she'd told AJ he was lovable. Thank goodness Bailey had been right there or he might have thought Emma meant it. She sort of did, but maybe he wouldn't figure that out. Or maybe he already had.

Darn the man. Emma balled her hands. Why did he have to be so nice and generous and well, lovable?

"Did you have enough to eat?" Lilah asked, sitting in a rocking Adirondack chair where she had a view of all the happenings in the backyard.

"Yes, the pulled pork sandwiches were great. The asparagus spears, too." But the delicious food couldn't compare to being included last night and tonight in the Cole family celebrations, a dream come true for an orphan like Emma.

"I hope you saved room for dessert. Bailey made shortcake from scratch. Marianne brought the strawberries and whipped cream."

"Sounds yummy." Emma patted her stomach. "But I'm going to need to go on a diet when I get home."

Lilah pshawed. "Nonsense. If anything you're a little thin. A couple extra pounds would be healthy. I'm sure AJ would agree, but let's leave him out of the discussion. It's a rare man who can say anything about a woman's weight without getting himself in trouble."

"Advice more men should follow." Emma picked up a garbage bag and tossed the paper plates from the picnic table inside. "I'm going to clean up so Bailey isn't left with a mess."

"Thank you, dear," Lilah said. "You fit right in, you know that?"

Emma wondered if her feet were still touching the grass. She didn't think so. "Thanks. That means a lot."

The words did. Emma wished she could stay in Haley's Bay forever, but nothing was real, not her being accepted into the Cole clan, not the kisses shared with AJ, not the feelings she was developing for her employer. Still, a bay-size part of her wished all of it were true. Especially dating AJ.

"Help Emma clean up." Lilah directed a pointed stare at Camden, Declan's twin sister.

The young woman wore her straight brown hair in a ponytail and no makeup on her pretty face. She dressed more like her brothers in oversize jeans and a long-sleeved T-shirt. But not even the baggy clothes could hide Camden's athletic physique and curves. Camden sighed. "I catch, gut, clean and fillet fish all day, Grandma. Isn't that enough? Let someone else help."

Lilah tsked. "You'll never get a husband thinking like that."

"I'm not in the market for a husband, Grandma. My life is fine the way it is."

"Well, I need more grandkids."

"Talk to Risa and Ellis. They've already got two and all the gear."

"Those children need cousins, not second cousins once removed, to play with. First cousins. Though if the rest of you keep taking your own sweet time, these kids will be old enough to babysit for you."

"Be glad you don't live in Haley's Bay," Camden said to Emma. "Or this grandkid talk is all you'd hear."

"Well, I'm not getting any younger," Lilah countered.

With a smile, Emma moved to a folding card table. The Coles weren't a perfect family, but they were real. In spite of their differences, they loved one another, even Mr. Cole and AJ, if either of them would put their stubbornness aside. The two men sat closer to each other. Progress? Emma hoped so. She picked up more plates and cups.

"I've been toying with a boating app," AJ announced.

"Lots of them on the market," Mr. Cole said.

Ellis nodded. "NOAA put out one with free nautical charts."

Her heart ached for AJ. He so wanted to impress his family, and when his efforts failed, he retreated, distancing himself or in this case, not saying a word. His actions had nothing to do with his family's rejection, but showed AJ's insecurities. The two of them might come from different worlds, but they shared something in common—loneliness. She hated how he'd separated himself from his family.

"What does your app do?" Declan asked.

Emma wanted to kiss the guy for asking. Not really, but AJ needed help from his family to find his way back home.

"Mine has charting and wind features as well as tides, and weather with animated radar," AJ explained. "The app is still in beta mode. It needs more testing."

"Come out with us tomorrow afternoon," Mr. Cole said. "We'll try it out."

Ellis nodded. "We can be your beta testers."

Please say yes. She clutched the garbage bag. They'd planned on going through Lilah's photo albums to scan and print pictures for the florist to use, but Emma could do that herself.

"Sure," AJ said finally. "That would be great."

Emma released the breath she hadn't realized she was holding. This was the first step for AJ to find his place here. She crossed her fingers, hoping he made the most of the opportunity.

AJ searched the backyard, but didn't see Emma. Bailey's cottage didn't offer many hiding spots. He doubted he'd find Emma under any beds. He smiled, eager to tell her about going out with his dad and brothers on the boat tomorrow after lunch. Knowing she'd be happy pleased AJ.

"Looking for Emma?" Declan asked.

"He's always looking for her," Grady teased. "I would be too if I were him."

AJ shook his head. "Have you seen her?"

"She's in the kitchen washing pots and pans," Ellis said. "My wife was delighted. She hates getting roped into KP duty. Says it ruins her manicure and dries out her skin."

"Not Emma." AJ glanced at the back door, wishing he could see her. "She's the definition of low maintenance."

"Ironic since you can afford to give her anything she wants," Ellis said.

"Sometimes that's how you know," AJ said. "Emma wants nothing from me."

Declan's eyes darkened. "She might be after your money. Being humble could be an act."

This was the perfect time to remind himself that Emma was acting the part of his girlfriend. This might be—was—temporary, but something had shifted between them today. AJ wasn't sure what. "She's not."

"And you know this how?" Grady asked. "When I was in Seattle with Grandma you didn't mention a girlfriend. Neither Bailey nor Camden knew and they talk to you almost as much as Grandma and Mom. Now you're bringing this woman home when you haven't been here in ten years."

"Emma is my assistant's best friend. Libby wouldn't steer me wrong." AJ looked at Declan. "Why the concern? You haven't cared what I've done for the past decade."

Declan rocked back on his heels. Ellis looked at the grass. Grady took a sip from his can of soda then glanced up. "Dad."

AJ looked at each of his brothers. "Dad?"

"Yes, me," his father said. "You boys get out of here. I need to talk to AJ alone."

Declan, Ellis and Grady scattered like ants on a picnic blanket, but not before Declan threw AJ a sympathetic glance.

His father sat in one of the camp chairs. "You went by the Candy Cave and saw Natalie."

AJ nodded.

"Did she tell you about her and Craig?"

Another nod. "Said they were separated, and he was seeing someone else. Wanted to know if I'd be interested in getting back together even though Emma was right there."

His dad whistled. "Not surprised by that. I'm assuming she didn't mention being the one who cheated?"

AJ's jaw dropped. "No."

"Saw her myself or I wouldn't have believed it. The guy dumped her as soon as Craig told her to get out. The Steeles are our biggest competitor, but I feel real bad for him. He's trying to get full custody of the two kids. Rough road ahead, but you sure dodged a bullet with that one."

"Yeah." AJ tried to wrap his mind around the fact Nat had wanted a second chance with him after cheating on her husband. But then again, she'd been wearing AJ's engagement ring when she went out with Craig. "I don't think I'll ever understand women."

"I gave up with your mother a couple decades ago," his father said. "Now Emma…"

His father's suspicious tone made AJ stiffen. "What about her?"

"Seems nice, but women have the ability to make us men stupid. Protect yourself, son. Have those fancy lawyers draft up a pre nup before your relationship goes any further."

He stared at his father as if seeing the man for the first time. “A pre nup?”

“Hell, yes,” his dad said. “I didn’t raise any fools though I had my doubts about Grady until recently. You’ve done well for yourself, son. Got a lot to lose. Don’t get married until she signs a pre nup. Promise me.”

His father had asked him for only three things: to stand up for his brothers and sister, to not go across the country for college and to take over the family business instead of moving to Seattle to work in technology. This was the fourth, and like the first, a no-brainer, especially since AJ never planned on marrying. Not Emma or any woman. “Sure. I promise I won’t get married without a pre nup.”

“Good. Very good.” His dad stood. “Looking forward to seeing what that app can do tomorrow.”

“Me, too,” AJ admitted. “And, Dad, thanks for the advice.”

His father nodded once. “Anytime, son. All you need to do is ask.”

Maybe Emma was right. Maybe things could change.

Chapter Ten

Sitting on the swing the next morning, Emma kept her feet firmly planted against the porch to keep from moving. She held on to Blossom's leash, an old dog tether Lilah had in the garage. The cat had pawed at the window through the night, making sleep impossible for Emma. That and her sudden fascination with watching AJ sleep, but there was nothing to be done about that oddity. She hoped being out here at least appeased Blossom, who explored as far as she could, sniffing the air and rubbing against what she could. "Enjoy the outdoor time, but this isn't going to be a habit."

"I can't believe Blossom kept you up all night." AJ leaned against the porch rail, a cup of coffee in hand. He'd seemed more relaxed when they returned from Bailey's house last night. Maybe the thought of going fishing with his dad and brothers this afternoon had put him into a good mood. No matter what the reason, seeing him happy pleased Emma. "I didn't hear a thing."

She sipped from her cup of black tea, needing a jolt of caffeine to get going.

"That's because you were exhausted from staying up the night before. It was my turn." A blue sky with only a few puffs of white stretched to the horizon. Boats, big and small, headed out of the harbor for a day at sea. "Another gorgeous day in Haley's Bay."

"Summer is like this." He looked like the poster child for vacation apparel in his board shorts, a T-shirt and bare feet. "Some rain from storms off the Pacific, but days like today make up for the wet winters."

"Sounds like Portland weather. Late summer and early fall is my favorite."

"September was mine. Sunshine and school."

She drew back. "School?"

"New notebooks and pens and batteries for my drafting calculator."

"You're such a nerd."

"Computer geeks r us."

The angle of the sun's rays gave him a golden halo around his head. Talk about gorgeous. Emma sipped her tea. The warm liquid did nothing to cool her down.

"I couldn't wait for school to start." He bent over and gave Blossom a pat on the head. "Summer vacation was too long for me. Always too much fishing. You'd think my old man would've figured me out back then."

She'd never dreamed of any foster parent figuring her out. She hadn't wanted them to know her that well. Not all were bad, but those were the ones she remembered. "I liked being in school, too."

She received a hot breakfast and lunch at school. Sometimes an afternoon snack if whatever foster parents put her in extended care after school.

Blossom chirped, sounding more birdlike than feline.

She stared through the porch railing at two hummingbirds hovering around a feeder.

"You can look, Blossom, but you'll never get a chance to catch them."

The words didn't deter the cat. She crouched into a hunting position, her gaze never leaving the birds.

"She's ready to attack," AJ said, sounding amused.

Emma tightened her hold on the leash. "I wonder if her owner let her outside. She seems to like it."

"Sunshine, a breeze, birds." He moved to the swing, then sat next to Emma, his bare leg brushing hers. Sparks erupted at the point of contact. "What's not to like?"

She could say the same thing about him, except a little space would be nice so she wasn't the first spontaneous combustion casualty in Haley's Bay. She scooted to the far edge until her hip bumped the armrest. That still didn't give her more than a couple of inches between them.

AJ put his arm on the top of the swing. "Good idea bringing the cat out here. Though I'm enjoying it more than her. A nice place for my morning coffee."

She raised her mug. "And tea."

Blossom looked at Emma and AJ. The cat meowed once, jumped onto the small empty space between them then nudged each with her head.

Emma laughed. "Blossom is jealous."

"Cats don't get jealous. She wants more space."

"She wants you for herself."

AJ gave the cat a pat on the head. "Nice kitty."

The cat crawled onto his lap, circled once, then lay down. He rubbed the cat. Purring commenced, loud like a generator during a power outage. "Not jealous, sleepy."

"Sleepy, yes, but staking her claim." As if on cue, Blossom stretched. "She's made herself at home."

"A totally different cat from the one screeching on the flight here."

Emma could say the same thing about herself. She sipped her tea.

AJ set his cup on the railing next to the swing. "I asked my grandma if she wanted to adopt Blossom, but she thinks she's too old. Doesn't want Blossom to get attached and then grieve when she dies."

"Cats do grieve. Blossom has been through that with the passing of her last owner."

"Sounds more like an excuse. My grandmother likes to travel to see her kids, grandchildren and friends. A cat would mean added responsibility."

"I don't blame Lilah for wanting to have the freedom to do what she wants without having to worry about a pet. I can't have an animal due to my job. Not many clients want a live-in nanny who comes with their own dog or cat."

AJ's gaze narrowed. "I thought you'd want my grandmother to keep her."

"Only if Lilah wants Blossom," Emma explained. "The cat needs to be with someone who wants to adopt her, someone who will love her the way she deserves to be loved, not out of some sense of obligation. That's why I keep saying a forever home. Animals get attached. Change is hard on them."

"I see that, but having my grandmother keep Blossom would have been the easiest solution to my problem."

Emma liked AJ, but sometimes the guy didn't have a clue. "Blossom is not a problem."

"She is until I find her a place to live. Excuse me, a forever home," he corrected. "And no worries. We made a deal. I'm a man of my word, but I might not be able to find Blossom a forever home for her until I get back to Seattle."

"That's okay. I'll take her back to Portland with me.

I'm going to need approval for an out of state adoption anyway." Warmth balled in the center of her chest at the thought of the cat having a family of her own. "I appreciate you keeping your word."

"No need to sound grateful. This was something you wanted. I'm not doing it out of the goodness of my heart." He sounded like a CEO again. "I'm getting something out of this in return."

"I hope having a pretend girlfriend has been worth it."

"Best spur-of-the-moment decision I've ever made."

"You think?"

AJ nodded. "No drama. No need to buy presents. No talk about the future. Might have to try fake dating when I get home."

"Go for it." Her voice was flat, not encouraging, but the idea of AJ with another woman unsettled Emma. She stared into her tea. "Don't forget the big donation to the shelter. Pretending hasn't come without a price."

"A tax deductible donation is better than blowing money on some sparkly bauble I'll see only once or twice."

"You sound so jaded."

"No. Just the reality of my situation." He rubbed his chin. "Something my father reminded me of last night."

"Your dad talked to you? What did he say?"

AJ stared over the edge of his coffee mug. "He wants me to have my lawyers draw up a prenuptial agreement for you to sign."

"You're kidding."

"Nope." AJ half laughed. "He said I'd done well for myself and have a lot to lose."

"You do," she agreed. "Your dad is a smart man. Another way the two of you are alike."

He rubbed Blossom, who rolled over so AJ had better access to her tummy. Emma envied Blossom's proximity to AJ. All night she'd thought about curling around his warm body. Of course once they touched, those thoughts would have turned steamy, but from afar, all she wanted was the closeness.

"Knowing he's concerned must make you happy."

"I never thought he cared," AJ admitted. "I was surprised."

"Your father cares. Your grandmother and mom have told you that. But this is proof from your father. A man who doesn't care about his son would never bring up the need for a pre nup. He'd let you marry a gold digger and let her steal your fortune."

"Gold digger nanny?"

She shrugged. "It works for illustrative purposes."

Blossom's purring stopped. The cat slept soundly.

The silence was soothing, the lack of conversation comfortable.

Emma sipped her tea, staring at the bay. A bird swooped down to catch breakfast. She wondered if one of the boats she'd seen motoring out of the harbor earlier belonged to the Cole family, and if they were having any luck fishing.

"My family believes we're contemplating marriage," AJ said finally. "We're going to have to come up with a breakup scenario I can tell them after we leave."

Emma's heart panged. She didn't want to think about going home to her studio apartment alone. Not when she liked being surrounded by family and dreamed of being surrounded by AJ.

The corners of Emma's eyes stung. She blinked. Once, twice. Okay, that was better. "Don't get ahead of yourself. We have a couple of days left here. Someone might figure out we're not really dating."

"Won't happen. If my dad's talking about a pre nup, we've convinced them."

She giggled. "Hard to believe."

"I know."

"You can tell them we got tired of having a long-distance relationship but I didn't want to move to Seattle and you weren't moving to Portland."

"That'll work unless you move to Seattle."

"I don't know what I'm going to do. But your family would never know if I moved." The thought of never seeing Lilah or any of the Coles again made Emma's hand shake. A good thing the party was on Saturday. Getting attached to people she barely knew was beyond stupid. "But I must admit having a fake boyfriend has been more fun than I thought it would be. I'd forgotten how nice it is to hang out with someone. I'm going to have to get out more, make new friends when I'm back in Portland."

"Are you talking friends or men?"

"Both," she said. "Until now I haven't been…something. Willing? Ready? I don't know. But I want a real boyfriend. Our spending time together has been really nice."

She expected him to smile, but AJ didn't. "How do you usually meet men? Online?"

"No. I'm too…"

"Old-fashioned."

"Yes. I don't date much due to my work and being more of a homebody, but I'd rather meet someone in person or through friends or the rescue shelter." Talking about meeting other men felt weird, somehow wrong. But he'd asked so she wanted to answer. "Though I should figure out if I'm moving to Seattle first. Wouldn't want to meet the man of my dreams and then move away."

AJ stared at the cat. "Long-distance relationships are tough."

He would know after Natalie. "I've never been involved

in one. But don't you go out with women all over the world?"

"Yes, but I only date casually wherever I might be," he explained. "That's different than being in a committed relationship and not seeing each other every day."

"A fake relationship does have some perks, then."

"I like knowing the expectations ahead of time."

"Doesn't that put a damper on the overall romance with no spontaneity, no surprises, no future?"

His gaze locked on hers. "You've surprised me."

"You've surprised me, too." Self-preservation screamed to look away but she couldn't. Fake relationship or not, something connected them, something beyond Libby, the cat, his family and this trip to Haley's Bay.

Emma's pulse rate kicked up a notch. Her body's response to a glance, a touch, his kiss was one of those surprises. And her heart…

His arm slipped from the back of the swing to around her shoulder. "What if we expand our agreement?"

The bass drum *boom-boom-boom* of her heart turned into a snare roll. She opened her mouth to speak, but no words would come. Her tongue felt too big.

"I want to kiss you," AJ continued.

She looked around. "No one's here to see."

"Exactly."

The implication of his words bounced through her like a basketball. "We're just pretending."

"I know that's the deal. I also know I said I wouldn't touch you when we're alone. But I want to. Badly. That's why I'm asking. There's chemistry between us."

So he felt it, too. The realization didn't make her feel any better. "That doesn't mean we have to experiment. Some chemical reactions are highly combustible. Others don't react at all."

"Aren't you curious which we'll be?"

Emma was, and that scared her. She had a feeling there would be an explosion of epic proportions. AJ Cole wasn't like other men she'd known. Thoughts of him filled her mind and dreams. At times he left her feeling warm and fuzzy inside, but then he'd put her on edge and make her want to scream with frustration. His kisses frightened her most of all because in his arms she found a sense of belonging, a place that felt like home, somewhere she might want to stay. Forever.

But she knew better. There wasn't such a thing as forever. Nothing lasted. Not home. Not family. Not love.

Warning bells rang in her head. She wet her dry lips. "Curiosity can have serious consequences."

"One kiss without an audience, just you and me."

"And Blossom."

"She's asleep. No one will know. Not even the cat. It's only one kiss."

Emma hesitated, torn between following common sense and giving into desire. "One kiss saved Sleeping Beauty and Snow White, changed their entire lives."

"You into fairy tales?"

"Not at all, just…"

"Using them for illustrative purposes," he finished for her.

She nodded.

"We're past the first-kiss life-changing stage."

Emma wasn't so sure about that. AJ's first kiss had changed the way she thought about him, and each kiss since then. Since meeting him, a part of Emma wanted to believe happy endings were possible. Silly. She should know better.

"You're also awake, not under a spell," he added. "No magic in your nanny bag, remember?"

True, except being with AJ felt magical at times. A kiss, not a practice one or a pretend one but a for-real one, would let her know…

Emma wasn't sure what, but she might figure out something important. She wanted a kiss without anyone watching, without any reason or motivation for either of them, mainly him, to *perform.*

One kiss. What did she have to lose?

Taking the initiative, she leaned forward and kissed him. Man, he tasted good. Warm like sun shining down on them, with a hint of coffee—French roast. Yummy

He pressed his mouth against hers, deepening the kiss. His arm came around her shoulders. She pressed against him, arms circling him, wanting to get closer, wanting more.

One kiss. Oh, boy, this was so much more than a kiss. His lips breathed life into her heart. His touch made her feel desired.

Real, pretend, she couldn't tell the difference. The lines had completely blurred, and she didn't mind one bit. She could get used to this.

He moaned. Or maybe the sound came from her. Emma wasn't sure what was happening. She had never felt this away before and didn't want the feeling to stop.

His kiss ignited a fire low in her belly and heat spread through her. Hunger and need took over. She ran her fingers through his thick hair. Wanting to get to the place where it was only the two of them, and nothing else mattered.

"Mmmeorrrrrooooowwwrrrrreeee."

Emma jerked back. Her butt hit the porch with a loud thud. "I guess it doesn't get more real than this."

Blossom sat on AJ's lap as if nothing had happened. He looked stunned. "Let me help you."

Emma took the offered hand and stood. "Told you she was jealous."

"Her tail got caught between us. She didn't like that."

"For someone who claims not to like cats, you sure do stick up for her."

"Why do you assume the worst when you like her?"

"I…" Emma wasn't about to tell him he was wrong, except the sinking feeling in her stomach told her that he was right. "Maybe because I love cats and you hate them, but Blossom likes you better. Not quite fair, is it?"

"She likes you, too. You're the one she uses for a pillow at night."

"I'm softer."

"You also smell better, but stop trying to change the subject. Let's talk about the kiss." He stared at her, desire clouding his eyes, his breathing uneven. "I'd call it highly reactive."

An experiment she wanted to repeat. "I'd concur with that finding."

"We need more data points to explore this further."

Anticipation hummed through her. More kisses sounded great to her. But real kisses, any kisses, would complicate an already-convoluted situation. "We can't. I work for you. Exploring any more would be—"

"Inappropriate."

Dangerous, but she'd go with his reason. "Yes."

"But that kiss—"

"Was amazing." She wasn't going to deny the truth. "But we were never meant to be involved in a real relationship."

"Relationships are too complicated."

O-kay. She was missing something here. Not surprising given her lack of experience. Time to figure out what he meant by exploring this further. They might be talking about two different things. "What are you suggesting?"

"A fling."

"You want us to have a *fling?*" The word tasted like sand in her mouth.

"Yes. Stop working for me. Let's have fun together."

"Here? At your grandmother's house?"

"This is the perfect place given the time we have left here, and we have my grandmother's permission."

Emma's stomach churned. AJ didn't want her. He wanted to have sex with her. Why should she be surprised? He was not only attractive, but a billionaire who dated casually. To him, asking the pretend girlfriend sharing his bed to be his real-life lover during vacation would make total sense.

But to assume she'd be game… He didn't know her at all. The realization both hurt and angered her. Emma's blood pressure spiraled. "Thanks, I'm flattered, but no."

"No?"

His amazement in that one word made her bite back a smile. Having so much money must mean people never said no to AJ. Well, if that were the case, this would be good for him because he was going to hear the word again from her. "No."

He started to say something, then stopped himself. "Care to give me more than a two-letter answer?"

"Sure." Emma didn't want to aggravate him but she could give an hour-long speech as to why a fling would be a bad idea. "Playing make-believe is fine, but a fling is a good way to get hurt if real feelings become involved."

"I'm not looking for something serious."

Emma had never been seriously involved. But that was only because she hadn't met the right man. Okay, up until this point she hadn't wanted to meet the right guy, but after getting to know AJ, what she wanted was becoming clearer. "You're not looking for a committed relationship?"

"That's the last thing I want," AJ answered honestly. "I'm not sure I will ever have interest in that kind of relationship."

"You don't plan on getting married someday."

"No."

Relief pushed aside any disappointment. Her affection for AJ was growing and yes, he tempted her, but they wanted different things from relationships and life. Getting romantically involved with him would be a mistake. "Marriage is something I want. Having a fling would be a bad idea. I don't think I'd be able to keep my feelings casual, and even if I wasn't seriously involved I might miss meeting the man I'm supposed to marry. Trust me, my saying no is the best thing for both of us."

No. AJ stood at the harbor, waiting for the boat. Emma's rejection stung. She'd been firm, but nice. Still he rubbed his chin as if he'd been hit with a left jab.

No was a word AJ heard in business negotiations, from the board of directors, from this family. *No* was Natalie's answer when he begged her to wait until he returned to Haley's Bay after his freshman year before marrying Craig Steele. *No* was AJ's answer to women who wanted to get serious.

Emma's *no* meant she didn't want to get started with him. Her unwillingness to have a fling intrigued AJ. The way she kissed back told him she was interested.

So what was wrong with her? Didn't she know what he could offer her? Emma needed some fun in her life. She didn't have to take everything seriously, including romance. He wanted her to be happy. He wanted her to see that she was an amazing woman who deserved to have someone take care of her in return.

AJ could do all those things if she said yes. She wouldn't regret a thing. He had no doubt she would be thanking him when they were finished. All he needed to do was convince Emma to go from his bed buddy to vacation lover, but how?

Challenges revved his brain and kept his adrenaline high. This would be one of the best because of the reward he'd receive at the end. He had two days to change her mind.

AJ smiled, forming a plan of attack. Definitely achievable.

A horn blasted. Declan waved from the stern. Their father stood behind the wheel driving the boat to the dock. Memories of being picked up like this when AJ was a kid rushed back. Weekends and summer days spent out on the water. His dad had taught him and Ellis, then they taught Flynn, Declan, Camden and Grady. Bailey got too seasick to go out on the boat. Plus her wanting to wear skirts and dresses annoyed their father. Maybe AJ wasn't the only outsider.

"Climb aboard," his father yelled over the engine. "We're wasting time."

AJ jumped on board. He looked around. "Where are Ellis and Camden?"

"Out with tourists."

A few minutes later, his dad steered the boat through the mouth of the harbor. AJ enjoyed the ride. He hadn't been on the water like this in over ten years. He lifted his chin, letting the wind whip through his hair and over his skin. Spray shot up, wetting his sunglasses.

Declan adjusted his baseball cap. "Remember your way around?"

"Yeah." AJ wiped the saltwater from his sunglasses. "Don't forget who taught you everything you know."

"You mean Dad."

Declan's lopsided grin told AJ that his brother was kidding. "Hey, I might not have been the best fisherman in this family but I was one helluva teacher."

The engine cut off. His father climbed down from the helm.

"That's why you'd be great working with the tourists who don't know one end of a rod from the other and think every single fish they catch is a salmon." His dad stood next to him. "I sure as hell don't have the patience."

"Me, either," Declan admitted.

"So where's this app of yours?" Dad asked.

"On my phone." AJ pulled his smartphone out of his pocket. He wasn't exactly nervous, but he felt a strange sense of uncertainty, a way he hadn't felt since talking to his first venture capitalist. "I'll send you the app to load onto your phone tonight. I want your opinions, what works, what doesn't, any improvements you would make."

"Will it work on my tablet?" Dad asked.

Things really had changed around here if Jack Cole used a tablet. "Yes. It will."

Declan leaned against the bridge. "So show us what this thing can do."

With a deep breath, AJ handed his phone to his brother. "Here you go."

Chapter Eleven

That afternoon, Emma removed another photo from the scanner/printer she'd set up in the guest bedroom while AJ worked on his laptop. So far, Lilah was none the wiser to what was going on and thought Emma and AJ were making the most of their afternoon together.

She was. Just not in the way Lilah thought.

Emma enjoyed pouring through the Cole family photo albums filled with decades of snapshots, looking for ones to use for the birthday party decorations. The images and the time spent with AJ's family helped her clarify what she wanted in life. Something she never imagined happening during a temporary job as a personal assistant. A sigh welled inside Emma. If only she had someone to love her how she wanted to be loved… Someday she would.

She returned the photograph to the album and removed another picture. The candid with Lilah and one of her great grandchildren illustrated the passage of time. Emma remembered seeing a similar shot of Lilah holding the baby's father, Ellis.

Emma scanned the photograph. "So your dad and Declan liked the app?"

AJ glanced up from his computer. "They thought the app needed fine-tuning. My dad gave me a couple great ideas that I'm trying to incorporate. Declan, too. I can't wait for Ellis and Camden to try it tomorrow."

The excitement in AJ's eyes matched the smile on his face. Today had been a good day for him. Talking about his dad didn't seem to change AJ's mood, either. Emma couldn't be more pleased. He'd come so far in such a short time. She wiggled her toes. "I'm so happy things went well out there."

"Yeah, me, too. It went way better than I expected." He shook his head. "Except my dad still wants me back in Haley's Bay permanently."

"Of course he does. You're the oldest. His plans and dreams for you are still alive in his head and heart."

AJ nodded, and for the first time, didn't look upset over his father's expectations. Definite progress. "My dad asked if I'd go fishing in the morning. Said we'd dock by noon so there'd be plenty of time to get ready for the party."

"Better not stay up too late tonight. Sounds like it'll be an early morning."

"No."

"What do you mean *no?*"

"I told my dad I was on vacation and wanted to spend the day with my girlfriend preparing for Grandma's party."

Emma placed her hands on her hips, though sitting downplayed her annoyance. "Haven't you learned anything?"

AJ grinned wryly. "Is this when you take away my electronics before going all Supernanny and Nanny McPhee on me?"

"How could you say no to your father?"

"I never liked fishing much."

"That's not the point. Spending time with your family is.

"I can show up if I want, but I'd rather help you."

"I've got everything under control."

"You could use an extra hand. I've got two."

"If you change your mind—"

"I'm too stubborn for that to happen."

"Guess I deserve that." Emma pulled the sheet from the printer and added the picture to the manila folder containing all the printouts. "This is the last one."

AJ placed his laptop on the bed, then picked up the folder. He thumbed through the pictures she'd spent the day gathering and printing. "These are great. Grandma is going to cry when she sees these."

The photographs covered almost all of the past eighty years of Lilah's life. Emma had taken the most recent shots last night at Bailey's house. "Happy tears I hope."

"Tears of joy." He hugged Emma. "Thank you. These pictures are going to make her birthday party more special."

"You're welcome." She loved being in his arms, but was careful not to look at his face, especially not his lips. She didn't want him to think she'd changed her mind about wanting a fling. She hadn't, even if she couldn't stop thinking about him that way. "I enjoyed seeing the Cole family over the years. Grady was a cute kid."

AJ drew back. "Grady?"

"You were cute yourself." She stepped out of his embrace. "Can you please take the folder and flash drive to Charlie? He's waiting to drive these to the florist. She's working on the decorations tonight so they'll be ready tomorrow."

"Sure, but what about the photo albums?"

"Your grandmother's at the beauty salon with Bailey, Risa and Madison. Lilah will never know I borrowed them if I can get them back in the study before she returns."

"I'll run the stuff out to Charlie, then help you. We'll be done in no time." AJ slipped on his shoes. "Maybe we can take a walk before meeting my family at the pizza parlor."

"Sounds good." Lilah organized the albums by year, the way she'd found them. "We make a good team."

He stopped by the door. "We would make a better one if you'd say yes."

"Yes?" she asked, though she knew what he meant.

"To some horizontal experimentation with skin-to-skin contact. Should I go on?"

"Please don't."

"It's for your own good."

"Oh, really?"

"Yes. You work too hard. It's time to up the play factor in your life."

"That's what you're going with?"

"Damn straight." Laughter gleamed in his eyes. "Come on, doesn't some hot sex with a billionaire sound like fun?"

His flirty tone made her laugh. She had to give him points for not giving up. She appreciated how he wasn't pushing her, but keeping things light and playful between them. "My job is to look out for you. I like working for you, I don't want to quit, and don't you dare fire me. We work well as a team without the hot sex, in case you haven't noticed. That's why the answer was no, is still no and will always be no."

He feigned being shot in the chest. "Rejected once again."

"Stop asking and I'll stop shooting you down."

"Where's the fun in that?"

"I had a feeling that's what you would say."

"Of course you did," he teased. "Next time I need a pretend girlfriend I'll make sure she's not so old-fashioned."

"I'm sure there are millions of women who would be more accommodating than me when it comes to having a fling with a handsome billionaire."

"So you think I'm handsome?"

Darn, she hadn't meant for that to slip out. Too bad he didn't want to date, instead of having a fling, but Emma wouldn't go out with him, either. She liked him too much already. Opening her heart when she would be saying goodbye to AJ on Sunday would not be smart. "What can I say? You are easy on the eyes."

"Hold that thought. I'll be right back after I give these to Charlie." AJ left the room with the file in hand.

Emma carried the photo albums to the study and placed them back in the bookcase. This idea of hers had worked out well. She had another, too. She would load every picture she'd scanned today for the party decorations and slide show onto a digital frame for AJ to give to his grandmother as a birthday present. Emma would give AJ a copy of the JPEG files to store in case anything ever happened to the frame or the house. Having a backup was important. She wished her parents had put photo negatives into a safe deposit box somewhere.

The song from Disney's *Beauty and the Beast* sounded on Emma's cell phone. The ringtone was from the Lundberg twins' favorite movie. Her breath caught in her throat. Every nerve ending stood at attention as if a five-star general was walking past and needed to be saluted. Trey.

Why would Abbie and Annie's dad be calling? Emma hadn't talked to him in three months, not since she'd quit and moved out. She didn't want to look back. Looking forward to being home alone didn't hold much appeal, either. She wanted to make the most of the present here in Haley's Bay. She had only two more days.

The song continued to play. She slowly pulled out the phone from her back pocket. If she took her time, maybe Trey would hang up. He had no reason to be calling her… unless something was wrong with Abbie or Annie.

Adrenaline shot through Emma. She grabbed her phone, then hit Answer. "Hello?"

"It's Trey." His voice sounded rough, on edge, the way he'd sounded after a solo visit to his late wife's grave. After that, Emma had made sure she and the girls accompanied him. "Abbie was hit by a car."

Not sweet Abbie with her pigtails and toothless grin. Emma tightened her grip on her phone. "How badly is she hurt?"

"She had surgery yesterday. They moved her from ICU today. She's listed in serious condition."

Emma collapsed against the nearest wall in the study, sinking to the hardwood floor. An elephant rested on her chest. The weight pressed down on her breastbone, as if it were real, not imaginary. She wasn't sure what hurt more, breathing or her heart. But nothing she felt compared to Abbie's injuries and Trey's worry. "Oh, no. I'm so sorry. Does the upgrade mean she's stable?"

Let her be okay, Emma prayed.

"Yes, she's better," Trey said. "But seeing her unconscious yesterday… I'm sorry for not calling earlier, but Abbie was in ICU. Only immediate family is allowed."

Emma wasn't family. She was the former nanny. Of course she wouldn't be allowed in. "I understand. How's Annie doing?"

"Scared."

"That's understandable." Emma shivered, a chill overcoming her. "I'm sure you're all worried right now."

Arms encircled her, drew her close into a cocoon of welcoming, comforting warmth. AJ. She didn't know where he'd come from, but she was thankful he was here.

She leaned against him, wanting to soak up his strength. He might be her pretend boyfriend and wannabe lover, but she considered him a friend. And she needed one desperately at the moment. Emma had gone through so much alone. She didn't want to do that right now. Or ever again. "Where are you?"

"The children's hospital."

"I've been to their ER. Stitches for little Max. An ear infection for Samuel. An MRI for Brooklyn. They're the best when it comes to kids."

"That's what I've been told." Trey's voice cracked. "Keely is here. She's helping me with Annie."

Keely was the new nanny Emma had found. "That's great."

"Yeah, but ever since Abbie woke up from the surgery she's been asking for you. Annie, too. The girls wanted me to call and see if you could come by today."

"Of course, I'd be happy to come to the hospital. I promised the girls I'd be there if they needed me." If the girls needed Emma, she had to go. She wanted to see Abbie and reassure Annie. Emma calculated the drive time back to Portland. Then realized she didn't have her car and also was obligated to AJ. She glanced at him. "At least I'll try to get there. I'm not in Portland."

"Go," AJ whispered. "It's not a problem."

Affection for the man next to her made her wish things could be different between them. She mouthed a thank-you, then returned to her phone conversation. "I'm in

Washington, across the river from Astoria, so it'll take me a little time to figure out a way there."

"As long as you'll come," Trey said. "It'll mean so much to the girls. And to me. The thought of losing Abbie..."

The pain in his voice stabbed her heart. A lump clogged her throat. She knew loss, that kind of paralyzing hurt and grief. Emma laced her fingers with AJ's, thankful he was here with her. She cleared her throat. "You're not going to lose Abbie. You said she's better. Stable. The girls need you to be strong, Trey."

"I know, but being here reminds me of Elizabeth."

Trey's wife, Elizabeth, had died of ovarian cancer. She'd been a stay-at-home mom who doted on her girls and her husband. Trey had never done more than give the twins an occasional bath, grill meat or wash a load of laundry until his wife had gotten sick. But Emma couldn't be Trey's support system again. That was likely the reason he'd fallen for her. "Focus on the girls. That's what Elizabeth would want you to do."

"I'm trying." He sounded so lost, like a rudderless boat adrift on the bay and heading toward the open water. "I don't know what I would do without Keely."

"I'm glad she's there to help you."

AJ squeezed Emma's hand, sending tingles shooting up her arm. She relished the feeling for a nanosecond, then refocused on the phone call. She liked Trey, appreciated what a good single father he was to his girls and how generous he'd been as an employer. He was handsome, but he'd never sent her blood boiling through her veins or made her want to give up her last breath for one more kiss like AJ.

But she realized with a start, the situation with the two men was similar. Both claimed they wanted her, but Trey wanted a fill-in wife and mother and AJ wanted a pretend girlfriend and vacation fling. Neither wanted her.

Not the way she wanted to be wanted. One man wanted her to complete his family. The other wanted her to be a willing casual sex partner. She didn't want to be either. She deserved...more. But until this moment hadn't known that. "Tell the girls I'll be there as soon as I can."

After a quick goodbye, she disconnected from the call.

"What's going on?" AJ asked, still holding on to her.

"One of the twins I used to nanny for was hit by a car. That was her father. She's in the hospital, doing better, but I promised the girls if they ever needed me I'd be there. I need to go. I'm sorry."

"Don't apologize. The jet will be the fastest way to Portland."

The room spun even though she was sitting. Emma leaned forward to keep from getting dizzy. "Th-thanks. That would be the quickest."

AJ used his finger to raise her chin. "You're pale and look scared to death."

She took a steadying breath. "I need to get to Portland. I'll be fine."

He didn't look convinced.

"Really." She tried to sound strong and in control. "I can fly for Abbie."

AJ's mouth twisted. "I doubt you've overcome your fear of flying since we arrived."

"I just don't like takeoffs," Emma clarified.

"Why not?"

The girls needed her. She scooted away from him. "There isn't time."

He pulled out his phone and sent a text. "There is time. The flight crew needs to be notified, a flight plan filed and the jet prepared for departure."

She'd forgotten flying had rules and regulations unlike driving a car. She wrung her hands.

"So why don't you like takeoffs?" he asked.

How hard could telling AJ be? They'd shared so much these past few days, moments beyond hot kisses and meaningful glances. She enjoyed being with him. Except her tight muscles and roiling stomach didn't seem to realize that.

"It's…" Her lips clamped together, as if tightened with a vise. She couldn't talk, not even if she wanted to tell him what had happened.

"Please, Emma." The concern in AJ's voice tugged at her heart. "Tell me."

She hadn't talked about what happened to her family since she'd stopped going to appointments with counselors and doctors. None of them understood what she'd experienced. No amount of talking or medicine would change the past. Her family and home were gone. Forever.

"Let me help you," he said.

AJ had protected Libby during the conference call on the jet. He'd made a large donation to the rescue shelter at Emma's request. His love for his grandmother and his family was clear, even if he wouldn't admit it.

Forget his Attila nickname. He wasn't a ruthless billionaire. The AJ she'd gotten to know was a thoughtful, generous, caring man. He wouldn't be able to help her beyond the use of his jet, but telling him why takeoffs affected her so badly was the least she could do to thank him for his getting her to Portland quickly.

"Libby told you I was in the foster system when I came to live with her and her parents, right?"

He nodded. "But she never told me what happened to get you there."

Emma inhaled deeply and blew the air out from her mouth. She did so again, mustering her courage and her strength. She could do this. With AJ at her side, she could do anything.

But she stared at the double-knotted laces on her tennis shoes, not wanting to see the familiar pity when people discovered she had no family. "When I was ten, my house caught fire. My bedroom was on the second floor. I remember being woken up by my brother, Michael. He was fourteen. I smelled smoke. Lots and lots of smoke. I could hardly see."

Emma rubbed her nose as if she could smell the scent now. "Mikey was a wrestler. Not that tall, but built solid and strong. He dragged me out of bed, pushed out the screen from the window, lifted me up to the sill and told me to jump."

"From the second story?" AJ asked.

"Mikey said there was no other way out of the house." Her hands trembled. She'd been terrified, clutching on to her brother's T-shirt with two hands, waiting for their father to come bursting into the room and save them. But he never came. It had been just her and Mikey. "I clung to my brother. Cried. He said he'd be right behind me. But I couldn't jump. Then he…he threw me out the window."

AJ sucked in a breath, gathered her closer. "Oh, Em…"

"As I fell, I heard screams. Awful, horrible screams." I wasn't sure if it was me or Mikey or my parents." She fought the urge to cover her ears. She knew the sound was in her memory and not real. "A loud boom sounded. An explosion. I expected Mikey to come to me, but he wasn't in the front yard. He wasn't anywhere. I looked back at the house to see it had collapsed. My brother, my mom and my dad were trapped inside. I never saw them again."

AJ held her, rubbed her arms, kissed her hair. "I'm so sorry."

"Me, too." She closed her eyes, thinking about her family, then opened them. "I don't remember what happened after that. I woke up in a hospital, but I've never forgotten that falling sensation. That's why I don't like to fly or go high on swings or ride roller coasters. I freak out and get sick."

"Understandable."

"After I recovered, I was put into the foster care system because there were no relatives to take custody of me. My parents had never written a will and appointed a guardian. I bounced around with different families for five years until Libby's parents became my foster parents the summer before my sophomore year of high school."

He caressed her cheek. "I noticed your smoke detector on the dresser, but had no idea."

The tenderness in his gaze made breathing difficult. "It's not typical dinner conversation. I've never told Libby everything. No one knows but you."

He brushed his lips across Emma's forehead. The gentle gesture warmed her cold insides. "Thank you for telling me. You've overcome a lot. You impress the hell out of me."

Emotion clogged her throat. She swallowed.

His gaze on hers, he looked like he wanted to kiss her. Her heart skipped a beat, maybe two. She could use a kiss. Desperately. Emma moistened her lips. Waited. Hoped.

AJ lowered his arm from around her. "Grab your purse and whatever else you need."

No kiss. Disappointment ricocheted through her. He hadn't wanted to kiss her, even though she'd wanted… No. She didn't want anything from him. Well, beyond a fast way to Portland.

He raised his cell phone. "With the birthday party tomorrow, I'm calling in the reserves to help."

"The reserves?"

"My brothers and sisters."

"But the party is my job."

"We're a team, remember? And in case you forgot, as I had until you reminded me, I'm part of a very large extended family. And so are you. It'll be fine."

Emma hoped so because all she wanted besides seeing the twins was to be a part of AJ's family. She tucked her hair behind her ears. "Thank you."

The limousine sped through town, a hair above the speed limit, but not enough to warrant a ticket from the officer on patrol, Grady, who waved as they passed. AJ had no doubt Charlie would get them to the airport in safe but record time.

In the back of the limo, AJ kept his arm around Emma. Her muscles remained tense beneath his palm. The tight lines on her face hadn't relaxed. She worried him. Hell, everything about this situation did from the injured child to Emma's tragic past. He patted her shoulder. "We'll be there soon."

"I'm sorry to leave you. I don't know if I'll be back tonight, but I'll try to return before lunch tomorrow."

Did she really think he would let her go alone? The thought boggled his mind. "I'm going with you."

Her lips parted. "But the party—"

"Is under control. Thanks to you."

Questions filled her gaze. Ones he wasn't sure he could answer if she asked. But the more he learned about her, the more he admired her. The more he wanted… "I want to help you."

And he would. Any way he could.

Her lips curved upward into a soft smile. "This is your vacation. Your first time home in ten years."

Her giving heart meant she thought of others before

herself. Whether that was the children she cared for or a person like him she'd met only a couple days ago. But someone needed to put Emma's needs first for once. He could do that. "My family understands."

"They think I'm your girlfriend."

"You are."

"Not really. Once we leave Haley's Bay..."

He brushed his lips across hers, fighting the urge to kiss her more deeply.

But she didn't need that now. "Don't think about that now. Lean on me. I'm right here. You're not going anywhere without me."

She rested her head against him.

The limousine turned into the airport and parked. Charlie hopped out of the car, then opened the passenger door. AJ followed Emma out of the car. Lights illuminated the tarmac outside the hangar.

She looked around, her eyes panicked. "Where's the jet?"

"No jet." He pointed to the waiting helicopter. "We're taking that instead."

"A helicopter?"

"It's not the same as flying in a plane. The momentum is different on take-off, more lift than propulsion. Might be easier for you. More distractions."

"This has gotta be costing you a lot of—"

"I've been thinking about getting a helicopter for a while."

"You bought this helicopter today?"

He nodded once.

Her eyes gleamed with gratitude. "Thanks."

"Just trying to help."

He'd spend as much money as it took to keep her from relieving a nightmare. "Let's go. The pilot is waiting."

She took a step toward the helicopter then stopped. Her body stiffened. “What if I get sick?”

“The pilot knows about your takeoff issues. He said we’re good no matter what happens.”

The look in her eyes made AJ feel like a superhero. “You think of everything.”

“Not always.” Except with Emma, AJ didn’t want to forget anything. He wanted to do things for her himself, be in charge of all the details. “But this was easy.”

He hoped the flight would be as easy for her. Buckled inside the helicopter with headphones on, AJ held Emma’s hand. The rotor spun. Blood drained from her face, leaving her skin ashen. Her free hand balled into a fist, knuckles white.

He understood Emma’s fear.

But if she didn’t relax she would make herself sick again.

Emma needed a distraction. He knew what might work. All he needed to do was wait for the right moment.

The pilot made his final checks. Almost time for liftoff. This was it. AJ lowered his mouth to Emma’s. So what if no one was around who needed to see them acting like boyfriend and girlfriend?

His lips pressed against hers.

So soft. And all his.

Yeah, kissing was the perfect distraction.

He wouldn’t mind being distracted like this for the rest of today. Tomorrow. Every day.

Self-preservation screamed to stop kissing her. But he couldn’t.

For Emma’s sake.

Liar. He wanted to kiss her. For him.

He paused. They were airborne. “Good?”

She looked around. A grin spread across her face. "Really good."

"Let's not slack off now. There could be turbulence or a cloud..." AJ brushed against her mouth and nipped her lips open.

He might not get her into bed, but that didn't matter. Having sex with Emma wasn't the reason that he helped her get to the hospital. He was her friend. No ulterior motives involved.

What was happening to him? Emma had gotten under his skin. Even that damn cat was growing on him. Letting them go was going to be harsh, and unwelcome.

The realization made him deepen the kiss. He would give all he could and take what he could get. For now.

At the hospital, Emma skirted past AJ, who held open the door to Abbie's room. A cartoon played on the television, one of the girls' favorites. Trey stood next to the bed. Keely, the new nanny, sat on a recliner with Annie on her lap. Abbie looked so tiny in the hospital bed, tubes and wires connected to her bruised and broken body. Bandages covered her face. Gauze wrapped around her head. A cast was on her left arm.

Emma's heart tightened. Goose bumps covered her cold skin. She fought the urge to rub her hands over her arms and forced a smile instead. "Hello, everyone."

Annie jumped up from the chair, ran and threw herself against Emma. "You're here. I knew you would come. Abbie, I told you she would come."

Emma hugged the little girl. Sticky fingers touched her skin. "It's awesome to see you, Annie. You've gotten taller."

"I've missed you so much. Abbie has, too."

"Well, I'm here now."

"Yay." Annie wouldn't let her go. "Just like you promised."

"It's important to keep your word."

"I remember."

Emma let go of Annie, then kissed the girl's forehead. "Of course you do. You're a very smart girl."

Annie led Emma by the hand across the room to the hospital bed. "Abbie's going to be fine. Right, Daddy?"

"That's right, pumpkin."

Trey looked as if he'd aged ten years since Emma had seen him last. His usually coiffed hair was disheveled, as if the strands hadn't seen a comb in days. Whiskers covered his normally clean-shaven face. But the worry clouding his gaze and the deep lines at the corners and around his mouth surprised her the most. He looked wary, exhausted, ten years older.

"Hey, sweet princess." Emma touched the injured girl's left pinkie, one of the few places that didn't have any bruises or cuts. "It's so good to see you."

Abbie's dry lips formed an *O,* then curved upward. "Emma."

A lump burned in her throat. "I'm here, baby."

"Annie said you'd come." Abbie's voice sounded hoarse and weak. "All I had to do was ask."

Emma's chest tightened. She picked up the water cup and stuck the straw in Abbie's mouth. The girl sipped. "I'm sorry you're hurting."

The straw fell from her lips. "Better me than Annie."

Tears stung Emma's eyes. "You're such a good sister."

"Like you taught me to be." Abbie moved her hand to hold Emma's.

Trey gasped. "She moved her hand."

Keely touched his arm, a gesture of comfort and sympathy. He wrapped his arm around her and pulled her close so her head rested against his shoulder. The two looked more like a couple than an employer and employee, but their relationship was none of Emma's business. She was here for the girls, nothing else.

"I need to get the doctor," Trey said, then walked out of the room.

Emma focused on Abbie. "Are you as tall as Annie now?"

"Taller."

AJ stood next to the bed. "So this is Abbie."

Abbie's eyes widened. Her dry lips parted. "It's Prince Eric from *The Little Mermaid*."

"I'm AJ," he said. "Emma's friend."

"It's Prince Eric," Abbie said again.

Annie studied AJ with a discriminating eye. "My sister's right. You look like Prince Eric."

From the expression on AJ's face, he didn't have a clue who they meant. Emma took the opportunity to study him. "You know…the girls are right. Well, if you transformed yourself into a cartoon character."

"Who is Prince Eric?" AJ asked, sounding confused.

Annie giggled. "Emma's favorite prince."

"My favorite from the Disney princess movies," Emma clarified.

Trey returned. "The doctor will be right here. This is the most alert Abbie's been. Thank you so much for coming, Emma. You brought a friend?"

"Oh, my goodness." Emma let go of Annie. "Where are my manners? I totally forgot to introduce all of you."

"You were concerned about the girls," AJ said.

Trey extended his arm. "Trey Lundberg."

The two men shook hands. "AJ Cole."

"That name sounds familiar." Trey's mouth quirked. "The tech mogul. The one your friend works for."

"Emma works for me, too," AJ said.

"I'm filling in for Libby." Emma didn't want to get into too many details. This wasn't the time with Annie plastered against her side and Abbie holding her hand.

"You've met Abbie. This pretty princess is Annie." Emma motioned to the nanny. "That's Keely."

"Nice to meet you, AJ." Keely stared at Emma. "Your coming so quickly means the world to the girls and us."

Us. Definitely a couple, especially if the sparkling diamond engagement ring on Keely's hand was from Trey. Emma had to admit the two looked good together.

Trey cleared his throat. "The doctor will be here shortly. Could you take Annie to the cafeteria for a few minutes?"

"Yes," Emma said. "We'll have a snack."

"Ice cream." Annie shimmied her shoulders. "I want ice cream. Emma loves ice cream."

"I didn't know that," AJ said.

Annie nodded. "Rocky road is Em's favorite."

Emma pushed a strand of hair off Abbie's face. "It's true. But do you know my second-favorite flavor?"

"Butter pecan," Trey answered, to her surprise.

"How did you know that?" she asked.

"There was always a pint of that and one of rocky road in the freezer. The girls only eat chocolate or cookie dough."

Annie tugged on Emma's arm. "Can we get ice cream now? Please?"

Emma leaned over the bed to whisper into Abbie's ear. "We'll be back in a few minutes. As soon as you feel better, I'll take you for ice cream. Okay?"

Abbie gave a half nod.

Emma held Annie's hand as they exited the room. The little girl looked up at AJ. "What's your favorite ice cream, Mr. Prince Eric?"

"Rocky road," he said.

"Just like Emma."

His gaze met hers, a tender glance full of affection. "We have lots in common."

Emma's pulse quickened. "Do you like butter pecan, too?"

"No, but I don't mind black walnut."

Annie beamed. "You both like nuts. I like peanuts."

"What about hot fudge?" AJ asked.

The girl nodded, her ponytails bouncing furiously.

"Emma likes chocolate, too." AJ winked. "I saw her having seconds of my grandmother's brownies."

"I only had two."

He laughed. "You could have had more."

Emma wished she could have him.

Wait. What was she thinking? She wasn't. That was the problem. Her worry about Abbie was no excuse. Kissing most of the helicopter ride had addled Emma's brains. She needed to be more careful around AJ. Much more careful.

"I'm hungry," Annie said.

Emma realized she'd mentally drifted away for a moment. Something she had a habit of doing when AJ was around. She looked at the little girl and fought the urge to sniff the strawberry shampoo scent in Annie's hair. But Emma couldn't get too close. She was no longer their nanny. "Let's find you some ice cream."

Chapter Twelve

In the hospital gift shop, AJ bought stuffed animals for both girls and a bouquet of flowers with Get Well balloons for Abbie. He returned to the room to find Trey and Emma gone. AJ gave the presents to the girls, earning him smiles, thank-yous and a hug from a bear.

Annie curtsied, cuddling her stuffed bear like a baby. "Thank you, Mr. Prince Eric."

"You're welcome." He bowed. "Fine princess."

Abbie's frog sat next to her on the pillow while a nurse checked her vitals. The girl stared at the flowers with a smile on her bruised face. AJ would make sure fresh flowers and balloons were delivered every day during Abbie's recovery.

"You didn't finish telling me about the ice cream," Keely said to Annie.

"We had two scoops of ice cream." The girl bounced from foot to foot, making AJ wonder if she needed to use the bathroom, but Keely didn't seem alarmed. "Two big scoops."

"Did you eat all the ice cream?" Keely asked.

"Every last bit. I had chocolate with whipped cream and a cherry. Emma and AJ both had rocky road. That's their favorite. But they didn't want whipped cream or a cherry. I don't know why they wouldn't want a cherry. That's the best part."

Keely toyed with Annie's pigtail. "Did the ice cream taste good?"

"Oh, yes. The best."

"Sounds like special ice cream."

"It was." Annie lowered her voice. "Especially since Mr. Prince Eric bought me a soda to drink."

"Wow." Keely touched the little girl's shoulder, reminding him of Risa interacting with her two kids. Emma had been attentive, but not as warm and fuzzy with Annie downstairs in the cafeteria. "Ice cream with a soda would be the best."

"I know." Annie held up her bear. "And he also got me this."

Keely shook her head. "So cute."

"Abbie loves her frog already."

"Frogs are very special," Keely said. "Just like bears."

"Special like you and Emma." Annie hugged Keely. "Though you get to be my new mommy, not just my nanny."

AJ watched the two and realized there was a slight disconnect, a distance, in the way Emma interacted with the two girls. Oh, she cared about Abbie and Annie. Emma's coming to the hospital at a moment's notice was proof of that, but Keely acted more like a mom while Emma seemed—he searched for a word—*guarded.* No, perhaps *professional* was a better description, since Emma was nurturing and affectionate. But not even that adjective truly fit, because someone who was only doing their job wouldn't be here or trying to get him to reconcile with his family. Maybe he was off base. Except...

Looking back on his three days with Emma, he noticed a contradiction. She wanted to know personal details and stick her nose into his business, but she offered nothing of herself in return. Granted, he hadn't asked many questions, but when he did, she was good about changing the subject or turning the focus onto someone else, mainly him.

Today, he'd dragged the information about her family out of Emma. She'd likely relented because she needed to steel herself for the flight on his jet, not because she wanted him to know anything about her.

The realization bugged him. He'd seen her go out of her way to help others and not ask for anything in return. She had to have needs...dreams, especially growing up the way she had. He wanted to make her dreams come true.

The door opened, and Emma walked inside the room followed by Trey. The two talked quietly, as if sharing a private moment. Okay, not so private given they weren't alone, but who knew where they'd been a few minutes ago. They seemed comfortable around each other. AJ's stomach tightened.

Trey must like nannies if he was marrying Keely. Had he also dated Emma? Was that why she didn't want to have a fling? She'd had her heart broken or didn't want to be hit on by another boss? AJ didn't like either scenario. He balled his hands, wanting to punch something. Well, Trey.

Emma walked toward AJ while Trey headed straight to Keely and the girls. "We spoke to the doctor," Emma kept her voice low. "Abbie's doing better. She'll be hospitalized for a while during her recovery, so I can see her once I'm back in Portland. There's no reason we can't return to Haley's Bay right now."

"You don't want to stay longer?" AJ asked.

"No." She glanced at Trey, Keely and Annie standing next to Abbie's bed. Hurt flashed in Emma's eyes. "It's time for me, for us, to go. The birthday party's tomorrow."

Emma spoke with zero emotion, treating this hospital visit like a job or item on the to-do list she kept in her notebook. Something was off, but AJ didn't know what.

He pulled out his cell phone and typed a message. "I texted the pilot."

"Thank you."

She glanced at the foursome. The longing in her eyes about broke AJ's heart. He touched her arm, wishing he could kiss her and make everything better. "What's wrong?"

"I'm ready to get back to Haley's Bay. That's all."

Emma might believe that, but he didn't. Something was bothering her. He leaned closer, placing his mouth right next to her ear. "Is it Trey and Keely?"

"Heavens, no." Emma lowered her voice more. "Trey told me about their engagement. I'm thrilled for them and the girls. We never… He wanted to, but I didn't. Everything's worked out for the best."

Laughter sounded from the other side of the room. Emma sighed with a wistful expression, not a look of jealousy.

"Something's still bothering you," AJ said.

"It's…" Emma shot a sideward glance toward Abbie's bed. "I'm not bothered. I'm envious of Keely getting a family. That's all."

Emma might not buy into fairy tales, but she had a favorite prince and, according to Annie over ice cream, knew all the princess movie song lyrics by heart. The nanny—his nanny—was a romantic who'd lost her family and wanted another.

AJ nearly laughed, and not in a good way. He could

give Emma anything money could buy. Hell, he'd bought a helicopter and hired a pilot to bring her to Portland today, but he couldn't give her the family she wanted.

Still, he wanted to help her. Who was he kidding? AJ wanted to take Emma home. Not back to Haley's Bay. To his home in Seattle. Where he wanted her to stay. With him.

This was never going to work. AJ combed his fingers through his hair. She wanted a family. He didn't want a relationship. Unless they… Maybe they could compromise. Business deals and mergers had been mediated. He'd compromised with internal projects. External ones, too. For a chance with Emma, he was willing to try anything.

Fifteen minutes later, after hugs and kisses and goodbyes had been exchanged in Abbie's room, Emma waited with AJ at the helicopter pad. She needed a nap, a good cry, a hug, a kiss and dinner. Not in that particular order. "I'm so glad Abbie's doing better."

"I hear the relief in your voice." AJ put his arm around her shoulder. "Just when I think you can't impress me anymore, Emma Markwell, you do. You're amazing."

"I don't know about that, but thanks. You're pretty amazing yourself." Somehow she managed to say the words without her voice croaking or cracking or squeaking. Maybe she could do without the nap. "Buying the girls presents was very sweet. The stuffed animals were adorable, and the bouquet was beautiful. Did you see how Abbie kept staring at the flowers?"

He nodded. "They seem like great kids."

"They are. A couple of my favorites."

"How long did you work for the Lundbergs?"

"Nine months." Thirteen days and four hours, but who was counting?

"Not that long."

Emma shrugged. "Some nannies stay in positions for years, until the kids no longer need them or the family can't afford them, but I've never worked for more than twelve months. Most of my assignments are shorter. That's my choice."

AJ straightened. "That's it."

"What's it?"

"I noticed a difference in how you and Keely interacted with the girls. I don't mean this in a negative way—it's something I noticed when you were in Haley's Bay, too."

"What are you talking about?"

"You hold a piece of yourself back."

"From you?"

"From everyone. The families you work for, the children you care for, the people you meet."

"That's not true. That's ridiculous." She stared down her nose at AJ, offended. "I put everything into being a nanny. I pour all of me into each child. Aren't I here now?"

"You are. That meant everything to the girls, but you keep walking away from families."

Her cheeks felt warm, her chest heavy. "I don't walk away. I tell them my availability from the beginning. It's their choice whether they want to hire me or to keep looking for someone longer term."

"Their choice? Before you said it was your choice," he repeated her words.

"No." She shook her head, more like a three-year-old. "Stop attacking me."

"I'm trying to help you the way you've helped me," AJ said. "Think about it. Think about all those kids you said you took to the ER. Think about Abbie and Annie."

"No. I…" Emma covered her face with her hands. Her limbs burned as if on fire. "Oh, no. You're right. That's exactly what I've been doing and I didn't even realize it. I gave my love for them a time limit. Those poor kids."

AJ cradled her in his arms. "It's okay."

"No, it's not." She rested her head against his shoulder, wanting to hide away from the world. Time for a career change. Something different. "I was supposed to be nurturing and caring and devoted—"

"You were all those things today with the girls. Annie said you were the best nanny ever, even better than Keely. I'm sure the kids never realized what was going on. You've been those things with my family and me in Haley's Bay, but for some reason you don't open yourself completely and let others in."

"I—I don't want to get too attached." So many things made sense now. She rubbed her face. "I think that's why I bolted when Trey said he wanted to date me. He gave me a reason to leave. I never stuck around long enough to see if things would be awkward or not. I just ran."

"That makes two of us. You ran from the families you worked for. I ran from my family and Haley's Bay."

"I'd laugh if it wasn't so sad." She shook her head. "We're a pair."

"A pretty good pair if you ask me. You helped me figure out things with my family. Now I've helped you."

"You did. But ouch, it kinda hurts."

"Should have warned you about that."

She kissed his cheek. "Thanks anyway."

"There's something else we need to work out."

"What's that?"

"Us."

Her shoulders sagged. She didn't want to rehash this morning's discussion again. "I'm not the fling type. Nothing else needs to be said."

"How about I'm sorry?" he asked. "I know a fling isn't for you."

"I've been worried I gave you the wrong impression by sharing your bed or kissing you back."

"You didn't. This is my fault completely."

His words brought a rush of relief. Maybe things could be different between them. She crossed her fingers. "An easy mistake to make when you haven't known someone long."

"It might not be long, but I know I want to spend more time with you."

Her heart stumbled. She was afraid to hope. Nothing had worked out before. Well, nothing except Libby and her parents. "We don't have much time left in Haley's Bay."

"True, but we have plenty of time after we leave."

"I'm confused."

"You're cute when you crinkle your face like that."

She touched the bridge of her nose. "It's just...we want such different things."

"You want marriage and a family. I don't want a relationship."

"Exactly." Hope deflated like a Mylar balloon with a pinhole. Slowly. She'd rather the whole thing just blow up. "It will never work."

"Not all relationships end in marriage," he explained.

"No, but that's always a possibility, right?"

"Maybe not."

"I'm more confused now."

"What if we got to know each other. Dated. Dinners, movies, art shows, a show on Broadway or beignets in New Orleans?"

"We live in different states."

"Dating would be easier if you moved to Seattle. That's where the first compromise comes in."

His tone bothered her. She narrowed her gaze. "You sound like you're negotiating a business deal."

"More like a relationship."

That got her attention. She couldn't believe he'd said the word. "You don't want one of those."

"If dating works out, and we decide to pursue something more, I would be willing to compromise."

"In what way?"

"I'd agree to a relationship with you if you forgot about having a family with me."

His words seem to be punctuated with a gong. The air felt heavy in her lungs. She struggled to breathe. "Are you serious?"

He nodded. "Move to Seattle. We'll get to know each other. Date for real. Then take it from there."

Unreal. Emma couldn't believe a man who made her realize something so crucial about herself could be so, so, so stupid and shortsighted and selfish. "Take it where? To a relationship with no chance of a future?"

"Marriage doesn't equal the future."

"No, but you're asking me to compromise on my dream so I can hang out, have you support me, fly around on your jet and sleep with you."

He flashed her a devilishly charming smile, one she wanted to wipe off with a tissue. "You have to admit it's a good compromise."

Not good. She rested her face in her hands. Not by a long shot. What if she fell in love with him and wanted more? He wouldn't give her more. He wouldn't ever give her his heart.

I like knowing the expectations ahead of time.

His words echoed in her mind. She wouldn't be surprised if AJ had this whole *relationship* thing planned out from beginning to end. Speaking of which… "How long do you see this lasting?"

"As long as we're having a good time."

That could mean four days or four years. This wasn't a compromise. This was a temporary arrangement for the benefit of one person—AJ Cole. She would wind up with nothing except a broken heart, a few memories, ticket stubs and shiny baubles he'd tell another woman he regretted buying. Her temper spiraled.

The helicopter approached.

"You are an amazing man, Atticus Jackson Cole. I thought you were my friend. I thought you'd figured me out even though I held back on you. But I was wrong on both counts. You are used to getting what you want. This time that happens to be me. But I'm not going to be flattered or compromised into something I don't want."

"Emma—"

"Let me finish." She didn't have much time with the helicopter landing. "Being with you in Haley's Bay has been wonderful. I'm not going to deny that. You've helped me learn so many things about myself, including what I want. I need to put myself out there if I'm going to fall in love, get married and have a family. I can't be afraid. I can't settle for less. I definitely can't compromise with some half-hearted, never-going-anywhere relationship designed to end when it's no longer fun."

AJ's jaw hung open. "You're as stubborn as my dad."

"As stubborn as you."

"I like you."

"I like you, too." She patted his hand. "This isn't a rejection. We both know what we want. They happen to be different things. That's okay."

"There's chemistry between us."

"Sparks ignite the flame, but someone needs to tend

the fire to keep it going." She squeezed his hand. "I need to find someone who will want to collect more wood and kindling and tend with me. Not use semantics to get out of doing the job or hire someone else to do it for him."

His lips thinned. "I thought you cared about me."

"I do." Shutting up was what she would normally do, but not any longer. She needed to open up. This was a good place to start. "I'm sure if I let myself I could fall in love with you quite easily."

He inhaled sharply.

"But I'm not a deal you can negotiate or company you can acquire with terms favorable only to you," she continued. "I'm not something that can be compromised. I agreed to be your pretend girlfriend and I will continue to do that. But do not touch me and you better not kiss me unless you want a black eye."

Six o'clock the next morning, AJ stood at the harbor waiting for his brothers and dad to show up at the boat. He hadn't planned on going fishing, but now that Emma had kicked him to the curb for the second time—hell, forever—he knew better than to hang around. She had the party under control. He was only in the way.

But he missed her already. Not because he felt a sense of loss that something he wanted wasn't around. He was missing the partnership. Half of being a team, of something… special. The thought of saying goodbye to Emma tomorrow was killing him. He couldn't let her walk away, but how could he stop her?

"Look what the cat dragged in." Ellis laughed. "Surprised to see you up this early."

"What the hell?" Declan slapped AJ on the back. "You look worse than some roadkill I've seen."

"Woman trouble, son?" his dad asked.

AJ nodded. He'd been running away like Emma, but he was ready to stop, change, set things right. Her words had been echoing through his head all night.

Until now I haven't been...something. Willing? Ready? I don't know. But now I want a real boyfriend.

Marriage is something I want, which is why having a fling is a bad idea. I can't keep my feelings casual.

She'd told him exactly what was going on, what she wanted, but he hadn't listened. He'd proposed the exact opposite to her twice. Idiot.

AJ was an idiot for trying to get Emma to have a fling she didn't want and a relationship with no future because he didn't want those things, either. He wanted the bigger dream. He just hadn't realized it yet. But now he did. Oh, man, did he.

He was head over heels for Emma Markwell. What he felt for her after four days was different than the aggrandized, childish love he'd felt for Nat and different from the lust he'd experienced for other women. Falling so hard so quickly was the last thing he expected to happen, but exactly what he needed. There had to be a way to make things right.

"I messed up with Emma." The anguish in his voice matched the pain in his heart. He hadn't planned on her touching that particular organ, but somehow she had and he couldn't imagine life without her.

"Come on," Declan said. "She's crazy about you. Buy her a dozen roses and a diamond and all will be forgiven."

"That won't work. Not with her," AJ explained. "I'm not sure what will. I only met her four days ago."

His father and brothers' jaws dropped in unison.

"Four days and I'm already in love with her," AJ continued. Emma had shown him how much was missing from his so-called perfect life. He'd been so focused on work and increasing his company's bottom line, he'd forgotten to live and to love. She and that cat of hers had been affectionate and devoted to him. He'd been happier in Haley's Bay, in the town he thought he hated, because of them. That had to be love, right? "Either that or I'm losing my mind."

"Sounds like love to me," his father said, resigned.

"But I screwed up and she wants nothing to do with me."

"Been there, done that, skipped buying the T-shirt." Ellis nodded. "Definitely love."

"I need to win her heart and get her back, but I don't know how." The words poured from AJ's lips. "I need your help."

His father put his arm around AJ's shoulder. "Let's get on the boat. Once we drop the lines, we'll formulate a plan. With all of us Coles working together, Emma doesn't stand a chance. She'll be yours before your grandmother blows out the candles on her birthday cake."

AJ sure hoped so. He would be happy if she agreed to give him another chance, but he liked his dad's outcome better.

The party was in full swing, and Lilah was the proverbial belle of the ball. Emma loved seeing the birthday girl, floating on air in a gorgeous lavender dress and a huge smile lighting up her face. Lilah danced from person to person soaking up the birthday wishes and love offered by family and friends. And she adored the pictures used in the party decorations. Lilah's happy tears had made up for Emma's sadness over leaving Haley's Bay tomorrow and having to say goodbye to the Cole family, including AJ.

"You've done well, girl." Mr. Cole stood next to Emma. "I don't think anyone will be able to outdo the soiree you put together. Thank you from my brothers and sisters and our kids and their kids."

"AJ's the host."

"I'm sure it wasn't my son or that capable city girl assistant of his who came up with the new theme at the last minute."

"Not last minute. Three days ago," Emma corrected. "As soon as I met your mother, I knew Lilah needed a unique and personalized theme. Something that was all her. Fortunately the vendors were willing to work with me at the last minute to make this an eightieth birthday party she'll never forget."

"Haley's Bay will never forget this. Great job." Mr. Cole headed to the bar.

Emma looked around at the family and friends enjoying themselves, especially Lilah. The nostalgic decorations, inspired by her photographs, brought laughter and tears. The food, based on recipes she'd cooked her family and neighbors over the years, started debates on who cooked the dishes better, Lilah or the caterer. The music, chosen from each decade of her life, kept people on the dance floor song after song.

Emma was both proud and miserable at the same time. At least AJ was enjoying himself.

He'd thanked Emma for her hard work, then walked away. Probably for the best. She'd shot him down, rejected him. Was it any wonder he'd run from her like he'd always run from his family and Haley's Bay before?

The two of them circulated separately the entire evening. He wore his host hat, visiting with guests and making sure Lilah was feted like a queen. Emma donned an imaginary event planner apron, overseeing the party schedule and keeping the DJ on track with announcements.

Being apart from AJ was good, she told herself. She

needed to get used to being apart from AJ after being with him almost nonstop since they'd arrived in Haley's Bay. He didn't seem to mind being away from her. Especially not now. He danced with Madison, who hung on his every word as well as his body. Emma tried not to care. Thinking about AJ hurt.

No worries. After tomorrow she would never see him again. The realization made her heart ache more.

"Wonderful job, Emma." AJ stood at her side. "If you decide you want a break from being a nanny, you should try event planning."

"Thanks." She had to force the word from her dry throat. "Lilah looks happy."

"Grandma is thrilled," he said. "She loved the digital frame with the pictures you uploaded. Thank you for coming up with the perfect birthday gift for her."

"You're welcome."

Talking to him hurt. Emma pressed her arms against her side. She didn't want to care about AJ. She wanted him to go back to the dance floor with Madison. Okay, not really. But chitchatting as if nothing had changed between them was hard. Especially since she was still supposed to be his girlfriend.

The DJ put on the song "What a Wonderful World."

"This was my mother's favorite song," she said without thinking. "She and my father danced to it at their wedding."

AJ extended his arm. "May I have this dance?"

She noticed his parents and siblings watching them. Madison, too. Emma couldn't say no if they wanted to keep up the charade. Only a couple more hours. She ignored the pang in her heart, took his hand and followed him to the dance floor.

He placed one hand on her waist as they took a traditional dance position. "I've had a change of heart."

"About?"

"Blossom."

Her gaze jerked up to meet his.

"I've found her the perfect forever home."

"Where?" she asked.

"With me."

Emma stumbled over her feet, but AJ kept her upright. "What are talking about? You don't like cats."

"I might not like cats, but I love Blossom. I spoke with the shelter earlier today. I'm adopting her."

Emma's heart tore a little more. A selfish reaction. She should be ashamed. Living with AJ meant Blossom would have the best of everything—food, toys, cat trees and veterinary care. "Diva Kitty hit the adoption jackpot."

"Glad you think so."

Emma nodded. But a part of her wished Blossom could stay with her. Being temporarily involved in a family as a nanny or part of an animal's life as a foster or shelter volunteer was no longer enough. She wanted a place to call home for longer than her typical three-month lease, furniture that didn't come with an apartment, a pet that she could provide a forever home to. How had her life become so…transitory? Was that her way of keeping her distance?

"I spoke to the shelter director this afternoon. Blossom's former owner built her an outdoor play area. He also took her to his office each day."

"Looks like you have a new carpool buddy."

"Yes, but I don't think Blossom's going to happy without you." AJ spun Emma around the dance floor. "Would you consider making our arrangement more permanent?"

She stopped dancing, unsure whether to be upset or happy he wanted to employ her after all they'd been through. "What do you want me to do? Be a cat nanny? Or do you want to continue the dating charade?"

"I don't want you to work for me. Though Emma Markwell, the billionaire's nanny, has a nice ring to it."

She gave him a look.

"I'll just come right out and say it." He cupped her cheek. "I love you, Emma."

Her heart slammed against her chest. Air rushed from her lungs. She held on to his hand, afraid if she let go her knees would turn to taffy again. "W-w-what?"

"I screwed up. But my family knocked some sense into me. Dad and Ellis told me they knew right away when they met their future wives, and I do, too. I can't let you go. Please give me another chance. And another chance after that when I screw up again. We Cole men can be dense, but I'm sure you'll straighten me out eventually. Please give me a lifetime of changes with you."

She struggled to breathe. "But that would mean—"

"A forever home for Blossom with me and you."

Emma sucked in air. Hyperventilating seemed inevitable.

"We haven't known each other long, but I hope you will someday feel the same way about me," he added.

"I…I…" Emma couldn't speak. She was stunned. Thrilled. Frightened to death. Her first instinct was to run out of the big white tent on the bluff and not stop until she reached Portland. Because what she wanted most in life were the things she feared losing again—a home, her things, a family, her pets. Things she could have with AJ.

Did she dare take that chance? Make the leap?

Self-preservation screeched no. She'd been listening to that voice since she was ten years old, and knew the reasons well, but seeing the Cole family, especially Lilah with her children, grandchildren and great-grandchildren, helped Emma to realize that the risk of loving and losing was natural. Living a solitary life with zero attachments and few possessions wasn't. She couldn't imagine walking away from AJ again.

He waited for her answer, his gaze never wavering from hers.

"You're serious," she said finally.

"Very."

She took a breath.

"I'm going to need a few chances myself. I'm far from a pro at relationships. I've lived with families as an outsider. You pointed that out. But I've seen the work needed to have a successful relationship. It's hard work. Often boring, not fun. That's part of what scares me. Good times aren't always guaranteed. Walking away isn't—shouldn't be—an option. At least not with me. I can't do that. You can't do that to me."

"I get that. I do. No pre nup, okay? My dad will understand. No walking away. We date, we marry then we live happily ever after through the good times, boring times and whatever else life brings."

She couldn't believe the words he was saying. "That's all I want. I'm finished keeping myself distanced. From the families I worked for, the animals I've fostered, even things I've purchased and where I've lived. I've kept my emotional liabilities and attachments to a minimum, but I don't want to do that anymore. Especially with you."

Hope filled his eyes. "Is that a yes?"

"Yes, I'm ready to take the leap, but only with you." The smile on her face grew by the second. "I'll give you another chance and another after that, but only if you'll do the same with me."

"I love you, Emma Markwell." AJ kissed her on the lips. "You can have as many chances as you want."

Something bumped against her leg. She looked down. "Blossom."

The cat purred.

Declan held on to the end of the cat's leash. "Only for you, bro. Only for you."

AJ laughed, then brushed his lips over Emma's again. "I'm going to like kissing you for real."

She nodded. "We're going to need a lot of practice."

"Wonderful, wonderful. My birthday wish came true!" Lilah hugged Emma, an embrace full of love, acceptance and rose-scented perfume. "Now all I need is for the rest of my unmarried grandchildren to find their true loves."

True love.

Emma sighed, resting her head against AJ's chest and feeling the beat of his heart against her cheek. That was what she'd found in Haley's Bay. True love and a family.

Blossom meowed.

Not to mention a cat.

"Well, don't look at us for help, Grandma," AJ teased. "We'll be too busy getting to know each other, then we'll need to talk about the future, wedding plans and where to honeymoon. But not until after we spend more time together and make things official."

Emma's heart overflowed with joy at the thought of getting married and being AJ's wife. She wanted to pinch herself to make sure she wasn't dreaming. Except none of her dreams had ever been this good.

"Not to worry." Lilah beamed. "These things have a way of working themselves out. Isn't that right, Blossom?"

As if on cue, Blossom meowed. The cat rubbed against AJ's leg, then head butted Emma's calf.

AJ rubbed the scruff of Blossom's neck. "Looks like our cat agrees with you, Grandma."

"I agree, too." Satisfaction filled Emma. She wiggled her toes. "Things do have a way of working out."

"When you least expect it," AJ said.

Emma's heart sighed. "I wouldn't have it any other way."

* * * * *

2 in 1
MARINELLI
50% OFF
your first parcel